Coming Home

Lori L. Howard

the Peppertree Press
www.peppertreepublishing.com

Copyright © Lori L. Howard, 2023

All rights reserved. Published by the Peppertree Press, LLC. The Peppertree Press and associated logos are trademarks of the Peppertree Press, LLC. No part of this publication may be reproduced, stored in a retrieval system, transmitted in any form or by any means, electronic, mechanical, photocopying, recording, or otherwise, without prior written permission of the publisher and author/illustrator.

Graphic design by Elizabeth Parry.

For information regarding permission, call 941-922-2662
or contact us at our website: *www.peppertreepublishing.com* or write to:
The Peppertree Press, LLC.
Attention: Publisher
715 N. Washington Blvd., Suite B
Sarasota, Florida 34236

ISBN: 978-1-61493-934-4
Library of Congress: 2023923137
Printed: December 2023

Dedication

For my husband Ed and the two Marines whose names I combined to create the focus character of this book: Eugene Lucas and Bill Jahn. "Top" Lucas (MGySgt, retired) served 30 years in the Marine Corps and Bill Jahn was there when the Marines hit China Beach on 3/8/1965.

I would also like to thank Dick Overton, another American hero who served with the Marine Corps in Vietnam. These three Marines each answered several pages of questions, and I learned a lot about them and Vietnam (the country as well as the conflict) while writing this story.

Thank you to my five "beta testers," who read the draft of this book in its entirety and offered feedback and criticism (and so much encouragement): my husband Ed, my sister Lisa Zubke, and my friends Jalene Rende, Linda Jahn, and Rick Vance.

• • •

Chapter One

Leslie forced her key into the rusty lock, something she would need to replace before selling this cozy bungalow that she had called "Home" for most of her life. She caught a whiff of lilacs coming from the side yard, indicating that spring had finally arrived, and announced aloud that she needed to cut some blooms in the morning. Billy was following behind, counting, and asked if Grandma might be looking down from Heaven. Leslie smiled at the thought. "I can't imagine her *not* watching us," she managed. Billy squinted into the sun, smiled and waved, then went back to counting sidewalk squares.

Leslie's mind was already on the tasks at hand. There were calls to make, mail to pick up, a ton of dirty laundry from the trip, and groceries to buy. First and foremost, she needed to make sure that they had syrup because Wednesday night is "waffle night" at their house. It would be nice to get back into a routine after eating out every day for two weeks. Being on vacation was fun, but coming home was a great feeling. Leslie cringed a little when she saw the floral arrangements covering every open space on the counters. Most of the flowers were dead and dry after not being watered for a couple of weeks. The kitchen smelled like a mixture of carnations and roses, with an occasional whiff of something less pleasing. Leslie set down her suitcase and started tossing flowers into trash bags, but when she uncovered the area where the answering machine sat, the blinking light made her smile. "Oh, Mom," she teased aloud. "Who else uses an answering machine these days?"

Leslie pressed the "Play" button, expecting messages of condolence and sympathy for her mother, but the first message was not to express sympathy at all: "Hello, Mrs. Lucas, this is Justine Wilson from the U.S. State Department. We have some great news for you. Please call back as soon as possible. You have my number." Leslie pressed the "Save" button and listened again. Why would someone from the State Department be calling her mother? They probably needed her to speak or give a presentation for one of the veterans' groups.

Leslie turned to watch Billy as he walked straight to his room, skipping the first step as always. She pressed "Return Call," assuming that she'd be leaving a voicemail since it was almost 5:00, but someone answered on the first ring. "Oh, Mrs. Lucas, I'm glad you finally returned my call!" the live voice said excitedly. "I'm so excited to be the one to give you this news!" Leslie explained that Susan Lucas was her mother and she had unfortunately passed away three weeks ago. "Oh, no! I'm so sorry to hear that," said the voice. "I'm Justine Wilson. Are you her daughter, Leslie?" Leslie confirmed that she was and wondered how this woman knew her name. Nothing could have prepared Leslie for what she heard next: "We have your father. He's being examined at Bethesda."

There was more to the conversation, but it was all a blur. Leslie called Melanie, Billy's babysitter who lived next door, and asked if she could stay with Billy at the house for a few days. Leslie tried to figure out what to tell Billy, but as long as he had Melanie and a supply of fruit snacks – the squishy ones, not the hard ones – he would be fine.

•••

Chapter Two

Leslie was trying not to drive too quickly as she headed east on the Ohio Turnpike, grateful for cruise control to keep her at a safe speed. Her boss was understanding about the extra time off and her babysitter was staying at the house with Billy so Leslie could meet her father alone. Having an autistic son meant screening everyone in his life carefully, but Melanie loved Billy dearly and knew how to handle his idiosyncrasies.

Leslie's brain teemed with so many questions and conflicting emotions that she had driven about two hours before she realized that she hadn't turned any music on. Her new Equinox had a great stereo system, and she cranked up the 80s station. She tried to clear her mind by singing at the top of her lungs, a pleasant distraction for a couple of minutes before more questions took over her thoughts. Where has my dad been? If he's alive, why hasn't he called? She even questioned whether she had actually received that call, or if it had been a dream. Since everything seemed to be a blur after Justine had said, "We have your father," could she have misunderstood? Was she going to Bethesda to pick up ashes or a live person?

Driving alone gave her plenty of time to think, something that didn't happen often, so her mind wandered into places in her memory that she was usually able to avoid. She thought about when she had met Mark in college, when he was so charming and generous. Late one Friday night, she was heading back to the dorm after researching a paper in the library and it started to rain. Always prepared, she pulled out her umbrella and picked up her pace. She was surprised when Mark ended up under that umbrella, heading back from a party at one of the fraternity houses. She was happy to shield him from the rain, even if he did smell like tequila, and was quite surprised when he asked her out.

Leslie had never dated in high school and wasn't sure how to handle the attention from Mark, but she soon found herself spending all her free time with him. When graduation loomed on the horizon, they decided to get married. Her mother, Susan, was worried that

Leslie would leave the area and start a new life elsewhere. As an only child who grew up without her father, Leslie had a close relationship with her mother; in fact, Susan's world revolved around Leslie. Mark seemed to understand and agreed that they would stay in southern Michigan. Leslie found a job at a local accounting firm and Mark went to work for a major insurance company. They were able to afford a nice home and discussed having a family. Leslie wanted to have children, but Mark made it clear that he did not want any kids.

For eighteen years, Leslie and Mark lived comfortably, each advancing steadily in their careers. Leslie enjoyed working 9-5, Monday through Friday, as that allowed her to enjoy her weekends. She and Mark loved going to football games on Saturdays in the fall. They had a cabin in the Upper Peninsula of Michigan, and Mark went up there occasionally with his friends to hunt. He didn't seem to be very good at it, though, since he never brought anything home besides dirty laundry and empty beer cans. Leslie did not understand why he enjoyed hunting and chose to spend Mark's hunting weekends with her mother. Leslie accompanied Susan to every patriotic celebration or event in the area, as she had done for most of her life. Her world was predictable and somewhat boring, but Leslie was comfortable with that. She accepted everything as it happened and continued her daily routine, complacent and secure, living just blocks from her childhood home. Her circle of friends seemed to get smaller and smaller as her friends moved away or became wrapped up with their careers and kids.

One day at work, Leslie felt nauseous, and her usual cures didn't help. She had eaten all her Tums and the office busy bodies started teasing that she was pregnant. She had taken birth control pills for more than 20 years, never missing a day, but had read about women who had become pregnant while taking The Pill. The pregnancy test that she picked up at the drugstore was positive, but before she told Mark she decided to have her doctor run a test at his office. It was also positive.

She told her mother before telling Mark, and of course Susan was thrilled. She asked Leslie to consider naming the baby after her dad if it was a boy, and Leslie agreed. "William Leslie Lucas" was a great name, and Leslie was named after him, so she thought it would be a great way to honor her father's memory.

Mark did not take the news well and initially he accused Leslie of getting pregnant on purpose. Eventually, he softened and seemed to accept that he was becoming a father. They talked about redecorating one of the bedrooms and about names for the baby, and Leslie felt closer to Mark than she had in several years. They discussed Leslie going back to work post-pregnancy as soon as the doctor cleared her, and Susan suggested that she could retire from her job at the library to be their full-time babysitter. Leslie remembered thinking that life was falling into place beautifully.

Before any concrete plans were made, Mark was suddenly relocated to Alexandria, Virginia, for work. He was evasive when Leslie questioned him about being transferred over 500 miles away, supposedly against his will. He was the Vice President of his company, and she knew that he had his choice about where he worked. The cooperative and caring side of his personality seemed to have vanished overnight, but she had a lot on her mind already. She had read how dangerous it is for women in their 40s to have babies, but she was healthy and more fit than most women her age. She put in her notice at work and packed up the house, weak with morning sickness and horrified at the thought of leaving her mother all alone. She knew that Susan would never leave Michigan for more than a few days, but maybe she could convince her to move to Virginia when she retired.

Thinking about her marriage to Mark as she headed to Bethesda, it dawned on Leslie that she had never planned ahead much until she became pregnant. Since she hadn't planned the pregnancy, she needed to educate herself about becoming a parent. Some of her friends were already having grandchildren, and everyone was more than generous with advice. Actually, *too* generous. Downright annoying. She read everything she could get her hands on and couldn't believe that *What to Expect When You're Expecting* had been around since 1984. There was a lot of research available about having a baby after 40, and most of it seemed to be negative. She shrugged it off, determined that this baby was going to recharge her marriage and hold their family together.

The birth went as planned, and this sweet little 8-pound gift arrived only two days after the due date. After seeing that the baby was healthy and had all his fingers and toes, Leslie slept well for the first time in months. Mark was uncharacteristically upbeat and agreed to name the baby after Leslie's father, who was Missing in Action (MIA) in Vietnam. William Lucas Mitchell ("Billy") had come screaming into the world with a healthy set of lungs, and Leslie found it fitting to name him after her father, the hero that she had never met.

Susan had spent almost a week in Virginia, helping Leslie with the baby and making sure they had what they needed. Although Mark was nice to her mother, Leslie saw him roll his eyes when Susan said she needed to get home "in case Bill shows up." Her mother wasn't even to the end of the driveway when he started: "Does she really think he's coming back? Has she ever been in for a psychological evaluation?" Leslie ignored the questions that she'd heard 100 times and walked away to check on Billy, who was a pleasant distraction.

Although it was difficult to be away from her mother, Leslie spoke to her on the phone every day and Susan's visits became more frequent. Their proximity to Washington, DC, was an advantage for her as she enjoyed the patriotic events and rallies, and she was quite active with any group related to Prisoners of War/Missing in Action (POW/MIA) service members. She was invited to speak to a group with relatives who disappeared in Vietnam, the National League of POW/MIA Families, and connected deeply with them. Logically, it was hard to imagine that Leslie's father was still alive, since he had been MIA for almost 50 years, but it was still possible.

Mark always had snide remarks about Susan's belief that her husband was still alive, since so many years had passed since he was last seen. Not much was known about Sergeant William Lucas at all, besides that he loved Susan, cars, his country, and the Marine Corps. Leslie noticed when Susan's visits started tapering off, and finally discovered the reason on one of the few trips she took back to Michigan with Billy. He loved these visits to Grandma's house because everything there was stuck in time. It was predictable and comfortable, and he seemed to be more "at home" there than at his actual home in Virginia.

One night after Billy was asleep in the bed that Susan had bought just for him, Leslie had questioned Susan about why her visits were less frequent. Initially, Susan claimed that she was just getting older and didn't want to drive that far, but Leslie didn't buy it. She continued her questions until Susan finally told her the rest of the story. A woman had called Mark and Leslie's house when Susan was there for a visit, while Leslie was at the grocery store. Susan had answered the phone, thinking it might be Leslie, and the woman asked for Mark. He grabbed the phone and went into his study, and Susan continued reading to Billy. When Mark came out of the study, he demanded that she never speak to Leslie about the call. When Mark left the room, Billy said matter-of-factly, "That was Teresa. She's daddy's girlfriend." Billy was not a child to make up stories, and Susan didn't ask any more questions. She didn't say anything to Leslie at the time because she was afraid that Mark would take Leslie even farther away than Virginia.

As her mother revealed the details and the fact that she was afraid of making Mark angry because he's "unstable," Leslie realized that the red flags were there and she ignored them...late nights and weekends at work, an increasing number of "business trips" which he never talked about later, and just odd behavior in general. As an accountant, Leslie had always handled the family's finances, but after Billy was born Mark had started a separate account to use for work, saying it would be easier when it came time for taxes. Keeping a house and raising a son who required extra attention was exhausting, and Leslie had little time or energy for anything else, so she had buried her suspicions and focused on what she could control.

After Susan told her story about what had happened, Leslie knew she had to take action. She asked her mom to watch Billy for a few days so she could go have a talk with Mark that might get too heated for Billy's comfort (or her own). Susan had new neighbors, a young woman named Melanie and her husband Steve, who was recently discharged from the Marines. She and Billy were going to take them some cookies and get to know them better, which would redirect Billy's focus about Leslie being gone for a few days.

Leslie drove back to Virginia in a fog, replaying events and dialogue in her mind – and occasionally aloud – that would have

given any woman plenty of reason to question her husband. She didn't call Mark to tell him that she was on her way, and he didn't expect her and Billy to be home for a few more days. Since he had been working so many extra hours, Leslie assumed that he would still be at work when she arrived. Her plan was to park in the garage and wait for him to come home, but that changed when she pulled into the driveway.

It was dusk, so her headlights weren't noticeable as she pulled alongside the black Lexus parked in her driveway, which she recognized. Tim worked with Mark and he and Trish were really the only friends that Leslie had in the area. They hadn't been to the house in months, so Leslie found it odd that they chose to visit when she was out of town. The car behind Tim's, a red Challenger, wasn't one that Leslie recognized, but she assumed it was another co-worker.

She used the side door into the garage, feeling like she was trespassing into her own home. As she opened the door into the kitchen, Mark was laughing louder than she had heard him laugh in years. For some reason – intuition, perhaps – she took out her cell phone when she set her purse on the counter. From the kitchen doorway, she could see into the living room and what she saw shocked her. There was a beautiful redhead sitting on Mark's lap in the living room, laughing with Tim and Trish like they were best friends. Leslie instantly felt betrayed, not just by her husband but also the couple that she thought were her friends.

The coffee table was full of bottles, and all four of them appeared to be drunk. There was only one light on and they didn't notice Leslie walking in with her phone, snapping pictures, until she was halfway across the living room. She set the phone down, fumbling it and almost dropping it in her haste. The laughter stopped abruptly and Leslie asked the woman, "Are you Teresa?" The woman seemed stunned and slowly nodded her head as Mark stood up quickly and dumped her on the floor. There was a confusing amount of conversation all at once, with Mark saying that he could explain and Tim realizing that it was late and Trish saying how nice it was to see Leslie again. Teresa was the only one who didn't speak, and she quickly headed for the door with Tim and Trish right on her heels.

Mark, who was obviously intoxicated, rambled on and on with his lies and grew angry when Leslie told him to stop lying. She decided to call her friend Katrina, who was a divorce attorney back in Michigan. Leslie knew what she had to do, but she was concerned how a divorce would affect Billy. She laughed at herself when she picked up the phone, realizing that she had pressed the "Record" button when she fumbled her phone, so she had a solid five minutes of recording the ceiling. She pressed "Stop" and stomped upstairs, with Mark right on her heels, spinning his stories and making excuses. She locked herself in their bedroom and almost deleted the ceiling video, but thought she might want to refer to it later.

Leslie texted Katrina the clearest picture of Mark and his girlfriend, then called Katrina before she could reply to the text. They didn't speak for long but agreed to meet for lunch in a few days to decide how to proceed. Leslie then called her mother to say she'd be back tomorrow and said Good Night to Billy but didn't tell either of them what had just happened. She was still a bit shocked, and wondered if that image of the redhead would ever get out of her brain. She finally drifted off to sleep, feeling more relieved than anything else.

When Leslie awoke in the morning, she showered and dressed, then cautiously unlocked the door. Mark wasn't there, so Leslie acted quickly. She drove into town and rented a U-Haul with a car dolly attached, and the young man who did the paperwork was nice enough to put her car on the dolly for her. It was a cumbersome set-up, but Leslie felt powerful behind the wheel. She packed up the majority of her and Billy's belongings, somehow finding the strength to get everything into the truck on her own.

After five hours of physical labor, Leslie called her mother to say that she was on her way and would be arriving late. Susan didn't question Leslie, but just listened patiently and reminded her to be careful. Mark called when Leslie was about three hours into her drive, and his tone was completely different. He argued that she couldn't prove anything and vowed to fight her for the house and cabin. Not surprisingly, he didn't want custody of Billy. Mark was clearly not prepared for the barrage of words that spewed from her mouth before she hung up on him, fueled by betrayal and frustration.

Somewhere along that drive, Leslie shed her mousy existence and decided that she deserved a better life as she headed back to the two people who mattered most in her world: Billy and Susan.

Just remembering that incident and reliving it made Leslie's blood boil, but Billy did not seem to mind the divorce. The judge gave Leslie full physical custody and ordered Mark to pay child support and alimony, since Leslie had quit working to care for Billy. They sold the house in Virginia and split the profit, and Leslie let Mark keep the cabin up north. Susan wanted Leslie and Billy to live with her and Leslie agreed to do it temporarily. She returned to work at the same accounting firm that she had left almost ten years ago and found that some of her old friends were still there, most with grandchildren and talking about retiring soon. She found a great school for Billy and was relieved that their neighbor Melanie was happy to be Billy's babysitter.

Susan worked at the library for a couple more years after Leslie moved back, then started to get sick a lot. By the time Leslie convinced her to go to the doctor, Susan was diagnosed with Stage 4 pancreatic cancer. She had already won a battle with breast cancer, joking that it was caught early because she had the world's smallest breasts. Through all her doctor's appointments and the surgery and chemotherapy, Susan continued her work on behalf of the POWs and MIAs from Vietnam. She was patriotic and wore red on Fridays to "Remember Everyone Deployed." She talked to Leslie about dying and begged her to keep the same home phone number and live in the same house just in case her dad came home. Leslie had agreed, but secretly planned on moving into something more modern as soon as the house was fixed up and sold.

When Susan finally lost her battle, Leslie was shocked at how much money her mother had saved over the years. She was a millionaire, working at the local library! There were several bank accounts, one being checks from the federal government and another the $2 million inheritance from her stepfather. There was another account for the money that Grandpa Lucas left her, in appreciation for her taking care of him in his later years. All of this was left to Leslie when Susan died…the accounts, the house, her mom's 1992 Buick, her dad's 1958 Chevy Impala, and more information about

Vietnam than the Vietnamese probably had. It was a lot to digest, and although Billy was 11 now – almost 12 - he was having a difficult time understanding that his grandmother was never coming back because he had never known anyone else who died.

After the funeral, Leslie and Billy took some time away and went to Orlando, visiting all the parks, but there was a lot to be decided when they got back. Walking into the house with all of that on her mind was enough, and this call about her father possibly being found made Leslie forget everything else she had planned to do. As she drove, Leslie was second-guessing what she had been told and felt silly for grabbing photo albums and paperwork and letters to bring along. It would be crazy to bring those items if she were just picking up his ashes. She hoped that they at least had something of his for her to keep, like dog tags or old letters.

...

Chapter Three

Leslie didn't remember the Ohio Turnpike turning into the Pennsylvania Turnpike, but she did remember stopping for gas and a cheeseburger near Pittsburgh. She loved the beauty of these hills and was merging onto I-70 before she knew it. She had grown stronger and more confident since divorcing Mark but certainly did not feel that way now. After Billy was born, Leslie became a planner, maybe even a bit of a control freak. The fact that she had not booked a hotel before she left was completely out of character, yet here she was, heading toward a city she hadn't visited in years to possibly meet her father for the first time.

When Leslie was about 20 miles from Bethesda, she stopped at the outlet mall in Clarksburg to make a plan. She called Melanie to check on Billy, who was too worried about Leslie to return to school. Leslie had predicted that this would be the case, and assured Melanie that two more days wasn't a big deal; he could go back on Monday. Melanie said they had just finished some craft projects, which Billy loved to do. He did not love to talk on the phone, though, so Leslie was surprised that he asked if he could speak to her. Hearing his voice always made life a little better, and Leslie relaxed a bit. Melanie said that "Justine from D.C." had called three times, and apparently she didn't have Leslie's cell number and needed to talk to her. Leslie wrote down the number and smiled about the fact that Melanie wouldn't give her number to anyone. After she hung up with Melanie, Leslie called Justine, who had driven over to Bethesda and wanted to meet there. Leslie said she needed to find a hotel, but Justine said, "No, honey, you have a place at Fisher House. Everything will be paid; you don't need to worry about a hotel." Justine gave Melanie directions to Fisher House 5 and told her that she would have to show her ID at the gate. She said she would meet her there whenever she could make it. Leslie entered the address in her phone and headed back out on 270.

Somehow, Leslie had forgotten how much she hated this traffic, and never understood how someone created this logistical nightmare of freeways, highways, and parkways. Either a genius or a maniac, she figured, or a little bit of both. Since it was almost 5:00, traffic was at its peak and she would just have to be patient. She could see that the cherry blossoms were everywhere, so she rolled down the window to smell them. They were one of the few things she missed about this area, but the lilacs in Michigan were a fair tradeoff.

When she pulled up to the Fisher House, Justine was waiting outside. She introduced herself and asked if Leslie had any problem getting through security at the gate, but she had only had to show her driver's license and they checked her name off their list. Justine had already checked Leslie in and handed her the room key. They spoke briefly about the drive, and Justine told Leslie that she could put her stuff in her room and leave her car parked for the duration of her visit. It was a 5-minute walk to the medical center, or they could take the shuttle if she was tired. "So, my father is alive?" Leslie asked. "Not just alive, but in great shape," Justine replied. "Well, physically, anyway. He doesn't remember anything, at least as far as they can tell, but they're doing a lot of testing."

Leslie walked back to the car in a fog, feeling like a robot, now with more questions than answers. If he doesn't remember anything, how do they know it's him? Is he going to understand that she is his daughter? Does he remember Mom? His family? What did Justine mean by "...as far as they can tell?" What kind of testing are they doing? Am I supposed to take him home with me?

She grabbed her new red suitcase, purchased for the recent Florida trip, and the blue Rubbermaid tote full of pictures, articles, and paperwork. She was wearing a white t-shirt, so she smiled when she realized the coincidental red-white-blue combination. As she headed back to the beautiful brick building that looked like an oversized home, more questions filled her mind. How long do they expect me to stay here? Why have I never heard about these Fisher House buildings? The questions kept coming, and she wanted a Coke and some answers. As she had learned repeatedly in her life, sometimes answers brought disappointment, and she was worried about being disappointed again.

Leslie really wished her mother could be here and was doing her best to hold back her overwhelming emotions. "Chin up," she could hear her mother say. She stood tall and proceeded through the lobby with her red patent suitcase, where she was greeted as if she were part of the Royal family. By the time she reached her room, she was feeling a little more at ease but still anxious. She was stronger and more confident with each passing year, but old insecurities were creeping in. What am I going to say? How am I going to get through this? She reminded herself that her success rate of making it through adversity was 100% and laughed when she realized that she'd probably read that on Facebook or on a poster at the office.

The room was perfect: not near an entrance or stairs or an elevator, warm and welcoming with a queen bed and patriotic decor. She quickly washed her face, ran a brush through her hair, and put on a fresh shirt. Mom had bought this sleeveless cobalt tank for her last year at Christmas, and it was Leslie's favorite color. Somehow, she felt closer to her mother just by wearing it.

She hung up the items in her bag that might wrinkle and went back to the lobby to find Justine. The staff members were incredibly pleasant and seemed to be familiar with Justine. As they walked out the front door, Justine said she would handle any reporters, and Leslie stopped in her tracks. "Why would there be reporters?" she inquired innocently. Justine smiled and explained, "It's not every day that someone who's been missing for over 50 years shows up. This is huge news, like he's returned from the dead." Leslie was trying to understand what reporters would ask and knew that she would be useless to them as her head was swimming with questions, not answers. She was trying to imagine this situation from someone else's point of view and wondered what people would think. She could barely understand it from the point of view of an only child who grew up her entire life without siblings or a father, sticking up for a mother who remained convinced to her last breath that Bill Lucas was alive. Against all odds, he was.

Leslie was starting to feel nauseous and reached into her purse for some Tums. She saw the light on her phone blinking, indicating that she had a text, so she checked it. Melanie had sent a photo of a great piece of artwork that Steve had helped Billy create: a Marine Corps emblem, glued pieces of colored paper making up the eagle, globe, and anchor on which he had written: "To Grandpa, Love

Billy." She choked back the tears, digging deep for the poker face that she had put on so many times in her life. Billy had no idea how much he helped her handle stress. "I'm ready," Leslie told Justine with a smile. "Let's go see my father."

Justine had already been to the Medical Center but had not seen Bill Lucas because he was going through a series of diagnostic tests to make sure he was healthy. She mentioned that someone had driven over from the National Security Agency (NSA) to set up an intelligence debriefing, but the agent was having a hard time interviewing him because he did not – or could not – speak to them. "Why would a truck driver be of any interest to the intelligence community?" Leslie asked. Justine laughed heartily and said, "He definitely was *not* there to drive a truck. You'll learn more in the debriefing set up in the receiving area. Military protocol."

Leslie walked the last couple of minutes in silence, feeling that every question brought more questions and few answers. Why isn't he talking? Shouldn't he be relieved that he's back, happy to see other Americans? Did Mom know that he wasn't a truck driver? She said it was the logical choice for him because he loved cars so much. Almost every picture Leslie had of her father had some type of vehicle in it, mostly his 1958 Impala that was still under a tarp in the garage. Leslie smiled at the thought of how happy he would be to see that car again. She had learned a lot about cars from their neighbor, Gary. He taught her how to change tires and spark plugs and oil, but she always paid someone to do it for her. Too messy.

Gary handed Leslie a dirty rag and told her to wipe the dip stick on it and then check the oil to make sure they had the right amount. Her cute little pigtails swung forward as she looked down at the rag, concentrating on getting all the oil off before putting the dip stick in again. "You have to put it all the way in, to make sure you get a proper reading," she reminded Gary. "That's right," he agreed. "Good job!"

Leslie pulled the dip stick out of the oil and held it up sideways. "Parallel to the floor," she mumbled as Gary watched patiently and smiled. "It looks pretty good, don't you think?" Leslie surmised. Gary suggested that he check it one more time for the sake of quality control. "Is that like getting a second opinion?" asked

Leslie. "Something like that," Gary replied. He wiped the oil on the rag and tested it again. "Careful," Leslie reminded him. "I don't think you're holding it parallel." Gary laughed and thanked her for the reminder.

"Looks like we're all set with our oil level," he declared as he wiped off his hands. "What's next?" Leslie cocked her head and thought about it. "Tires?" she asked excitedly. "Can I check them?" Gary pulled the tire gauge out of his toolbox and handed it to her. "Do you think you can do it this time?" he laughed. "Remember, we're checking the pressure, not flattening the tires." Leslie rolled her eyes and walked to the front of the Impala. "That happened one time," she reminded him as she kneeled to check the tires. For each tire, Leslie called out a number to Gary. "24!" she yelled. "Perfect!" he replied. After she checked all four tires, it was Gary's turn to yell out the numbers. "We have a good system!" Leslie announced proudly when he was finished.

...

Chapter Four

As she and Justine walked through the Medical Center front doors, Leslie was awestruck by the size of the facility. The entrance was striking, a white building with gold doors surrounded by black panels. The main building looked to be about 20 stories high, rising above the parking structures and other buildings like a skyscraper. It was quite impressive, and Leslie had to work to keep her jaw from dropping open.

Justine went to check them in and get their Visitor badges while Leslie took everything in. She saw a sign that said "Vending," and remembered that she wanted a Coke. Justine handed Leslie a badge to pin on and said she'd have a "more permanent one tomorrow." Leslie didn't even ask what she meant, and said she was going to buy a Coke. Justine said, "No, come with me. We have Coke in the debriefing area." They walked down a narrow hallway that looked like it went nowhere, and Justine pulled a U.S. State Department badge out of her purse. She used it to scan her way into a room at the end with a "Staff Only" sign. Leslie felt like she was in an episode of "The Twilight Zone." Inside the room, she was welcomed by a distinguished older man in a gray herringbone suit who introduced himself as "Jim Carlson." Leslie thought he looked familiar but assumed that he just had a common look. Justine smiled and greeted him with "Isn't it close to your bedtime, General?"

The lounge was sparse but comfortable, and Jim asked Leslie to have a seat while Justine went to get her a Coke. He explained that he was in Vietnam with her father and had been part of the team that recently extracted him from the Marble Mountain area. "What do you mean, 'extracted?' He didn't want to come back?" He didn't answer the question directly, but Jim Carlson definitely answered some questions that she'd been wondering about for years.

Leslie listened in awe as Jim described how her father was discovered in a monastery, working and living as one of the monks. The Americans who spotted him had attempted to speak with him, but he disappeared before they could get his name. When they returned to Florida, they made several phone calls, trying to get someone to check into it. They were Vietnam veterans and had heard rumors in the veteran community of American POWs being used for free labor until they died, having never seen their families again. A young Congressman from Sarasota, also a veteran, listened to their story and convinced the Veterans Affairs Committee to put together a team and investigate. Jim was part of that team, and they flew into Da Nang, armed with the names and pictures of all known POWs and those listed as MIA. The team found the American, verified his identity as that of Marine Sergeant William Lucas, and convinced him to return to the United States.

George Martin and Ron Linden returned to Vietnam with a tour group of Americans who wanted to see the beauty and peace of the country, a stark contrast to the last time they were there together. They had reconnected through Facebook over 40 years after serving together as part of 1st ANGLICO, and when a tour was advertised in George's hometown, he asked Ron to go with him. "I'm not saving your ass this time," Ron had replied to the email that George sent. "Semper Fi!" was George's only response, and three months later they boarded a plane in Tampa.

The flight took forever, but it gave George and Ron some time to catch up and talk about the miserable time spent in the jungles of Vietnam. Other members of the tour group joined in to hear the stories about leeches and monsoon rains and the various ways that the old Marines had adapted to their environment. When the plane landed in Da Nang, the two men held back tears and took it all in, bracing themselves for whatever memories surfaced.

By Day Three on their itinerary, George and Ron were tired of hearing the politically correct and historically inaccurate stories that the tour guide was sharing. They took advantage of dim lighting inside Marble Mountain to ditch the group and take a tour of their own. As they moved slowly through the displays of beautiful statues and candles, Ron mentioned to George that he had read about POWs who were kept inside the mountain and worked to death, brainwashed into thinking their country knew about them but didn't care to come for them. They initially agreed that it would be impossible with all the people who frequented the area but started to believe it more and more with each cave and stairwell they discovered.

There were monks still living inside the mountain, and one in particular looked a little out of place. He was working on a marble carving when they saw him the first time but disappeared quickly when George tried to take his picture. When they spotted him again, George attempted to communicate with him. "Do you speak English?" he asked. "You don't look Vietnamese; you look like an American." The mysterious stranger bolted from the room again, and each time Ron and George attempted to speak to him he disappeared.

"We have to tell someone," Ron urged. They found their tour guide and told him what they had seen, and he laughed at them. "Old wives' tale," he stated presumptuously. "There's no way that POWs still live in this mountain." Arguing didn't get them anywhere, nor did threatening, and both men were unable to enjoy the remaining ten days of their trip. They had to move on to Hue the next day, and another destination each day after that. By the time they returned to Florida, they had started to doubt what they'd seen, but the idea of this possibly being an American POW continued to plague them.

Leslie sipped the Coke from Justine, who left the room before she could thank her. "Was he a prisoner?" Leslie asked. Jim explained that Sergeant Lucas was officially listed as "Missing in Action," never as a POW, and did not appear to be held there against his will. He didn't want to escape because he doesn't seem to remember who he is, and Jim suggested that Sergeant Lucas may have no recollection of his identity or perhaps the English language. There were psychologists, neurologists, and linguists all trying to work with him to get any information. He can see and hear, but so far no words had come out of his mouth. "How did you know who he was, then?" Leslie asked. Jim pulled out a small box from the desk that contained her father's dog tags, some pictures, and tattered letters wrapped in plastic. He explained that these items were not in Sergeant Lucas's possession; they had been locked in a safe by the abbot of the monastery where Sergeant Lucas was found. When the team first showed up and began surveillance, they asked to speak to the abbot and were told that he was 95 years old and on his death bed. Sergeant Lucas had been extremely close to the abbot and stayed at his bedside until someone else came into the room, then he'd disappear again. None of the other monks knew the true identity of the American, nor did they ask. They were there to be enlightened, not burdened by anyone's past.

In a death bed confession, the abbot admitted that he had objects locked away that proved the identity of the one he saw as a son, the one he called "Erden" (Treasure). His true name was William Lucas, and he was a United States Marine. Since Jim and the team were there during this time, one of the team members who spoke Vietnamese was able to get more information from the abbot, who passed away a short time later. The new abbot was able to retrieve the objects – including the deceased abbot's personal journals - from the safe and brought Sergeant Lucas to the team. He was obviously grief-stricken by the abbot's death but seemed to understand why he had to go back to the United States. He only nodded his head or used facial expressions to show his emotions or reactions; they had yet to hear him speak.

Jim had not yet seen the full report so he didn't know all the details, but the fingerprints matched those on file for Sergeant Lucas. He asked Leslie if they could get a blood sample from her to test against his, and she agreed readily. She wanted to make sure it was her father before she got too excited. This was getting more and more intriguing by the minute, and she still had not asked about his truck driving.

• • •

Chapter Five

Justine came back to escort Leslie to the lab for bloodwork, and Leslie was surprised that everything in the hospital stayed open so late. "We have to take care of our troops," Justine explained. "Their needs don't always fit into a schedule." Leslie asked about Justine working so late, too, and she simply replied, "Same."

When the phlebotomist drew a third vial of blood and declared it to be the last one, Leslie asked why they needed so much blood. The phlebotomist looked at her computer screen and shrugged. "Just a lot of routine tests, especially since you're new to our system," she commented. Leslie's growling stomach took priority over any questions or reaction, and Justine whisked her off to the cafeteria as the blood was sent to be tested. Leslie couldn't remember when she had last had any bloodwork, since she rarely went to the doctor, but the lab made her think about her mother and all the tests and treatments she had endured.

Leslie wasn't sure if the food was better than average hospital food, but this sure beat what they had served at the hospital where she spent so much time visiting her Mom. Justine had opted for a Cobb salad and sweet tea and she watched with amusement as Leslie wolfed down her turkey and mashed potatoes with gravy. Leslie was halfway through eating when she looked up and saw Justine staring at her, so she slowed down and took a drink of her Coke.

"So, when do you get to go home?" Leslie asked. Justine said she would go home after escorting Leslie back to the Fisher House, and Leslie asked if she would be able to see her father tonight. Justine explained that they would have to wait for the blood tests, which should be back late tonight, and suddenly Leslie realized how tired she was. Driving 500 miles while mentally and emotionally processing the situation at hand was catching up to her, and she wanted to talk to Billy. She suggested that they go back now so Justine could go home, which brought a glowing smile to Justine's otherwise serious face. "Whatever you want," she said. It was almost 9:00.

On the walk back to Fisher House 5, Leslie asked Justine about her job and her life. She had worked for the State Department for 9 years, had no kids, no husband or boyfriend, and basically her job was her life. The only things that she did outside of work were exercising and working on getting her Masters in Social Work (MSW). Most of her courses were online and this was her last semester. She had walked right into this job after serving four years in the Marine Corps, since her clearance was still active, but she was ready to have a life of her own. Leslie was fascinated and commented about what a great coincidence it was that her father was also in the Marine Corps. Justine laughed and said, "Nothing in the State Department is a coincidence. They pair agents with appropriate cases."

They walked into the Fisher House lobby and Justine shared nods with the receptionist and told Leslie that she would meet her there in the morning so they could go back to the hospital. Leslie walked into her room, threw her purse on the bed, and collapsed into the recliner by the window with her phone. She had a great view of the tiny parking lot, which was full when they walked through, and wondered which car was Justine's. She stood up and looked out, but nobody was in the parking lot or getting into a car. She assumed that Justine was talking to the receptionist at the front desk, whom she seemed to know, so she probably didn't leave right away. Leslie called Billy while she continued to watch the parking lot.

Melanie answered the phone and commented that it's funny to answer a house phone instead of her cell phone. Leslie said she would eventually get rid of the house phone and answering machine, but it was easier to get Billy to talk on the old phone that sat on their end table because he liked it. Billy was eager to talk to Leslie and Melanie only had time to say that he was doing fine before he was on the line. "Mom, can I talk to my Grandpa?" he asked excitedly. Leslie didn't expect that question, and she laughed at Billy's excitement to meet his grandfather. She explained that he was in the hospital and instantly regretted saying that when Billy asked, "Is he going to die, like Grandma?" She reassured him that everyone dies eventually, but not everyone who goes to the hospital dies there. They were just doing tests and his grandfather would be able to leave soon, she explained. "Did you tell him about me?" Billy continued. "Is he excited to meet me?" More explaining, more questions. Leslie realized that he came by this inquisitive side naturally, always asking questions non-stop just like his mother.

She steered the conversation to what Billy and Melanie had done that day, and in the middle of a sentence he said, "Oh, no. It's 9:00. I have to go to bed. Good night!" He gave the phone back to Melanie, who reminded him to stop at the bathroom first, and off he went. Melanie asked Leslie how things were going and told her that a local reporter had come to the house earlier. Melanie told the reporter that Leslie was out of town, and finally had to call her husband to come and scare the persistent paparazzi away. Steve said he had read something on one of his Facebook groups about a Marine Corps hero being found and was doing some research. "Your dad was a bad ass, huh?" asked Melanie. "Probably as much as a truck driver could be," Leslie answered. "Good one!" Melanie answered, which Leslie did not understand. Melanie had to go because Billy was asking her to turn out the light, and Leslie thanked her for being so great with Billy.

After she hung up, Leslie realized that not one car had left the parking lot while she was on the phone. She grabbed her key and walked down the hall and out the front door. The lot was still full; no cars had left. Where did Justine go? Back to the hospital? Was her car in another lot? As she came back in, she said Hello to the receptionist, who looked up from her texting as if she had been caught with her hand in the cookie jar. "Is everything okay?" she asked, walking toward Leslie, who just nodded and mumbled something about being tired as she headed back to her room. She set her phone alarm for 7:00, put on her night gown and brushed her teeth, and fell asleep immediately. Even those unanswered questions in her head couldn't keep her awake tonight.

•••

Chapter Six

Leslie woke up at 6:30, thinking she needed to get ready for work, and sat up. The bed was so comfortable that she had slept through the entire night, which was rare for her. She turned off the alarm and went to the window. Most of the cars were gone from the parking lot and she thought back to last night. She needed to ask Justine what kind of car she drives.

Leslie showered, put on a red t-shirt like she did every Friday, and took her time getting ready. She was rarely allowed this luxury and felt a tinge of guilt about being happy to have some time alone. She loved her son, but it was a lot of work being a single parent of a child with special needs. It could be a lot worse, she reminded herself, as Billy's place on the autism spectrum was considered "mild" and he was labeled as "High functioning." She thought about some of the exhausted parents that she saw at the Autism Support Group meetings that she used to attend. She was luckier than most, but many of them did not seem to grasp the meaning of a "support" group and Leslie had to stop attending.

Her phone buzzed with a text from Justine, who asked if she was eating breakfast there or wanted to grab something at the hospital. Leslie replied that she could wait to eat at the hospital if Justine would be there shortly and went over to the recliner to wait. She watched a couple of families leaving, one with someone in uniform, and felt like her red shirt meant even more in this environment. She and Mom had worn red shirts every Friday for three years, showing support and raising awareness for military families and their deployed loved ones. About 10 minutes passed when Justine knocked on her door. Leslie had not seen her pull in, so she was not expecting it. She put her phone and key in her purse and opened the door. Justine was also wearing a red shirt, which warmed Leslie's heart. They walked out, nodded at today's receptionist, and headed over to the hospital.

The walk seemed shorter today, and along the way Justine explained that she expected the reporters today. She told Leslie to tell them that she knows nothing, and Leslie commented that it should be easy because she really doesn't. As if on cue, an unshaven young man with brown curly hair approached and asked if her name was Leslie Mitchell. "Yes, I'm Leslie," was all she said as she wondered how this unkempt man could be a reporter. Didn't they wear suits and always look like they were on their way to an opera? Justine grabbed her arm as they went through the front door, pushing it closed on the curious man, and Leslie saw others with microphones and cameras coming. There were several security guards at the front doors who were not there yesterday, and Justine clarified that it's normal to have extra security when they expect uninvited guests.

They grabbed Leslie's new "permanent" badge from the front desk and headed down the hall to the same debriefing room as yesterday. Leslie didn't see Jim, and asked if he'd be in. "Oh, he's upstairs with your father," Justine said. She grabbed some paperwork and sat down with Leslie. "What do you want for breakfast? I will have it brought to us." Leslie just wanted some toast and scrambled eggs with cheese, and maybe some sweet tea. Justine said she'd have the same and called the cafeteria to order it.

As they waited for their breakfast, Justine explained that the blood tests were back, and this was definitely Leslie's father. Leslie was relieved, but then realized that she had not brought the Rubbermaid tote with her. The pictures and paperwork were in there, and she said she would go back after they ate breakfast to get them. Justine offered to have someone retrieve the tote from Leslie's room and one of the security guards could bring it over, if that was okay with her. Leslie described the tote and where it was, and Justine called next door to have it brought over. There was a knock on the door, and Justine looked out the peephole. She opened it and a nice older lady from the cafeteria brought their food over to the small table.

They ate in silence as Leslie started to realize that she could get used to this, not paying for anything and having meals brought to her. Since Leslie always seemed to be the one looking out for others, it was usually difficult to allow anyone to wait on her, but this felt nice. Justine finished her food, unlocked a drawer in the desk, and pulled out an extremely old and worn folder. She placed it next to an open notebook on the desk and placed a pen next to it. She opened another drawer and took out a small black box with buttons on it, then turned to Leslie. "Are you ready to find out more about Sergeant William Lucas?" Leslie nodded. She was ready.

Justine picked up the black box and said, "This is a micro-recorder. I need to record this conversation, but first I need to get your consent to do that." Justine slid a consent form across the desk and Leslie signed it. For some reason, she immediately started feeling sick to her stomach. Justine pressed the record button and said, "This is Justine Wilson, United States Department of State. Today is Friday, April 19, 2019. I am speaking with Leslie Lucas Mitchell, daughter of Sergeant William Lucas, in Debrief Room A at Walter Reed Medical Center. Ms. Mitchell, some of the information that I am about to divulge is still considered to be classified and must not leave this room. The consent form that you signed spells out the consequences of sharing this information. Do you have any questions?"

Leslie's mouth said No, but her brain had non-stop questions. What is happening? What did my father do? Justine opened the file and explained that it was her father's SRB (Servicemember Record Book), which contained his training and dates of service and any punishments he may have received under the UCMJ (Uniform Code of Military Justice). Justine said, "Before I tell you what's in here, can you tell me what you have been told about your father? Specifically, about his training or military service?" Leslie closed her eyes to think about what she'd been told and started spilling. "Well, he went to college in the fall of 1962 and started dating Mom the following summer. He wanted to be a History teacher, but he also loved foreign languages and wanted to travel the world and visit historic places. A lot of his friends were enlisting in the military while he was in college. There were tons of protests on campus about the war in Vietnam when he went back for his senior year in the fall of 1965, and he was drafted that November. He was only 6 months from finishing college, and could have taken a deferral, but he wanted to serve his country. Mom said he made a deal that he would waive his deferral if he could choose his branch. He chose the Marine Corps."

Justine was taking notes, although the conversation was being recorded, and she looked up from her notes. "I don't blame him,"

Justine interjected with a smile. "Do you know when he left for Vietnam?" Leslie didn't know, but she said she thought he went to Japan for about a year and then came home to Michigan before heading to Vietnam. During that time at home, her parents got married and she was conceived. Her dad went to Vietnam and her mom sent him a letter telling him that she was pregnant. He wanted to be home for the birth, but things kept happening. He was declared "MIA" just before her first birthday. She had that letter in her tote.

Susan finished bleaching the cloth diapers and gave them a rinse in hot water before hanging them on the line. With Leslie down for a nap, she had time to get some chores done and had made a long list. With Leslie's first birthday only a few weeks away, Susan had a lot to do. She started thinking about how wonderful it would be for Bill to be home for his daughter's first birthday, but decided she'd settle for getting a letter from him.

Two months ago, she had donned her most beautiful pink dress and dressed Leslie up in a darling little dress that matched hers. Susan had been counting the days and marking them off on the calendar, and went to the airport on the day that Bill had promised to be home to see them. When he wasn't on the flight, Susan called everyone who might know something, including her friend Linda, whose husband had been home on leave the week before and should still be there. There was no answer, no matter how many times she called, and nobody at home when she stopped at their house. For two months, Susan had called everyone and anyone, but had no real answers. She had received a handful of letters from Bill, but they were dated before the day that he was supposed to leave Vietnam.

A knock on the door brought Susan back to the moment, and she looked out the window to see a dark blue car that she did not recognize. She opened the door and a Marine Corps captain greeted her. "Mrs. Lucas?" he inquired. "Yes, I'm Susan Lucas," she answered quietly. "Are you here about my husband? Is he dead?" The Captain handed her a sealed letter addressed to her, with the return address simply "The White House." He cleared his throat and explained that Sergeant Lucas was officially Missing in Action, and that they would be in contact with any further developments. Susan thanked him and closed the door.

As she read the letter from President Nixon, she felt as if she were someone else, watching a movie of a poor wife who just wanted her husband to come home. She thought of all the women who had received death notices and counted her blessings. Bill was missing, still alive, and just needed to be found. At that moment, she vowed to never give up on her husband coming home. She decided to take everything one day at a time and went back to planning Leslie's birthday party.

"When were you born?" Justine asked. "July 4th, 1967," Leslie declared proudly. "I have been patriotic since birth." They were interrupted by a knock on the door, and Justine switched off the recorder. One of the receptionists from Fisher House was there with the tote. Leslie thought to herself that they really have "Customer Service" figured out and thanked her for bringing it over so quickly.

"We'll go through some of your belongings shortly," said Justine, "but first I would like to set the record straight about your father." She clicked the recorder back on and opened the SRB. "William Leslie Lucas enlisted in the United States Marine Corps in November of 1965, during his senior year at the University of Michigan. When he was drafted and given aptitude tests, he scored off the charts, nearly perfect, on the DLAB (Defense Language Aptitude Battery). He had an affinity for learning languages that was rare and had taken French and Spanish classes in high school and college. He also knew a little Morse Code from his time as a Boy Scout. No arrests, no drug use. He was a gold mine for the military and was sent to the Defense Language Institute in Monterey, California, to learn Vietnamese. They polished his Morse Code skills and he went through the Basic courses for Vietnamese quickly, then went through the Advanced Vietnamese and French courses. He was given the MOS (Military Occupational Specialty) of 2571, which was a Cryptologist/Radio Operator. He was in Okinawa for a couple of weeks for intelligence training, but the rest of that first year was spent at DLI in Monterey." This was all new to Leslie, but she was fascinated and urged Justine to continue.

"When your dad came home on leave with orders to Vietnam, when your parents got married, he actually went back to DLI first for another school. He went through Basic and Advanced Russian and received the highest test scores in the history of the school.

When he wasn't in class, he was at the gym or outside. He was very physical and loved boxing. He boxed, he ran, and he lifted weights that he made himself. He was an expert with any weapon that was handed to him but wasn't interested in ribbons or medals or anything that labeled him."

Leslie said her neighbors had discovered some information on the internet about her dad and made a comment that he was "quite a bad ass," and Justine said some records are open to the public and people are starting to find out how much Sergeant Lucas did. She winked and said, "Yes, he was quite a bad ass." Leslie laughed, then thought to herself that her mother wouldn't have liked hearing that he was actually in California instead of Okinawa or Vietnam. "So, when did my dad actually go to Vietnam?" she asked.

Justine explained that Bill arrived in Vietnam on 20 April 1967, attached to 1st Radio Battalion, 3rd Marine Division, III Marine Amphibious Force. He was on Team 2, a small Signals Intelligence unit in Chu Lai. Sergeant Lucas was an Expert Rifleman and liked to be part of the action, but he was so valuable to the intelligence mission that they tried to keep him out of harm's way and tried to protect him as much as possible.

Justine was interrupted by a buzzing sound and a door opening. It was Jim Carlson and he seemed to be in a good mood. He saw that Justine had the SRB out and asked how things were going. "Hey, General. I'm just telling Leslie about Sergeant Lucas getting to Vietnam and how he liked to be part of the action." Jim's face lit up with a smile and he said, "That's either the smartest or luckiest man alive…and still alive!" He chuckled to himself as he walked into the next room, shaking his head.

Justine continued, explaining to Leslie that several times her father would disappear for hours at a time to go on his own unplanned reconnaissance missions. He would come back with intelligence, sometimes stolen equipment that he had recovered, and occasionally a live prisoner that he had captured.

Staff Sergeant Pirada paced back and forth in front of the ¾ ton van that was fitted with his platoon's intelligence collection equipment, begging his lieutenant to give him ten more minutes to find Sergeant Lucas. "Sir, I'm aware that the enemy's position has been confirmed to our northwest, but we can't send in air support yet. Lucas is out there." After being granted ten minutes, Pirada directed PFC Tillotson and PFC Mackey to go find their squad leader. They were back in five minutes with a sweaty Sergeant Lucas and one terrified Viet Cong soldier. "Luke, you're killing me!" Staff Sergeant Pirada yelled as he called the Lieutenant back. "Commence fire, sir. All clear."

Mackey and Tillotson led the VC prisoner to the holding tank where he would be interrogated while Sergeant Lucas explained to Pirada what had happened. "There were three of them, Staff Sergeant. I took care of the other two, but this one started crying and begged me to take him alive. He might have some valuable information." While Pirada started his routine speech about the dangers of going out on patrol alone, Lucas laughed and rolled his eyes. "I'm heading to the chow hall," he stated casually. "Killing makes me hungry." As Pirada continued his expletive-filled tirade, Lucas promised to share the intel he'd collected after he filled his stomach.

"Wow, so my neighbors were right," Leslie commented. "My dad *was* a bad ass." Justine laughed and clicked the recorder off. She said she wanted to check in with Jim Carlson for an update and asked if Leslie wanted something to drink. Leslie asked for some sweet tea and noticed that Justine took the SRB with her when she left the room.

While she was gone, Leslie remembered that her Rubbermaid tote had been delivered and was sitting on the counter. She took off the lid and looked inside for some pictures that might help her fill in this story. She had just grabbed some of Mom's albums and a few loose pictures out of her old cedar chest, most of which she hadn't seen in years. She thought she had placed the letters on top of the pictures when she put everything in the tote, but the pictures were on top. Where were the letters? Did she forget them? They were probably under the other paperwork. She set the pictures back inside when she heard Justine coming back.

•••

Chapter Seven

Justine returned with Leslie's tea and asked if she needed a break. Leslie said she wanted to continue with her father's SRB, as she liked hearing about his experiences. Before Justine opened it again, she said, "So, you know that your father was a restless kind of guy, right? He liked to be part of the action and participated in a lot of short Search and Destroy missions, but he also enjoyed helping the locals." Justine turned on the recorder and explained that the Marine Corps had an extensive pacification program in place. Shortly before Sergeant Lucas arrived in Vietnam, the Marine Corps had intensified and restructured that program, calling it the Combined Action Program (CAP). The idea was to be embedded with the villagers to protect them and assist with any development of their village, while also gathering needed intelligence. With his language abilities, Sergeant Lucas could communicate with those who spoke Vietnamese or French, which was usually the older locals. He established a school, built by Marines, in part to build trust but also to make sure that everyone received an education.

"Well, my dad wanted to be a History teacher," Leslie said. "I guess this was as close as he got." She was feeling more fascinated by her father, learning all this new information, but of everything she had heard so far this was her favorite part. Mom would have been so proud, and Leslie wondered how much her mother had known about the school.

Justine explained that Sergeant Lucas taught school early in the morning, and then worked 10 to 12 hours gathering intelligence or going on patrol with the local soldiers. He was fully embedded in their community and he befriended a local Buddhist monastic, or monk, named Thich Dinh Ky. There was a monastery in a pagoda right next to the school and he visited often, but lived at Marble Mountain. "Is he the one who saved my father?" Leslie asked, feeling like she was putting it all together. "Yes, he is the one who saved your father and protected him all this time," Justine replied. "Unfortunately for us, he passed away and we can't ask him any questions, but we're still hoping to find more information from the extraction team's report."

Justine explained that the school seemed to be the outlet that Sergeant Lucas needed, as he became involved with the children of the village. He stopped his rebellious private missions and turned down some temporary orders to help with a secret mission to South America in the fall of 1967. He was scheduled to return to the United States in January 1968.

"Are you sure?" Leslie asked. "According to Mom, we went to welcome him home in April, but he wasn't on the plane. Her letter declaring him MIA states that he went missing in April. What happened?" Justine paused, then answered, "The Tet Offensive happened. It was brutal and we lost a lot of men. Your father was originally scheduled to leave on 20 January 1968, but he requested to put it off for two weeks. The Tet Offensive changed a lot of plans, including scheduled flights, for weeks. At the end of February, he was issued orders out of Vietnam for 20 April 1968, giving him exactly one year in country. Two days before he was scheduled to leave, there was significant activity near Chu Lai and a lot of Marines died. Team 2 was wiped out, or so it was believed, and three of them are still listed as MIA. Your dad is one of the three." Justine turned off the recorder and made some notes.

Leslie's heart ached for those other families, as the odds of finding the others alive were statistically low. Those men would be in their 70s, possibly even 80s, and finding one of them still alive – her father – had been improbable. "So, this is a big deal. All those reporters outside want to tell the story of a tough old Marine who defied the odds."

Justine warned her again about talking to reporters. "Americans have come a long way when it comes to our Vietnam veterans," she said, "but reporters these days are no longer interested in reporting facts. They thrive on controversy and will create some if there isn't any available. I assume that they'll focus on your dad's training and body count, then make up some controversy, probably that he was a rogue spy, and then talk about him abandoning his family." Justine paused to check her phone that had buzzed. Leslie knew that Justine was telling the truth; she had seen so much of that exact issue in the past couple of years that she had stopped watching the news. "So, what exactly do you mean by his 'body count'?" she asked. Justine said they'd talk about that later; she had just received authorization for them to go see Sergeant Lucas.

•••

Chapter Eight

The elevator ride up to her dad's room seemed to take an eternity. Justine seemed excited, too, although she spent most of the time reminding Leslie that her father doesn't seem to recall his past and still has not spoken actual words, so they don't know what languages he remembers. Leslie knew a lot of tricks that she had learned from Billy's speech therapist and thought she might be able to help. "The general consensus was that Billy would never have normal speech," Leslie explained. "I learned a lot about language development and how to celebrate the smallest victories."

"I don't give up easily," Leslie continued as they left the elevator, "especially when it comes to my family." She smiled, knowing that Mom would be proud, and had to suppress her emotions again. There was nobody in the hallway, which was odd for a hospital, and all the doors were closed. In every hospital she'd ever been in, everything and everyone is displayed for the whole world to see. All the doors are open, and you see things you really may not want to see. This was different, but she liked it. No accidental mooning here.

There was a security guard by her dad's door, and she had to show him her badge and ID. He wrote something down and nodded at Justine, who smiled and pushed open the door. Bill Lucas was sitting up on the edge of his bed, looking out the window with an excellent view of the garden area. He was tan and thin, wearing a white t-shirt and some olive drab shorts that were way too big. He turned to them and immediately looked away, but Leslie had already noticed the brown eyes with long lashes, just like hers. Justine whispered to Leslie that she had read that Buddhist monks are not allowed to touch women. Since he seems to have lived at the monastery for 50 years, there was an assumption that he followed their beliefs. To be respectful, the hospital used as many male nurses as possible to care for him. Leslie's hope that there might be a "Welcome" hug dissolved, but she approached him anyway. "Hi, I'm Leslie, your daughter. I've been waiting to meet you for 52 years."

Bill stood up and stared at Leslie for a second, sizing her up, obviously trying to understand what was happening. His big brown eyes seemed to change shape and they welled up with tears as he walked toward her. To her surprise, he embraced her in a bear hug and simply said, "Oh!" Justine squealed with delight and pulled out her phone. "Are you recording this?" Leslie asked. "No, I'm calling General Carlson," Justine said. "He can see what's happening on the monitors."

By the time Jim Carlson got there, Leslie had let her wall of emotions come down and was crying like a baby. Justine was having a hard time holding back tears, and a few slid down her cheek as she witnessed the precious moment that this 52-year-old woman met her father for the first time. Bill Lucas didn't say anything else, but he appeared to be aware of what was happening and his eyes brimmed with tears. He regained his bearing when General Carlson entered the room, and they exchanged nods. Jim Carlson was carrying Leslie's Rubbermaid tote and set it on the counter.

"Where should we start?" he asked Justine. She hesitated, not wanting to offend someone she admired so deeply, but this wasn't supposed to be their responsibility. "Should we be doing this?" she asked. "With all the therapists involved, I don't want to step on anyone's toes." Jim Carlson laughed. "We're Marines, and that's kind of what we do. Do you know how many of my friends from Vietnam didn't get adequate help? They followed a standard treatment plan, regardless of their problems or their progress. They all just fell into the 'PTSD' category, no matter what got them there, and some of them are no better off today than they were 40 years ago. I have some vested interest in this particular Marine, and we're going to help him recover his memories…or at least teach him about the life he once had and find out if he wants it back. Are you with me?"

Justine wasn't used to the retired General speaking so passionately about someone. He was dependable and loyal, and had a slightly soft side, but this was unusually soft. Cottony soft. She knew that he was trusting her with this vulnerable situation, and she didn't want to let him down. "I'm in, sir. I guess we should start at the beginning."

• • •

Chapter Nine

While Justine and Jim talked, Leslie opened the tote and laughed when she saw that the letters were back on top of the pictures. She didn't say anything about it, but decided she would ask Justine about it later. As she was pulling out photo albums, she asked Bill if he understood what she was saying. "Nod your head up and down if you understand me, like this," she told him as she nodded her head. He nodded his head and Leslie smiled, then asked Justine how to proceed.

"We should make an outline for this," Justine told Leslie and Jim. "Sergeant Lucas is going to need as many pictures, as many details, as we can find. Does his sister still live in Virginia?" Leslie wondered how they even knew that, since her Aunt Judith had only moved there a few years ago, just about the time that Leslie had left Virginia. "She lives in Fredericksburg, probably just over an hour from here," Leslie replied. "I haven't called her yet to tell her about my dad." Justine asked if she might have photos of Sergeant Lucas as a child, and Leslie knew she did because her aunt brought up the subject at Mom's funeral.

Leslie stood by the casket at her mother's funeral, surrounded by several beautiful flower arrangements, during the family viewing. "Mom, what happens with all these flowers after everyone leaves?" asked Billy, who was always thinking ahead. "We'll take most of them home, honey," Leslie explained as she squeezed his hand. "It will make the house more cheerful." Aunt Judith had overheard their conversation and offered to take all the flowers to her house. "That's thoughtful of you," Leslie replied, "but we can manage. If there is an arrangement that you really like, you're welcome to take it."

Aunt Judith stepped closer to Leslie and stared into her face, which Leslie did not expect, so she laughed nervously and looked away. "You're just like your mother," Aunt Judith whispered angrily. "She was so selfish." Leslie usually backed down when it came to

Aunt Judith and her mean nature, but today was not the day to push Leslie's buttons. "Give me one example," Leslie shot back sharply. "Well, when my father died, he left all his money to your mother," Aunt Judith began. "Do you know what I got? Pictures. Not just of me, but of your mom and dad and everyone else." *Leslie argued that memories are quite valuable and pictures show those memories, but Aunt Judith was undeterred.* "Your mom was jealous that I received the pictures and she tried to buy them from me," *she continued.*

Before Aunt Judith could say another word, Billy spoke up. "Do you still have the pictures? When you die, can my mom have them?" *Leslie wasn't sure if she should scold Billy or thank him, but she was surprised that Aunt Judith agreed that Leslie could have them. As her aunt walked away, mumbling something about her only brother marrying "that woman," Leslie clenched her teeth and reminded herself that this day was about her mother. She was having a hard enough time keeping it together, and allowing Aunt Judith to get under her skin would make it worse.* "Come on, Billy, let's go find a snack," *she suggested cheerfully.*

Leslie cringed at the idea of talking to her aunt again so soon; she had just seen her a few weeks ago, after not hearing her condescending voice for months. Aunt Judith had called to talk to Leslie on their home phone just before Susan died, so she would have to call Melanie to get the number from the phone's history. Justine suggested that they break for lunch so Leslie could call her Aunt Judith, and they could regroup with a plan afterward. Leslie and Justine left together, but Jim said he would meet them downstairs after he spoke briefly to Sergeant Lucas. As the door was closing, Leslie heard Jim say, "Okay, Erden…" She asked Justine why he was calling him that, and Justine explained as they got in the elevator: "That's who he thinks he is. He was the abbot's righthand man, and I'm sure he's still coming to terms with the fact that Ky died recently; he was all he had…or so he thought. Imagine what he's experienced, after the trauma of the war. I assume that he had complete amnesia, somehow lost his ability or his will to speak, and now he is being told that he is someone completely different than the peace-loving Buddhist he had become."

Leslie thought about how awful that would be and wondered how much he really understood. They came out of the elevator and headed toward the cafeteria, and the Director of Security stopped Justine. "We've been turning away reporters all morning, Ms. Wilson. Are you planning on having a press conference?" Justine said they were talking about doing that this afternoon, and she would keep him informed. He shook Leslie's hand and said, "Congratulations on your father being found. He's a true American hero." Leslie thanked him and smiled as she thought to herself, "Also, he's a bad ass."

When they reached the cafeteria, Leslie realized that she really wasn't hungry and just opted for chicken noodle soup and crackers. She ordered a large Coke and closed her eyes as she sipped it. Ah, the simple pleasures in life. Justine picked up a chef's salad with Ranch dressing and decided to get a Coke instead of her usual sweet tea because it seemed to make Leslie so happy. "Oh, this is good," Justine said. "I haven't had a Coke in weeks. I might need the sugar and caffeine if the General makes me talk to the press this afternoon. That's always draining."

Leslie blew on her soup and asked Justine what she was going to tell them. "The truth," Justine said. "Your dad disappeared in Vietnam in 1968 and was taken to a Buddhist monastery at Marble Mountain to be nurtured back to health. He didn't know who he was, and they let him be someone else. We didn't know he was alive until those veterans spotted him on a tour and we sent in a team to investigate. The leader of the monastery died soon after our team arrived, and now Sergeant William Lucas is back. Tada!" She met Leslie's gaze and took a deep breath. "Wow!" Justine finally managed. "That sounds like a story just waiting to be exploited. Those reporters are going to shred me out there, especially since many of them know about his past."

This was Leslie's chance to learn more about what her father had really done. "Okay, I know that he wasn't a truck driver, but I'm still thinking about your 'body count' comment. Did my dad kill a lot of people?" At first, Justine seemed to change the subject as she brought up the greatest Marine sniper in Vietnam, Carlos Hathcock, who had once spent four days moving 1500 yards to kill an NVA general. She explained that Hathcock had 93 confirmed kills, but in order to have them count as "Confirmed," a third party had to be a witness...someone other than the sniper's spotter. In his estimation, Hathcock killed over 300 enemy soldiers. Sergeant Lucas was on track to break that record, having 75 confirmed kills and 100+ unconfirmed in a short time, but after Leslie's birth and opening the school his focus was redirected and his interests shifted.

Justine suggested that having a child, seeing that precious little baby in the picture his wife sent, gave him a new perspective. Maybe he became more aware of his own mortality. Perhaps witnessing the deaths of so many fellow Marines contributed to that, and he just wanted to make sure that he got home to see his wife and daughter. "Do you think he knows what he did?" Leslie asked. Justine admitted that she had no idea, but explained that this was General Carlson's area. He was tasked with "debriefing" Sergeant Lucas and gathering any useful intelligence. They had to be sure that he isn't a double agent or that he didn't go AWOL, and that the amnesia is real. As much as she hated to say it, she informed Leslie that they had to walk a fine line between welcoming home a survivor or a traitor. She voiced her concern that the liberal media was going to take the "traitor" route, but Justine assured Leslie that she believes her father is a survivor and an American hero.

•••

Chapter Ten

As Leslie walked with Justine to the debriefing offices, she could see that some equipment was in the lobby, staged for the afternoon press conference. There was a podium on a dolly, waiting to be wheeled to its destination, along with microphones, chairs, and bottles of water. The Director of Security approached when he saw them. "Ms. Wilson, the forecasters are calling for rain late this afternoon, so if we're doing this outside then we should do it by 3. Will any of the family members be joining you?" Before Justine could answer, Leslie said, "Yes, I'll be there." Justine said they would discuss it, but plan on one family member being there. As they continued walking, Justine commented, "Look at you, jumping right into the fire. Your mother would be so proud."

They opened the office door and Jim Carlson was there, just finishing his sandwich. "Peanut butter and jelly, sir?" Justine queried. He laughed and patted his stomach. "Every damn day!" Justine reminded him that he packs his own lunch, so he could pack something different. "At my age, I enjoy my routine with no surprises. If I made a ham and cheese sandwich, I'd probably forget by lunchtime and it would surprise me. I'll stick with peanut butter and jelly."

"Some surprises are welcome," said Leslie, "like getting that phone call from Justine to tell me my dad is still alive. How did you handle the surprise of finding him?" Jim explained that some surprises are indeed welcome, but it was more of a discovery than an actual surprise, since all they knew when they left for Da Nang is that it was an older American man.

As the Extraction Team landed in Da Nang, they discussed their plan of action. Jim handed out the laminated hand-drawn maps he had made after years of being in the Marble Mountain area, and the team asked him a lot of questions. He had been there so many times that he personally didn't need a map, so he used his time to take some pictures of the area and reread the statement from the two veterans who had supposedly seen the American. "What if he's just someone who visited Vietnam and decided he liked it?" he asked nobody in particular. "It might not be such a bad place if people weren't trying to kill you."

The team discussed how they would divide and search, wearing t-shirts that identified them as part of a tourist group so they wouldn't arouse suspicion. They spotted the American on the first day, and it didn't take long to get the head monk to confess that he had been hiding that particular American since the late '60s. He had proof in his safe, and ordered one of the monks to release the contents of the shoe box that he had kept in there for years. Inside were photos, a knife, some letters that had basically turned to cloth, and a rusted snuff tin containing the dog tags of the American.

As Jim pried open the snuff tin, he thought about how exciting it would be to discover that this was one of their men who had either gone AWOL or been captured. The dog tags were wrapped in tape, and when he finally was able to read them he fell into a chair. "Oh, my God, Luke, it's a fucking miracle," he mumbled. "Susan was right." The other team members were completely silent for several seconds and someone finally asked, "Who's Luke?" Jim was in shock and only managed to whisper, "My friend."

"If I woke up tomorrow with my head sewn to the carpet, I wouldn't be more surprised than I was that day," he laughed. Leslie and Justine laughed, too. It was nice to break the tension that she was feeling about calling her Aunt Judith, who was always rude and selfish. There was not one pleasant memory that she could conjure up about her aunt, who just seemed so miserable. She married into money and she flaunted it, but she had never worked a day in her life. She didn't have any kids, but she had two ankle-biter dogs and two housekeepers and Leslie felt sorry for all four of them. When Aunt Judith had rolled into town for Susan's funeral in a new Lincoln Navigator that had been painted fuchsia, though, Leslie was able to laugh through her tears. Aunt Judith was always over-the-top and thought everyone was jealous of her.

"Do I really have to get those pictures from my aunt?" Leslie asked. "She's just such a horrible person." Jim said he'd be glad to talk to her, which made Leslie feel better. She liked Jim and felt like she had known him for a long time. How nice that he would talk to someone he didn't even know so she didn't have to do it! Leslie said she was calling home to get her aunt's number, and Justine and Jim went into another room to give her privacy.

It took Melanie a little while to answer the phone and the answering machine didn't pick up. When she finally answered, she apologized but she had put the phone on mute and turned off the machine because of all the calls from reporters. They were watching cartoons, and Billy noticed that the phone lit up so she looked at the number and saw that it was Leslie. Melanie suggested that Leslie call her cell phone when she wanted to reach her from now on and asked how things were going. Leslie explained everything and could tell that Melanie had been spending a lot of time with Billy. So many questions! She asked Melanie to tell Billy everything, since he was watching his favorite episode of "Sponge Bob" and did not have time to talk.

Leslie asked Melanie to scroll through her home phone's history for Aunt Judith's number. "Oh, you're calling to give her the news?" Melanie inquired. "That's nice of you, considering how she treats you." Leslie explained that she needed pictures from her father's childhood so they could put together a chronological timeline for him, so she had to do it. Melanie commented that she liked this "brave new Leslie" and that she would text her Aunt Judith's number as soon as she found it.

•••

Chapter Eleven

Leslie was staring at the number that Melanie had just texted and took a deep breath as she punched in the numbers on her phone. She secretly hoped that Aunt Judith wouldn't answer so she could just leave a message. Unfortunately, she picked up immediately. "Hello, Leslie. Are you calling for motherly advice? I knew you would, after being so weirdly close to your mom all those years." Leslie took a deep breath and began, "My dad is alive. I'm at the hospital in Bethesda, Maryland, and I need to get some pictures from you." Aunt Judith laughed heartily and said, "I hope they have a Psych Ward there. I wondered if you'd pick up where your mom left off." Leslie could feel that familiar lump in her throat and paused. Before she could say another word, Jim Carlson snatched the phone out of her hand.

"Judith, this is Jim Carlson. How about you stop being a bitch for one minute and listen? Our Extraction Team went to Vietnam a couple of weeks ago and brought back your brother. He's in great physical condition, but he has no idea who he is. We need as many pictures as we can find, starting with his childhood. You're probably the only one who has them, since you took all the photo albums that your father had." As they talked, it was obvious to Leslie that Jim knew her Aunt Judith. Leslie listened intently, mouth wide open, and handed Jim a pen to write down her aunt's address when he asked. By the time the call was over, Leslie was pacing.

"Have you met my Aunt Judith before?" she asked. Jim admitted that he had known Judith for years and couldn't understand how she and Bill came from the same family. Jim had met her at her mother's funeral when he was home on leave in 1970. "Wait...You knew my Grandma Lucas?" Leslie asked as she was trying to put it all together. "Not really," Jim explained. "Here's the story: Your dad and I were friends in college. He was the smartest guy I'd ever met; I was a year ahead of him. I knew that when I graduated college, I wanted to be commissioned a Marine Corps officer. I had been planning that for most of my life. When I met your dad, he had so many interests that he had trouble picking a major. Languages, history, political science, regular science...he loved learning and really wanted to do something. Very high energy. When he came back to campus that second year, all he talked about was your mom. He was smitten, to say the least."

Leslie sat down and closed her eyes. This was getting weirder by the second. Justine appeared in the doorway and was watching and listening. Jim continued, telling Leslie with a slight crack in his voice that he was probably responsible for her dad's interest in the Marine Corps. Leslie reminded him that both of her grandfathers were Marines, so her dad probably had some interest before he even met Jim.

Jim talked about the plans they made, how Bill wanted to teach History and promised that he would mention the contributions of the Marine Corps as often as possible. After graduation in May 1965, Jim was commissioned and left for flight school. Bill was drafted while Jim was at flight school, and with both of them going to different training and Jim flying missions all over the world, they missed each other's weddings. By the time they met again in Chu Lai, it had been almost two years since they had seen each other.

Jim carried his helmet under his arm as he strolled across the tarmac, already sweating before he made it 50 yards. A thin shirtless Marine ran toward him, carrying a canteen and a towel, which confused Jim until he recognized Bill and laughed. "I figured you would need this when you finally decided to land," Bill shouted above the noisy aircraft. "Had to. I ran out of fuel," Jim replied. After a brief hug, Jim took a swig from the canteen and closed his eyes. "Beer! How did you manage to get it cold?" Bill teased that Jim didn't have the clearance for such information as they walked to the mess tent.

After catching up on life since they had last seen each other, Bill turned the conversation to Jim's flying. "It's cool that they made this airstrip like you're landing on a carrier, huh?" Bill asked. Jim agreed that it was a great idea but admitted that he preferred landing on the actual carrier, at least during the day. "When can I go up?" Bill inquired. Jim laughed, thinking it was a joke, but stopped when he realized that it wasn't. "There's only room for two people," he explained. "Me and my bombardier." Undeterred, Bill argued that he had spent a lot of time studying the specifics of the aircraft and knew that he would be a great bombardier.

Jim and his assigned bombardier were already putting in more hours than anyone else, and they both were committed to their mission, so finding extra air time was nearly impossible. One day, Bill showed up, ready to fly, and Jim's bombardier was nowhere to be found. "Please tell me that you didn't hurt him," Jim inquired. Bill laughed and simply replied, "He's fine. I just found things he likes more than flying." Jim never asked, but instead enjoyed his friend's companionship and admired his abilities. They were a great team, and Jim always looked forward to the days when Bill was able to bribe the assigned bombardier into doing something else so he could go up in the air with Bill.

"Your dad was driven, trying to win the war all by himself. By today's terms, he would have been labeled ADHD and probably medicated. I took him up in the air with me several times. He loved jamming enemy transmissions, and he was the best. On the ground, he would get a fix on enemies by triangulating signals and communicating their locations to air support or artillery. He kept a pad of paper with notes and tally marks for targets that were hit. He was everything I expected him to be, although he did get carried away sometimes. He'd get a slap on the wrist and the next day he'd be right back at it."

Jim shook his head and laughed. "That lucky SOB." He paused, reflecting on Bill's antics and results, and his mood softened. "One day, after receiving a letter from Susan – your mother - with the birth announcement and picture of you, he just changed. It was like a switch turned off. He didn't want to go up in the air, didn't beg to go on extra patrols, and suddenly realized that he could die out there. He needed to make sure that he got home to you, especially since Susan's dad never got back to her. He showed your pictures to everyone who would listen: fellow Marines, soldiers, and even the villagers and school children. He was so proud."

Leslie cocked her head and thought about that for a few seconds. "If he was so excited, why didn't he come home to see me right away?" she asked. "If he got there in April 1967 and probably received the birth announcement in late July or early August, couldn't he have come back to the United States sooner?" Jim explained how difficult it was to let someone so valuable go home that quickly, but also suggested that her dad could have come home sooner than his original plan of January. "Since he had spent his first four months there being destructive, he vowed to spend four months being *constructive* and helping the children of the village. That's why the plan for January." He winked and said, "Plus, I'm sure he didn't want to miss Bob Hope and Raquel Welch coming to Chu Lai for Christmas."

That made sense to Leslie, and she mentioned that Justine had already explained what happened with the timeline after that point. "So, you were over there the whole time that my dad was?" Leslie asked. "Not continuously," he replied. "I was in 6 months before him, learned to fly the Intruder while he was in Monterey the first time, and already had been in Vietnam for several months when your dad arrived. I was back in the States on leave when your dad went missing, but I was on the next flight back to Vietnam, to be part of the search team. I flew for hours at a time, questioned everyone, and tried to find the monk that he had befriended to ask him questions. The monastery was deserted, and we assumed the Communists did it because they don't like Buddhists. Also, the Vietnamese are elusive as Hell when they want to be."

Jim and Linda sat on the front porch, drinking their morning coffee and taking in the aroma of lilacs blooming. "It's great to have you home for a couple of weeks," Linda professed. "Now that you've relaxed for a week, I have a few projects for you." Jim laughed, knowing that she would have a list somewhere, and watched a blue sedan drive past slowly. "Government vehicle," he observed aloud. "Probably delivering bad news in the area." Linda squeezed Bill's hand and said she hated seeing those cars. "I'm just glad they aren't coming to tell me any bad news," she stated as she stood up. "I am going to find that list," she teased. "Do you want more coffee?" Jim said he was fine, just going to read the paper and sit outside.

Linda went inside and Jim closed his eyes, feeling the cool air and enjoying the smell of decent coffee and lilacs. He opened his eyes when he heard a car pull up; it was the government sedan. The driver got out and Jim stood to greet him. "Hey, Williams, what brings you out to my neighborhood?" *he asked casually.* "I'm not MIA, am I?" *Lieutenant Williams didn't laugh and put his head down.* "No, sir, but I just received word that Sergeant Lucas has gone missing. I thought you would want to know." *Jim's mouth was wide open for a few seconds before questions started flooding out of it.* "Unfortunately, I don't have many answers," *Lieutenant Williams apologized.* "It just happened yesterday. That's all I know." *Jim thanked him and put his head in his hands.*

Linda came outside with her list and saw the government sedan pulling out of the driveway. "Wrong address?" *she asked. Jim looked up at his beautiful wife with horror in his eyes.* "What happened?" *she inquired.* "Bill's gone missing," *Jim replied slowly.* "I have to go find him." *He walked past Linda and straight to the refrigerator.* "Drinking beer at 10:00 isn't going to help," *she offered as she followed him inside.* "What are you going to do?" *Jim paced back and forth in the kitchen, drinking the beer.* "I need more answers," *he finally managed.* "If anyone can find him, I can."

As he went to pack his bag, Linda sat down at the table and cried. She thought about Susan and the baby, whom they had met just two days ago. "Should I call Susan?" *she called out. Jim ignored the question and Linda could hear him throwing things around.* "Are you leaving today?" *she asked as he returned to the kitchen.* "I'm leaving now," *he replied.* "I have to find him." *Linda threw her arms around Jim's neck and kissed him goodbye, knowing that this could be the last time she saw him. She watched him drive away, sobbing, trying to ignore that sick feeling in her stomach that she would never see their friend Bill again.*

•••

Chapter Twelve

Leslie observed Jim's expression curiously and asked, "You don't think it was your fault that he went missing, do you? Did you think he was dead?" Jim admitted that he did think it was his fault, but he just couldn't imagine anything killing Bill, since he seemed bulletproof. Jim had sent letters to Susan and to Bill's parents, and they continued to write back and forth for months. Judith was 19 when Bill went missing, and she seemed like a sweet little sister. "She wrote to me, too," he explained. "She told me how proud she was of her brother and that she would never give up hope that he would be found alive. When Rose - your Grandma Lucas - was sick the next year with cancer, Judith was at her bedside, taking care of her. Doctors didn't know as much about cancer back then, and Rose died in 1970. I met Judith at the funeral. She was pretty, but she thought she was some kind of pinup girl. Everyone was wearing black, as you should to a funeral, but Judith was wearing pink. She justified it by explaining that she just didn't look good in black."

"Ugh. Classic Aunt Judith," Leslie said. "If Aunt Judith doesn't look good, the world just isn't right. Everything is about her, and she still wears mostly pink." Leslie tried to picture Aunt Judith at the time, when she would have been 21. "Was she pleasant to you?" Leslie asked. Jim laughed and was obviously choosing his words carefully. "She was more than pleasant," he said. "Downright flirtatious. I found it completely disrespectful. It was her mother's funeral, for Pete's sake. Judith kept finding reasons to talk to me and asked me questions about Bill's disappearance. She vowed to do whatever was necessary to help find her brother, but Bill Sr. - your Grandpa Lucas - thought the same thing I did, that your dad was too tough to die. We assumed he was a POW, but we didn't know where."

Jim tried to keep in touch with Susan and Bill Sr and even Judith, but things took an odd turn with her. The letters she wrote started to get racy, as she seemed to fantasize that she and Jim would get married when he finally "came back from the war." Leslie cocked her head. "I thought you said you were married." Jim's jaw clenched noticeably. "I was divorced by then," he explained, and continued to talk about Aunt Judith. She had too much time on her hands, taking care of Bill Sr. after Rose passed away. Judith caught on to the fact that Jim felt guilty about Bill's disappearance and thought that somehow he could have prevented it, and she tried to manipulate that guilt.

"If only he had listened to me about going home earlier, or about changing his path to be an officer," he began. Leslie interrupted, "No, you can't take that on. He was drafted. He wanted to serve his country and he did. Even if you were there with him, you couldn't have prevented this. You need to let that go. If you need to see a therapist about it, you should." Jim laughed. "Back then, we just didn't do that. It wasn't considered masculine, or accepted at all," he said, "but in the past 20 years I have seen therapists, analysts, shrinks of all kinds. I realize their worth, but none of them could make me feel better. Do you know why I took this job? I get to work with people who are still looking for POWs and those who went MIA. I have found hundreds of our Marines and soldiers, most of them deceased, but finding Bill Lucas was the best thing I could ever have imagined happening. I might finally be able to retire."

Justine gasped and ran to the desk calendar. "I am writing this down. What day is it?" Leslie looked at her phone. "April 19th," she said. "How appropriate that tomorrow is the 20th," Justine mused. She had never heard all the details about Sergeant Lucas and told General Carlson that he could rest easy now. She agreed that he should retire and enjoy life while he still has some energy, then asked what in the world he was going to do with himself. Jim smiled and said he was considering selling his place in D.C. and moving back to Michigan to spend some time with an old friend.

His smile faded quickly when Leslie asked, "So what exactly happened with my Aunt Judith?" Jim took a deep breath and reminded Leslie that Judith had started rumors that she and Jim were a couple, despite Susan and Bill Sr. telling everyone it was not the case, since Jim wasn't even around to defend his name. Judith met a guy who had been discharged from the Navy early due to his parents dying in some type of accident, and the parents were quite wealthy. She always wanted someone to pay her way, as her parents had done, and she saw the dollar signs in that man's eyes. She tried to set up a confrontation between Jim and her new boyfriend, wanted them to fight over her, and Jim laughed. "Imagine, some squid thinking I was going to fight him to impress her. To this day, I think he married her to make me jealous. They moved to the Detroit area, leaving Bill Sr. without anyone to care for him. He had a lot of medical issues and needed help. It's a good thing Susan was there to help him."

Jim claimed that the more time that passed after Bill's disappearance, the less patriotic Judith became. She supported Jane Fonda when she went on that "humanitarian trip" to Hanoi, and even started participating in protests. When the war was over, Judith sent Jim a nasty letter that he burned over a campfire. "She wrote horrible things about me killing babies and tried to turn that knife in my heart about Bill being MIA, then she had the nerve to go with her father to the unveiling of the Wall and pretend to be patriotic again. She's a horrible person."

"Tell me about it," Leslie commiserated. "Mom and I went to the Wall shortly after it opened, during Spring Break of my freshman year of high school. Aunt Judith told Mom that she shouldn't go, that it was a waste of time. She never let up on Mom for believing that my dad was still alive. You would think that she would appreciate Mom's loyalty and dedication to her brother, but she is a psychopath. Did you ever see her again?"

"I actually saw her a couple more times," Jim answered, "and each time your mom tried to keep her away from me. Your mother was a wonderful lady, and I truly admired her devotion to Bill. The next time I saw Judith was in 1989 at the University of Michigan commencement ceremony." Leslie smiled and said, "What a coincidence! That's when I graduated from there." Jim shook his head. "No coincidence," he explained. "Your mom invited me. I actually sat between her and your Grandpa Lucas during the ceremony. It started a tradition for me, and I haven't missed a commencement at my Alma Mater since that day."

Leslie didn't remember Aunt Judith being there, so Jim explained that she had been there until he showed up. She tried to make a scene about him being there, claimed that he broke her heart, and Bill Sr. told her to go home and stop embarrassing him so she stormed out.

Jim didn't see Judith again until 2005, when Bill Sr. passed away. This time, it was Jim speaking up for Bill Sr., who had left all his money to Susan and his home and car were willed to the church. All he left for Judith were personal effects, including the photos. At the funeral, Judith stood up in front of everyone and accused Susan of having an inappropriate relationship with her father so she could have all his money.

"I remember that there was some confrontation at the funeral, but I was in the bathroom or something," Leslie recalled. "Mom never told me the details. She just said that she had offered Aunt Judith half the money for the pictures. Judith wouldn't give her any photos and mentioned to me at Mom's funeral that I could have them when *she* dies." Jim suggested that we could make that happen sometime this week and Leslie laughed. "What exactly did you say to her that day?" Leslie asked.

Jim looked down like he was disappointed. "Let's just say that I did not conduct myself that day as a Lieutenant Colonel of Marines should have. I stuck up for your mother and grandfather, put Judith in her place, and she left in dramatic fashion as always…in tears." A light bulb went off for Leslie, and she said, "Oh, my God! You were the officer in dress blues at my Grandpa's funeral! I knew I had met you before!" Leslie remembered the incident vividly, seeing someone push back against Aunt Judith and loving it. "That was 14 years ago. Have you seen her since that day?"

Jim said that he had not, but he had no reason to see Judith. He probably would have seen her at Susan's funeral if he had attended, but he was in Vietnam. "I knew that your mom was sick and I should have reached out to her more often, but things have been so busy. With all these tour groups going to Korea and Vietnam, we are getting dozens of reports of possible POWs and MIAs, so we're heading over there every other month. I apologize for not being there."

Leslie reassured Jim that it was okay; he was doing something important. "So, are you meeting my Aunt Judith somewhere?" she asked. "Yes, in fact I need to leave," Jim answered. We're meeting in

Quantico, at the Museum of the Marine Corps. I still don't think she believes me, but I have some pictures of the mission as proof. I don't want her up here, since we're supposed to have a press conference this afternoon. Justine can handle that. She's better at it than I am."

∙ ∙ ∙

Chapter Thirteen

The door shut behind Jim and Justine continued to stare at it. "I really think he's going to retire," she said. "I thought that day would never come. Do you know that he's been working for this country for over 50 years? 40 years as a Marine Corps officer and nearly 13 years with the State Department. Rarely takes vacation. No family. Just a man with a mission."

Leslie thought about that and wondered what happens when someone finally accomplishes a life-long mission or a goal that seemed unattainable. Not being a person who is very driven, Leslie was clueless about the subject, as she had always just let life fall into place. She firmly believed that Jim's mission all these years was to find Bill Lucas, and that was quite an honor. He had accomplished that goal and had been part of the group that retrieved him. She hadn't really thought about it until now, but her dad must have been terrified by the whole situation. What if he didn't want to return to his life? What if he was happy being "Erden," a handy man who lived with Buddhist monks?

Leslie wondered how much Jim had told Bill about his early life, and asked Justine about it. "As far as I know, General Carlson has only worked with generics like name and date of birth, and simple history like where Sergeant Lucas grew up and who his family was. Neither of us is usually involved with the healing process because we are part of the recovery team. This situation is different because there is some history and some personal investment. It's uncharted territory."

Leslie thought about the reporters and the questions they might ask. She had a feeling that they would be asking questions that were upsetting and was secretly glad that Jim would not be there to hear those questions. He and her father had both been through enough. She didn't realize that Justine was thinking the same thing.

"We have to talk about the press conference," Justine commented. "We need to make sure that we're on the same page. When those reporters spot a weakness, they're like sharks. Are you sure you want to be there?" Leslie said she wouldn't miss it for the world and asked who else would be there besides the two of them. "There is always some type of subject matter expert there, sometimes several," Justine replied, "but I don't decide who is there. That is done by someone at a much higher level. I do know that your father will not be there, as we are trying to protect him from additional stress."

Leslie knew that was for the best but wondered how many members of the media would treat this like someone claiming that they captured an alien or perhaps Bigfoot. If the reporters can't see him, he doesn't exist, right? She didn't know what to expect, but she was ready to stand up for her father. "Are you doing all the talking, or am I supposed to get up there, too?" Leslie asked. Justine said she would not put Leslie in an uncomfortable situation, but she knew that her mother would have jumped at the chance and thought she might want to fill in for her. "If you decide to talk to them, you can bail out at any time. You can defer a question to me or someone else on the panel, or just say that you don't know or aren't comfortable answering a question. You've been through a lot, too, and honestly you don't have to say a word." Leslie appreciated Justine's offer and said she would play it by ear.

Justine had to get some notes ready for the press conference, and Leslie said she would look through her tote for a few pictures to take out there with her. "By the way," she asked Justine, "Who took the letters out of the tote and then returned them?" Justine stared at Leslie for a moment and then asked her to clarify what she meant. "Well, when I packed the tote at home, I put in the letters last, as kind of an afterthought," Leslie explained. "When the lady from Fisher House brought the tote over, the letters were not in there. When I looked again in my dad's room, they were mysteriously back."

Justine explained that they have to be thorough and they have agents who work various jobs so they can watch people. One of them probably browsed through the letters. "So, that lady at the front desk, the one who obviously knows you, is an agent?" Leslie queried. "She seemed mysterious, like she was covering for you last night when you left but didn't really leave. Do you have a special room there? Did you really go home?"

Justine sat back and smiled at Leslie. "Look at you, being a super sleuth. You are definitely more observant than most people. Taking your questions in order, yes, yes, and no. Yes, she works for us and she was probably responsible for taking the letters out. She must have come back and replaced them when we went upstairs to see your dad. I will ask her, but she probably should not have done that. Yes, I have my own room at Fisher House and nobody has ever figured that out before you. No, I did not go home. I plan to do that tonight, though. I'm impressed by your observation skills. Maybe you should be working for us." Leslie was proud of herself for being so perceptive, especially at a time when she was a bit overwhelmed, but simply answered, "No, I'm just an accountant." They laughed and Justine went to work on her notes while Leslie looked through the pictures she had brought. While she browsed through the photos, she decided to call Melanie to let her know about the press conference and tell her to watch the news.

•••

Chapter Fourteen

Jim Carlson was cussing his way through Friday afternoon traffic behind the wheel of his government-issued black Impala, eager to get to the Museum. He got off 495 near Wakefield Park to avoid some of the traffic, but that was busy, too. He was thinking about how much he liked this car and couldn't believe Chevrolet was stopping production on such a great vehicle, when his phone rang and interrupted his thoughts. "Sir, it's Overton. I finished translating some of Ky's journals and these are pure gold." Jim pressed the orange "Record" button on his dash to record the call. "What do you mean, 'pure gold'?" he asked. "Did you get some good intel? Do you know how Sergeant Lucas ended up at Marble Mountain, over 60 miles away from his base of operations?"

Agent Overton said that it was all in the journals, in extreme detail, and it was going to take weeks to translate everything because it was all hand-written. He was looking for other linguists who knew French and Vietnamese so they could help him, as the journals were a combination of both languages. "There are entries back to the end of WWII, when Ky was a young man. I skipped over the earlier stuff to get to anything I could find about Sergeant Lucas. Ky was quite fond of Lucas, looked at him like a son. I went to April 18, 1968, the day that Sergeant Lucas went missing and got some answers. It was supposed to be a day of celebration at the school that Lucas had started, but the VC got wind of the plans and decided to cancel them." Overton read the translated journal entries for three days and Jim had so many different emotions that he wasn't sure how to react.

"16 April 1968: The teacher and five others were on the way to a Farewell ceremony at the children's school when they encountered an ambush of VC mines. Villagers raced to help the Americans. The three men in the first Jeep could not be saved, but the teacher and two others received injuries that could be treated. We took them into the school, making sure that the children did not see them. The ceremony was cancelled and we moved the blown-up Jeeps to a remote location and covered them with canvas and branches.

VC returned and searched our pagoda but not the school because the children were there. They asked where the teacher was, but we remained silent despite the beatings they gave us. They burned our pagoda and we slept at the school. The villagers have given us food and some clothing for the injured Americans."

"17 April 1968: A long night of treating wounds and not sleeping. A farmer from the village will drive us in his truck to the Mountain of Marble during tonight's darkness. There is a hospital there, and our patients need medicine and to be hidden from the VC. The teacher woke up but does not remember anything that happened or who he is. The other two have not opened their eyes, but they make sounds and will survive their injuries. I told the teacher that he needed to be quiet and he has obeyed my wishes. We will treat them and return the men when they have healed."

"18 April 1968: Shortly after arriving at the Mountain of Marble, our other two patients woke up and thought they were war prisoners. The teacher calmed them down and they stopped trying to run. They ate like animals and after receiving medicine they slept for many hours. There are many men at the mountain hospital and we are doing what we can, but many of them will not survive. It is cool and wet inside the mountain, which brings relief from the warm days but also invites infection. I have taken the personal items from the teacher and other two men and hidden everything so they are not discovered by the VC. The teacher does not know his name, but I am hopeful that his memories will return as he recovers."

Jim pulled off on Hampton Road and sat in the parking lot of the Fire Station. Agent Overton asked if he wanted to hear any more, and Jim's voice was so quiet that Overton had to ask him to repeat what he said. "No, thank you, I've heard enough." Jim put the car in park and laid his head on the steering wheel. He couldn't remember the last time he cried, but the tears flowed freely as he fumbled for some napkins in the glove box. He had been to Marble Mountain so many times after Bill went missing. He went inside, checked every face in the hospital there and unzipped every body bag. How could he have missed three men? What happened to Mackey and Tillotson if they survived the VC ambush? He was grateful that his old friend had survived but couldn't help feeling like he had failed those other Marines.

Jim regained his bearing and headed over to Quantico. He had to pull himself together, focus on the fact that his friend was back from the dead and needed his help more than ever. Visiting the Museum always motivated him and put life back in perspective. He was not looking forward to seeing Judith, but his mood would at least shift out of sadness, probably to anger. She was a horrible woman and had a way of making everything about her that really turned him off. Jim wondered if she was even capable of being happy that her brother was found alive, or happy about anything really.

He pulled into the parking lot and stepped out to gaze at the impressive building that serves as a reminder of Iwo Jima. He remembered the fundraising and the hard work that came before this dream of a museum became a reality, but the effort was definitely worth it. They did an amazing job with the displays and there are dozens of great docents who are happy to tell their stories and teach the history lessons of our beloved Corps.

Jim looked at his watch. Judith should have been here by now, and he wasn't sure that he wanted to be seen inside with her. He had a reputation to uphold, after all. He pulled out his phone and the slip of paper on which Leslie had written her aunt's phone number and address. He punched in the numbers and after 5 rings she picked it up. "Are you almost to the museum?" Jim asked. She said that she had decided not to come, that she and her friend Karen had been doing facials and drinking wine before heading out for some dinner. She and Karen agreed that he was just trying to get the pictures for Leslie.

Jim took a deep breath. "So, you're saying that you don't believe that we found your brother?" he asked. "That's what I'm saying," she answered. "And you're not bringing the pictures?" Jim asked, his voice (and blood pressure) rising a bit. "You're 2 for 2," Judith laughed. "I'm going to need some proof. Also, what's in it for me?" He could hear someone laughing in the background and asked where she was. "I'm already out to dinner with friends," Judith answered. "Not really sure when I'll be home. Stay in touch." There was a click and the phone went silent.

Jim was so full of frustration that he had walked in circles around his car several times before he even realized that he was doing it.

How could anyone be friends with that monster? He reached into his left front pocket and pulled out his other phone. "Hey, it's Carlson. Got a minute? I need you to ping this phone number's location." He read Judith's number from the scrap of paper. "Really? That's her home address. Okay, do me a favor and get the local news affiliate for that area. Click them in on a 3-way call so you know what I'm doing. I'll hold." Jim knew that Judith was an attention whore and if she wanted attention, she was going to get it.

He felt so stupid for falling for her lie and should have known that she agreed too readily to meet him in Quantico. He wasn't very nice the last time they had seen each other, so maybe this was her way to get back at him. Before he could analyze further, a woman's voice came on the line. "This is Sherry at Fox News. How can I help you?" "Hi, Sherry," Jim began. "I'm not sure if you realize this, but one of our Vietnam Veterans was recently found alive. There is a press conference at Walter Reed in about a half hour." Sherry said that she was aware, and informed Jim that they already had two people there for the press conference. In fact, she claimed that reporters from every news outlet within 200 miles would be there.

"Well, I happen to be one of the people who rescued Sergeant Lucas and just discovered that he has family in your area. You could be the first to get an exclusive interview." Sherry said that she would love to interview him, but he said, "No, not me. Sergeant Lucas has a sister who lives in Fredericksburg. I have her address. Write this down." Sherry seemed to be quite interested. "Oh, that's even better! No offense, of course, but we like to get the reactions of family members. I'll send someone over right away. Thank you!" There was a click and she was gone. Jim could hear the laughter on the other line after the reporter hung up and smiled. "Hey, see how many other reporters you can send over there," he suggested. "Newspapers, TV, whatever. Thanks!"

Jim got back behind the wheel and headed north. If traffic would give him a break, he could make it back before the end of the press conference.

…

Chapter Fifteen

Leslie followed Justine out to the front lobby of the hospital. The podium was set up inside because rain was expected, and security was limiting the number of reporters who could come in. The area was roped off and there were 6 chairs near the podium. Justine chose the chair closest to the podium and set down her notebook. "You should probably sit by me," she said to Leslie. "If you want to leave at any point, just let me know and slip out of the roped area. I don't want you to be traumatized by this."

Leslie laughed and couldn't imagine that it would be traumatizing. They were telling a happy story, right? Well, the ending was happy. She set her water bottle on the floor in front of her chair but didn't want to sit down just yet. She looked around and wondered who else was coming. She asked Justine if she had heard yet who would be sitting with them. Justine explained that there would be three doctors with various specialties, plus there was always a chair for General Carlson. Leslie did the math in her head. "There is no way he'll be back in time, even with the press conference's late start. I imagine Aunt Judith is giving him a fit right now." Justine said it was standard protocol, something they always did, even if they knew he wouldn't be coming.

Two of the doctors arrived in uniform, and they appeared to be a couple. They introduced themselves to Leslie and Justine and mentioned that they were neuropsychologists specializing in TBIs (Traumatic Brain Injuries) and listed their credentials. It all ran together like alphabet soup and Leslie laughed nervously. She had always considered herself to be above average intellectually, but she felt way out of her league. How is it that these two people were not only trained in the military but were also physicians with advanced degrees? She had no idea what to say, so she thanked them and sat down to wait for everyone else to arrive. She looked down at her red t-shirt and wondered if she should have changed into something nicer but felt satisfied that this sent the right message.

The reporters and photographers were entering, one at a time, and they all scrambled for the seats in the front row. Leslie counted 32 chairs, 4 rows of 8, and asked Justine if she expected that many. "Oh, there will be a lot more than that," Justine laughed. "They'll be holding them back at the doors, and some of them will probably still be there when you go back to your room tonight." They were taking pictures of Leslie and looking around, probably wondering where her dad was.

The third doctor arrived in a stereotypical white lab coat and greeted Leslie. He flashed his badge, said, "Backstage pass" with a laugh, and then apologized. "I'm sorry. I should be more serious, but this is my first press conference and I am really nervous. Let me try again. Hi, my name is Dr. Michael Edwards. I am a Psychotherapist who specializes in Psycholinguistics, and I am truly fascinated with your father. I would like to work with him long-term, so I hope you're taking him back to Michigan because that's where I'll be heading in a couple of weeks." Leslie smiled. This doctor didn't make her feel stupid or give a list of credentials. "Hi, I'm Leslie Mitchell. This is my first press conference, too. Have a seat."

Dr. Edwards waved down the row at his two colleagues and sat down next to Leslie. A photographer immediately took their picture and he said, "Oh, boy. I've seen this happen. By tomorrow, we'll be a couple in the headlines. We're probably jetting off to a private island when the press conference is over." Leslie laughed, maybe a bit too loudly because Justine turned around from the podium, where she was looking at her notes. Leslie took a drink of her water and looked out at the crowd as Justine started the press conference.

"Good afternoon. My name is Justine Wilson, and I work in the Military Recovery section of the U.S. Department of State. Approximately one month ago, we received a tip that an American - possibly a veteran of the Vietnam War - was spotted alive in the Marble Mountain area of Vietnam. We sent in an experienced team, led by Brigadier General James Carlson, USMC Retired. The team located the American and identified him as Sergeant William Lucas, MIA since April 1968, and they brought him home. He is in excellent physical health, but we are still working to find out exactly what happened. Behind me, I have his daughter, Leslie Lucas Mitchell, as well as three physicians whose areas of expertise match Sergeant Lucas's needs. Each person will have a turn to speak and we will take questions at the end. Dr. Edwards, would you like to go first?"

Dr. Edwards stood up quickly and replied excitedly, "Of course! Thank you, Justine." His enthusiasm and energy were contagious. He addressed the crowd: "Good afternoon, I'm Dr. Michael Edwards. I have been a Psychotherapist for 22 years, treating those who have suffered trauma, with the majority of my patients experiencing severe PTSD. I help those with emotional or psychological issues figure out what's causing the issues and prescribe appropriate changes, which are specific to each person and each trauma. For the past 10 years, I have worked exclusively with military members here, treating active duty and veterans. Being a military veteran myself gives me an insight, an empathy if you will. Having studied languages since I was a child, I became enamored with a lesser-known field of psychology called Psycholinguistics, focusing on the relationship between psychological factors and language. Certain trauma, whether physical or mental, usually affects language. You may or may not know that Sergeant Lucas was a linguistic genius. In addition to his native English, he spoke four or five other languages, and he could communicate in Morse Code. Quite impressive. When you learn a language, you use the receptive skills of listening and reading and the productive skills of speaking and writing. We are still doing tests, but at this point Sergeant Lucas has lost his productive skills. He is non-verbal, but we have speech therapists and medical doctors looking into the reason. We are expecting a full recovery and will update you as we make progress. Thank you!"

The press was in a frenzy, standing up and asking questions, but Justine took the microphone and reminded them that they would have time for that after all speakers had a chance to address them. Dr. Edwards sat down and asked Leslie how he did, but she was hung up on what he had said about her father being a 'linguistic genius.' Did her mother know that? Leslie was still convinced that Mom thought he was just a truck driver. Justine introduced the military neuropsychologist couple, who went to the podium together, and Leslie whispered, "You did great!" Dr. Edwards sat back in his chair and relaxed as he examined the reporters. "They're like sharks," he whispered to Leslie, "but we're in a big boat and they can't reach us." He started drawing on his pad of paper, a boat with sharks around it and them on top. Leslie smiled and nodded; she appreciated the analogy. Seeing Dr. Edwards succeed with his first press conference gave her more confidence that she would be successful as well.

She listened to some facts about Traumatic Brain Injuries that Mr. and Mrs. Lieutenant Colonel Neuropsychologist shared and realized that she hadn't even tried to remember their names. She thought about Billy and how he did not relate to some people. He had explained that we have limited space in our brains and we have to choose what takes up that space. Billy was wise beyond his years. Leslie already knew a lot about TBIs from attending presentations and seminars about PTSD with her mother. Mom had explained that "When your dad finally makes his way back home, he most likely will have PTSD and we need to know how to help him." The irony of the situation was overwhelming, and Leslie wondered how Mom knew all these years that he might be found. Did she really know, or was she desperately holding on to that dream so her heart didn't completely break?

Leslie realized that all the presentations and seminars that she attended with her mother were worth every minute. She may not have realized it then, but her mother was preparing her for this very situation in every way possible. Her mother had made sure that Leslie was educated, had refused to sell the family house or get rid of anything that had memories tied to it, and had amassed a small fortune that gave Leslie the choice to never work another day in her life. Mom had never spent a dime of her inheritance from her stepfather, Grandpa Baglia, and had never spent any money from the government or from Grandpa Lucas. She pinched every penny, and rarely bought anything new for herself. Leslie decided that her mother had to be the most unselfish person in the history of the world.

•••

Chapter Sixteen

Out of the corner of her eye, Leslie spotted a familiar figure. It was Jim Carlson, making a beeline to the podium. She exchanged looks of confusion with Justine and wondered how he got the pictures and returned so quickly. The applause of a few reporters made her realize that the neuropsychologists had finished. Leslie took a deep breath as Justine went back to the podium, ready to speak, but surprisingly Justine said, "Thank you. I believe we have a member of the extraction team here who might like to tell you about the discovery of Sergeant Lucas."

Without missing a beat, Jim Carlson walked to the podium and raised the microphone. Leslie noticed that his jaw was clenched and his brow was furrowed; he looked furious. The sharks in the audience were obviously excited about his appearance on the stage and cameras flashed. He looked out as he gripped the sides of the podium. "Good afternoon. My name is Jim Carlson, retired Marine Corps Brigadier General, and I work for the Department of State in Military Recovery. It is our mission to find and recover all missing or deceased members of the military and bring them home. Typically, we bring home remains, usually ashes. Sometimes, we bring home nothing. We follow all legitimate leads and it has been many years since we brought home a live body. Not just *any* body, but Bill Lucas, a friend of mine for over 50 years, since before we became Marines. We were friends in college and he enlisted about 6 months after I was commissioned. When Sergeant Lucas went missing in 1968 it almost killed me. I felt incredible guilt that one of these psychologists would probably label as 'Survivor Guilt,' and drank myself into a stupor every night for years. That guilt cost me my marriage, which was too new to withstand the fallout, and almost cost me my military career. My sole focus in life was to find Bill Lucas. I finally stopped drinking after being sent to a residential treatment facility to work through my problems, but sadly I also stopped believing that I would ever find Sergeant Lucas."

Jim seemed to pause to collect himself, then went on. "I left the military after 40 years. My plan was to retire and fish, but at my retirement ceremony someone mentioned this new section of Military Recovery, probably sarcastically, and my interest was piqued. I checked into it, and they seemed happy to have me on the team. I have done a lot of things for many people, but occasionally I wondered what had happened to Sergeant Bill Lucas. I'm pretty sure I was in shock when they handed me his dog tags and I saw him, but it was difficult to accept that he did not recognize me. I even checked the index finger on his left hand to see if it was him. He has a crescent-shaped scar on the top of that finger, something we used to tease him about years ago. It's still there, and maybe one day I'll be able to tease him about it again. We're still not sure what happened to Sergeant Lucas, but we are going to get him back 100%. In order to make sure he has round-the-clock care, this is my formal announcement that I will be retiring as of today. I've accomplished my mission. Thank you."

The members of the press were applauding as Jim went to take his seat, but then he seemed to remember something. He stepped back to the microphone and said, "Oh, and Sergeant Lucas has a sister named Judith who lives in Fredericksburg. I'll be sharing her address after the cameras are off, if you want to contact her." Leslie found herself clapping in delight. She wondered what had happened at Quantico earlier and where the pictures were, but she was happy for Jim and for her Dad.

Justine stepped up to the microphone and said, "Well, that is some news, General. Good luck to you in retirement. We do have one more speaker, the daughter of Sergeant Lucas, Leslie Lucas Mitchell." Leslie took a deep breath and stood up. "You got this," whispered Dr. Edwards, and she knew that she did. She moved the microphone back down and looked out at the cameras and reporters. "Good afternoon," she began. "I probably should have prepared a speech, but how do you follow that? I am Leslie Lucas Mitchell, and I met my father for the first time today. He went missing when I was 9 months old, just a few days before he was due to come home, never having met me. My mother never gave up hope that he was still alive, and we both put up with a lot of ridicule over the years for her belief. As some of you may know, she passed away 3 weeks ago so she just missed the chance to find out that she was right. I am going to take my Dad home and help him recover his memory and hopefully help him make some new ones." She paused, trying to swallow the lump in her throat, and took a deep breath. "I'm not trying to steal anyone's limelight here, but I think I'll retire, too. Thank you."

As she turned around, the tears started to flow. She did not want to cry in front of everyone and put her head down. Dr. Edwards handed her a tissue and whispered, "You did great! Take a drink of your water and just breathe. Don't show those sharks any weakness." Leslie tried to pull herself together as quickly as possible. The questions were filling up her head again. Now what happens? Can they ask me as many questions as they want? Are there things I'm not supposed to tell them? Good Lord, did I just quit my job on national TV?

Justine returned to the podium. She addressed the reporters and reminded them that they each had one question, which they could direct at whomever they chose, but anyone on the panel reserved the right to pass the question on to someone else if they didn't want to – or could not – answer the question. She started at the back of the room, and luckily the first two questions were directed at the neuropsychologists. The third question came from an older man who seemed to know Jim Carlson. "General, where exactly did you find Sergeant Lucas?" he asked. Jim didn't bother standing. "In a monastery at Marble Mountain," Jim said. Nothing more. Dr. Edwards leaned over to Leslie and said he was warned to give them only enough information to answer the question…nothing more. She nodded in agreement.

Leslie realized that her phone was vibrating so much that her purse was moving. She took it out and looked at it. She had several missed calls and texts. She scrolled through to make sure none were about Billy, as a text from Melanie popped up: "We're watching you on the news! Billy is jumping up and down on the couch, yelling USA! USA!" Leslie smiled and looked up. Everyone was quiet, looking at her. "Could you please repeat your question?" Justine asked. One of the reporters asked, "Miss Mitchell, when will your father go home with you and where will he live?" Leslie said, "I'm not sure...eventually, and wherever he wants." She wanted to say more but thought about what Dr. Edwards had said.

The next reporter also directed his question at Leslie: "What was your aunt's reaction to her brother being found alive?" Leslie laughed and said, "She doesn't believe it," and Jim Carlson winked at her. "Maybe she will now," he added. One of the other reporters said someone from his news station was at Judith Beech's home to capture her reaction to the news conference, and that would be available later. Leslie was anxious to see it and texted Melanie back, asking her to record anything she saw about them on TV. She knew that Aunt Judith was going to turn this into a money issue, but she wasn't sure how.

The next few questions went to Dr. Edwards, who handled the reporters well, and then came the question that Leslie couldn't believe took so long, directed at Justine: "When can we speak to Sergeant Lucas?" Justine said she had no way of knowing that, but she was sure that he would talk to them as soon as he could. Jim Carlson looked at the clock on the wall and said they would take one more question and then they would call it a night. He pointed to a young man in a blue suit who looked like he still might be in high school and said, "You, sir. What is your question?" The young man stood up and thanked Jim for choosing him. "Sir, if I may be so bold, after all you have done for this country, what would you consider to be your greatest accomplishment?" Jim was trying to keep his emotions under control and simply said, "This."

Justine stood up and thanked the press for coming and was reminded by several of the reporters that General Carlson promised to give them the address for Sergeant Lucas's sister in Fredericksburg. He reached into his pocket and read the name and address to everyone before Justine could stop him. The cameras were still rolling.

Dr. Edwards exclaimed, to nobody in particular, "I love that guy!" Leslie stood up to leave and he told her to stay on the boat until the sharks were out of the water. He was kind of odd, but funny. She stood up and waited with Justine, Jim, and the three doctors until the members of the press had cleared. Security guards were posted at the doors and the maintenance team wasted no time putting everything away. Dr. Edwards told Leslie that he would like to set up a time to meet and discuss her dad's prognosis and handed her his business card. Leslie promised to call him the next day. Justine thanked all three of the doctors for being there and headed back to Debrief Room A with Leslie and Jim. "Come on, retirees. We have a lot to figure out."

Leslie headed back to the debriefing office with Justine and Jim, happy to have her first press conference out of the way. Jim patted Leslie on the back and said, "You did a great job up there. Never tell them more than they ask or they'll start a feeding frenzy. They're like bears or mountain lions. They sense fear and will tear you apart." Leslie laughed and wondered how many other animal analogies there were for members of the press. "Thanks, Jim. I am glad to have it out of the way." Justine told her to get used to it because everyone was going to want to hear this story and she was going to be bombarded.

Once inside the office, Justine grabbed some bottles of sweet tea and Coke and set them on the table. "Okay, General, where are the pictures?" she asked. The furrow returned to Jim Carlson's brow and he said, "She didn't bring them. She didn't even show up! She said her friend told her that it was a trick, that I was just getting the pictures for Leslie." His jaw was clenched for a moment, then he laughed. "I sent a reporter to her house to record Judith's reaction to the press conference. Let's turn on the TV." He turned on the TV and it was right there, as if by magic.

They watched as the reporter showed up at Judith's door and explained why she was there. Judith and her friend Karen were doing facials and apparently thought it was a big joke prompted by Leslie and Jim. She asked the reporter and camera man to come in, pointing out the lavish decorations that she had just purchased in the foyer. The reporter asked her permission to put what they recorded on national television and Judith agreed, obviously sticking to her belief that this was a farce.

Judith's hair was clipped back and she had on her facial mask, unaware that the whole nation could see her. The reporter told Judith about the press conference and asked her to turn on her television so she could see for herself. Judith mocked everything that the reporter said, telling her that her brother died 50 years ago. She expressed her disbelief that they were taking their joke this far, just to get some pictures that she didn't even want. It was all on national television for the world to see, and Leslie loved the fact that everyone was watching this play out live. Years of Aunt Judith's tormenting and rudeness clouded her ability to feel sorry for her. She had bullied Leslie and mocked Susan, left Grandpa Lucas alone when he needed her, and refused to give some pictures of her dad to Jim Carlson...pictures that she just admitted she didn't even want!

The press conference came on TV at the Beech home. Judith and her chubby little friend Karen set their wine glasses down and stared at the screen. The cameraman continually panned from the TV to the women's reactions, then to the reporter. When Jim Carlson saw his face on the screen, he said, "Listen to this handsome devil; he's sharp." They all laughed and when he gave Judith's address out to the whole world, he said, "Oops. I didn't mean to do that." The camera man was focused on Judith and caught her reaction and subsequent tantrum in its entirety. She was screaming and yelling at the reporter, the camera man, and even at Karen. She kicked them all out and slammed the large mahogany door, clipping the back of Karen's foot and sending her sprawling on the front porch. The recording ended there and that reporter was on the screen, commenting about what had happened.

Jim pressed the "Mute" button and looked at Leslie. They laughed until they cried, and Justine finally spoke up. "So, she didn't come to meet you and we don't have the pictures. How are we going to fill in the first 20 years of Sergeant Lucas's life? Is there anyone else who might have pictures?" Jim Carlson said that he had a few from college, and Leslie said she could look through the albums that her mother had to see if there were any. Otherwise, they would have to figure out how to get the pictures from Aunt Judith.

"Wait a minute," Justine said. "I just remembered something that Susan told me a few years ago. She was a pretty serious scrapbooker, as I recall. Before Mr. Lucas - Bill Sr, Grandpa Lucas, whatever you call him - before he died, Susan was taking care of him a lot. She took many of his pictures to the library and made copies, and she made a few scrapbooks. Did you find those, Leslie?"

Leslie said that she didn't look through any of the scrapbooks because she assumed they were just the ones that Susan made of everything Leslie – and then Billy – had ever done. She knew where they were in the house, though, and she could look through them when she got home. She mentioned that there was a presentation a few years ago at the library where Susan worked, about preserving memories in digital form. As far as she knew, Susan had paid the speaker to digitize all of her scrapbooks, but she didn't know where the thumb drives were that she had them put on. She had laughed about her mom turning her scrapbooks into digital form, thinking it was kind of ridiculous. She explained that she hadn't had time to go through everything yet, as they were just returning from their much-needed vacation when she got the call from Justine.

Jim Carlson's face lit up. "So, you might have copies of all those pictures at home and we won't need your aunt's cooperation. We need to know as soon as possible." Leslie agreed and said she would check as soon as she got home. Justine said she still couldn't believe that General Carlson didn't drive down to Fredericksburg to punch someone in the throat. "It could still happen," he said with a wink.

• • •

Chapter Seventeen

Jim excused himself and said he needed to go send an email, notifying his "superiors" that he was retiring. "You have superiors?" Justine quipped. "Well, I have people who keep track of what I do," he replied. "They're going to have to find someone to replace me on the team." Justine frowned and thought about how different it was going to be without General Carlson, then turned to Leslie and stated, "We need to plan this out. If you are retiring, you'll have more time to devote to your dad's recovery, and I believe it would be better for him to do that in Michigan. Is there a VA hospital near you?" Justine inquired.

Leslie explained that there is a great VA hospital in Ann Arbor, and that many of the University of Michigan Medical Center doctors also treat the veterans. "The hospitals are right next door to each other," Leslie explained. "Since my dad went to U of M, maybe I can take him on campus to see if that helps his memory, too." Obviously, a lot has changed but some things really had not. Leslie was thinking aloud: "Football games are still played at the Big House, the brass block M is still there in the Diag…" Justine looked at her funny. "What's a Diag?" she asked. Leslie explained that it's a popular gathering place on campus, named after the way sidewalks run through it diagonally. "Do you really think that will be a memory for your dad?" she asked. Jim Carlson walked in and without missing a beat he said, "There were all kinds of protests in the Diag when I was there. I think that's a great place to take him." Leslie smiled and Justine gave her the "thumbs up" before turning her attention to Jim.

"Did you send your email, sir?" Justine asked. "Yes, and I recommended you as my replacement," Jim replied. "Do you have a pilot's license?" Justine said she was flattered, but did not like to fly, much less have the license, and Jim said it probably wasn't a necessity. "If all of you are going to Michigan, maybe I should follow," she teased. "There are federal offices in Detroit. Maybe I can transfer there." Jim suggested that she look into Ann Arbor, not Detroit, and she agreed to do that.

"We really need a plan for Sergeant Lucas," Justine suggested. "I guess this is your last day, so let's figure something out." General Carlson said he decided to give a two-week notice because he knew that his access to Bill Lucas would be limited if he didn't have the clearance and authority that he has now. "So, we have two weeks to get things in place for him to go home," he said. "In the meantime, I am tired of my old friend being held here like he's a prisoner. His status is being changed to 'Outpatient treatment' so he doesn't have to stay here 24 hours a day. He's physically healthy and I don't believe he is a threat, so I will be taking him home with me at night. I'll make sure he is back here for appointments, and I plan to wrap up any loose ends while he's in those appointments."

Justine started taking notes. "Okay, that's a start. Are we authorized to do that?" Jim Carlson said he had given this country over 50 years of his life and dared anyone to question his integrity or his motives in making this decision. He would talk one of the doctors into signing off on the decision. "What time are you meeting with Dr. Edwards tomorrow?" he asked Leslie. She explained that she was calling him tomorrow and didn't know. "Did you know that he is going to Ann Arbor, too?" she asked Jim. "Good grief! Is anyone going to be left here?" Justine asked. "Quit your whining and join the group," Jim replied. "There's nothing for me here, and Leslie wants to take her dad back home. Dr. Edwards found out three months ago that he was transferring to Ann Arbor. I would suggest that whether you decide to stay here or transfer, you find someone to spend time with. It is not healthy to be married to your job. I missed out on so much, threw away a marriage and never had kids or pets because I couldn't be tied down. Don't do that to yourself."

Justine liked this softer version of the retired General who intimidated so many people. Compared to a couple of her drill instructors, though, he was a kitten. She thanked him for his concern and showed him and Leslie an outline that she had created. At the top of the page, it read *Get Sergeant Lucas His Life Back*. She held it up, like elementary teachers hold the book when they read to the class. "Okay, class," she said with a grin, "The first step is to find out if he wants it back." Leslie agreed, said she had thought about that, and General Carlson said that was ridiculous. Justine reminded him that there was some "dark time" in Sergeant Lucas's life that might really haunt him, some that they might not want him to recover.

General Carlson stood up. "The man was doing his job. It wasn't his decision to kill those people; we were ordered to do so by the government." Justine reminded him not to shoot the messenger, that she's also a Marine and understood why they did what they did. "He is a legend in the Marine Corps, sir, and I agree that he was doing his job. Just imagine that for 50 years you think you're a servant for monks, loving peace and praising Buddha, and someone tells you – or you suddenly remember - that you once killed over 100 people. I'm concerned for his emotional well-being if or when that happens."

General Carlson apologized for getting so defensive and grabbed one of the Cokes on the table. He took a big swig and suggested that they gloss over that part initially, fill in his family information first, tell him that he served in the Marine Corps, and then skip ahead to what happened and what he's been doing for the past 51 years. Later, when the time felt right, he would tell him more. He warned that they would have to be protective of what information got to Sergeant Lucas before he was ready, and Leslie said she should be able to handle that since she wasn't going to be working.

"Okay, perfect," said Justine. "Next item: Do we call him Erden or Bill? He has been called 'Erden' for years and responds to that name." Jim Carlson said he would ask him, explaining that his real name is 'William Leslie Lucas' and his nickname is 'Bill.' Leslie interjected that she was just going to call him "Dad." She liked how it sounded, and never even realized how much she wanted to have a father in her life. She asked Jim Carlson how much her father really understood of what she was saying, and he said, "Actually, very little if you're speaking English. He does understand Vietnamese, but mine is rusty, and of course French. I didn't learn much French, but I know a few things, mostly inappropriate. Since he can't speak, I am finding that asking him "Yes" or "No" questions in Vietnamese seems to be the best way to communicate. Part of the problem is that many years ago, Buddhists took vows of silence and just never said a word. From what I have read, not using your voice for extended periods causes the vocal cords to atrophy. We don't know if he decided to stop speaking, or if he forgot how, or if his brain injuries caused him to lose his speech. Whatever the issue, we are going to have to figure out how to get him back to speaking so he can tell us everything that he remembers. The journals recovered from Ky's safe should give us more information, too."

Justine said she thought they had a good start and suggested that they plan more the next morning. She said she would call someone to drive Leslie back to her room, but that they would be using a different entrance. General Carlson said he was heading upstairs to get Bill Lucas and take him home. Leslie knew that she wouldn't get much sleep tonight, worrying about her father and her meeting with Dr. Edwards. She felt better about the situation now, but more questions were filling her head. Did Dr. Edwards have more information? What if he disagreed with their plan of action? When was he leaving for Michigan? What should she wear?

• • •

Chapter Eighteen

Leslie waited for the car to take her back to the Fisher House and wasn't surprised when a black Impala pulled up. She half expected to see Jim Carlson behind the wheel, but it was a much younger man in jeans and an olive drab tee shirt. He jumped out and showed Leslie his badge. "It's an honor to meet you, ma'am," he greeted her. "I'm Todd Jameson." She asked if he knew where she was going, and he said, "Of course. Fisher House 5. I will make sure you're safely inside and that nobody bothers you while you're there." That seemed a bit much, so she joked, "Oh, like a bodyguard?" He smiled and nodded. "Exactly. We need to protect our assets. Plus, there's a full moon tonight and that always makes everything worse." He opened the back door and Leslie said, "I'd really rather sit in the front seat." He opened the front door and waited for her to strap in, then shut the door and ran around to the driver's seat. He explained that he would text her his number so she could let him know when she was ready to return to the hospital in the morning, and she said she would write down her number for him when they got there. "It's already in my phone, ma'am," he replied. Of course it was.

They drove out of the parking lot and passed the driveway to the Fisher House. "Oh, no. Are you kidnapping me?" Leslie asked, confused about why they passed the entrance. She probably watched too many movies about this type of situation, and he could sense the fear in her voice. "I'm sorry, I should have explained. There are reporters out there waiting for you, and a couple of them are hanging out by the Fisher House buildings. One of our agents is having them removed so we're circling around and coming in from the other side of the base." Having them removed like ants or cockroaches? Leslie was amused at the mental image this created.

She wanted to ask Todd some questions about himself but realized that she was too tired to make small talk. She needed to soak in a tub or something. There was a buzz and the words "All clear" displayed on the dashboard screen. "Okay, we're good to go," Todd announced. He flipped the car around behind Fisher House 3 and into their small parking lot. They walked across the lawn to Fisher House 5, into the back door and past the front desk. Leslie noticed that there was a different woman working at the desk. Todd walked Leslie to her room and said he'd text her shortly so she knew what number to text in the morning. She thanked him and went inside, then spent the first ten minutes checking to make sure that nothing was missing. She didn't like the fact that the other agent, disguised as a front desk worker, had been in here when she was gone. It felt like a violation.

Her phone buzzed and she pulled it out of her purse. "Reply to this number in the morning when you're ready to go. Please, not before 6 AM." Leslie laughed. Before 6 AM? She didn't even like to be out of bed by 8 AM. She took off her shoes and fell on the bed with her phone. She had 8 texts and 11 missed calls. None were from Melanie, but she saw two calls from Mark. What did he want? He had become quite a deadbeat dad, rarely calling to talk to Billy, and never asking to see him. Why was he calling her?

Leslie dialed Melanie's cell number and never heard it ring. "Hello, TV star!" Melanie answered. Leslie laughed. "Hi, Melanie. How's Billy doing?" Melanie said he was fine, just starting to miss his mom. She put Billy on the phone and he told Leslie everything he did that day, what he ate for each meal, and what he planned to do tomorrow. He asked when she was coming home, and she said she was planning to spend tomorrow at the hospital and then drive home on Sunday. "Did you meet my Grandpa? He's your dad, right?"

"Yes, I met your Grandpa," she replied, "And yes, he's my dad. You know, like your dad in Virginia." Billy sighed. "Well, I hope your dad wants to spend time with you, not like my dumb dad." Leslie wanted to agree with him, but she reminded him that he should show respect for both of his parents. She also reminded him that he had to go back to school on Monday, after being off for 3 weeks. "Oh, yeah! I can tell everyone that my Grandma died but now I have a Grandpa!" He handed the phone back to Melanie and went to brush his teeth.

"Well, that seemed to pull him out of his slump," Melanie said. "He was really excited to see you on TV and asked if that older man was his Grandpa. I told him he was Grandpa's friend, and he was tickled to find out that grandparents have friends, too. Such a funny kid. So, who was the doctor sitting next to you that you were chatting up?" Leslie blushed and was glad nobody could see her. "Oh, that's Dr. Edwards. He's a Psychotherapist who is working with my dad, helping him get his speaking skills back. A Psycholinguist, actually." Melanie's "Uh-huh" was quick, and she wanted to know when Leslie would see him again. "I don't know," Leslie answered, "but I'm supposed to call him tomorrow so we can meet and discuss my dad's prognosis." Melanie seemed excited, and the questions continued. "Oh, so you're meeting with him privately? Is he married? What are you going to wear?" Leslie laughed, wondering honestly what she was going to wear. "Good night, Melanie! It's been a long day."

Leslie dragged herself off the bed and changed into her pajamas. She washed her face and brushed her teeth, then looked at the texts on her phone, most of them from her handful of friends who were congratulating her. One was from her boss, asking if she was seriously not returning to work, and she made a mental note to call him tomorrow. She plugged in her phone and was asleep as soon as her head hit the pillow.

Just after 3:00 in the morning, Leslie heard some yelling outside and sat up. She looked out the window and saw Todd Jameson chasing someone over the stone wall between the building and the parking lot. Had they been looking for her? Was he serious about being a bodyguard? Leslie knew that he had a room there and felt safe. She realized that she had left a light on, so she got up to turn it off and double check that the door was locked. She set her alarm for 7:00 and wondered if Justine actually went home or if she was down the hall.

...

Chapter Nineteen

Leslie awoke to the sound of her phone's alarm. She had slept like a rock and somehow felt that today was going to be a great day. She took a leisurely shower and spent a lot of time picking out the right outfit, hoping that she would meet with Dr. Edwards today. The khaki slacks and white shirt showed off the tan she had from her trip to Florida, and she decided to put on a little bit of foundation and some eye liner. She was pleased with her look and tried taking a selfie with her phone so she could show Melanie what she decided to wear, but she wasn't very good at it so she decided to stand in front of the mirror and take a picture of her reflection. She sent it to Melanie and instantly received a "Thumbs up" in approval.

It was just after 8:00 when she texted Todd to ask him if he was ready. There was an immediate knock on the door, and she was pleasantly surprised to see Todd when she looked out the peephole. "What did you do, sleep out here?" she asked. "Only since about 3:30," he replied. "I can't believe the paparazzi was outside your window." Leslie thanked him for chasing them away, and he suggested that she consider finding someone "to help with those vermin" when she returned to Michigan. She said she would be fine, since she had some neighbors who were quite protective.

They drove to the private entrance of the medical center in silence, as she was ravenously hungry and thinking about what she wanted for breakfast. She thanked him and said she was probably leaving tomorrow but would be back soon to pick up her dad. He handed her a Marine Corps challenge coin and asked her to give it to her father, and waited until she was inside the building before driving away. *Good Lord, how many Marine veterans are there?* she wondered.

Leslie felt odd being alone and went to the cafeteria to get some breakfast. The French toast looked delicious, and the long shape reminded her of the pain perdu at that restaurant she loved in Savannah. It really was tasty, and in the process of shoving a big chunk in her mouth she looked up to see Dr. Edwards smiling at her. "The French toast is great, isn't it? I got the same. Mind if I join you?" She blushed, not able to say anything until she chewed up her mouthful of French toast. He didn't wait for an answer; he sat down across from her.

She took a drink of her tea and greeted him. "Good morning! I guess this means I don't need to call you today," she managed. He launched right into his analysis and prognosis of her father, using a few phrases with which she was unfamiliar, stopping to clarify when she asked what he meant or if her facial expression reflected confusion. It was all quite fascinating, but there were so many variables that it seemed like a daunting task. As Leslie understood, her father's speech issues could be physiological or psychological, self-imposed or not, and could be age-related. Once they could determine the cause, they could figure out what languages he remembers and try to get him back on the road to communication. Dr. Edwards said that it could take years.

Leslie thanked Dr. Edwards for his explanation, but respectfully disagreed about the course of action. "Why is it important to determine the cause? He can make sounds, so maybe he just needs to relearn English. Nobody probably spoke English to him for over 50 years so maybe he just doesn't remember. I read about a Hungarian soldier who was found in a Russian mental hospital 50 years after being a POW from World War II, around 2000. He didn't communicate because he couldn't speak Russian, but eventually regained his speaking when he was around others who spoke Hungarian." Dr. Edwards said he was familiar with that case and it was a great lesson for anyone studying linguistics. The soldier had lost his ability to converse, but the language still played in his head. When he spoke, the words were basically what his high school English teacher would call "Stream of Consciousness." Whatever went through this mind was what came out of his mouth, so he had to relearn social discourse and how to answer questions directly. It was a fascinating situation.

"So, how do you think we should approach this?" he asked. "What's your recommended course of action?" he asked. Leslie suggested that they put together a timeline of her dad's life, using pictures and places that might jog his memory, and use simple words that relate to those pictures and places. For the time that he was at the monastery, they could use the information in Ky's journals to fill in the blanks. "I'm not aware of said journals," Dr. Edwards admitted, clearly intrigued. "Go on." Leslie worried that perhaps she wasn't supposed to tell him about the journals. She explained that the abbot who saved her Dad kept detailed journals which are being translated by government linguists because the journals were written in Vietnamese and French. Dr. Edwards said he would love to get his hands on them, just as Jim Carlson walked up to the table.

"I trust that you're talking about something appropriate," Jim stated calmly. Dr. Edwards explained that he was just informed about the journals written by the abbot that could give some insight to Sergeant Lucas's life during his time at the monastery. He offered to help with the translations, admitting that his French was much better than his Vietnamese but he could read both. The information in the journals could give significant background information about the status of Sergeant Lucas's current communication walls as well as the progression of his language skills. He argued that he and his fellow psycholinguists might be better suited to do the translations, since they might pick up on psychological clues as well as linguistic ones. Jim Carlson stared at him for a second without responding.

Leslie was watching Jim's face and asked if he was okay, since he looked exhausted. "Full moon last night," he explained. "Did you know that Buddhists have a ritual during every full moon? I was looking for candles and flowers all night. I ended up cutting some cherry blossoms in my yard and I stole some tulips from the neighbor's garden. Did you know that if you open tulips all the way, they resemble lotus flowers? I didn't even know that I had incense in the junk drawer in my kitchen, but your dad found it and we burned it at dawn. My place smells great, but I didn't sleep much. I'm exhausted."

Leslie laughed at the mental picture. "Where's my dad now?" she asked. Jim said he was in with one of the Speech Language Pathologists, and Dr. Edwards said he should go join them. He asked Leslie to call him @ 2:00 so they could meet about their plans. She said she would, and when he was gone Jim laughed. "Look at you, grinning from ear to ear," he said. "I might be tired, but even a tired old man can see how you light up around that doctor. Are you wearing eye liner?"

Leslie changed the subject and asked if she could spend some time with her dad today, as she needed to go home soon to find the pictures and see Billy. "Of course," Jim replied. "Maybe we can go somewhere for lunch after your dad's appointments. Do you like Vietnamese food?" Leslie had no idea, as she couldn't remember ever eating Vietnamese food. Jim said that as long as she likes noodles, rice, and pork, there should be something she could eat. Leslie nodded. Noodles were one of her favorite foods.

They walked together to the office and Leslie was surprised that Justine was not there. Jim said he told her to take a couple of days off, and said he was going to miss working with her when he left. "When are you leaving the area, and when am I supposed to take my dad home?" Leslie asked. Jim said they should go talk to the Social Worker in charge of her dad's care and see what she thought. He told Leslie that she should go home tomorrow, and not worry about her dad because he was in capable hands. She already knew that but thanked him for his loyalty to her dad. "Semper Fidelis," Jim said. "Always faithful. Marines take care of their own."

•••

Chapter Twenty

Jim went in the other room to make a few phone calls and Leslie realized that her Rubbermaid tote was still there. She made a mental note to take it with her when she left the hospital tonight, since she didn't know for sure when she would be back again. She opened the tote and took out the photo albums and loose pictures. Seeing pictures of herself as a child brought back bittersweet memories, as Mom always supported her and made sure she had everything she needed but Leslie never had a father figure. There were some male teachers and fathers of her friends who were extra kind to her and tried to fill the void in some way, but she had always held them at arm's length.

Leslie realized how much she was like her mother, who had never met her biological father because he died on Iwo Jima. Grandma Betty remarried when Susan was only five, so most of her life she at least had a stepfather. Leslie used to wish that her mother would remarry so she could have a stepfather, but she realized that her mother must have truly believed that her dad was still alive so she couldn't remarry *because she was already married*. Although Susan never showed a trace of wavering from that belief, Leslie often wondered if her mother privately had doubts or thought her husband was dead. It was an incredible love story, one that she planned to tell the world as soon as she could put it into words.

She teared up quickly as she breezed through the albums, remembering the great birthday parties that her mother threw for her and all the places they visited. There were several trips to Washington, D.C., and vacations to Florida in the winter and Mackinac Island in the summer. Her mother always had someone stay at the house, just in case Leslie's dad showed up, which everyone thought was sweet but sad. Upon seeing the photos, Leslie reminisced about her first trip to Mackinac Island in 1977, when she fell in love with lilacs. Beautiful, fragrant lilacs.

Leslie settled in next to Grandpa Joe on the ferry to the island, watching the Mackinac Bridge getting farther away. Yesterday was the last day of fourth grade and she already missed her favorite teacher, but today started summer vacation. "Have you been out here for vacation before?" she inquired. Grandpa Joe squeezed her hand and smiled. "Yes, many times, for vacation and for work," he replied. "It's like going back in time...no cars, just horses." Leslie squealed with excitement. "I love horses! Mom, have you been out to this island?" Susan explained that she used to go out every summer. "Your dad went out here when he was a Boy Scout, and stayed in the Scout Barracks," she added. "He always wanted to go back, but..." Grandma Betty changed the subject. "They have the oldest lilacs in the world, Leslie," she gushed. "Wait until you get a whiff." Grandpa Joe laughed. "They help cover up the smell of the horses," he explained with a wink.

Leslie laughed as she watched hills and buildings come into view. Grandpa Joe was the only tour guide she needed, sharing that Mackinac Island was first a National Park and then the first State Park and explaining that the British and French both wanted the island at some point. "We'll go up to that fort on the hill to learn more about the history," he promised, as he pointed out the large white fort. Leslie was excited to see the fort and the lilacs and the horses. "We should do this every year," she suggested as their ferry pulled up to the dock and they disembarked. The scent of all those lilacs was overwhelming, but there was another scent in the air. "What's that delicious smell?" she asked, looking in the shop windows for clues. "Horse poop," teased Grandpa Joe, who was elbowed by Grandma Betty. "That is Mackinac Island fudge, sweetie," she explained as she shot a stern look at Grandpa Joe. "Watch, they're pouring it on the slab right now." Leslie was mesmerized by the process and the smell. "Horses, lilacs, and fudge," she murmured as she watched. "This is Heaven."

Leslie smiled as she remembered the beginning of her relationship with the island and all it had to offer but closed that album and looked for one that might have older pictures that she could show her dad. There was an envelope with photos of her parents on the day they were married, and Leslie beamed as she sorted through them. Both of her parents were beautiful and could easily have been models. The pictures weren't great quality, but black and white photos seemed to capture expressions better than color photos. There was sheer joy in their smiles, and she felt that deep down her Dad had to remember this love of his life.

She put the pictures back in the envelope and set it aside as Jim Carlson came back in the room. "We're all set to meet with the Social Worker, but since today is Saturday apparently that's an issue for some people. I set it up for 8:00 tomorrow morning, hoping that you could do that before hitting the road." Leslie agreed that it was a good idea but asked if they should invite anyone else. Jim said the Social Worker was calling everyone involved with her dad's rehabilitation to request that they attend. He told Leslie that he has trust issues, so he would call Justine himself and suggested that Leslie check with Dr. Edwards when they talked this afternoon.

"What do you have there?" he asked. Leslie showed Jim the photos and she could tell that he was getting choked up as he went through them. "They were so young," he finally managed. "So full of life and dreams. Your dad could have been or done anything he wanted." Leslie tried to lighten the situation and said, "I'll bet nobody ever thought he would end up being a Buddhist handy man." Jim laughed. "No, but you can bet he was good at it."

Jim sat down and looked quite serious. "I had a talk with your dad last night. Well, I talked, and he listened and nodded," he began. "I explained again that he had a life before, and that he was injured and it caused him to forget that life. It was difficult, since I didn't know all the right words in Vietnamese, but he seemed to understand. I wanted to know if he wanted that life back and he did not respond, except for some unintelligible noises, like some type of clicking." Leslie laughed at the mental picture, but then apologized. She could tell that Jim was choosing his words carefully.

"I realize that I need to ask 'Yes' or 'No' questions, since he can't tell me what he's thinking, so I had to guess. To make a long story short, he wants both. He wants to know about his past, but he likes the calm and peaceful life that he has led at the monastery. He understands that you're his child and that he had never met you before yesterday. I explained that his wife died, but since he has lived with men who don't have wives he seemed more surprised than sad. We are going to have to stay open-minded about his reactions and not let our expectations tell us what is appropriate. I found myself feeling disappointed that he didn't seem sad about Susan's death, but he doesn't seem to remember the emotional attachment. He was pretty excited to know that he has a grandson, though."

Leslie listened intently and realized that this made sense. She found it interesting that her Dad's reactions were similar to what some autistic people exhibit and felt that she could handle the necessary changes in expectations, as she sometimes had to do that for Billy. "They are going to get along great," Leslie replied. "But what do we call him? Did you explain that the name he uses is not his given name?" Jim said he had explained that but couldn't really get a response. His own plan was to use both initially, and gradually use "Bill" more and more.

Jim said he hadn't really thought about everything that has changed in the past 50 years, but having someone around who has basically lived in a cave made him look at things differently. "Your dad is fascinated with the garage door opener and the TV remote. He obviously didn't have much technology at the monastery. I'm no technical guru, and don't use my laptop much, but he kept opening it and closing it. It was like having a large toddler at my house. Wait until he hears about the internet!"

Leslie laughed and said, "This is a lot like having a toddler, but more complicated. For some things, we are reminding him how to do what he already knew how to do at one time. For others, it's more complicated and will require more explanation. We need to figure out what he likes to eat and wear, and possibly how to drive again." Jim seemed deep in thought. "It would be great if he still had that '58 Impala," he said. "I would love to drive that again." Leslie was confused. "The Impala is in my garage," she said. "Mom didn't get rid of it." Jim stood up. "Are you kidding me?" he asked. "She told me years ago that she was going to sell it to your neighbor, the guy who kept it running for the parades." Leslie explained that Gary was allowed to come and go in their garage and he worked on the car (and anything that broke at their house), but the Impala was left to her when Susan died. Jim said he was really looking forward to taking Bill for a ride, and Leslie said she would let him drive if she could go with them. She hadn't been in the car in a couple of years, so it might be fun. She needed to find the title and make sure it was insured.

∙ ∙ ∙

Chapter Twenty-One

Leslie's phone rang and she looked at the screen. Aunt Judith. Ugh. Leslie let it go to voicemail and told Jim that her aunt was calling. He said she had called him last night, and of course he didn't answer, but she didn't leave a voicemail. "I still can't believe Judith wouldn't bring me those pictures," he said, shaking his head. "I wonder if she's ever done anything for someone else without getting something out of it for herself." Leslie asked Jim if he could imagine being married to someone that miserable, and he said there was only one woman he could imagine being married to.

"What ever happened to Linda?" Leslie asked. "Have you seen her since you split up?" Jim said he ran into her once when he went back to Michigan, and all he knew was that she had remarried and had a son. He claimed that he wasn't sure if she was even still alive. Leslie thought about how sad it was that Jim never married again, and suggested, "Well, now that you'll be retiring, maybe we can find a girlfriend for you." Jim laughed. "It's too late for me, but what about you? When was the last time you went on a date?" Leslie couldn't remember and commented that she had been too busy with Billy and her mom to worry about such things.

They were interrupted by Jim's phone buzzing. He said, "Oh, your Dad is done with his Speech-Language Pathologist. Now he gets to see the Otolaryngologist. Want to go with me to walk him over to his appointment?" Leslie said she would love to go and asked, "What the heck is an otolaryngologist?" Jim explained that it was the technical term for an ENT (Ear-Nose-Throat doctor). They were trying to rule out any physical complication that would prevent Bill Lucas from speaking, and this was the second opinion. The first ENT claimed that there was nothing he could find that would prevent speaking and suggested that it was a psychological issue rather than physiological. "Today's ENT specializes in Laryngology," Jim explained, "so apparently he focuses on diseases and injuries that affect your voice box and vocal cords. Basically, he is the 'T' in ENT."

Leslie visualized the doctor being Mr. T and the thought made her smile. She had learned a lot in a couple of days and was fascinated by the number of specialists available to diagnose and treat her father. "It's a good thing I'm retiring, since I assume that my Dad will have a lot of appointments," she thought aloud. Jim said he would be around to help and would be happy to take Bill to any appointments. Leslie suggested that Jim also find a good therapist to deal with all of this, but Jim shrugged it off. "I needed a therapist years ago, but my life has more purpose now than it did then. My friend has been found alive and I brought him home. He may not know who he is and getting his memories back may or may not happen, but the burden has been lifted. If I died today, I could rest in peace."

Leslie commented that she couldn't handle any more death for awhile and Jim apologized for being so insensitive about her Mom passing away so recently. Leslie knew he didn't mean anything, that he was just making a point, and told him not to worry about it. "Have I even thanked you for finding my Dad, for giving up living your life to find him?" she asked. "If not, then I'm doing that now. Thank you, from the bottom of my heart. You're a true friend and I admire that you take your 'Semper Fidelis' so literally." She hugged Jim and could tell that he was getting choked up again. "Maybe I do need a therapist," he admitted.

They headed upstairs to get her dad and Leslie found herself getting excited. "I'm going to see my Dad," she beamed. "Do you know how many years I've been waiting to say that? I like the way it sounds." Jim voiced his regrets that he never had any children, and Leslie said she would adopt him as her second dad. "Billy would be thrilled to have two more grandfathers, since the one he has lives so far away," Leslie said. "I spent my whole life not having a dad, so having two might make up for all those years I had none." Jim said he would like that and hoped that there was a house for sale near them. "I don't know of any real close," Leslie said, "but I have a friend whose daughter is a real estate agent. We'll find something."

They stepped out of the elevator and Bill Lucas was there by himself, just waiting for them. Jim was angry at first, since someone was supposed to be with Bill at all times, but then he pulled out his phone and took a picture of him sitting in the chair. "Evidence," he told Leslie. "This proves that he isn't a flight risk, that he doesn't need a constant companion." Bill's face lit up when he saw them; he stood quickly and bowed slightly with his hands together. "It's a sign of respect," Jim explained. Leslie smiled and said "Hi!" and she and Jim were both shocked when Bill responded, "Hi!"

•••

Chapter Twenty-Two

Leslie and Jim exchanged a look and laughed. This was certainly unexpected, and Jim asked Bill in English, "So, you're talking now?" Bill smiled, but didn't seem to understand, so Jim asked him the same question in Vietnamese. Bill shook his head and Leslie was a little bit disappointed, but not completely. He had just mimicked her speech, and she knew from teaching Billy how to talk that this is how it starts. She felt hopeful that this was just the beginning.

Jim explained to Bill that they were going to see an Ear-Nose-Throat doctor, and Leslie wondered if any other language used the word 'otolaryngologist.' Bill kept smiling at Leslie, but never said anything else. He walked quickly, with a purpose, and Leslie found it hard to keep up with him. He stopped at a potted plant in the hallway that appeared to be dying and pulled off the dead leaves. He looked up and saw a skylight, then moved the plant under the light. She admired his love for plants and wondered if he could help with her garden. She knew he would love the large Buddha statue sitting in it, which Mom had put there many years ago. It was supposed to bring luck, but Leslie didn't think it worked... until now. Maybe her luck was improving.

They reached the ENT's office and Jim checked in with the receptionist. She asked if all three of them would be seeing the doctor, and Leslie said they would. There was no waiting, and they were taken back immediately to see the doctor. This was another military doctor in uniform, an Air Force Colonel who appeared to be almost as old as her father. Jim started explaining the situation, but the colonel interrupted him. "Thank you, sir, but I have been briefed about Sergeant Lucas and I'm looking forward to working with him today. Please have a seat." Leslie didn't like the doctor's rude approach and she could tell that Jim didn't, either.

There were only three chairs, as they had not expected Leslie, so Bill Lucas sat on the floor cross-legged. Leslie realized that he must have understood the command to sit, or perhaps it was the voice inflection that he interpreted. The Colonel called out to his receptionist to bring another chair and when she brought it to Bill, he bowed his head slightly but averted his eyes away from her. Jim told him to sit down in Vietnamese, and the doctor asked Jim what language he was speaking. He said it was Vietnamese, but that Sergeant Lucas also understood French and little bit of English. "Have you tried Russian?" the doctor asked. "I read through his dossier and saw that Russian was one of his languages." Jim said that he had not tried Russian and the doctor asked Bill: "Kak vas sovut?" Bill stared at the doctor, then looked at Jim.

"That 'dossier' probably didn't state this, but Sergeant Lucas currently doesn't speak," explained Jim. "He is not able to answer an open-ended question like that." The doctor commented, "Oh, you know Russian, too?" Jim admitted that he knew a little, but 'What's your name?' is quite basic so he recognized it. He explained that Bill would answer 'Yes' or 'No' questions by nodding or shaking his head, and that he had been called 'Erden' for 50 years and identified with that name. The doctor tried again: "Vas sovut Erden?" Bill looked confused, so Jim told him in Vietnamese that the doctor was asking if his name is Erden, but he was speaking Russian. Bill nodded and Jim asked if he understood the Russian words. Bill shook his head, indicating that he did not. Jim said, "There you go. He doesn't remember any Russian."

For the rest of the appointment, Jim translated the doctor's questions into Vietnamese for Bill and there was a lot of nodding. There was no indication that Bill was physiologically unable to speak, although his vocal cords were a little tight. According to Mr. T, as Leslie would remember him, there was hope that with some speech therapy Sergeant Lucas could completely regain his speech. The Colonel believed that his injuries ruptured the connection between his thoughts and actions, which was a little out of his realm of study. He recommended working with Speech Language Pathologists and Psychologists who were experienced with Traumatic Brain Injuries. Jim explained that they already had all those people looped into the Care Plan, and he and Leslie thanked the doctor and escorted Bill out.

In the hallway, Leslie asked Jim why he didn't mention that her Dad said "Hi" earlier and Bill turned to Leslie and said, "Hi!" again. Jim laughed but then explained, "That arrogant SOB doesn't need to know. Giving him that information would ensure a longer stay here, so they could run more tests. We need to get the green light as soon as possible for your Dad to leave this facility so he can go home and continue his treatment there." Leslie understood and smiled when she thought of her Dad going home, but she had a lot to do before he arrived.

It wasn't quite 11:00, a little early for lunch, so Jim suggested that they stop in the debriefing office for a few minutes. Jim went to use the restroom and Bill noticed the pictures sitting out. Leslie tried to explain that the man in the pictures was him, first pointing to him and then the picture and saying, "That's you." When he looked confused, she pointed at the picture and said, "Erden." He was intrigued and looked closer at the pictures.

Jim came back into the room and explained to Bill that the lady in the picture was Susan, the wife he had told him about. Bill sat down and stared at the pictures. Leslie said, "She was beautiful, and she loved you so much." Jim translated, and Bill's eyes filled with tears. "Do you think he's remembering?" Leslie asked Jim. "No, I just think he sees how in love these two people are, and he's struggling to understand that it's a younger version of him." Leslie felt like she was intruding somehow and excused herself to use the restroom.

Bill continued to look through the pictures but kept coming back to the one of him and Susan sitting on the front of his car. Jim explained that the car was his first one, that it was still at his house, and they would see that soon. Bill didn't seem interested in the car, and Jim explained again that Susan had recently died. Bill walked to the window and looked out, as Leslie returned to the room. "What happened?" she asked. "Look at the picture in his hand," Jim said. "It's the one of your parents sitting on the Impala. I think the pictures are already bringing back memories for him."

Jim asked Bill if he was hungry, but there was no response. Leslie put her arm around Bill and gave him a little squeeze. She saw a tear roll down his cheek and tried not to think of how sad it was that her parents had just missed each other. "Let's go eat," she said. He nodded his head, and she knew he understood. They were going to get through this, and she looked forward to the day when they could have a normal conversation so she could ask what he was thinking. Jim grabbed his sunglasses and keys, and they headed out to lunch.

Leslie sat in the back seat and watched her Dad take in the sights as they drove down the road. There was a lot squeezed onto the small base, but things were more spread out in the surrounding neighborhood. Riding with her dad was similar to taking Billy to an unfamiliar place, his head turning as he strained to see, but this was a much quieter experience. Billy asked a lot of questions, and her dad just took it all in. Jim was trying to tell him what some of the more obvious landmarks were and explained that they were going to a restaurant that would serve food he might like better than what he was getting at Bethesda. "I think the food is great at the medical center," Leslie commented, "but I don't know what he typically ate at the monastery." Jim said the place they were going was authentic, and the people who worked there were all Vietnamese.

They pulled up to the pagoda-style restaurant and Bill looked nervous. Jim explained that it was just a place to eat, and they walked inside. They were taken to a table in the middle of the restaurant, but Bill shook his head and didn't want to sit there. Leslie asked if they had something in the back or a corner, since her father was shy around strangers, and they were offered a corner booth in the back. Jim and Leslie thanked the waitress and sat down. Bill did not want to sit between them, and Jim explained that he needed to have an avenue of escape. He had spent years running away from people, and probably didn't like to feel trapped. Leslie adjusted easily to what others might consider inconvenient or quirky. Raising Billy had taught her to be accommodating, even if she didn't always understand the reasoning.

There were pictures on the menu and Bill seemed quite excited by some of the choices. He pointed to the Pho, and Jim said he would order that for him. Leslie said she would have the same, as it looked simple with noodles and brisket and broth. The waitress who came to the table appeared to know Jim and spoke to him in Vietnamese. He ordered for everyone, and Bill seemed to understand the conversation. His smile was genuine and Leslie felt that bringing him here was a good idea.

The food didn't take long to get to the table, and Leslie watched her dad and Jim pick up their chopsticks like experts. She was glad that there were spoons because she didn't know how to use chopsticks, but Jim said he would teach her later. They ate in silence, a common practice for Buddhists, and Leslie enjoyed the quiet time. She watched how her father enjoyed his meal and decided to expand her cooking skills to include some Vietnamese dishes. Since she wouldn't be working, she would have time to experiment. She wondered how Billy would handle a change to the menu, but it wouldn't hurt to try.

After the Pho, Jim ordered Mango Cake for dessert. Leslie was surprised when she was served a glob of sweet rice with peanuts and sesame seeds, with no mango or cake at all. Jim explained that it was just shaped like a mango, and Leslie was proud of herself for being open-minded enough to give it a try. Bill obviously enjoyed it, pausing between bites to close his eyes and revel in the deliciousness. Leslie noted that it really was like being with Billy, except much quieter. She offered to pay for the meal, but Jim told her that she was being "ridiculous." She could get used to this idea of having two Dads.

The ride back to the hospital was quiet, and Jim explained to Leslie that Bill would want some time alone to meditate when they got there. He suggested that she call Dr. Edwards a little earlier than planned, giving her something to do. It was almost 1:00 already, so she agreed that she would call him when they got back. She thought about what she was going to say when she called and felt silly that she really wanted to know all about him.

"Thinking about that doctor?" Jim asked, looking at her in the rearview mirror. "He isn't married, you know." Leslie said she wasn't worried about that, and Jim said he was letting her know, just in case. "Thank you," Leslie replied. "I'm starting to reap the benefits of having two dads." They laughed, and so did Bill, which made Leslie laugh even harder.

•••

Chapter Twenty-Three

As they walked through the lobby when they returned to the hospital, Leslie noticed that the stage and podium were set up again. "Another press conference?" she asked Jim. He said he hadn't heard anything and kept walking. When they were inside the debriefing offices, Jim and Bill went to the back room and Leslie checked her phone in the front office. She was 40 minutes early but decided to call Dr. Edwards anyway.

He picked up immediately with a cheerful, "You're early!" Leslie wasn't expecting that reaction and it made her laugh. "Hello, Dr. Edwards! I am calling to see when we can meet to discuss my father." He asked her to please call him 'Michael' and said he didn't have an appointment until 3:00, so the sooner the better. He explained where his office was, and Leslie yelled to Jim that she would be back, but Jim was already deep in meditation with his friend Bill and never heard what she said.

Leslie stopped in the restroom on her way to see Dr. Edwards. She used the restroom, wiped her oily nose, and checked for food in her teeth. Her hair looked nice, and that eyeliner really did make her big brown eyes pop. She shoved a mint in her mouth and walked to the elevator, whistling. The head of Security saw her and said, "Good afternoon, Ms. Lucas. How are you today?" Leslie felt wonderful and replied cheerfully: "Good afternoon! I feel great!" He laughed, but Leslie thought he looked frightened so she decided to work on being cheerful without being scary. She didn't have a lot of practice.

She reached the office of Dr. Edwards and told the receptionist her name. "Oh, honey," the sweet older woman cooed, "he has been expecting you all day. You go right in." Leslie thanked her and caught a whiff of lavender as she went by the desk. She opened the office door slowly and Dr. Edwards stood to greet her. "Hello, hello! Have a seat!" he said. "Would you like something to drink? Water? Tea? Vodka? Whatever you wish." She thanked him and said that water would be fine, especially if they have some that isn't refrigerated. "Are you kidding?" he asked. "I drink mine at room temperature, too. Let me grab a bottle for you."

He grabbed a bottle from the cupboard and handed it to Leslie. "Let's talk about your dad. Did I tell you that I am fascinated by his case?" Leslie explained that he had shared that with her, but she was glad to hear it. Leslie told Dr. Edwards that she and Jim had sat in at the ENT appointment and it was his opinion that this was not physical or physiological; it was a psychological issue. Dr. Edwards said he assumed as much and asked if Sergeant Lucas had said anything today. "Yes, he did!" Leslie gushed. "When I saw him this morning, I said 'Hi' and he said it back to me. We didn't tell the ENT."

Dr. Edwards laughed and said he was impressed but asked why they didn't share such a breakthrough. Leslie explained that they didn't want to do anything to change the plans in place, and the goal was to get her Dad discharged as soon as possible. Since he was not speaking and nobody had heard him say anything besides her and Jim and Justine, it was best that everyone assume that he can't talk and let him go home. "I love it!" Dr. Edwards replied. "Brilliant but somehow devious! But I am also one of the doctors in his Care Plan, so why are you telling me about it?" Leslie explained that since he is going to Michigan shortly, too, he would still be part of the Care Plan. She suggested that he should take the lead in the Care Plan because he is the link between his treatment at Bethesda and Ann Arbor.

"I like how you think," he said, "and I will work on that. You're heading out first thing in the morning to go back home, right?" Leslie explained that she had planned to do so, but General Carlson had scheduled a meeting with the Social Worker for everyone at 8 AM. She asked if he had received anything about it, and he said that he was included in a group email and wasn't sure if he was going to attend. "Well, if you're hoping to take the lead on this, you should definitely be there," Leslie explained. "Having everyone from his Care Team in one place is great for communication, so we can all be on the same page." Dr. Edwards agreed to be there and said he would check to see if anyone was left off the group email so he could invite them.

Leslie asked where he was from in Michigan and was surprised to find out that he grew up only about 20 miles from her and had graduated high school two years after Leslie. He was commissioned an officer in the Air Force when he received his Bachelor's degree, and Air Force life allowed him to complete his Masters and PhD. He had been an Air Force doctor until just a couple of years ago, when his chosen field of Psycholinguistics was not an approved military path. Rather than settle with a position that he didn't want, he chose to resign his commission and continue as a civilian in the field that he loves. He admitted that he makes more money as a civilian, but still has trouble figuring out what to wear to work every day.

They laughed at how close they grew up to each other years ago and Leslie commented about what a small world it was. She suddenly noticed a beautiful picture on the shelf behind his desk. "Wow! That woman is gorgeous!" she gushed. "Who is that?" Dr. Edwards explained that it was his mother, and the picture was taken about 6 years ago. His father had passed away unexpectedly almost 10 years ago, just before Dr. Edwards came to Bethesda, and he was going back to Michigan in part to be near her. "My mother is in her early 70s and I don't have any brothers or sisters to help take care of her. I worry about her more and more."

Leslie said that she was an only child, too, and explained how lonely it was growing up without a father or any brothers or sisters. Sometimes, she felt bad that Billy was an only child, but it just worked out that way. They talked about Billy and her mother and Leslie's divorce, and time just flew by. He was so easy to talk with, and Leslie was sad when the receptionist buzzed and said his 3:00 appointment had arrived. Leslie thanked him for his time, apologized if she was talking too much, and opened the door to the lobby. There sat her Dad and Jim, smiling. "Is this your 3:00 appointment?" she asked. Dr. Edwards said that was doctor/patient confidentiality and smiled.

Jim and Bill stood up and walked into Dr. Edwards' office, and Leslie followed behind. As he walked into the office, Bill smiled at Dr. Edwards and said, "Hi!" Leslie and Jim laughed, and Dr. Edwards felt like he was part of a secret club. He felt honored to be part of this group and asked Jim if he minded translating what he was saying. Jim said he didn't mind but thought that Dr. Edwards knew

Vietnamese. He explained that he could understand if someone else spoke and he could read it, but he can't speak it very well. "Ah, the old 'receptive and productive' issue, huh?" Jim asked. Dr. Edwards was quick to reply. "Yes, sir, and I am also an expert in sarcasm." Leslie smiled and took a seat to observe the process. Jim agreed to translate but encouraged Dr. Edwards to use the words that he did know so he could practice his Vietnamese.

Leslie watched as Dr. Edwards tried to get to the cause of the problem, and she admired his desire to really pinpoint the issue. He would ask questions in English, interjecting an occasional word in Vietnamese, and Jim would translate to Bill. Dr. Edwards was cognizant of the need for Yes and No questions, but there were some questions that were open-ended so he had to be creative. He checked Bill's vocal cords and explained that there were people who took vows of silence and when they spoke again, their voices were quite different because their vocal cords had tightened. Some even lost their voices entirely. Since he had heard Bill say "Hi," he knew that he could speak, but that somewhere there was a disconnect.

Dr. Edwards tried some exercises and asked Jim if anyone else had asked Bill to draw pictures to express his thoughts or feelings. Jim said that a few doctors had tried to get Bill to write words, but as far as he knew there were no requests for pictures. Dr. Edwards grabbed some white paper from the printer and a pencil from his desk, and asked Bill to draw a picture, any picture. Jim reiterated the request in Vietnamese, but Bill had understood and he was already drawing. The first picture was a garden and Leslie thought it was beautiful. She wasn't surprised when Dr. Edwards pulled out one of the tiny black recorders and started speaking into it; everyone in the building seemed to have one of those things.

"Patient is non-verbal but seems to have mental pictures that he is expressing as drawings," Dr. Edwards said. Jim pulled out his phone and was scrolling through some pictures. "I think I know what that picture is. Let me find it."

Bill finished drawing the first picture about the same time that Jim found it on his phone. The picture was the garden near the area in Marble Mountain where they found Bill. Dr. Edwards was thrilled, and asked Jim if he could load all the photos that he took there onto a thumb drive so he could compare them to future drawings. Jim said he would, as Bill started another drawing. This one portrayed the abbot who saved Bill, probably his last image of the old monk as he was lying on his deathbed. Jim said, "Oh, that's Ky. He's the one who wrote the journals." As they watched Bill draw his picture, Dr. Edwards asked Jim if he could get him a copy of the journals and Jim promised to do what he could. He was still waiting for some translations, but they were too slow for his taste and he might need to intervene. Dr. Edwards said that between the two of them, they could probably translate the journals themselves.

Bill appeared to be excited to have paper and pencil in hand and he produced drawings of a large Buddha statue, a small room with candles and an altar, and another garden with beautiful flowers. There wasn't much noise in the room as the drawings were produced, except an occasional statement by Dr. Edwards into his recorder. Jim kept scrolling through the Photo Gallery on his phone to see if he had other pictures to match the drawings. Leslie just watched as her father produced several beautiful drawings.

When Bill was tired of drawing, he put down his pencil and looked up. Dr. Edwards said he thought this was incredible progress and suggested that Jim find a sketchbook for Sergeant Lucas. They discussed what Leslie had already talked about, getting her Dad discharged and back home as soon as possible, and they all seemed to agree that this would be the best plan for his recovery. Leslie felt hopeful that her Dad would be back in Michigan in just a few weeks and was glad that she would only have to make the drive back here one more time, when she came to take him home.

Dr. Edwards was putting his notes and recorder in his desk and Jim wanted to be sure that they would be on the same page at the morning meeting. In mid-sentence about how they would need to convince the other members on the Care Plan team, Jim stopped talking. He had noticed the same picture behind Dr. Edwards that Leslie had asked about. "Who is that?" Jim asked quietly. "That's Dr. Edwards' mother," Leslie replied. Isn't she beautiful?" Jim was entranced. "Oh my God. That's Linda."

Everyone stopped and time seemed to pause briefly. Leslie spoke first: "That's Linda? Your ex-wife?" Jim nodded as he walked toward the picture. "This is your mother?" he asked Dr. Edwards. "Yes, sir, but you must be mistaken. She was never married before.

She and my father were married a long time, but he passed away years ago," Dr. Edwards explained. Leslie suggested nervously that everyone has a doppelganger somewhere, an exact look-alike, and perhaps this was the case. "What's your mother's name?" she asked Dr. Edwards. "It's Linda," he said, "but I think that's just a huge coincidence. She and Dad were married for almost 40 years."

Jim picked up the picture and smiled. "Does she still live in Clinton?" Dr. Edwards said that she did, but she was currently on a cruise with some friends. His face went from confused to amused and he asked Jim if this was a prank, if perhaps Jim used his intelligence connections to get that information about his mother. Leslie thought about the fact that Jim was aware that Aunt Judith lives in Virginia and wondered if Dr. Edwards might be onto something. Jim put the picture down and said quietly, "Maybe she just looks like my Linda. Probably a case of mistaken identity." He motioned to Bill to go out the door and they walked out.

Before Leslie followed, she suggested to Dr. Edwards that he ask his mother if she knows Jim Carlson. He said he would text her as soon as they left, and asked Leslie what she was doing for dinner. "I have no idea," she said. "I'm just following Jim's lead. We had a great lunch earlier at a Vietnamese restaurant, not far from here. I had Pho and Mango Cake." Dr. Edwards said that sounded delicious, since he loves mangoes, and was disappointed to find out that the name comes from the shape, not the contents. "Well," he said, "if you don't have any plans, I know a great Japanese restaurant with beautiful gardens about 20 minutes from here. Your Dad and General Carlson are welcome to come along." Leslie thanked him and said she would let him know, then ran to catch up to Jim and her Dad, who were waiting by the elevator.

Jim was staring at the elevator door, as silent as Bill. The door opened as Leslie walked up and they all stepped in. Jim appeared to be in shock. "Is it her?" Leslie asked gently. Jim nodded and stared at the wall. She could tell that he was trying to keep his bearing and she didn't want to push. "I'll find out more," she promised. "Maybe we can get part of your life back." Jim squeezed her hand and closed his eyes. "She probably doesn't even remember me," he muttered quietly. Leslie dared him to find anyone who could forget him and squeezed his hand back. She had to do something about this and was anxious to hear what Dr. Edwards found out from his mother.

They stepped out of the elevator and Leslie could hear a lot of activity in the lobby. As they walked through on their way to the office, Leslie waved at the head of Security. He seemed to be working with some of his people on another upcoming press conference. She wondered about the service members with injuries who were sent here and assumed that the press conference was for one of the wounded warriors. She didn't have much time to think about it, as she worked to keep pace with Jim and her Dad.

They got to the office and Leslie asked Jim if he needed some time alone, if perhaps he wanted her to take her Dad for a walk. Jim said that would be great and explained where there was a meditation garden on the property. While he explained to Bill that Leslie was going to take him to the garden, Leslie grabbed a couple of bottles of water to take with them. On the way out, Leslie mentioned to Jim that Dr. Edwards had invited all of them out to dinner at a Japanese restaurant, if he was interested. She suggested that it might be a clever way to get more information about Linda, but Jim just shook his head and walked into the other room. Leslie grabbed some paper and a pencil, just in case her Dad wanted to draw. She carried a huge "Mom purse," big enough to hold drinks and snacks and art supplies because one never knows.

Leslie turned to Bill and said, "Okay, let's go for a walk." He smiled and walked out with Leslie. As they walked through the lobby, Leslie saw a flash and looked toward it in time to see the head of Security react by ushering the photographer out the door. She thought about how weird it was that reporters were still hanging around trying to get a picture of her Dad and wondered how long this fascination from the media would go on. They walked to the garden area and Leslie found some benches to sit on. She sat down and asked her Dad if he wanted to sit, but Bill shook his head and said "No." Another word! That's three…Oh, Hi, and No. Leslie laughed out loud and thought to herself that this really is like having a toddler.

Bill found a spot in the grass and sat down, legs folded like a pretzel. He put his hands on his knees and closed his eyes, so Leslie took out her phone to check messages while he meditated. She texted Dr. Edwards to let him know that her Dad just said "No," and asked him if the Vietnamese used the same word. He didn't reply immediately, so she used a translation app on her phone and affirmed her guess. She assumed that most languages used some variation of 'no.' She was proud of herself for learning something new.

She took a picture of her Dad meditating and sent it to Melanie, asking her to show Billy. Melanie replied that Billy was being a handful today, missing his mom, and asked if Leslie could call. She pressed the Call button and asked if everything was okay. Melanie said she wasn't feeling well and Leslie reminded her that she would be there tomorrow night. "Do you have a cold or maybe the flu?" Leslie asked. "Do you want me to call Mrs. Lutz, the backup sitter?" Melanie said she must have eaten something that didn't agree with her, as she threw up a few times today, but didn't have a fever. "Could it be morning sickness?" Leslie asked excitedly. Melanie groaned and said she wasn't sure if she was ready for that, but she would take a pregnancy test to rule out that cause.

Before Leslie could reply, Billy was on the phone. "Mom! I saw that picture of my Grandpa! He's skinny! Why is he sitting on the ground? Is he asleep?" Leslie explained that he was meditating, which is just a term for relaxing and thinking peaceful thoughts. She told him that he should try it and suggested that he be nice to Melanie because she doesn't feel well. He was excited when Leslie informed him that she was coming home tomorrow night and said he couldn't wait to see what she brought him. Leslie didn't go away often, but she always brought home a surprise for Billy.

Maybe she could stop at the gift shop tomorrow before leaving the area. She could see that they had some cute things in the window, and they probably had something unique for Billy. He said he had to go try meditating and handed the phone back to Melanie. Leslie said she would see them tomorrow evening, but advised Melanie that if she really felt sick she should call Mrs. Lutz. Melanie said she would tough it out and have her husband come over to play with Billy for a little while. Leslie thanked her and hung up, truly grateful for Melanie, who loved Billy and treated him like her little brother. She would be a great mother.

•••

Chapter Twenty-Four

Leslie noticed that a monarch butterfly had landed on her Dad's shoulder and snapped another picture with her phone. The door to the garden opened and Dr. Edwards came strolling out. "Is he meditating?" he whispered to Leslie. "Yes, and attracting butterflies," Leslie whispered back. "Absolutely at peace with the world. I love that."

Dr. Edwards watched Bill for a few minutes and Leslie asked if he had heard from his mother. He had not, but explained that reception is unreliable when you're out in the ocean, so that is to be expected. Leslie really wanted to know if this was the same Linda, so she asked if there was anyone else who would know. Leslie didn't have siblings, but she assumed that if she did, they would know things like that. "What about a sister? Does your mom have any sisters?" Dr. Edwards said that she does have one, his Aunt Helen. "They aren't very close now," he said, "but they were when they were younger. Aunt Helen lives out in California and is quite a free spirit, and Mom is controlled and a little regimented." He looked in his phone to find Aunt Helen's number. "Let's find out right now," he said, pushing the green phone icon.

Dr. Edwards put his phone on Speaker so Leslie could hear the conversation. Aunt Helen seemed happy to hear Dr. Edwards' voice. "Oh, Michael! What a nice surprise! I saw you on TV at a press conference. You seem so comfortable in front of the camera; I told you that you should have been an actor. Wait...did something happen to your mother?" He explained that his mother was fine, just out of town on a cruise, and he had a question that he wanted answered right away. "What? Your mother is on a cruise? Is she finally starting to have fun?" she laughed. Dr. Edwards agreed that it was about time she had some fun, but then he looked serious. "Aunt Helen, was Mom married before she met my Dad? I mean, married and divorced."

There was an uncomfortably long pause. "Yes," she finally responded, "she was married to a Marine. I think his name was Jim or John, or something similar. Why do you ask?" Dr. Edwards took a deep breath. "Was it Jim Carlson?" Aunt Helen thought that sounded right, but asked why he was inquiring, since that was so long ago. "Well, did you see the older gentleman on TV with me, who was part of the team that found a Vietnam veteran alive and brought him home? That is Jim Carlson. He is a retired Marine Corps Brigadier General and one heck of an American." Aunt Helen gasped and exclaimed, "I knew he looked familiar! I couldn't decide if I had met him or if he was from one of my dreams. Does your mother know?"

Dr. Edwards explained that he had texted her but had not yet received a response. Aunt Helen suggested that her sister might not be answering because that man broke her heart. His drinking caused a lot of problems, so she divorced him and found a man who didn't drink. Dr. Edwards could not remember ever seeing his father drink alcohol, even if his mother had a drink. "Wow. Why didn't she ever tell me about him?" Aunt Helen said there was no reason to tell him, and that people try to forget those who break their hearts. "As much as he drank," she added, "I'm surprised that the man is still alive."

Dr. Edwards explained that General Carlson got some help after losing his marriage and almost losing his career. "Well, at least he was able to salvage one of those things," Aunt Helen commented. "But she never stopped loving him. Even after being married to your Dad for years, she never let it go. It almost caused a divorce for your parents early in their marriage." She suggested that he talk to Linda about it and advised him to tread lightly for fear of opening up old wounds. He thanked his aunt for the information, then ended the call and turned to Leslie with a troubled expression.

"Well, it's true. General Carlson was married to my mother and broke her heart." Before Leslie could reply, a voice behind them said, "I didn't mean to hurt anyone. I really loved her." Leslie and Dr. Edwards turned around to see Jim Carlson, who had come out a different door and had not wanted to interrupt the phone conversation. "How much did you hear?" asked Dr. Edwards. "All of it," Jim replied, "and I deserve whatever horrible things your aunt and your mother have to say about me. I was a narcissist, so full of myself, unable to live a normal life because I made a mistake. I signed off on the request that Bill Lucas submitted to extend his stay in Vietnam, which was outside the chain of command and totally unacceptable. I could have prevented all of this by forcing the command's hand to send him home when Leslie was born. I kicked myself in the ass for 51 years, but he's home now. We can't change the past."

Dr. Edwards' phone buzzed and he looked down. "It's my mother," he said. "She texted back and said she knew a 'sweet gentleman by that name when she was younger.' She wants to know why I'm asking." Leslie spoke first. "Give me your phone. Jim, you sit down next to Dr. Edwards and I will take a picture of the two of you. Dr. Edwards can send it to his Mom." Dr. Edwards insisted that she call him 'Michael,' and Leslie said, "Okay, Jim, sit next to Michael. Both of you smile." She took the picture and handed the phone back. "Now, Michael, please send this picture to your mother," she requested. Jim and Michael exchanged looks and Michael said, "Why not?" at the same time that Jim said, "No, don't." Leslie put her hand on Jim's shoulder. "Hey, you got this part of my life back," she said, motioning to her Dad, "so let me help you get part of your life back. What do you have to lose? You've lost almost as many years of that relationship as I have of this one."

"And...sent," Dr. Edwards announced. "Do you think I should have sent an explanation?" Leslie laughed and asked if there really was an explanation and Bill Lucas seemed to be done with his meditation. Jim apologized to him about making too much noise and asked if they were too loud. "No," Bill replied. Leslie was amused at the shocked look on Jim's face and said, "He said that to me when we got here. Isn't it awesome?" Dr. Edwards high-fived Leslie and Jim, and Bill put his hand up to receive his high-five as well. "Wow, this guy learns fast," Dr. Edwards stated. "I told you that he was a genius," Jim replied. "We should have him back to normal in no time."

Jim and Bill walked to the door as Leslie and Michael followed. "Did you ask them about dinner?" Michael asked her. "We would love for you to buy us dinner," Jim replied. "Maybe we could all go together to find more clothes for my friend here." Leslie wasn't sure if her Dad would be comfortable with all of them going, but said it sounded like fun. "Maybe if you like shopping," Jim answered. Leslie loved shopping and couldn't understand why people didn't like it. Searching for bargains is like a treasure hunt and finding something that you really like at a low price is such a feeling of accomplishment. Now that she was technically a millionaire with all the money that Mom left, she knew that she didn't have to pinch pennies but still planned to do so, just for that feeling.

"It's still a little early for dinner, so maybe we can do some shopping first," Leslie suggested. "Get it out of the way. I have access to the joint account that Mom kept of hers and my Dad's, so I can pay for his clothes out of that." Jim scoffed and said he had plenty of money, but Leslie reminded him that he would need it to buy a house in Michigan. She would have to check what was available in their area.

"How about you, Michael?" she asked Dr. Edwards. "Will you be buying a house or staying with your Mom?" He explained that his father had inherited a huge old house in Saline, which he then passed on to him. "I work on projects to update it every time I go back to Michigan," he explained. "Soon I'm hoping to have time to enjoy it a little more."

Leslie thought about how nice it was going to be, having these men around. Billy had spent a few years not having much of a male role model, and now he was getting two...maybe three.

•••

Chapter Twenty-Five

General Carlson won the "Who's going to drive?" argument and Leslie sat in the back seat of his Impala with Dr. Edwards. Jim looked in the rearview mirror. "No funny business going on back there," he warned as he drove out of the parking lot. Leslie noticed that Michael blushed a little, which made her smile. She looked out the window and saw cones and barricades being set up for something. "What's going on out there?" she asked. Jim said, "Probably part of that press conference," and asked Dr. Edwards where the restaurant was so he could head in that general direction and stop to buy clothes on the way.

They found a Target that didn't look too busy, and Leslie decided that she would look for something that Billy might like. She said she was heading to the Toys to grab something for Billy, and Jim said he was taking her Dad to the restroom and would meet them over there. She headed to the Toy section with Michael, who asked a lot of questions about Billy while they walked. Leslie explained that Billy is a high-functioning autistic 11-year-old, almost 12. He likes Legos and Minions and cars. "What about GI Joes?" Michael asked. "Does he have any of those? I still have all of mine from when I was a kid." Leslie didn't think she had ever bought one for Billy but thanked Michael for the suggestion and said she would keep it in mind.

They had just started looking at toys when she heard a commotion and a man yelling. "I think that's Jim," she thought aloud, looking for the source of the yelling. There was no reply from Michael, who took off running in the direction of the commotion. Leslie followed but couldn't keep up. She came around the corner of an aisle and saw quite a scene. The reporters had apparently followed them and had surrounded her Dad and Jim. Michael went through them like a bowling ball, knocking a couple of them down, and got to Bill. "Es-tu blessé?" he asked. Bill shook his head but said nothing. "He's not hurt," Michael said to Leslie. "Let's get him out of here." Leslie grabbed her Dad's hand and she could tell that he was scared. Michael tried to get Jim out of the crowd, but one of the photographers was actually trying to block Jim's path so he couldn't get past. Leslie watched in awe as that 75-year-old Marine drew back his fist and leveled the guy. It was impressive, and it distracted everyone for a few minutes so the foursome could make it out of the store and to Jim's car. None of them spoke right away.

As he started the car, Jim took out his other cell phone and said, "Hey, I need a favor. Sergeant Lucas and I need to do some shopping. Target. That one is fine. Yes, now. I don't know. Bomb threat. Thirty minutes? Okay, thanks. I owe you." He rubbed his knuckles and said, "We're going to a different Target not far away. Apparently, there has been a bomb threat and they're clearing the building." Leslie and Michael looked at each other and laughed. "That's awesome!" announced Michael, giggling like a child. "I wish I had that kind of power." Jim looked at him in the rearview mirror. "I'm losing most of my connections when I leave this job," he said. "We might as well take advantage of them while we can. Let's go shopping."

Jim drove around and backtracked a little to ensure there was nobody following him, and eventually pulled into the parking lot of another Target. People were streaming out the front door and there were two firetrucks and a police car with its lights flashing. Jim pulled around to the Receiving door and parked. He looked at his phone. "Okay, all clear. We have 30 minutes to shop." They went inside and Leslie asked Michael if he could pick out something for Billy in Toys while she helped Jim get some clothes for her Dad. As they were walking, Leslie asked Jim, "Isn't it illegal to call in a fake bomb threat?" He laughed. "Nobody actually called in a bomb threat. The firemen and police cooperate with us to do these things when necessary. Most of them are veterans and they play along. They just need something to tell the press, so they'll tell them that it was a bomb threat. Let's go find your Dad some clothes."

Leslie found clothes and handed them to Jim, who asked Bill what he liked. They had to find underwear and socks and a few pairs of shoes. It was quite chaotic, but they got what they needed and Michael met them at the self-checkout. He had Legos and GI Joes, plus a whole set of SpongeBob DVDs. "Did I tell you that Billy loves watching SpongeBob?" she asked. "No, just a lucky guess," Michael answered. "I also love watching SpongeBob." Leslie laughed and rang everything up as Michael put it in bags. Jim looked at his phone and announced, "Okay, 3 minutes. Let's go!" Leslie inserted her card to pay, and the four of them hurried out the back door. Leslie thought the whole experience was thrilling and couldn't help but notice that her father was actually laughing. What must he be thinking?

They threw all the bags in the car and got in. "To the restaurant!" Jim announced. He drove slowly around the building to the front, just as the fire trucks were leaving. One of the fire fighters saluted Jim, who nodded in acknowledgment. Jim explained to Bill what was going on, then asked him if he liked Japanese food. Bill nodded his head and seemed excited. Leslie admitted that this was the most adventurous day she'd had in a long time, maybe ever, and Jim advised her that she needed to get out more. Leslie realized what a sheltered life she had been living and agreed that she needed to be more adventurous.

The restaurant was beautiful, a pagoda-style building like the Vietnamese restaurant but with more ornate decorations. Michael asked to be seated in the garden if possible and they were ushered immediately to an area with a beautiful view. There were cherry trees with their blossoms, but also lilacs, azaleas, wisteria, and tulips. That's just what Leslie could identify; there were several other flowers that she did not recognize. The colors and scents were overwhelming, and Leslie could see how much her Dad loved this spot. She was looking forward to working in the garden with him when they got home.

Leslie looked through the menu as Michael explained the dishes to her, and she settled on a beef rice bowl. He ordered for her and himself in Japanese, which really impressed Leslie. The waitress then looked at Bill and asked if he was ready to order (in Japanese). Bill nodded his head and Jim ordered for them. He then asked Bill if he understood what the waitress had asked him and Bill nodded again. Jim remarked that it was odd, since Japanese was not one of the languages that Bill had been taught. Michael was thrilled because he spoke Japanese pretty well. "Now I can ask him questions in Japanese!" he bragged. "But how did he learn Japanese?"

Bill got up from his seat and motioned for Leslie to follow him. They walked around to see the various plants and flowers, with

Bill bowing to each one to show his respect. Jim and Michael were alone at the table and Jim said that he wanted to apologize for what happened between him and Linda. "That all happened before I was born," Michael said, "but it would be nice for you to apologize to her yourself. I think it would mean a lot to her." Jim nodded and said he wanted to do that. "I love my Mom and I loved my Dad, but they didn't have the greatest marriage," Michael said. "We were comfortable, and she never went without material things, but now that I think about it, there was always an emptiness, like something was missing." Jim nodded and admitted that he was probably responsible for that. He was grateful that Leslie and Bill were heading back to the table so he could change the subject. Just as they sat down, their food arrived. Leslie looked around and asked where the utensils were. "Right here, silly," Michael said, as he handed her some chopsticks. "You expect me to eat rice with chopsticks?" she asked. "Sounds like a great diet plan."

As Jim and Bill started eating, Michael showed Leslie how to hold her chopsticks and grab the food. "For rice," he explained, "you have to get a glob of it together. It's actually easier with regular white rice because it's sticky." He was a good teacher and very patient with Leslie. She picked it up well, but the waitress felt sorry for her and brought some "American silver" for her to use. Once she could concentrate on the food instead of trying to get it to her mouth, Leslie realized that it was delicious. She had Vietnamese food for lunch and Japanese for dinner. She was with three men who know about a dozen languages among them. What a life, she thought. I could get used to this.

•••

Chapter Twenty-Six

When they were almost back to the medical center, Jim asked Leslie if she wanted to be dropped off at Fisher House. She wanted to get her Rubbermaid tote full of pictures and letters that were still at the medical center, so they pulled into the back entrance and parked. Security guards were everywhere and sections of the property were roped off, so Jim suggested that Leslie get her tote tomorrow morning. Michael said he wasn't going inside and he could drop her off if she wanted, so Jim explained to Bill what they were doing. Bill got out to hug Leslie when they stopped at Michael's car.

Jim popped the trunk so Leslie could get the toys that she bought, and Bill's eyes lit up. "Oh!" he exclaimed and shut the trunk before Leslie could get her things. She laughed and went around to Jim's window to ask him to pop it again. Bill watched as Jim pushed the button to pop the trunk, clearly amazed at the technological marvel. "I guess if you lived inside a mountain for 50 years, there are new things to discover that we take for granted," Jim observed. Bill closed the trunk and came back to pop it open himself. Michael grabbed the bags of toys before Bill could close it again. He and Leslie walked to his car, leaving Jim to deal with Bill and the trunk. "Au revoir!" Leslie shouted, proud to remember something in French. "À demain!" Michael yelled to Bill. "What does that mean?" Leslie asked. "Until tomorrow," answered Michael. Of course, Leslie thought. I knew that.

Michael put the toys in the back seat and opened the passenger door for Leslie. "Thank you! I love the color of this Tahoe," Leslie gushed. "What year is it?" Michael said it was a 2018 model, and he loved the shade of blue, which is his favorite color. "Mine, too," said Leslie. "I drive a blue Equinox." She explained how to cut over to Fisher House 5 and they watched all the security guards and extra barricades along the way. "Must be someone pretty special," Leslie commented. Michael explained that everyone who works at the hospital receives a daily email of events, but he had not seen anything that might explain the extra security or barricades. "I hope

I get to see what's going on tomorrow before I leave," said Leslie. "If not, you'll have to text me to let me know what all the fuss was about." Michael said he would definitely do that if he found out, just as they arrived at the front door. He quickly jumped out and ran around to open her door, then grabbed the toys from the back seat. "Billy is going to love these," he said. "Do you need me to carry them in for you?" Leslie assured him that she could handle the bags, but she appreciated the offer. "Okay, I'll see you in the morning then," he responded, waving as he headed back to his door. Leslie smiled, flattered at the gesture. "À demain!" she called out as she turned to go inside. She was already excited to see him in the morning.

When Leslie entered the lobby, the agent/desk attendant stood up and approached to help Leslie with her bags. "Good evening!" the desk attendant called out. "Anything I can help with?" Leslie said she was fine but thanked her for the offer. "Hey, do you know what all the commotion is about at the medical center?" Leslie asked. "There's extra security, and now they have put up barricades." The agent shook her head, and Leslie whispered, "I know where you really work. You must know something." The agent walked back to her spot behind the welcome counter and replied matter-of-factly, "I have no idea what you're talking about." Leslie laughed as she walked to her room. Of course.

Once inside the cozy little room, Leslie looked at what a mess she had made in just a few days. She set the toys by the door, part of her system when she packed up to leave on any trip. Once something is ready to go, it gets staged by the door. She looked through her clothes, trying to find something that looked nice but would also be comfortable while driving. Since this would be the last time she would see her dad or Jim or Michael for a few weeks, she decided to wear something nice to the morning meeting and set aside something comfortable to change into for the drive.

Leslie took the pad of paper out of her purse and started her "Don't forget..." list, another part of her personal system. She had forgotten phone chargers, shoes, clothes, snacks, and even an alarm clock in past hotel rooms. Making a list was always helpful. If she put all her clothes into the drawers or all her shoes in the closet, she always remembered them, but she learned her lesson about using the in-room safe on a trip with Mark. She never used those.

Mark closed the door and sprawled across the king-sized bed. "Ah, luxury resort," he sighed. Leslie was busy unpacking her suitcase, hanging some clothes and putting others in dresser drawers. "You're literally the only person on this earth who uses hotel dressers," he laughed. "We're only here for a weekend. It's okay to live out of your suitcase." Leslie rolled her eyes. It wasn't her idea to drive 300 miles to Niagara Falls, just to watch some waterfalls. "I don't like wearing wrinkled clothes, even if it's just to watch some water flow over a cliff," she explained. "You're free to do as you please, but I'm putting my clothes away. Why not use the facilities that we're given?" Mark sat up and gave her that childish expression that made him look like a chimpanzee. "By all means, let's use the facilities," he teased. "Here, I'll do my part." He walked over to the safe and read the directions aloud, then pulled $500 out of his wallet and put it inside. "There we go," he announced. "Now, I'll go use the other facilities."

As the bathroom door closed, Leslie tried to open the safe to retrieve the money but she didn't know what numbers he had chosen. "What's the combination?" she called out. Mark didn't answer so she finished putting away her clothes. When he came out of the bathroom she asked again but he wouldn't tell her. "Why are you so worried about money?" he inquired. "We make plenty of money and your mom is loaded." Leslie was tired of that same argument and suggested that they go find some dinner.

She paid for dinner that night and for everything they bought the next day, which was the norm. By the time they headed home on Sunday, she had completely forgotten about the safe. When they got home and she was putting everything away, she asked Mark if he remembered to get his money from the safe. He had not, so she called the hotel and explained the situation. Mark didn't remember the combination, but the manager explained that the hotel staff can open it anyway. Unsurprisingly, they claimed that no money had been found in that room's safe. Leslie didn't pursue it because she couldn't be sure that Mark was telling the truth about forgetting the money. She just chalked it up to a lesson learned.

The phone ringing in her room startled her, but it was a welcome distraction from any thoughts about Mark. Leslie answered hesitantly, as she didn't know of anyone who had this number.

"Hi, Leslie; it's Justine. I heard you had an eventful day." Leslie was happy to hear Justine's voice, but she knew that Justine was supposed to be taking the day off. "Hi, Justine. Aren't you supposed to be relaxing?" Justine laughed and replied, "Now, how would you have been able to get into that Target if I was relaxing? I told you, this job is my life. Are you going to be at the morning meeting?" Leslie said that she would be there and shared that she was wearing something nice because she wanted to leave a lasting impression. Justine advised that she would be there at 7:30 to escort her over because of all the beefed-up security and Leslie asked if she knew what was going on with that. "Of course I do," Justine answered. "Big surprise. I'll see you in the morning."

Leslie hung up, wondering what the surprise could be, but continued packing. She decided to take the Target bags and the outfit that she was going to wear while driving out to her car, since she wouldn't need those tonight. The agent at the desk watched and smiled, but she didn't say anything. Leslie put the outfit on the front seat and the bags in the back, looking around for any clue about what was happening at the medical center. She returned to her room and called to speak to Billy and Melanie briefly before getting ready for bed. Melanie was feeling a little better and Billy was excited that Leslie was coming home the next day. The conversation was short and sweet because Leslie was exhausted. Although she was happy to be going home to see Billy, she thought about how much fun she was having with Michael and her dad and Jim. Target runs would never be the same again.

•••

Chapter Twenty-Seven

Leslie awoke to the sound of the alarm clock at 6:30. She had slept soundly through the night and woke up feeling refreshed. After a quick shower, she straightened her hair and put on a little bit of makeup. She dressed conservatively in a navy blue short-sleeved dress that hung enough to hide flaws but was still flattering. She put on her navy flats that matched perfectly and the red/white/blue necklace that Mom had given her for her birthday. She looked in the mirror and was proud of what she saw. She was much younger-looking than a lot of women her age. Well, normal women... the ones who didn't have personal trainers or makeup artists or plastic surgery.

She thought about turning on the morning news but didn't want to get distracted. She packed up her clean clothes and put the bag of dirty clothes in her big red suitcase. She was checking her "Don't Forget..." list when there was a knock on her door. She looked at her phone. 7:30 on the dot. She opened the door and Justine seemed excited to see her. "Good morning!" she beamed. "Are you ready to go?"

Leslie had her suitcase and toiletry bag, and Justine followed her to her car to put them inside. "Why don't you just wait until you come back here after the meeting?" Justine asked. Leslie explained that she could tell them that she was out so they could start cleaning the room and Justine laughed. "You really are considerate," she commented, "but they have plenty of open rooms." Leslie put her bags in the car and said something about hoping her shoes wouldn't get wet on the walk over to the hospital. Justine pointed to a golf cart and said, "No worries. We're taking that so we can dash over and get settled before they start the meeting. Let's go!"

Leslie thought the "day off" had been a good idea because Justine seemed rejuvenated. They zipped over to the medical center, past barricades and security guards and through waiting reporters. They pulled up to the front and security guards rushed them inside, but Leslie's purse had to be inspected. She handed her bag to the guard and said she didn't know she was going to be searched and showed him the mace in the inside pocket. He said she was all set and told her not to be afraid to use that if the situation arose. Leslie thought that was odd advice, but she thanked him and rushed inside with Justine.

The podium and stage were set up and the lobby was even cleaner than usual. The floors had been polished overnight and there were no trash cans visible, which Leslie found unusual. Maybe they were being sanitized or replaced. She and Justine grabbed their badges from the Visitors' desk and stopped at the debriefing office to grab some sweet tea from the refrigerator. Leslie asked if she should take her Rubbermaid tote now (so she wouldn't forget it) but Justine said it would be safer there. They would stop in after the meeting so she could retrieve it. Justine grabbed some paperwork and Sergeant Lucas's file, and they headed up to the conference room where the meeting would be held.

Jim Carlson was already there with Bill Lucas, both sipping hot tea as Jim spoke and Bill nodded. They stood up when Leslie approached, and Bill hugged her and smiled before sitting back down. He was dressed in slacks and a polo shirt and Leslie told Jim he did a good job, and that she thought her dad looked great. "You look great, too, kid," Jim said with a wink. "Thank you," she replied with a smile. He was such a gentleman. Justine sat down on the other side of Leslie, but Jim suggested that Justine sit next to him so Dr. Edwards could sit next to Leslie. Justine said she had some things to discuss with General Carlson anyway, and as she moved seats Dr. Edwards showed up as if on cue. "Good morning," he said energetically. Leslie stood to greet him and wondered how he always had so much energy. "Wow! You look amazing, Leslie. That necklace really complements your dress." Leslie thanked him and blushed a little as she noticed that Justine was watching and smiling.

Dr. Edwards had a list of everyone whom he believed should be at the meeting, and as they arrived he checked them off. There was a fairly even mixture of military and civilian doctors, and Leslie wondered how many of the civilians were prior military. Once everyone had arrived, the door to the conference room was shut and the Social Worker in charge of her dad's Care Plan addressed the room. She asked everyone to tell the group their role in this Care Plan and give their prognosis for recovery. Jim requested that everyone also mention what languages they speak, as he was conducting a survey and putting that in his records as well. Leslie and Justine both gave him the same puzzled look, but he ignored their glances.

As the doctors went around the room, Leslie was fascinated with the level of expertise contained in that small space. The general consensus was that Sergeant Lucas had suffered a severe traumatic brain injury (TBI) that caused amnesia. He didn't seem to remember his native language or have any memories of his early life as a Marine. Dr. Edwards did not share that he had any knowledge of Sergeant Lucas saying words, but he did share that he had spoken to him in Japanese and he understood. Although the meeting was being recorded on a small portable device as well as on camera, Leslie was amused at how furiously a few of the doctors were taking notes. Others seemed disengaged, clearly having given up on being able to help this particular patient.

When everyone was finished, the Social Worker asked Leslie if she had anything to add. She wasn't expecting to speak, but she decided to address the room. "Good morning. I haven't met most of you. My name is Leslie Lucas Mitchell, and I am the daughter of Sergeant Lucas. I grew up not knowing my father for the first 52 years of my life, but my mother never lost faith that he was alive. I may have just met him, but I have been waiting my whole life for this and I will do whatever it takes to help him regain his memories and his speech. He is going back to Michigan with me as soon as he is medically cleared and will continue treatment at the VA Hospital in Ann Arbor. Dr. Edwards will be moving there in a couple of weeks, so it is my recommendation that he be the connection between here and there. Continuity and stability are so important with anyone who has a TBI, as you know, so I believe that it's important that at least one member of this team is part of his continued Care Plan."

Jim spoke up. "Well, there will be two of us. I will be there, too, but in a personal capacity since I will no longer be employed by the U.S. Department of State." He smiled and added smugly, "I will be retired." Some of the doctors laughed and the Social Worker said she would find someone at the VA Hospital in Ann Arbor to take over the Care Plan of Sergeant Lucas as soon as he was cleared to leave there. She thanked everyone for coming and for their input.

Jim looked at his watch. "We need to go," he said. "Justine, Leslie, Dr. Edwards. We have to get downstairs." Justine picked up her belongings and told Leslie she had a blank journal for her so she could write about this process and her progress. Leslie thanked her and admitted that was a great idea but wondered why they needed to head downstairs. Justine said the General had a surprise for her, but that's all she would divulge.

Jim picked up his notes and asked Dr. Edwards, "Do you know why I asked everyone what languages they speak?" Dr. Edwards stroked his chin and guessed, "So you would know what languages *not* to use when you were speaking to Sergeant Lucas?" Jim patted him on the back and exclaimed, "Oh, you're sharp! That is exactly what I was doing."

The five of them walked past the elevator and to the stairs. The door to the stairs was locked, but Jim had the key and let them all inside. "It's only one flight of stairs, so why take the elevator like everyone else?" he asked. The stairs came out right next to the debriefing office, where they dropped off their belongings. Jim told Leslie that she could leave her purse there if she chose, but she didn't like being without her purse and decided that she'd take it with her. They walked out to the lobby and Leslie could see the front of the podium clearly. "Is that the Presidential Seal of the United States?" she asked. "Looks like it," replied Justine. "Let's go get a closer look."

As they approached the podium, Leslie could see that it was indeed the Presidential Seal on the front, and she asked Justine if the President was going to be there today. Justine looked at her watch. "He should be arriving any minute," she said. "Let's take our seats." Leslie stared at Justine like she just grew another head. "We're staying to watch the show?" she asked. "No, honey," Justine replied. "We *are* the show. Come on!"

The seats on the stage had names on them so there was no guessing about where to sit. Jim Carlson was behind the podium, slightly to the left, and Bill, Leslie, Dr. Edwards, and Justine filled out the left side. Behind the podium, slightly to the right, the name card read "Commander in Chief," followed by "First Lady" and then the names of four men that Leslie didn't recognize. Justine explained that those were the other members of the extraction team that went over to recover Sergeant Lucas. Leslie was excited to be able to thank them for their part in this, but she was super excited to see the President.

There were Secret Service agents everywhere, most in suits and all with earpieces. Leslie wondered where they would land the President's helicopter and felt silly for wondering when she realized that the White House was only about 10 miles away so they would probably arrive by car. She sat down and glanced at Dr. Edwards, who appeared as if he'd seen a ghost. "Michael, are you okay?" she asked. "Not really sure," he answered. "Why am I up here?" Leslie reminded him that he was the one who was going to make sure that her dad received the proper care when he switched facilities, and Michael seemed to snap out of his stupor a little. "We must have done really well with our first press conference if this is what we're doing for our second one," he commented. Leslie laughed and agreed.

The reporters and cameramen were being admitted one at a time and their bags were being searched thoroughly. Leslie thought of the mace in her purse and pushed the bag under her chair. She looked over at her dad, who was getting an explanation from Jim about what was happening. She interrupted briefly to make sure that nobody was going to expect her dad to get up there and speak, and Jim said that everyone had been briefed about the situation. Bill really seemed excited to be there, so Leslie relaxed a bit and took out her phone. She texted Melanie and asked her to please turn on the TV and find this press conference and set up her DVR to record. Melanie texted back that she was at the doctor's office and would call Steve so he and Billy could watch it and record it. "Good luck there!" Leslie texted back, and Melanie replied, "Same to you!"

Leslie took the mirror out of her purse and saw one of the Secret Service men watching her closely. She checked to make sure she didn't have anything in her teeth and that her hair was in place, then did a quick check to make sure none of her nose hairs was sticking out. Getting old was funny and sometimes embarrassing. Errant eyebrows grew in the middle of her forehead, and occasionally the hair in her nose had to be trimmed. Why doesn't anyone tell you these things are going to happen when you get older?

"Can I see that mirror?" Michael whispered. "I need to make sure I don't have anything in my teeth." Leslie laughed and handed him the mirror. "You should text your mom and tell her what's happening," she suggested. He said that he already had, but she had not responded. "Maybe there's a delay in the texts getting to her out in the ocean," he suggested. "Or perhaps there is shuffleboard on the Lido deck." Leslie snickered and said that it was hopefully being recorded at her house, but it would probably be something that anyone could look up later on social media.

The reporters filled in seats quickly and appeared to be disappointed that their spots were also assigned. Their names were not on the seats, just their networks or organizations, and they were trying to change them at first. Each of the two seating sections had a Security Guard from the medical center assigned to it, and they had outlines on clipboards that showed the correct seating order. They were quite efficient at getting people to their assigned places and announced that once seated they must stay there or be escorted out. These guys were not messing around and Leslie could have watched the process all day. It was fascinating.

The four men from the extraction team arrived and greeted Jim Carlson and Bill Lucas. Leslie walked over to thank them for bringing home her father and wasn't surprised to find out that they were all military veterans. She was surprised, though, when Jim Carlson told them there had been little improvement and that her dad still isn't talking. One of them joked that "Sergeant Lucas took his vow of silence pretty seriously" and Leslie saw a slight wink from Jim. She remembered what he had said, that if her dad shows improvement then they will keep him longer. Jim probably told the team the same thing, and they were putting on a bit of an act in public because you never know who is listening.

The extraction team took their seats and Leslie returned to hers, as did Jim and Bill. The reporters were settling down and it was surprisingly quiet in the lobby. Justine approached the podium and adjusted the microphone. She kept looking at her phone, obviously getting messages from someone, and cleared her throat. "Ladies and gentlemen of the press and distinguished guests, allow me to introduce the President of the United States." Everyone stood as music played from a speaker behind them. The President walked down the hallway where the debriefing office was, followed by his wife and a few Secret Service agents.

Leslie's first impression was that he was taller than she expected, and his wife was even more beautiful than she looked on television. "Wow," she whispered to Michael. "She's gorgeous." He nodded his head in agreement and whispered back, "More impressive is that she speaks five languages." Leslie smiled and looked over at her father, who seemed to be taking it all in pretty casually. Cameras were flashing and people were cheering. Everyone in the medical center seemed to have wandered over to see what was happening.

The President shook everyone's hands on the way to the podium, and said to Jim, "Hey, General. Great to see you again!" He shook Bill's hand and said, "Welcome home, Marine." Bill nodded and smiled, his eyes fixed on the First Lady. "Bienvenue à nouveau aux États-Unis," she said. Bill's eyes lit up and he hugged her. Michael whispered to Leslie, "She knows that he speaks French, so she welcomed him back to the United States." Leslie was so proud and was starting to feel a bit overwhelmed. She fought back tears as the President shook her hand and said, "Your father is a true American hero and we just wanted to give him a hero's welcome." Leslie expressed her gratitude to him and to the First Lady, who warmly took Leslie's hand and smiled. Leslie thought that this was the most beautiful woman she'd ever met and couldn't believe everything that was happening. It was as if she were watching herself in a dream.

When all the handshaking and greetings subsided, everyone but the President sat down. He took the Podium and addressed the members of the press. Leslie appreciated that he glossed over the fact that her father had killed a lot of people because she wasn't sure how well he understood what was being said about him. She didn't want some things being told to him until the time was right, and it might be quite awhile before anyone explained it to him.

• • •

Chapter Twenty-Eight

Before Leslie could firmly grasp what was happening, her dad stood up and the President put some type of ribbon or award around his neck. Everyone was clapping, then the President left the podium as his press secretary took over to answer questions. Another beautiful, intelligent woman. Leslie was feeling a little insecure and out of place but didn't remember much that was said. She sure hoped she could watch the whole thing later when her mind was clear.

Everyone from the stage filed out down the hallway to the debriefing office, where there were drinks and snacks set up in anticipation of the visitors. Whoever set it up was quick, Leslie thought, since she was just there a half hour ago and nothing was set out. She debated whether she should take the time to eat or use this unique opportunity to talk to the President. Her stomach growled, sealing the decision that she needed to eat.

The extraction team, including Jim Carlson, stood in a circle to talk and Justine joined their conversation. Bill Lucas sat down next to Leslie. "Are you hungry?" Leslie asked. He nodded his head and Leslie was excited that he understood...or at least seemed to understand. She pointed to the food that was set out and asked what he wanted. Michael translated: "Qu'est-ce que tu voudrais?" he asked. Leslie hadn't even realized that Michael was next to her, but she appreciated his translation. Bill looked over at the table to check out what was offered. Leslie walked over to the table to get a closer look, putting some grapes and a croissant on a plate. She set the plate down and said, "Pour moi," pointing to herself to indicate that this plate was for her. She was proud that she remembered some French, especially when Bill quietly said, "Le même" and pointed to himself. Leslie wanted to jump up and down and tugged Michael's sleeve. "Did you hear that? He said 'le même.' That means 'the same' in French!"

Michael hadn't heard it and asked Bill to repeat what he said while Leslie grabbed a plate for her dad. "Le même," Bill said, pointing to Leslie's plate. Leslie filled a plate for her dad and handed it to him, along with a napkin. Bill bowed his head over the plate and was silent, assumingly in some type of prayer or meditation. He ate quietly while Leslie delighted in the fact that her dad communicated with her. Michael started to talk but Leslie put her finger to her lips and shook her head. As Jim had told them, Buddhists believe it is impolite to speak during a meal and she wanted to show some respect for her father's beliefs. Michael understood and grabbed a plate for himself. He had some strawberries and a thick slice of banana bread, which looked delicious to Leslie.

The President, who had been speaking with his wife, approached Jim Carlson and spoke to the group for a moment while the First Lady mostly smiled and nodded. Justine came over to get something to drink and set a sweet tea in front of Leslie, who mouthed "Thank you." Leslie had only met Justine a few days ago but felt like she was going to miss her when she left there. Michael went to grab napkins and some tea for himself and for Bill Lucas, who nodded in acknowledgement. He seemed to really enjoy the grapes and croissant but did not drink the tea until he had eaten everything. Leslie assumed that it was another ritual and added that to her list of things to remember. Michael took care of their empty plates and came back with another slice of banana bread for Leslie. "I saw you eyeing my banana bread," he teased. "This one is for you." Leslie thanked him, but before she took a bite, she offered a piece to her dad. He looked at it curiously and popped a piece into his mouth. A huge smile spread across his face and his eyes lit up. Leslie laughed at his reaction and wondered if he'd ever had banana bread. She ate some of it and offered more to him but he waved it off and stood up. She followed his gaze and saw that the President and First Lady were heading over to the table.

Bill Lucas stood as the President approached, obviously out of respect, and Leslie thought it was a good idea. She stood and greeted the President, who told Leslie that he had been briefed on the situation. He would make sure that her father received all pay and benefits that were owed to him, and that his medical care would be completely paid by the VA. Leslie expressed her appreciation and shared that it meant a lot to her that he and his wife had taken the time to come over and honor her father. With the First Lady translating, the President then spoke to Bill Lucas about what a great American he is. Leslie asked if she and her father could take a picture with them and they were happy to pose while Michael snapped the photo.

The President looked at his watch and said he had to leave but hoped to see them again when they accepted his invitation to the White House. Leslie noticed that Michael had been staring at the First Lady during the entire interaction, and as they left Leslie commented, "She sure is beautiful." Michael nodded his head. "Her French is incredible," he noted. "You'd think that was her native language!" Leslie wondered if anyone else got this excited about languages.

Jim Carlson came over to speak to Leslie and asked how she liked the surprise. She said this was the most incredible thing to ever happen to her, besides finding out that her dad was still alive. They talked about what would happen from here and when Bill Lucas might be able to leave. Jim had less than two weeks until retirement, and his goal was to leave there in two weeks with her dad. Leslie said she would need at least a week to get the house in order and catch up on calls and mail, plus wrap up any loose ends at work. She could then return to pick up her dad and finally take him home.

Leslie asked Jim where her Rubbermaid tote was now, and he pointed to a cabinet. "Did you have time to get copies of everything?" she asked. Justine laughed. "You're good," she said. "You know he did." As Jim retrieved the tote from the cabinet, Leslie thanked Justine for everything and wished her well with finishing her degree and finding a life that made her happy. Justine said this was a good start, seeing this Marine going home, and she hoped that Leslie would stay in touch.

Jim handed the tote to Michael and asked him to put it in his Tahoe and drive Leslie back to Fisher House. He winked at Leslie and said he would see her soon, then explained to Bill (in Vietnamese) that Leslie was leaving now and they would see her again soon. Bill hugged Leslie and she did not want to let go. She had waited years for this but had lost hope that it would ever happen. She finally had her father, and was just trying to accept the reality that he would be coming home to Michigan. With Jim Carlson looking after her, it was like she got a two-for-one deal when it came to having a father. She felt like she had won the lottery. Maybe better.

She had so much to do, so she needed to get on the road. She and Michael walked briskly to his car. Some of the paparazzi were still out in front, and Leslie could see that people were taking pictures of her and Michael as they passed through the lobby. "I can't wait to see the headlines tomorrow," Michael commented. "They are going to have us sneaking off for a romantic getaway this time." Leslie laughed and considered the thought. "Well, I hope we're going somewhere tropical, at least," she teased.

They walked out to Michael's Tahoe and he set down the tote so he could get out his key fob and unlock the door. Like a true gentleman, he opened Leslie's door for her before putting the tote in the back seat. As he drove to Leslie's car, Michael said he had checked the weather forecast this morning and it looked like clear weather all the way back to Michigan. She had already checked it out but thanked him for being so thoughtful. He said there was some construction on the Ohio Turnpike, and she reminded him that she had just driven through there a few days ago. He added that he isn't a huge fan of Ohio, but they do have great rest areas, which made Leslie laugh.

They pulled into the parking lot at Fisher House and Michael drove right over to Leslie's car. "How did you know this was mine?" she asked. "You said you drive a blue Equinox," Michael answered. "It's the only one here." Leslie remembered telling him that but didn't have a lot of experience with men actually listening to what she said. All she could manage to say was, "Oh, right." She realized that she was going to miss him and tried to remind herself that this was her dad's doctor and she was being silly.

"So, you'll let me know when you're coming back to Michigan?" Leslie asked. "Of course! I will keep in touch about your dad's progress and the plans for my transition to working in Ann Arbor," Michael answered. Leslie reminded him that she was going to put together a timeline of her dad's life and had to find more pictures and anything that might trigger some memories. As Michael put the tote in her car, he suggested that it would be helpful to create a PowerPoint presentation – or something similar – that could be viewed over and over. Leslie remembered attending a seminar with her mom about doing exactly that.

Leslie commented that her mother may have already started that project and it was just a matter of finding it. "I hope your mother was more organized than mine," Michael replied. "She loses everything, then just buys more." Leslie said that her mother was fairly organized and felt sad for Michael's mother. She suggested that his mother might have never recovered from having her heart broken by Jim Carlson, and Michael agreed that it made sense. "I'm a psychologist, for goodness sake," he said. "How did I miss the obvious signs that my own mother had experienced a serious loss or trauma? It's so obvious, now that I think about it." Leslie suggested that it might not be too late to fix it, that they might be able to get some happiness back for Jim and Linda. Michael promised to get more information from his mother if she was willing to talk about it, and Leslie intended to do the same with Jim Carlson.

Leslie knew that it was time to get home, but she felt so important there. She had been treated like a millionaire from the moment she arrived, with people waiting on her and a private shopping trip and paparazzi chasing her around. As she drove off, waving to Michael and already missing these new people in her life, the thought occurred to her that she was, indeed, a millionaire. She could get used to this.

•••

Chapter Twenty-Nine

As Leslie made her way north out of Bethesda, traffic was a little lighter than it would be during the week, but it was moving slower than she wanted. She made sure that her phone was connected to the system in her car and listened to her voicemails. There were several, some that didn't require a return call and a few that did.

Leslie decided to start with the person she least wanted to call: Aunt Judith. The phone rang only once. "It's about time you returned my calls," Aunt Judith's obnoxiously loud voice blared. "For a short time, I was the only family you had. Now that your dad has returned from the dead, though, I guess you don't need me." Leslie had always cowered from Aunt Judith's condescending remarks, but this new chapter of her life seemed to give her more courage and strength. "Hello to you, too," Leslie replied. "To clarify, I have a son, so I do have another family member. Also, my dad returned from Vietnam, not the dead." Silence on the other end of the line. Leslie enjoyed it.

"Well, I guess you have everything you need now," Aunt Judith continued. "Did Jim tell you about our relationship, and how he broke my heart?" Leslie laughed. "He told me what really happened, and that you didn't meet him to share the pictures of my dad," Leslie replied. "Oh, right, the pictures," Aunt Judith bragged. "I guess you still need those." Leslie explained that she didn't really need them, as she had other pictures, and Aunt Judith suggested that she might be willing to reconsider the offer that Susan had given her. Leslie wasn't sure what the offer was and asked for clarification. "Well, your mom got all my dad's money," Aunt Judith whined. "He liked her more than he liked his own flesh and blood. All I got were pictures of Bill's childhood from before I was even born, then pictures of my childhood. Do you know that they didn't even take pictures of me until I was almost 6 months old? There is not one photo of my birth." Leslie explained that having a child was a busy time, and having a five-year-old and a baby probably made life rather chaotic. "That's bullshit," Aunt Judith replied. "He was just their favorite. They probably wanted another boy and didn't even want me. Anyway, your mom said she'd give me half my dad's money for the pictures. If you want them, you're going to have to fork over some money."

Leslie said she would consider an offer and that she'd get back to her about that. "I do have one question, though," Leslie said. "Why haven't you asked about your brother, who has been missing for 52 years?" Before Judith could answer, Leslie gave her the update. "He's doing well physically, and Jim is returning to Michigan to help my dad get his voice back. There is a great psychologist who studies Psycholinguistics and is going to find the problem and solve it. My dad will be returning to Michigan in a couple of weeks. It's going to be a lot of work, so I am retiring to be with him full-time." Leslie stopped, waiting for a response. "Let me know about the money," Aunt Judith blurted out before abruptly hanging up.

Before placing another call, Leslie switched on the 80s station and played some music to calm down. About halfway through the second song, a call came in and disrupted Leslie's singing. Her aunt's name came up on the screen and it felt satisfying to press the "Deny" button for the call. Leslie had no desire to speak with a woman who didn't even seem to care about her brother returning from Vietnam. Why would she be calling right back, after just hanging up? How was Leslie going to get those pictures without giving her aunt a lot of money? She turned up the music to distract her from the endless questions and finally relaxed a bit.

Although Leslie didn't really want to place the next call, she felt a sense of obligation. Mark was her ex-husband, but also the father of her child so she could never really get away from him. It rang five times before he answered. "Oh, hey," Mark answered. "Are you back in Michigan yet?" Leslie explained that she was on her way, still in Maryland heading north, and Mark wanted to know if her father was with her. "No, he's probably not coming up for a couple of weeks," Leslie explained. "Why do you ask?" Mark said he always wondered if Bill was still alive and wanted to hear some of his "war stories." Leslie tried not to let him get to her, but this was out of the question. "Wait a minute," she began. "You always said that Mom was crazy, that there was no way my Dad was still alive. What do you really want?" Mark said he had a friend who writes for a major publication, and Mark told her that he had a personal connection to this story. He was planning to go to Michigan in a couple of weeks to see if he could get her an exclusive feature.

Leslie was furious, but what came out of her mouth was laughter. A bit maniacal, but it was still laughter. "My Dad is in no position to talk about what happened. He has amnesia and doesn't even remember how to speak English!" Mark started to explain himself, but Leslie cut him off. "Your son – who is fine, by the way - is so excited about meeting my Dad, since his other grandfather can't seem to find time for him. I am hanging up now; I've had my fill of selfish people for today." Leslie pressed the red phone icon on her dashboard to end the call. She had put up with so much from Mark and just thinking about their one-sided relationship made her blood boil. She didn't realize at the time that she deserved so much better, and so much of her life was wasted with Mark. In contrast, she had so much fun these past few days with people who had never even met her. They weren't using her or seeing what they could take from her like Mark or Aunt Judith, but instead had given her something that she thought was never attainable: her father.

Leslie really enjoyed helping others, but it was rare for them to reciprocate. She seemed to have taken after her mother in that respect. Mom had been the stable force in her life, always giving and expecting nothing in return, except Leslie's promise that she would keep the house in case her father came home. Leslie felt awful that she had almost broken that promise, that she had intended to remodel the house and move somewhere else less than a week ago. Meeting her father, Justine, Jim, and Michael was an integrity check, reaffirming her promise to her mother. There would be some remodeling, but they were staying put. Leslie planned to give her father the best home possible, after all he had been through, taking life one day at a time. She felt confident and hopeful for the first time in years.

• • •

Chapter Thirty

Leslie decided to stop at a rest area for something to drink and to change into her comfortable clothes. She pulled off at the South Mountain Welcome Center; she had stopped here before, but she didn't remember it being this beautiful. The view was captivating on the mountain, and the flowers were really starting to bloom. She paused to smell the roses, but they were not a fragrant variety. Just beautiful, which still made Leslie smile.

As she walked into the lobby area, an older heavyset woman tapped her husband's arm. "That's the lady whose father was found in Vietnam, the one we saw on TV." She smiled warmly at Leslie and said, "Congratulations on your father coming home!" Leslie couldn't believe that someone recognized her and thanked the woman before rushing into the restroom. She changed her clothes, washed her face, and headed out to the vending machines. There was a small crowd there, led by the sweet old woman who had recognized her, and they all wanted to talk to Leslie and take her picture. Leslie looked at her watch. She had only been in the restroom for 12 minutes. She got her Coke out of the machine and talked to a couple of people as others took pictures with their phones, but she needed to get home to her son. Her heart swelled as they wished her well and waved goodbye.

With her mood elevated, Leslie got back on the road and decided to make some more calls. She called work to leave a message, knowing that they were currently closed. She left a voicemail for her boss, letting him know that she would be in tomorrow afternoon to talk about retirement. She felt too young to retire and had always assumed that she would do that when she was old enough to collect Social Security. Leslie considered what she would do with all her free time and looked forward to being more active with Billy's school and scouting. She decided to call him next, to remind him that he had a Scout meeting next weekend. He was always excited about Boy Scouts, and she appreciated how accommodating they were with him.

Leslie called home and Billy picked up on the first ring. "Mom! Melanie is going to have a baby! I am going to help her, so I hope it's a boy!" Leslie laughed and said that was wonderful news, and she knew he would be a big help. She told Billy that she was on her way home and reminded him to get his backpack and lunch pail out tonight because he had school in the morning. He would have to go to bed soon after she got home, but she promised that they would spend a lot more time together now that she wouldn't be going to work anymore. "Like, ever?" he asked. "Like ever," Leslie affirmed. "You and I will be helping your grandpa and spending a lot of time doing fun things with him. Also, you have a Boy Scout meeting next weekend, so that's exciting, huh?" Billy said it wasn't as exciting as Melanie having a baby or his mom coming home, or his grandpa being found, but it was exciting. He decided to go find his backpack and handed the phone to Melanie.

"Congratulations!" Leslie gushed. "How do you feel?" Melanie said she was excited, but still felt sick to her stomach. "Eat some of those Club crackers on the top shelf of the pantry," Leslie suggested. "That's what helped me through." Leslie asked how Steve took the news. "Oh, he's super excited," Melanie replied, "but he's a little worried about the extra expenses that a new baby brings. Leslie assured Melanie that they would have everything they need because she was going to help them. Melanie asked how she would handle that if she was planning to quit her job and Leslie laughed. "Let's just say that Mom set me up for life, and I plan to make sure that those who are near and dear to me are included," she replied. Melanie thanked her and mentioned that Billy was excited about his mom coming home. "Did you get a chance to stop and get something for him, or should I send Steve to the store for you?" Melanie asked. "Oh, I was able to run into Target and grab something," Leslie replied. "I'll tell you all about it when I get home. Best Target run ever!" Melanie said she would help Billy get his things together for school in the morning, and that she would see Leslie when she got there.

Leslie smiled as she hung up, feeling truly happy for Melanie and Steve. She knew they were going to be great parents, since they were so patient with Billy. She wanted to do something special for them but wasn't sure what that would be yet. She decided to turn on some music and just drive, leaving any other calls for later. She loved this station that only played hits from the 80s, but there were a few songs that she honestly never remembered hearing. When something came on that reminded her of Mark, she turned the station to something happier. She thought of all the red flags that she missed with him, and how that relationship had soured her. It seemed that having a man who respected her was just a fantasy, as she didn't know many women who bragged about how respectful or fun their husbands are.

Her thoughts were interrupted by her phone ringing. "Michael Edwards" came up on her dashboard, and she pressed the green phone icon. "Hello?" she answered in her most charming voice. "Well, hello!" Michael replied. "I just wanted to check in with you to see how your drive is going." Leslie told him about the calls that she had made, and stopping at the welcome center, where she was recognized. "Oh, you're probably going to get that for awhile," Michael suggested. "You also may get some invitations to be on talk shows and I'm sure your local news and newspaper will want to do a story. Heck, probably national news and even some magazines." Leslie said she really didn't want all that attention, but he said it was positive attention and it might be beneficial because it could be seen by others who could help her. "Who else do I need to help besides you and Jim?" Leslie asked. Michael suggested that her father would need some great counselors...social workers, psychologists, psychiatrists, speech therapists, and whoever else could help. He said he had received the approval to leave Bethesda earlier than expected and would probably be there in about a week so he could put a team in place before her dad arrived.

Leslie said she would probably be returning to Bethesda after he had already left to pick up her father, but Michael suggested that Jim could drive her dad back. "We can discuss that as it happens," he explained, "but what I really called about is that I heard from my mother and she was a mess. It turns out that she never got over General Carlson and doesn't even blame him. She thinks it is wonderful that they found your father and wants to see them both again. Apparently, she also knew your dad. This just keeps getting crazier." Leslie was happy for Jim and Linda, hoping for a reunion, and suggested to Michael that they assist in making that happen. Michael agreed that they needed something special but wasn't sure what to do. Leslie said she would think about it and asked Michael if he had told Jim. "Not yet. He intimidates the crap out of me, to be honest," Michael admitted. "Can you tell him?" Leslie said she would call Jim and talk about it, then call Michael back tomorrow. She hung up reluctantly, wishing their conversation would last longer, and felt like her heart was beating out of her chest. Speaking to Michael elevated her heart rate as much as briskly walking the 2-mile loop in her neighborhood, but without sweating. Maybe she needed to talk to him more often.

Leslie pressed the buttons on her dashboard to call Jim Carlson. "Hello," he answered gruffly. "You're not home yet, are you?" Leslie said she was just about halfway, but she had just spoken to Michael and had some good news. "So, you've only been gone a few hours and you've already called Dr. Edwards?" Jim inquired. "No, he called me," Leslie corrected. "He spoke with Linda, and she wants to see you again." There was no response, so Leslie asked if he heard her. "I heard you," Jim replied, "but I'm not sure if I can believe that. I don't deserve it."

Jim pulled up to the house just as the sun was going down. He was exhausted and hadn't had a drink all day. He couldn't remember the last time he had eaten a decent meal, as he was putting in so many hours of flying, so he was relieved to be home where he could have home-cooked meals and sleep in his own bed. He had missed Linda horribly, but he hadn't been very conscientious of calling her because he felt like a failure. His friend Bill was still missing and Jim was giving up hope that he'd ever see him again.

With the recent death of Ho Chi Minh in Hanoi, Jim wondered if he should shift his search efforts farther north. "I wouldn't be surprised if Bill had something to do with that," he mused as he walked up to the door. He was surprised to find that it was locked and began knocking as he called out Linda's name. He didn't have a key and didn't remember ever locking the door. After a few minutes of knocking, Jim walked around to the back door and tried that. It was also locked. He finally found an unlocked window and crawled through. He walked from room to room, impressed at how incredible the house looked.

Linda had kept herself busy. The kitchen was nicely decorated and different furniture and throw rugs adorned the living room. Jim felt guilty when he realized that he hadn't sent Linda any money or letters for months, and wondered where she got the money to redecorate. The kitchen had the black and white floor tile that he'd seen in a restaurant. He opened the refrigerator and there was no food or drinks. He frantically opened cabinets, starting to panic a little. Where was Linda? Had something happened? Was this someone else's house now?

Jim noticed the envelope on the kitchen table with his name on it. He tore it open and his heart sank. "Dear Jim – After not hearing from you for four months, I went to stay with my sister. I'm not sure how divorce works, but I'll figure it out. This isn't the life for me. I put up with the drinking, but I can't handle not talking to you and wondering if you're dead. I never want to see you again. – Linda."

"She said she never wanted to see me again," Jim said slowly. "Well, sometimes we say things to convince ourselves," Leslie offered. "I don't think she meant that. She didn't know if you were dead or alive. Haven't you ever heard that 'Time changes everything'?" asked Leslie. Jim replied with the same tone Billy uses when he needs reassurance. "Do you really think it's possible that Linda would forgive my selfishness?" he asked. "Sometimes, the things we want most seem unattainable but then something happens to remind us that anything is possible," Leslie explained. "A week ago, do you think I believed that I would ever meet my dad? I could never thank you enough for that, but I can try to help you get part of your life back, too. I will talk to Linda first and then we'll figure it out, okay?" Jim's voice was barely audible. "Thank you, Leslie," he managed. "You're a good kid."

•••

Chapter Thirty-One

Leslie was deep in thought about how to set up the reunion between Jim and Linda, enjoying the beautiful scenery through Pennsylvania. When she crossed into Ohio, she knew she was more than halfway and stopped near Youngstown to get gas and something to eat. She enjoyed the cheeseburger and fries, something she rarely ate, and decided to get another Coke to keep her awake on the drive. She had so much to think about that the trip went quickly, and before she knew it, she was in her own driveway.

She had been gone for weeks, except for one sleepless night after receiving that call from Justine, and she had a lot to do before her father got there. She hit the button on the garage door and Billy came running out before she could pull in. She parked in the driveway and got out to hug him. He ran around to the passenger door and looked in. "Awww...I was hoping that you brought my grandpa with you," Billy lamented. "I told you that he wasn't coming with me this time," Leslie explained. "You need to work on your listening skills." Billy quickly changed the subject and asked if Leslie had brought him anything. "There are two Target bags in the back seat for you," Leslie explained. "Go grab them." Billy seemed to forget that he was sad about his grandpa not being there and grabbed the bags from the back seat. He ran inside with the bags and Leslie called after him, "Don't worry. I'll get everything else!"

Melanie came out to ask if Leslie needed help, but Leslie said she had to take it easy now that she was pregnant. "Good grief," Melanie replied. "You're not going to start that already, are you?" They laughed and Leslie handed her the small bag with her toiletries in it. She pulled out her suitcase and threw her purse over her shoulder but decided to come back for the Rubbermaid tote. As she walked into the house, Billy was running out. "Mom, thank you! How did you know I wanted GI Joes?" he asked excitedly. "I didn't," Leslie answered. "A new friend of mine, one of your Grandpa's doctors, picked those out." Billy said he couldn't wait to meet him so he could thank him, and Melanie teased, "And when are we going to meet that new friend?"

Coming Home

"Soon," Leslie said with a smile. "He is coming back to Michigan and will be helping Grandpa here," she told Billy. Billy said that was cool and ran off to play with his GI Joes. Leslie said she had a lot to tell Melanie but wanted to get the tote out of the car first. She walked out to get it and stopped just outside the door. There was a little black car pulling into the driveway that she didn't recognize. "Hey, Melanie, do you know who this is?" Leslie called out. Melanie replied that the same car had been driving by quite a bit the past few days but had never pulled in until now.

Leslie watched as a young woman got out, dressed like she was going to a formal event. "Are you Leslie Lucas Mitchell?" she asked. "Yes, I am," Leslie answered. "May I help you?" The woman claimed to be a reporter from a local station and Leslie laughed. "Look, I just got home after driving all day. Do you have a business card? I can call you when I'm ready to answer your questions." The young woman said she would appreciate that, and shared that her grandfather knew Leslie's dad. She felt personally connected to the situation and wanted to help in any way she could. Leslie appreciated her approach and asked for her name. "Jennifer Tillotson," she replied proudly. Leslie felt like she had heard that name and wondered if she had read something that Jennifer had written. "How long have you been a reporter?" Leslie asked. "This is my first week, honestly, and I have been driving by to see if anyone was home since I heard about your dad on the news. I hope I didn't creep anyone out." Leslie assured her it was fine, and promised to give her a call in the next couple of days. Jennifer thanked her and drove away.

Leslie searched her brain, trying to remember where she had heard that name. She grabbed the tote and locked the doors. She would just leave her car in the driveway for the night. She had a lot of running around to do the next day, starting with taking Billy to school. As she walked up the steps, Steve came running across the lawn. "Hi, Leslie. Is everything okay? That car has been driving by for three days." Leslie said it was just a young reporter, harmless and new, and flashed the business card at Steve. "I am going to call her when I have settled back in," she said. "Nice girl."

Steve took the tote from Leslie and they walked inside. "What's in here?" he asked. Leslie explained that there were letters, pictures, and papers about her father that she had taken with her to Bethesda.

She shared with Steve that she needed to put together a timeline for her dad, starting at his birth, and those items would be handy. Steve suggested that he and Melanie could help and set the tote on the dining room table. "Oh, by the way... Congratulations!" Leslie said to Steve. "I understand you're going to be a father." Steve could barely contain his excitement and warned Leslie that he would probably be asking her a lot of questions, since his parents didn't seem to know much about raising kids. Leslie hadn't really talked to him about his childhood and didn't want to pry, so she told him that she would be happy to help.

Billy and Melanie came into the dining room and Billy was excited to show Leslie what they had done while she was gone. "Come on, Mom! I'll show you what we did!" Billy gushed. He grabbed Leslie's hand and pulled her upstairs. On his bed, his backpack and planner and lunch pail were arranged neatly. His pencils were laid out, three of them sharpened, along with his ruler and scissors and some notebook paper. Next to that was his outfit for the next day, one that matched, including socks and underwear. His shoes were on the floor next to his bed.

Leslie was impressed. "So, you had Melanie set all this out for you, huh?" she asked. "No, Mom, I did it myself!" Billy insisted. "Melanie just helped me sharpen the pencils and match my shirt to my pants." Leslie was shocked and asked Melanie if that was true. "Yes, he took his time to make sure it was right, but he did it himself," she confessed. Leslie hugged Billy and said she was so proud of him, that he was really growing up. Billy was proud of himself and replied, "I did this before I knew that you bought me the GI Joes. Do you think I predicted that you would get me something so cool, so I tried extra hard?" Leslie laughed and said she didn't realize that he even understood what 'predicted' meant. "Yeah, I'm pretty smart for someone who's 11, going on 12," Billy bragged. Leslie hugged him again and agreed. She had missed him.

"Well, kiddo, it's almost time for bed," Leslie said with a yawn. "Do you want to hear a little more about my visit with your Grandpa?" Billy said he did, and Steve said he did, too. They all went downstairs to the living room, but Leslie first stopped in the kitchen for a bottle of water. She told the three of them everything about the trip, except for the part about Jim and Linda. She didn't think Billy would really understand and decided that she would leave those details out. He would surely have questions for which she had no answers. She wanted to speak to Linda before telling anyone else, since it was rather personal.

Leslie wrote a check to Melanie for babysitting and thanked her and Steve. Melanie looked at the check, then blinked a couple of times and looked at it again. "You know that I was only here for four days, right?" Melanie inquired. Leslie replied that she was aware, but she wanted to take care of the people she could. Steve looked at the check. "$500 is too much. We can't accept this." Leslie argued that they can and that she would be paying Melanie a lot more to babysit so they could put away as much money as possible for the baby. They thanked Leslie and headed home, hand in hand.

Leslie turned her attention back to Billy and told him that she was happy to be home. "When will my Grandpa be here?" asked Billy. "I'm not really sure, but probably two weeks," Leslie replied. "We have a lot to do before then." She walked upstairs with Billy so he could brush his teeth and put on his pajamas. She tucked him into bed and headed downstairs to put away the stuff from her trip and make a list of what she needed to do tomorrow. Her mind was elsewhere, though, as she kept thinking of where she had heard that name. Tillotson…Tillotson…Tillotson and Mackey! That was it!

She grabbed the business card from the kitchen counter and dialed Jennifer's number. She answered immediately and Leslie blurted, "Jennifer, this is Leslie Mitchell. I hope it's not too late to call." Jennifer, who sounded even younger on the phone, assured Leslie that it wasn't too late. "I just remembered the connection with your last name," Leslie continued. "There was a 'Tillotson' with my dad when he went missing, who was also injured and taken to Marble Mountain." Jennifer was intrigued. "That is interesting," she said slowly. "My grandfather went missing about the same time as your dad, but nobody seems to know what happened to him. He's still listed as MIA."

Bill Lucas had finished cutting yellow frangipani blossoms and was heading back to the safety and coolness of the abbey when he saw a young man running away from the mountain. It was one of the men who had arrived with him about a month ago, but he couldn't remember his name. There had been another one, too, but

Bill had not seen the one they called "Mackey" for several days. This was a dangerous place, and only the local monks in traditional uniforms were to be trusted.

As Bill watched, an old pickup truck raced after the young man. The resounding blasts of an AK-47 caused Bill to panic and he risked his own safety by yelling at the young man to run. As the truck bore down on him, Bill shouted at the young man to get down, but his words were drowned out by the sound of the truck as one round after another pelted the shirtless man and he fell in a bloody heap.

One of the monks grabbed Bill by the hand and pulled him inside, spilling the cut blooms outside the door. He rushed Bill into the abbot's quarters, where he was hidden inside a closet and told to stay quiet. It seemed like hours passed before the abbot came to retrieve Bill, shovel in hand. He handed Bill the shovel and led him out into the dark night to the spot where the body lay awkwardly. The rain had washed off most of the blood, but it was obvious that the young man was dead.

After saying some calming words, the monks who had come to help wrapped the body in sheets and the abbot pointed to a spot for Bill to dig a grave. Although they offered to take turns, Bill somehow felt that this was his duty, and he singlehandedly dug the hole. They lowered the body into the shallow grave and replaced the dirt. A bowl of fruit and some lotus flowers were put on the spot.

Over the next few days, each monk visited the grave and paid their respects, but Bill was forbidden to go out during daylight for several days because he was told that he was in danger. At night, he brought more lotus and frangipani blossoms, and placed a small marble statue at the site. It was sad to have witnessed this horrible death, and Bill spent many days wondering why anyone would want to kill that young man.

...

Chapter Thirty-Two

After speaking with Jennifer Tillotson, Leslie knew she had to find out more about what happened to Jennifer's grandfather, whom Leslie believed was the Tillotson that was with her dad. There was so much to do that she decided to start some lists. She had things to do tomorrow, so she made a list titled "Monday." She had to take Billy to school, pick up the mail on hold at the post office, do some laundry, get groceries, catch up on the voicemails from the home phone, pay some bills, and stop by her office to discuss retirement. She added "Call Dad and Jim" at the end of the list, which made her smile. She never thought this would happen, that she would retire early to spend time with her father. She certainly never imagined that she'd be doing it without Mom around.

Leslie had held back her emotions for several days, still grieving for her mother but trying to stay strong when she met her father. Now that she was home where she was comfortable and free to be herself, she relaxed in her mother's recliner and let the tears fall. The chair still smelled like Mom, a little bit of gardenia and a hint of rose. There was a tissue box on the end table, so Leslie grabbed a handful and blew her nose. She had to laugh at the crocheted tissue box cover that Mom had used for years. She would wash it by hand in the sink and let it air dry. It must have meant a lot to her, and Leslie felt a little guilty for thinking about getting rid of some possessions that her mother held onto so dearly.

Leslie didn't really understand it when she was younger, but now she realized why Mom kept as many things as she could. The love of her life was missing and presumed dead, but Mom's heart couldn't accept it. She was so loyal and found joy in simple things like that tissue box cover and making scrapbooks to preserve memories. She kept everything that made her feel loved, and Leslie was sure that her mother kept every birthday and Mothers' Day card she had ever received. She preserved those precious times in pictures and arranged them in scrapbooks and photo albums. The thought of Mom putting together her scrapbooks made Leslie smile.

She needed to look for as many of those works of art that she could find, and then put them in chronological order for her Dad.

Leslie felt better after letting herself cry for a few minutes and grabbed her notepad to start her next list. "Things to do before Dad comes home" she wrote at the top. Before she wrote anything on that page, she added "Find scrapbooks" to her "Monday" list. She assumed they were in totes in the basement but wasn't sure exactly where. She only went down there when it was absolutely necessary, and since Mom had hired an electrician to move the washer and dryer to the kitchen, it was rare that Leslie had any reason to go to the basement. Maybe she had watched too many scary movies, but basements terrified her.

Leslie looked around the room and started thinking of things she would have to do before her dad came home. She wrote "Remodel Mom's bedroom" and considered having someone help her with that. She knew that Melanie was creative, so maybe she would help. Leslie thought about all the cleaning and redecorating that she would need to do and started listing all those projects. She would also need to put together the scrapbooks and photo albums and come up with a type of presentation that she could show her dad over and over. Steve said he and Melanie would help with that, which would be great. Being a Marine Corps veteran himself, he could probably offer some insight and suggestions that would be helpful when it came to the part about serving as a Marine. Jim could be helpful with that part, too, but it would be difficult for him to do much since he was so far away.

Leslie thought about Jim and what a great person he was, looking after her dad and retiring to come back home with him. She may have lost a parent, but she felt like she had gained two others. Jim had told her enough about his life that she felt sorry for him. He made it out of Vietnam physically intact, but emotionally and psychologically scarred. He had been through a lot and Leslie wanted to help him find some sense of normalcy and happiness. She wrote "Talk to Linda" on her list of things to do before her dad arrived, and decided that if there was time, she would do that tomorrow.

She turned off the lights and made sure the doors were locked. She grabbed her toiletry bag and suitcase and headed upstairs, leaving her lists on the kitchen counter. She was happy to be home, excited to start this next chapter of her life and spend more time there. Billy was at a crucial age, just starting the roller coaster of adolescence. Melanie had mentioned that he was talking a lot about a girl at school that he had missed while he was gone on vacation, and Leslie wondered why he hadn't said anything to her about a girl. Maybe she would ask him when she dropped him off in the morning.

She looked in at Billy and smiled. The nightlight that he had bought on their Florida trip cast a soft glow in the room and she could see his angelic face, sound asleep without a care in the world. The aroma coming out of the room wasn't so angelic, though; it smelled like a locker room. She decided to add "Buy deodorant for Billy" to her list, but it was downstairs. She was confident that she'd remember, since she would have to walk past his room in the morning.

Leslie put her suitcase in her room and grabbed some pajamas to get ready for bed. She took her toiletry bag into the bathroom because her toothbrush was in it and was changing into her pajamas when she heard her phone buzz. It was after 10:00, and Leslie had a reputation for going to bed early, so she was surprised that someone would be texting her this late. She looked at the message and saw Jim's name. She clicked on the message: "Your dad shaved his legs. He saw it on TV. I let him know that men don't do that. Talk to you tomorrow."

Leslie laughed harder than she had in a long time. She finished getting ready for bed and put away the rest of her toiletries. She took the empty bag back to the bedroom and set it on her suitcase. Her bed was made, but she was fairly certain that she had forgotten to do it when she left to go to Bethesda. She pulled back the blanket and there was a note on her pillow: "Mom – I made your bed while you were gone. Melanie helped me. Love, Billy." Leslie smiled and put the note on her dresser. She would thank Billy in the morning.

It felt so nice to be in her own bed with her perfect pillow and blankets that were just the right thickness. She made sure that her phone was plugged in and her alarm was set, then clicked off the light. She couldn't help thinking about how great Melanie was with Billy, and how grateful she was for her young neighbors who were going to have a baby. Leslie knew that they didn't have any extra money, so she tried to think of how she could help without making it weird. Although Leslie had told Melanie that she was going to pay her more for babysitting, how often would she need a sitter if she was no longer working? She needed to really think about what she could do for them.

Leslie decided that she would start by looking in the basement for Billy's baby items. She knew that Mom saved just about everything, so she was sure that the crib and changing table were down there. The basement was huge, and Leslie hadn't been down there in months, so it was going to take some time to go through everything. Maybe she could fix up a space for Billy to play down there, since his room was so small. There was so much to do, but she would have a lot more time to do it now that she wouldn't be going to work. Leslie thought about how life can change so quickly. One day, you're sad, saying goodbye to your mother and remembering all those years and memories together. Less than a month later, you're excited, retiring early and making plans to welcome home the father who missed all those years and memories. She thought about a poster that a co-worker had given her: "Sometimes the bad things that happen in our lives put us directly on the path to the best things that will ever happen to us." Leslie drifted off to sleep, ready for that new path and wondering if that poster was still hanging in her office.

•••

Chapter Thirty-Three

The alarm went off and Leslie was on her feet, ready to go. Although she was technically going into the office, she wasn't planning to actually work, so she chose a casual outfit. As she headed to the shower, she caught a glimpse of activity outside the window and stopped. It was barely light out, but there were several vehicles parked out in front with news logos on them. At first, Leslie wondered how they knew she was home, but then saw that she had never pulled her Equinox into the garage. Oh, brother. She had so much to do today.

Standing in the middle of the driveway was Steve, her young neighbor. Leslie assumed that he had things under control and continued to the shower. It felt great to be home, showering in her bathroom with consistent water temperatures. She was drying off when Billy knocked on the door. "Hang on, buddy, I'm almost done," she said. "Mom, there are people outside in vans and Steve is yelling at someone," said Billy through the door. Leslie assured him that everything was fine and got dressed quickly. She grabbed the hair dryer on her way out of the bathroom and greeted Billy with a quick "Good morning!" as he rushed past her. "Good morning! Gotta pee!" he yelled back. Leslie went to her room to dry her hair and was surprised when she heard the shower turn on. Billy usually needed coaxing to take a shower in the morning.

As she dried her hair, she watched Steve directing the traffic, not allowing anyone to pull into the driveway. Gary, the neighbor on the other side of Leslie, joined Steve in the driveway. Leslie hadn't seen Gary since Mom's funeral and made a mental note to go over there as soon as she got the chance. She threw on a little bit of makeup and went downstairs to make some breakfast and pack Billy's lunch. He came down while she was making scrambled eggs and asked if he could buy lunch at school instead of taking his lunch. "Do you know what they're having?" asked Leslie. "What if you don't like it?" Billy showed her the menu that was stuck to the refrigerator with magnets. "They're having chicken nuggets today," Billy explained. "I think I want to try them." Leslie didn't even know how much lunches were because Billy always took his lunch. She gave him a $5 bill and told him to put it in his pocket.

The toast popped up and Leslie buttered it and put two slices on a plate with scrambled eggs. When she set it down in front of Billy, he said, "Thanks, Mom. I missed you." Goodness gracious. How long had she been gone? "I missed you, too, honey," she replied. "Eat your breakfast while I run out and talk to Steve and Gary for just a minute, okay?" Billy sat down to eat and Leslie walked outside. Reporters jumped out of their vehicles as if they were synchronized, and it was a little intimidating. They walked quickly across the lawn, trying to be the first to talk to Leslie, and Steve was yelling, "Get off the lawn!" repeatedly and chasing them away.

Gary was laughing at Steve, and he got to Leslie before anyone else. "These people are like vultures!" he said. "I saw on the news that they found your dad, and Steve has been keeping me informed. I think that's great. How can I help?" Leslie explained that she had a lot to do, starting with taking Billy to school. She asked Gary if he could tell them that she had a reporter who was covering her story, and that maybe she could do a press conference later in the week. "Wow, planning your own press conferences now, are you?" he asked. "Maybe you should consider putting in a fence, and possibly a security system." Leslie said she would add it to her list, thanked Gary and waved at Steve. As she walked back to the house, she noticed Billy looking out the window and hoped that he wasn't afraid. He had come a long way, but he still had some social issues and did not like strangers in his yard.

He met her at the door. "What do they want?" he asked, more calmly than Leslie would have expected. She explained that this was big news, Grandpa Bill being found, and everyone wanted to be the first to get the story. "But it was already on the news," Billy replied. "Melanie even kept the newspapers from the last few days because it's in there, too. Mom, your picture was on the front page!" He grabbed the newspaper pile that Melanie had started and set them down in front of Leslie. She was surprised at the number of articles and pictures, and some had information about her dad's time in the Marine Corps. There was one of her and Dr. Edwards, and Leslie smiled. She would call him later, but she had a lot to do today.

Coming Home

She put her lists in her purse and snagged a bottle of sweet tea to take with her. Billy grabbed his backpack and they rushed out the door, which Leslie made sure to lock. As they backed out the driveway, Leslie stopped to thank Steve and Gary. "Hey, have you ever put in a fence?" she asked Steve. He said that he had, but it's not a one-man job. He had some friends at work that might be willing to help, though, so Leslie asked him to pick something out and talk to his friends. "I'll pay you guys to do it," she explained. "Just name your price. Gary, can you look into a good security camera system?" Gary said he would be happy to do that and asked about how much she was willing to spend. Leslie said she would spend whatever was necessary for a good system. "Fair enough," said Gary. "I'll get right on it."

Leslie rolled up the window and drove off, and about half of the news vehicles followed her. "We're getting a fence and security cameras?" Billy inquired. "Isn't that going to be expensive?" Leslie assured him that they could afford it, since Grandma left them more money than they could probably spend. "Are we rich?" Billy asked excitedly. Leslie thought about if for a few seconds and replied, "Yes, you could say that." Billy's eyes opened wide. "Woohoo!" he yelled. "Can I get a Playstation 4?" Leslie reminded him that his birthday was coming up soon and suggested that he make a list of what he really wanted. Billy asked if he could have a birthday party so his friends could see him opening the Playstation 4.

It was Leslie's turn to be excited. "You want to have a party, with all those people in your house?" she asked. "Mom, I only have, like, five friends," Billy replied. "I think they would be okay." Leslie said they could talk about it more later and told Billy that she wanted to ask him some questions. "Whatever you want," said Billy, still excited. "Shoot." Leslie asked if he thought that his body smelled different and explained that as we get older our bodies change and do funny things. "Are we having a sex talk?" Billy asked. Leslie said that he had already learned what he needed to know last year in his Health class, but she noticed that his room smelled a little funky. "Do you think maybe you need to start wearing deodorant?" she asked gently. "That would be cool!" Billy announced with more excitement than Leslie had anticipated. "Can I pick it out?" Leslie said she would prefer that he did and suggested they do that today after school.

They pulled into the school parking lot, but instead of just dropping Billy off, Leslie parked her car so she could go inside. Billy said he would see her later and ran off, which made Leslie feel a bit sad. It's part of him getting older, she reminded herself. As she walked into the school, she was met by the principal, Mrs. Golden. "Mrs. Mitchell, how great to see you back! Where is Billy?" Leslie explained that he ran off somewhere, and that she needed to make some changes to his Emergency Card information. "I want to express my condolences about your mother," Mrs. Golden replied. "She was a great woman, and we will miss having her help us with our annual fundraiser. Oh, and I saw you on TV with the President. That must have been exciting." Leslie explained that it wasn't so much being with the President that was exciting; it was the reason for it. "My father finally came home from Vietnam," Leslie gushed. "I finally got to meet him." Mrs. Golden congratulated Leslie and suggested that her dad come to the school in the fall for Veterans Day. Leslie didn't want to explain the problem with her dad's speaking, so she just thanked Mrs. Golden for the invitation and said she would ask him.

Billy returned and hugged Mrs. Golden, who smiled and patted him on the back. She remarked that he'd been gone for 3 weeks, and asked if he had done all of his homework. Billy replied that he did and explained that a lot happened in those 3 weeks. "My Grandma died, I went to Florida, my Grandpa was found, and we're rich. I'm getting PS4 for my birthday, and I'm buying deodorant tonight!" Leslie laughed. "Yes, we've been busy," she agreed. "Now get to class and remember that I'm picking you up after school!" Billy ran off, waving goodbye. Mrs. Golden was smiling at Leslie. "You know, that's a lot for a child like Billy to handle all at once," she began. Oh, here we go, thought Leslie. "Mrs. Golden, I appreciate your input, but my son is handling everything like a champ. Excuse me…I have a lot to do."

Leslie walked into the office, feeling proud that she stood up for herself and for Billy. She knew her son better than anyone else, and he was fine. The secretaries greeted Leslie like a celebrity, and Leslie thanked them for sending flowers for her mother's funeral. They asked about her vacation and her dad, and she let them know that she would no longer be working and needed to change some of the information on Billy's emergency card. They had already crossed out her mother's name for Billy's secondary contact and asked who Leslie wanted as a replacement. She gave them Melanie and Steve's information, and then added Jim Carlson's name and number, explaining that he was her dad's caretaker. "You may have seen him at the press conferences, if you watched," Leslie explained. "He was the distinguished older man in the suit." One of the secretaries fanned herself with a file folder and asked if that "hot old man" was single. Leslie laughed and said he was taken, then requested that they send a reminder to Billy at the end of the day that he was being picked up and should not ride the bus. She thanked them for taking care of everything and left the office.

...

Chapter Thirty-Four

As Leslie walked back to her car, she could see that two of the news vehicles had followed her to the school and were waiting for her. While she admired their dedication, she did not like the invasion of her privacy. She decided to just answer their questions. A clean-shaven young man approached her with his camera man and shoved a microphone in her face. "Are you Leslie Mitchell?" Leslie confirmed that she was, and the reporter asked how she felt about her father being found. "Seriously?" asked Leslie. "You're following me around to ask that? How do you think I feel?" She regretted that she had given him the opportunity to ask. "I was just asking, given the fact that he killed so many people. There's a rumor that he went into hiding rather than going on trial." Leslie couldn't believe what she was hearing. "I don't know where you heard that, but it's not true. My father did what he was trained to do, and he was not 'in hiding.' He had amnesia after suffering a significant head trauma. Who is your source for these lies?" The reporter flipped through his notes. "A family friend named Mark Mitchell." Leslie was furious. "That is my ex-husband, who cheated on me and I left him. Not exactly a credible source." She got in her car and slammed the door. What is wrong with people?

She left the parking lot and headed to the post office to pick up her mail. At least the reporters weren't following her anymore. She turned up her music and tried to forget the rude reporter's words. She wanted to strangle Mark. A "friend of the family"? Hardly. She walked into the post office and several strangers congratulated her and asked how her father was doing. Leslie had spent a lifetime feeling somewhat invisible and all this attention made her feel uneasy. She liked the fact that people were interested in her father, though, so she made sure to be respectful and acknowledged all the well-wishers.

When Leslie got to the counter, she showed her ID and asked for her mail that was being held. To her surprise, the postal worker brought out two huge bins of mail. "That can't all be mine," Leslie said. "There must be some mistake." They looked through the contents and it was mostly hers, with some addressed to her father. "Looks like your dad is already getting fan mail," said the postal worker. "Do you want to open a P.O. box for him?" Leslie declined and said that he would be living with her, so anything addressed to him should have the same address as hers. "Okay, have a great day," said the postal worker as he pulled up his sleeve to reveal a USMC tattoo. "Tell your dad I said 'Semper Fi'!" Leslie thanked him and said she would. She stacked the bins on top of each other and carried them out to the car, wondering how long it would take her to get through all of it. Billy could help her sort it later.

As she was loading the boxes into the back of the Equinox, Leslie's phone started ringing. She closed the back door and looked at the phone. "Hello, Michael," she said excitedly. "Why are you out of breath?" he asked. "Are you that excited about my call?" Leslie laughed. "While it is exciting to hear from you, I was just loading all the mail into the back of my car," she replied. "I don't know why, but in less than a month I received two huge boxes full of mail." He said that it would probably get worse before it gets better, as people across the country – maybe even other countries – would hear the story and want to connect in some way. She told Michael about the reporter at the school, and he suggested that she not speak to them. "The best thing to do is hold a press conference," he advised. Leslie agreed and told Michael about Jennifer Tillotson, the reporter whose grandfather also went missing in Vietnam. "Tillotson? Isn't that one of the Marines who was with your dad the night they were ambushed?" Leslie confirmed that they had the same last name, but she wasn't sure if it was the same guy. Michael said he would be meeting with Sergeant Lucas today and would ask him if he remembers anything about Tillotson.

"Hey, speaking of remembering," Leslie replied, "have you talked to your mother any more about meeting with Jim?" Michael said his mother was ready to meet whenever Jim came back to Michigan, and Leslie suggested that perhaps *she* should meet with Linda before Jim did. "Are you sure you want to do that?" Michael asked. "My mother can be quite a handful." Leslie assured him that it would be fine and asked him to have his mother call at her leisure. "Just give her my cell number and tell her to call whenever it's convenient," Leslie suggested. He said he would do that and added that it must be nice to be retired and not have a schedule. Leslie said she wasn't officially retired yet, but she was on her way to the office to take care of that. Michael wished her luck and said he would talk to her again soon.

Leslie thought about how easy it was to talk to Michael and reminded herself that this was her father's psychologist and he probably talked to everyone this openly. It was such an incredible coincidence that Michael's mother was Jim's ex-wife, and it seemed odd that just a few days ago she had not yet met any of these people. She wondered what she would be doing today if all of this hadn't happened and laughed when she realized that she would simply be on her way to another Monday at work. There was a lot to do in the next couple of weeks, but what was she going to do with all her time after her dad was home and things were settled down? She needed to find some hobbies.

Leslie was thinking about what she would do with all her spare time as she drove the short distance to her office. She walked up to the door, possibly the last time she would travel up this sidewalk, and wondered if her boss had listened to the voicemail she left. She opened the door quietly and discovered quite a surprise. The office was decorated for a celebration, and it was all for her. There were balloons and streamers and a giant sign that read "Good luck, Leslie!" with everyone's signatures and well wishes written on it. There was a beautifully decorated cake and vases of flowers on the table in the conference room. Leslie did not expect any of this and tears welled up in her eyes.

Her boss, Joel Candren, walked out to greet her. "Hi, Leslie!" he sang out. "We've been waiting for you!" Leslie's co-workers filed out of their offices and cubicles to say Hello and Goodbye. "Are you sure it's for real this time?" Fran, one of the older ladies, asked. She had been there when Leslie left the first time.

The past few months had been such a blur for Leslie with turning 40, finding out she was pregnant, and Mark's untimely transfer to Virginia. She had to pack up their house, reassure her mother that it wasn't the end of the world, and say goodbye to the job and co-workers she'd had for eighteen years. She dreaded the move and leaving the comfort and familiarity of this office. There would be no more hectic tax seasons or monthly potlucks or her boss reminding everyone that "the most important part of accounting is quality control."

Marie, who loved children and had several (everyone had lost count), greeted Leslie when she arrived for her last day. "Honey, you should be glowing with love," she gushed. "You're going to have a baby. Everything else is just details." Leslie hugged Marie and said she would glow when she stopped throwing up. "Get used to throwing up," advised Fran. "Kids do it a lot. You'll become a pro at wiping it off your shirt...and probably your furniture." Leslie thanked her for her advice and smiled. "And off the sheets and the floor," Fran laughed as she went to make copies of her reports.

Everybody had words of wisdom for Leslie's pregnancy. Eat this, don't eat that. Drink plenty of water, don't drink any water. Don't get stressed out or it will affect your baby. How could anyone expect her not to be stressed out? She had taken her contraceptives consistently and was aware that they're 99% effective. Being a person who deals with numbers daily, she easily did the math and knew that there was that 1% chance (or 9% with attributing factors) that she could still become pregnant. She could wonder why she was part of that 1% or overanalyze how it happened all day. Deep down, though, it wasn't the pregnancy that was stressful. Leslie was actually excited and knew that her mother would be there to make sure Leslie could handle the baby. The stress came from Mark suddenly getting transferred to Virginia, forcing Leslie to leave behind the life and people that she loved, her support system. It just didn't seem right.

"Nobody is making me do anything this time," Leslie assured everyone. "I am leaving because my dad will need me around full-time...plus my mother left me a small fortune." Everyone cheered and laughed, and they all packed into the conference room. Leslie hadn't eaten any breakfast, so she was glad to see the cake, which was a perfect "first day of retirement" breakfast food. Joel cut the cake and asked Leslie if she wanted to say anything before she left them for good. Leslie swallowed hard and said, "Thank you all for standing by me and never judging me and my decisions." Fran interrupted, "Oh, we were judging but that's what families do." Leslie fought back tears and said she was going to miss them, but she had a lot of catching up to do with her dad. Joel suggested that

Leslie make a huge deal out of every holiday, every celebration, and every small victory with her dad. "I can't imagine what he has been through," Joel added, "but please let us know if there is anything we can do for him. Seriously, anything." Leslie said she would as she took a bite of the cake. It was so light and fluffy, and the frosting was perfect. "I think I will start by making a huge deal out of this celebration," she commented. "I love you guys." Leslie was amused by the thought that there had probably never been a bigger mess of accountants eating cake at 10 AM and crying together. She wondered if she had ever truly appreciated how much they were like a family and made sure to speak to everyone before she headed to her office to retrieve her belongings.

Joel followed her down the hall. As Leslie packed things up, he picked her brain about the best choice for her replacement. "No contest," said Leslie. "Adrianne is the best accountant you have." Joel laughed. "Well, except for you," he replied. "No, myself included," Leslie replied. "I know that you've kept me in this position because I know how *you* want things done, but you should really listen to her ideas." Joel agreed and said he was going to miss Leslie, but she promised to keep in touch and possibly come back and visit. "Are you sure you're going to be okay financially?" he asked. "More than okay," Leslie replied. "My mother was a closet millionaire. She had more money than she could ever have spent. I had no idea, and I've been an accountant for years." Joel rubbed his chin and shook his head. "So…will you be needing an accountant?" he asked. Leslie laughed at the idea. "No, but thanks for the offer," she replied. "I feel confident that I can handle it. If not, I'll call you."

Leslie finished packing up her belongings and asked Joel if she needed to sign anything. "No, I'll take care of everything," he explained. "Did you get all your pictures and posters, or did you leave any for your replacement?" Leslie said she had everything except one poster that she decided she didn't need anymore. She thanked everyone and as she headed out to the car with her box, she yelled out to nobody in particular: "What's the most important part of accounting?" Several voices yelled back: "Quality control!" and Leslie laughed. She knew she would miss them, but she could always stop by to catch up. She headed home to unload her boxes and cross a few things off her list…and add a few more.

Coming Home

Leslie pulled into her driveway and hit the button on her garage door opener. She was startled at first to see a man standing in her garage with a tape measure, but then realized it was just Gary. She pulled into the garage and got out to unpack her mail and the items from her office. "Hey, Gary, what are you doing?" she asked. Gary said he was figuring out some details for her security system and Leslie just nodded her head, not really sure why he was measuring. "Can you give me a hand with these boxes?" she asked. "There was a lot more mail than I expected, plus I packed up my office at work."

Gary stacked up the two boxes of mail and Leslie carried the box from work with balloons tied onto both handles. "Wow, that was nice," Gary commented. "Did they have a party for you?" Leslie smiled. "Yes, there was even cake," said Leslie. "Cake for breakfast is a great start to my new retired life. I'm going to have time for my son, my dad, and even my neighbors." Gary set the boxes down on the dining room table. "Well, I hate to tell you this, but I won't be around to enjoy that. I'll be moving as soon as I get my house packed up." Leslie was surprised because she knew that Gary loved living here, although he missed his daughter, who had recently moved to Colorado.

"Is everything okay?" Leslie asked. "You've never mentioned moving, and I didn't even know that your house was up for sale." Gary said that everything was fine and his house had not been up for sale, but he received a call last night that changed everything. "Some guy called out of the blue from out of state and said he really likes my neighborhood. Offered me almost double what my house is worth. I thought it might be a scam at first, but somehow that money was in my bank account this morning. I didn't give him my account number, just the name of my bank. He said he knew the right people to get the money in my account and sure enough, it was there first thing this morning. I don't know why someone who has $350,000 to spend would want to live in my house, but the paperwork is supposed to arrive for me to sign today. I thought about you and your dad, and how much of each other's lives you missed, and realized that I want to spend as much time as I can with my daughter. I'll get your security system installed before I head out to Colorado."

Leslie was staring at Gary, trying to process what he said, imagining what it would be like without him as a neighbor. She couldn't remember a time when he did not live next door. He had always been their handyman who fixed whatever was broken and plowed snow from their driveway without ever being asked. "Wow!" Leslie finally managed. "I'm happy for you, since you'll get to see your daughter more often, but honestly I can't imagine not having you next door. I hope the new neighbors are nice, but it is odd that anyone with that type of disposable income would want to live in our neighborhood, with all these older homes. Did the man tell you his name?" Gary thought about it for a minute. "He did," Gary answered, "but I don't remember right now. Let me think about it while I finish taking these measurements, and I'll let you know if it comes to me." Leslie thanked Gary and started unpacking the boxes as he headed out to the garage. She hoped it wasn't some crazy person or a reporter, and she couldn't imagine having anyone else for a neighbor. She would really miss having Gary around.

Leslie set aside the box from work and concentrated on sorting the mail. She dumped out both boxes on the table and grabbed a trash bag. She had four categories...junk mail (straight into the trash bag), regular mail, her dad's mail, and "unsure." She had sorted through most of it when her phone rang. "Hi, Leslie, it's Jennifer Tillotson. I did some research, and my grandfather apparently was attached to the same unit as your dad. Isn't that crazy?" Leslie was impressed that Jennifer had found the information so quickly. "Hi, Jennifer. That really is crazy. I guess it wasn't unusual for people in the same area to be assigned together back then. I talked to my dad's psychologist a short time ago and he said he would ask him about it today." Jennifer was hoping that it might help them find out exactly what happened to her grandfather, and Leslie agreed. "I was thinking about this story that should be told about my dad, and maybe about your grandfather," said Leslie. "I am wondering if you would like to have the exclusive story. There have been two press conferences, but nothing here yet. What do you think?"

Jennifer was obviously excited. "That would be awesome!" she answered. "I think it would be beneficial to have an official press conference locally. That would appease some of the vultures and allow you to give everyone a general idea about what is happening.

It might keep you from being stalked and accosted every day. Do you want me to set that up for you?" Leslie agreed and asked Jennifer to set it up, trusting her to arrange everything. It seemed like a good deal, giving Jennifer exclusive rights to do an in-depth story in exchange for her setting up the news conference. Leslie said she would let Jennifer figure it out and asked her to call when it was arranged. "Thank you! Thank you! Thank you!" Jennifer shouted. "This is a great way to start my career in journalism!" Leslie laughed. "Thank you for handling it," she replied. "I don't know much about how things work when it comes to reporters and the press. I look forward to hearing from you."

Leslie hung up and smiled. She was getting better at having others do things for her, but it did not come naturally. She continued sorting the mail and wondered what to do about the pile for her dad. It was addressed to him, and she didn't want to do anything illegal by opening his mail, but he couldn't read it yet. Or could he? Had they asked her dad to read anything? She knew that he could not speak or write, but he could hear and see. Leslie searched her memory for anything that was said about testing her dad's ability to read but couldn't remember it being mentioned.

Leslie decided to text Michael, since they had already talked this morning and she didn't want to bug him. It was short and sweet: "My dad received a ton of mail. Can he read at all?" She set the phone aside, assuming that it would take awhile for a response. Gary opened the door into the kitchen. "Hey, I remembered the name of the guy who's buying my house…I'm pretty sure he said 'Jim Carlson.'"

· · ·

Chapter Thirty-Five

Leslie couldn't help but laugh. "Are you sure it was Jim Carlson?" she asked. "Yeah, pretty sure," Gary replied. "Do you know him?" Leslie grabbed one of the newspapers that Melanie had saved, the one with Jim Carlson at the first press conference. "That is General Jim Carlson. He and my dad were friends in college and he was part of the extraction team that brought my dad back." Gary was relieved to hear that it was someone who already knew Leslie and ducked back out the door to finish what he was doing in the garage.

Leslie picked up her phone and texted Jim: "You bought my neighbor's house? How will I ever find a handyman like Gary?" Jim texted back: "Yes, nice guy. I'm pretty handy, plus your dad will be there. Heading out for lunch and then to the appt with Linda's son. Call you later." Leslie took her junk mail to the trash, thinking about Jim's commitment to her father. She had heard the Marines' motto of "Semper Fidelis" many times, and knew that it means "Always Faithful," but never realized how seriously some of them must take that commitment. Jim could've bought any house in any city, but he chose to live next door to her dad, the friend he thought was dead. The friend he rescued who didn't recognize him. We should all be so lucky to have a friend like that.

Her phone rang and interrupted her thoughts. It was Billy's school, and Leslie answered right away. "Hello, Mrs. Mitchell. This is Mrs. Golden, Billy's principal. I just wanted to let you know about a situation." Leslie felt sick to her stomach. "What happened?" she asked. "Is Billy okay?" Mrs. Golden assured her that Billy is fine, but a little upset. Apparently, some of the other students were asking Billy about his "vacation," and he was talking about his grandfather being found. One of the boys, who has been in trouble for bullying other students, told Billy that he was lying and Billy punched him in the throat. Since it was Billy's first time doing something like this, he was just given a warning. "MY Billy punched someone? There has to be more to the story," Leslie said. "I'm not saying that he's an angel, but he's never displayed that type of aggression." Mrs. Golden said that it's part of middle school, and really nothing to worry about. Leslie asked about the other boy, whether he was okay, and Mrs. Golden assured her that his pride was hurt more than anything. Leslie thanked her and hung up. Yesterday, he was a little boy excited about Sponge Bob and today they were discussing deodorant and he's getting in fights? Leslie was glad that she wasn't getting this call at work and was anxious to hear Billy's side of the story.

Her stomach reminded her that it was time to eat some lunch, so Leslie made a peanut butter and jelly sandwich. She decided to explore the basement to see if she could find more photo albums and scrapbooks, so while she ate her sandwich she found a flashlight and some bug spray...just in case. She used to tease her mother when she discovered that the umbrella hanging at the top of the basement stairs was to protect Mom from spiders falling from the ceiling. Her mother had apparently experienced a spider fast-roping down from the ceiling, so whenever she headed downstairs, she took the umbrella and put it up like it was raining spiders. Leslie opened the basement door and laughed when she saw the umbrella there. Oh, why not, she thought. She took the umbrella off the hook and hit the light switch.

As Leslie descended the stairs into the basement, she had intended to open the umbrella to protect herself from the spiders that she was sure to encounter. There was no need because the basement was completely finished. The walls were drywalled and painted, the floors were tiled and covered with large area rugs, and the old fireplace had been restored. There were strings of lights, probably the old Christmas lights that Mom said she didn't want to throw out just because they bought new LEDs, hanging on ceilings and walls. There was new furniture and a bedroom that Leslie never knew about. She remembered Mom talking about her "craft room" in the basement, but she thought it was just some boxes of craft supplies. Her fear of the basement had kept Leslie from enjoying this area that her mother had spent so much time fixing up. She heard Gary come in upstairs and came back up.

"Hey, did you know that my mother had redone the basement?" Leslie asked. "Sure, I did," Gary answered. "Who do you think did the tile, the drywall, and the painting? She wanted it to be a surprise for you, and it was almost finished when she got really sick. Cool, huh?" Leslie threw her arms around Gary's neck. "Thank you for helping her! When did you do this?" she asked. "Mostly when you were at work," Gary replied. "I tried to get the fireplace completely restored while you were on vacation, but I ran out of time. It looks finished, but there's some work to be done on the inside." Leslie went back downstairs with Gary and asked him to show her what he had done. He said the bedroom was for Billy, since he was getting older and might want more privacy. Leslie joked that this must have cost a fortune. "I don't know about the materials because your mother bought everything. We had a deal that she would pay me for doing the work, but she never got a chance," Gary said, his voice trailing off. "She got sick and things happened so quickly." Leslie asked how much she owed him for all that work and Gary said not to worry about it. "I have plenty of money," he said. "If money could bring your mother back, though, I'd give up every penny. You only meet someone that loyal, with such a good heart, once in your lifetime."

A week ago, Leslie would have agreed, but she thought of Jim Carlson. "I suppose," she finally managed. She felt overwhelmed by this grand gesture of her mother's. Gary said that he needed to go pick up the security system and Leslie asked if he needed cash up front. "I'm telling you, kid, I have plenty of money," he insisted. Leslie requested that he bring her the receipt so she could reimburse him and Gary said he would. He went up the stairs and Leslie stood in the basement, in awe of the transformation. It was beautiful!

She walked through slowly and stopped in the Craft Room. There were tons of photo albums and scrapbooks, and Leslie looked at the labels on the shelves. They were arranged in chronological order, labeled with dates and places and events. Jackpot! Since the first label was "B.B. (Before Bill)," Leslie assumed that there were photos of her grandparents, too. Judging by the labels, she was fairly sure that Mom had copies of all the photos given to Aunt Judith. Leslie pulled out the chair at the desk that Mom had used as a crafting table. Next to the desk was an old card catalog that Mom had kept when the library got rid of it. The labels were date ranges, and Leslie opened the drawers to see what was inside. There were thumb drives in each drawer with dates that matched the albums on the shelves. Jackpot #2! Mom had digitized the photos!

Leslie couldn't believe that her mother had done all this and never told her. She wondered what other surprises she might find and started opening the desk drawers. She laughed at the office supplies, since some were probably 30 years old, and didn't even know what a few of the items were. There was a small lockbox in the back of the top drawer, but it wasn't locked. Leslie opened it and at first she thought it was empty. She was closing it when she noticed a small key taped inside. She pulled off the tape and removed the key, but the letters on it were too small to read without her glasses so she put it in her pocket and decided to do that later. She walked through the rest of the basement, checking out all the work that Gary had done, before heading back upstairs.

Leslie looked at the microwave clock. She still had about an hour before she needed to pick Billy up at school, so she looked at her list and decided to listen to 3 weeks' worth of voicemails on her phone. She grabbed a pad of paper to write down the names/numbers for the calls she needed to return. She went to Mom's answering machine, which was full, and hit the button to bring up those messages. There were condolence messages about her mother, congratulatory messages about her father, a few from reporters, and two of those pesky messages about her car warranty expiring. Leslie wrote down the names and numbers for everyone and decided that she would return those calls tomorrow. She grabbed the grocery list from the refrigerator and added several items, including deodorant for Billy.

She grabbed her keys and headed out the door. There was a silver car parked in front of her house, and two people were just sitting in it when she pulled out. She knew that Steve would be home soon from work, and he would assess the situation. She made sure to close the garage door and backed out of the driveway, feeling more relaxed than she had in a long time. Her first day of being officially retired was turning out to be quite productive, and she remembered the journal that Justine had given her to document her dad's progress. Leslie thought it might be interesting to get another journal to document her own progress and decided that she would add that to her list.

The pick-up line at Billy's school threatened to throw a wrench in Leslie's positive day, and she wondered how such a simple task could be a nightmare every day. Drive up, get your kid, and drive away. It seemed cut-and-dry, but with middle school kids nothing really is that easy. Leslie watched Billy walk out of the school, talking to everyone on the way out, several of them shaking his hand and slapping him on the back. What was this? A cute little girl hugging Billy? Leslie smiled as she watched him blush and told herself not to make it a big deal.

Billy opened the car door and before Leslie could ask how school went, he said, "Mom, I'm sorry that I got in trouble. That kid said I was lying, and I wasn't." Leslie laughed at his guilty conscience and assured him that she wasn't mad, but she did want to hear what happened. Billy explained that people were asking him questions about his trip and about Grandma's funeral, and he told them that his Grandma left but his Grandpa showed up to take her place. He always knew how to put things in perspective. "This mean kid named Shawn said I was lying. He's a bully, Mom. He's mean to everyone, and I don't like that." Leslie explained that bullies are usually cowards, but they are mean so people will leave them alone. Billy said that he tries to walk away from bullies, but this time Jenna was watching and he didn't want her to think he was afraid. "Oh, Jenna was watching?" Leslie inquired. "Any chance that Jenna is that cute little girl with the peach-colored shirt that just hugged you?" Billy blushed and said that it was. Jenna was still out there on the sidewalk, waiting for her ride. Billy rolled down the window and yelled, "Do you need us to take you home?" Jenna waved and said, "No, thank you. My mom will be here soon. See you tomorrow, Billy!"

Billy waved back and yelled, "Okay! See you tomorrow!" Leslie wondered how long this had been going on and thought it was pretty darn cute. "Is that your girlfriend?" Leslie asked. "Mom! We're just friends!" Billy replied. "Okay," Leslie answered. "Whatever you say. Let's go get some deodorant."

They drove out of the parking lot and headed toward Target. Billy asked if she could call some people so they could shut it down like she did with her dad. "Oh, I didn't make that happen," Leslie explained. "That was Grandpa's friend, Jim Carlson. By the way, he is going to be our new neighbor. He bought Gary's house." Billy was confused about where Gary would go, but he decided that it would be fun having Grandpa's friend next door. "I didn't know that Grandpas had friends," he laughed. "What kind of stuff do they do?" Leslie said she wasn't sure, probably play with GI Joes and drink coffee. Billy liked the idea.

They worked their way through Target quickly, crossing things off the list. She remembered to get the journal and Billy asked about it. He wanted one, too, and Leslie thought that was a great idea. She was trying to be a little more lenient with Billy, giving in a few times when he asked to get something that wasn't on the list. She knew that they needed to have more of a conversation about the altercation earlier but was putting it off until later. They spent eleven minutes in the deodorant section, smelling all of them...some two or three times. When he couldn't decide between two of them, Leslie threw them both in the cart and said he could trade off. "I like this new rich Mom," Billy declared. "She lets me buy extra stuff."

Leslie rolled her eyes and headed to the checkout line. People were staring at her, and one older gentleman with a "Vietnam Veteran" hat asked if she was the one whose dad was found at Marble Mountain. "Yes, sir," she replied proudly. "Tell him I said, 'Welcome Home,'" the man said with a smile. It made Leslie think of some of the rallies and conventions that she attended with Mom, and how tired she grew of everyone telling each other "Welcome Home."

Leslie was ashamed that she ever felt that way. She thanked the man and forced herself not to get emotional in front of Billy. They went through the Self-Check line and zipped out of the store. "Is Grandpa famous?" Billy asked. Leslie thought about it but admitted that she wasn't really sure. "He probably will be, once everyone knows the whole story about his life," Leslie explained. "But for me, he is just my Dad." Billy nodded his head and said, "For me, he is my Grandpa but also my hero."

•••

Chapter Thirty-Six

Billy didn't elaborate about what happened at school on the way home, and Leslie decided that she would talk to him about it later. He did mention Jenna again, and it turns out that she was new to the area and lived just around the block from them. "I feel sorry for her, Mom," explained Billy. "Kids my age can be so mean. I helped her find her classroom and then invited her to sit with me at lunch. She's really smart and she thinks it's cool that I'm in Boy Scouts." Leslie agreed that it is cool, and asked Billy what badge he wanted to work on. He thought about it for a minute and replied, "I think I want to try Signs, Signals, and Codes. I can learn Morse Code, braille, sign language, and lots of other cool stuff. One of the other Scouts said I can even make up my own secret code!" Leslie could tell that Billy was excited about it and said she would help him with that.

"So, now that you don't have a job, you can do more stuff with me, right?" he asked. "Of course," said Leslie, "but I think I've always done a lot with you." Billy agreed that she did, but when Grandma got sick they had to spend a lot of time helping her and they didn't do many fun things together. "Well, that changes today," Leslie promised. "We will be doing more fun things, but for the next couple of weeks I will really need your help to do some things around the house. We can make it fun, though." Billy said he wanted to help and asked what they needed to do at the house. Leslie explained that Gary was putting in a security system and Steve was putting in a fence, but there was a lot of redecorating to do to turn Grandma's bedroom into a space for a Grandpa. "What if Grandpa doesn't want to live with us?" asked Billy. "What if he wants to live next door with his friend? I heard that adult friends do that. It's called 'being roommates' or something like that. That's a funny way to say it."

Leslie hadn't even considered that option, but she wanted her father to live with her. She said they would need to do a lot of redecorating, and she was going to need Billy's help. She explained that there had been some renovations already at the house and asked Billy if he knew that Grandma had done some designing in the basement. Billy never went in the basement because, as he put it, "it's not normal for people to be under the ground unless they're dead." For some reason, though, he seemed excited to see what his Grandma had done to the basement when they got home.

They pulled into their driveway and Leslie was pleasantly surprised to see her neighbor Steve outside with one of his friends from work. Billy rolled down the window. "Hi, Steve! I tried that throat punch thing on a bully, and I got in trouble at school!" Steve slapped his forehead and headed over as Leslie pulled in the garage. Billy took his backpack inside and hung it up, part of his usual school day ritual. Steve introduced his friend from work, Tyler, and explained to Leslie that Tyler was going to help him put the fence in. They had the measurements and were going to get some quotes. "Thanks for taking care of that, Steve," said Leslie. "What do you know about the bully at school and the 'throat punch'?" Steve laughed and explained that Billy had talked to him about Shawn. Steve's advice to Billy was to try talking to the bully first, but if that didn't work, punch him in the throat. Apparently, it can be an effective tool to shut someone up. Leslie asked him to teach her how to do that some day when life calmed down a little.

Billy came back outside and explained the situation to Steve. "Did you try telling an adult before resorting to violence?" asked Leslie. "Mom, I told on him, like, 100 times. They wouldn't do anything so I had to stand up for myself." Leslie asked if that was why so many kids were patting him on the back today after school. "I'm popular now," said Billy. "I stood up to the worst bully in school and made him cry. Sometimes, that's all bullies understand." Leslie knew that as a parent, she should not condone violence, but she thought about the years of being bullied herself. "You know, Billy," she started, "I should be scolding you about doing that, but I am actually proud that you stood up for yourself. Kids aren't always nice, just like adults, and sometimes when you feel like there is no other way to get your point across..." Billy finished her sentence: "Boom! Throat punch!" Steve high-fived Billy and said he shouldn't have to worry about Shawn anymore. Leslie thanked Steve and asked him to let her know when he had the quotes for the fence. She reminded him to keep track of the time he was spending on this, so she could pay him fairly.

Leslie was glad to have Steve as a neighbor, teaching Billy how to stand up for himself and helping her whenever she asked. There was a definite improvement in Billy's self-esteem since Steve started spending time with him, and Leslie wondered how it would be to have a man around full-time to influence Billy. "Earth to Mom!" Billy yelled. "You zoned out for a minute." Leslie apologized and said they needed to get the bags into the house and put everything away. "That doesn't sound like fun," whined Billy. Leslie replied that it's fun if you skip and proceeded to skip into the house with her bags. Billy laughed at how silly she looked and tried to do the same but wasn't coordinated enough to skip while carrying bags.

He carried the bags inside, set them on the kitchen counter, and fished through the bag with his deodorant in it. He took the cap off one and sniffed it. "Oh, I am going to smell so good!" he claimed. Leslie laughed and explained how to put it on, reminding him that if he sweats a lot he should reapply it. Billy pulled his shirt off, rubbed some deodorant under his arms, and put his shirt back on while Leslie watched. He put the cap back on and grabbed the other stick of deodorant. "I'll go put these in the bathroom so I can wear some tomorrow," he announced.

Leslie started putting things away while he was upstairs. When he came back down, she asked Billy if he had any homework. "I have SO MUCH homework!" he replied. "I think the teachers are mad at me for going to Florida." Leslie suggested that was ridiculous and told him to get started. He asked if he could see the basement first, since he would be thinking about that so he wouldn't be able to concentrate. Leslie laughed and opened the door to the basement. "Okay, let's go," she said. "I want you to be able to concentrate."

Billy grabbed a flashlight from the kitchen before heading down, "just in case." When he got to the bottom, he obviously could not believe the difference. "This is awesome!" he yelled, running around. "Look at all the Christmas lights on the ceilings! I love it down here!" Leslie showed him the bedroom that was intended for him, so he could have some privacy as he got older. "Why would I need that?" he asked innocently. "I don't need to be away from you; you're my mom." He hugged Leslie and she closed her eyes, savoring the moment. He was almost her height, wearing deodorant and growing up so quickly. She thought about how lonely her mother must have been when she moved away, and how lonely she would feel when Billy moved away.

Billy broke away and asked if he could do his homework at Grandma's desk in the Craft Room. Leslie said that would be fine, so they headed upstairs so he could get his backpack. He left the flashlight on the kitchen counter and Leslie used it to see the small letters on the little key in her pocket. She was surprised to read the name of the bank where her mother had her accounts all these years and wondered why she would need a key at a bank. Did people still have boxes at the bank for their valuables? She decided that she would go there tomorrow and ask about it.

As she was thinking about the key and the bank, Leslie could hear her cell phone ringing from inside her purse. It was Michael, and Leslie tried to answer nonchalantly. "Hello, Michael, did you get my text earlier?" she cooed. "Hi, Leslie!" Michael answered. "I received your text, yes, but I want to inform you that you're on speaker phone. Your father and General Carlson are here." Leslie really didn't like being on speaker phone. She remembered that her dad had an appointment there, and laughed when Jim said "Hello, Leslie," and her dad said, "Hello." "What is going on there?" she asked. Jim spoke first. "Hey, Leslie, we have discovered that your dad can mimic sounds and will repeat short sentences. It's a lot of fun. He will say anything…just like a kid!"

Leslie heard her dad say, "Like a kid!" and she laughed. "Michael, what do you think of this?" she asked. He said it was significant progress, but there was even more. Michael had given her dad a simple book written in French – a children's book - and he seemed to be reading it. When Michael asked if he understood what he was reading ("Vous comprenez ce que vous lisez?"), the answer was "Oui!" This was excellent news! "Did you try having him read English?" Leslie asked. Michael replied that he did try, but her dad didn't seem to recognize the words.

Jim chimed in that he was teaching Bill simple objects and there were some sounds that he couldn't seem to imitate. Michael explained that every language has specific sounds like that, and someone who doesn't hear English much will forget how to produce those sounds, like the "th" in "thanks." Leslie heard her dad say "Tanks!" followed by Jim Carlson's laughter. "Well, at least you guys are having fun with this," she said. "It sounds like we're heading in the right direction. Can you take me off speaker phone now?" Jim said, "Okay, bye!" and Bill added "Bye!" before Michael spoke.

"Okay, just me now," he said. "Is everything okay?" Leslie explained that it was, but she really didn't like being on speaker phone. "Did you ask my dad about Tillotson?" she inquired. Michael said that he had not, but he had pulled some photos and was going to ask him before the appointment was over. He explained to Leslie that he had given her phone number to his mother, as they had discussed earlier, and Leslie should expect a call. She knew that he didn't want to say much about his mother because Jim was there, so she thanked him and said she would be expecting a call. She wanted to tell him all about her day, but she knew that Jim and her dad were there so she told Michael that she would talk to him later and hung up.

Leslie thought about what a day she'd had and decided that this was a great time to start her journal. She grabbed it and started writing but had not yet written a full page when her phone rang again. It was a Michigan number, one that she didn't recognize, so she assumed it was Linda. She answered, "Hello, this is Leslie," and the gentle voice on the other end did not match how Michael had described his mother. "Hello, Leslie. This is Linda Edwards, Michael's mother. He asked me to call you." Leslie wasn't really sure what to say, or honestly why she wanted to talk to Linda, but she managed to find her voice. "Hi, Linda. Thank you for calling. I realize that you don't know me, but..." Linda cut her off, "...but you wanted to know what happened between me and Jim?" Wow. This woman did not mince words. Leslie admired that. "Sort of. I met Jim less than a week ago. Did you hear about him bringing my dad back from Vietnam?" Linda said that she read it in the paper on her cruise and saw it on the news yesterday. She explained that she and Jim were friends with Leslie's parents at one time, but after her dad went missing, life just fell apart.

Leslie had expected to hear bitterness or anger, but Linda just sounded sad and Leslie felt sorry for her. Billy was calling for Leslie from the basement and Leslie asked if Linda could come by tomorrow so they could talk some more. Linda agreed that would be nice and promised that she would. Leslie was about to hang up but remembered that she hadn't given Linda her address. Linda laughed when Leslie told her the address. "You live in that same little house?" she asked. "I begged your mother to let me redecorate that place for her years ago."

Linda arrived at the birthday party looking like someone from a magazine cover. Her teased hairdo, recently dyed auburn, complemented her fair skin and closely matched her lipstick. The bright green baby doll dress with huge white and yellow daisies was fun and fashionable, and other guests couldn't help but stare at this gorgeous woman. "Who's that foxy lady? Is that you, Ann Margaret?" Susan teased. "Just Aunty Linda here to celebrate," Linda responded with a smile. "Where's the birthday girl?" Susan pointed to the stairs. "Still napping," she replied. "Shouldn't be long now."

Linda headed for the stairs. "I'm going to get that little crumb snatcher," she announced. "It's her first birthday. She should be here." Susan walked up the steps behind Linda, laughing at her friend's directness. Before she could ask if Linda had heard from Jim, Linda inquired about the worn handrail. "Don't you think this old thing should be replaced? I've been spending a lot of time doing projects and I can help with that." Susan said it was fine, but Linda was already on to the next project. "Was this wallpaper here before?" asked Linda. "I would love to change it. The color bums me out."

Susan seemed to understand what was happening. "Linda, have you heard anything from Jim?" she asked. "It seems like you're trying very hard to focus on things you can change." Linda pursed her lips as she opened the door to Leslie's room but did not reply to Susan's statement. Leslie had just awakened and squealed with delight. Linda picked her up and planted a huge kiss on Leslie's cheek, leaving perfect auburn lip imprints. "Happy first birthday, sweetie!" she gushed. "Let's get you downstairs to the party."

Leslie explained that the house probably looked exactly the same and that she needed to redo Mom's bedroom for her dad, so it was finally going to get redecorated. Linda apologized for how awful she was to Susan, who was exactly right about what was happening. "Let's just say that I owe my current career to Jim," Linda admitted.

"I learned to do a lot of home projects while he was at war. I was just too immature to handle the loneliness and his drinking." Leslie commented that everyone deserves another chance and laughed at the irony as she headed downstairs to see what Billy wanted.

...

Chapter Thirty-Seven

Leslie helped Billy with his math homework and headed back upstairs to finish writing in her journal. She had read that writing in a journal helps people figure things out, but for her it was a good way to keep track of what was happening. With so much changing in her life, she was going to forget some things and this journal might help refresh her memory later. She caught a glimpse of someone running across her lawn and went to the window.

Steve, her neighbor, was running out toward the street. Leslie recognized the silver car as the one she saw earlier and walked outside. The car drove away slowly as Steve read the plate number aloud. He pulled out his cell phone and texted someone, then saw Leslie walking out. "Hey, Leslie. Looked like two guys. I chased them away earlier. I will see if one of my friends at the police station can run the plate." Leslie thanked him and commented about how she would feel better once she had the fence and security system in place. "We should have the fence installed no later than next week," Steve said. "Do you still have weapons in the house?" Leslie blinked a couple of times and asked what he meant. "Weapons. Guns. Your mother had weapons in the house when she lived there alone," he explained. "I even took her to the range a few times to practice. Do you know how to shoot?"

Leslie was finding out that her mother did a lot without her knowledge, but guns? She asked Steve if he knew where they were, and they went inside. He showed Leslie the gun case in her mom's bedroom closet, which was locked. He said the key should be in her nightstand, along with a small handgun. They opened the nightstand drawer, but all Leslie saw was some tissue and several old pairs of nylons. Steve pulled out the nylons and there was a small revolver under them. "Is it loaded?" she asked. Steve checked the cylinder. "Yep. Locked and loaded!" he claimed. Leslie thought about Billy and shared her thoughts with Steve. "Billy would never come in here," he explained. "He doesn't like to go into other people's bedrooms and he doesn't like anyone to go into his room."

Leslie knew that he was right and asked Steve to put the gun back in the drawer. "Weapon," corrected Steve. Leslie had no idea what the difference was and replied, "Whatever. Let's just keep this door shut." Steve suggested that Leslie consider going with him to the range so she could learn how to shoot and feel more comfortable around weapons. She said she would think about it, but she had a lot to process today. Steve asked where Billy was and laughed when Leslie said he was in the basement. Before Steve could respond, Leslie said, "It's different. My mother had Gary do all kinds of projects down there." Steve walked down the stairs and saw Billy doing his homework at the desk in the Craft Room. "Hey, little man! I thought you didn't like the basement!" he teased. Billy jumped up when he saw Steve. "Hi, Steve! I like it now! Look what my Grandma did!" He showed Steve the whole basement, even the bedroom that was redecorated with Billy in mind. Leslie explained that her mother never got a chance to pay Gary, and asked Steve if he could come up with an estimate of what she should pay him, based on what was done.

Steve said he would do that later, but right now he had to get home to help Melanie with dinner. "How's she feeling?" asked Leslie. Steve said she had wicked morning sickness and they were ready for that to be over. Leslie remembered her own experience with morning sickness and warned Steve that some women have it throughout their entire pregnancy.

Steve thanked Leslie for raining on his parade and left. "What parade?" asked Billy. "What does he mean?" Leslie explained that it's an expression that means someone was having fun and you ruined it. "Wait. Steve wasn't laughing or anything," said Billy. "How did you know he was having fun? Who do you think invented that expression? Someone from an actual parade?" Leslie said he asked a lot of questions for someone who hadn't finished his homework as she started up the stairs. "You're raining on my parade!" he yelled after her. "Excellent job!" Leslie replied, laughing. "Now, finish your homework!"

She was going to continue writing in her journal but decided that she could do that when she went to bed and set it aside. She filled a pot with water and put it on the stove to boil. Tonight's menu was macaroni and cheese with hot dogs, and whatever fruit or vegetable sounded good. Leslie had so much changing in her life that it felt reassuring to prepare the same meal that she had made every Monday night for a long time. As she mindlessly gathered what she needed to make dinner, her thoughts turned to her mother and the secrets that she had kept…all the money she had, the basement, guns…what else? Leslie couldn't help but think about the key in her pocket. What if it unlocked a huge vault full of gold bars? It could be just about anything.

When the water started to boil, Leslie poured the macaroni into the pan, wondering about the bank key. Her phone rang and she saw that it was Michael. "Hello, Michael!" she answered. "Hello to you!" he answered. "I don't know what you said to my mother, but she thinks you are so nice!" Leslie laughed and said, "Well, maybe you haven't noticed, but I AM nice. Your mom was sweet, but a little defensive when it came to Jim. I invited her to come by for a visit tomorrow." Michael laughed. "Well, prepare to listen to her suggestions for how you should decorate. That's what she does, you know." Leslie admitted that she did not know, but she really needed help and looked forward to it.

Leslie changed the subject and told Michael about retiring and Billy's throat punch and deodorant, then the surprises that she kept finding from her mother. "So, she had the pictures digitized?" he asked excitedly. "That's awesome!" Leslie said she wasn't 100% sure, but the drives were labeled and she would take a look tomorrow after going to the bank. "Checking on your accounts?" he asked. "No, I found a small key in the desk downstairs," Leslie replied. "It has the bank's name on it." Michael said he had several patients who used safe deposit boxes at the bank to keep original copies of important documents like birth certificates, so that's probably all it was. Leslie agreed and had to hang up because the macaroni was done.

She called Billy upstairs and they ate together, talking and laughing about the basement and what a nice surprise it was. Billy said he wasn't ready to sleep down there yet, and Leslie said he never had to sleep down there; they could use it as a guest room. Billy finished his homework in the kitchen while Leslie turned on the national news in the living room and decided to call Jim to check in on her father.

Jim was happy to hear from her and admitted that it was kind of fun to have someone around. "It's kind of like having a large toddler, though," he laughed. "He repeats the most random stuff." Leslie heard her Dad say, "Random stuff," and thought it really was like having a toddler around. "Is he okay, though?" she asked. "Tell me honestly if you think he'll ever be able to talk to us." Jim didn't hesitate at all. "He's doing great," he bragged. "It's like something just clicked and he's coming back to us." Leslie asked if Michael showed her dad the pictures that he had and Jim said he did, but Bill didn't seem to remember those two men. "Give it time," he advised. "His memories, good and bad, are all locked up in there." Leslie thanked him for taking care of her dad and said goodnight, then went back to the kitchen as Billy was putting his books away.

"Are you finally done with your homework?" asked Leslie. "It's almost time to get ready for bed." Billy said he was done, but he just needed time to relax his brain for a minute after all that thinking. Leslie suggested that the best way to relax his brain was to eat a little bit of ice cream, and Billy asked if everything was okay. "Sure, everything is fine," Leslie answered. "Why do you ask?" Billy explained that he didn't remember her ever letting him eat ice cream right before bed. "When Grandma got really sick, she did things differently," he said. "She said 'No more rules' because she didn't have time for rules." Leslie thought about it for a second and asked, "So, because I am being spontaneous, you are worried that I'm sick?" Billy said he wasn't sure what 'spontaneous' meant, but he was a little concerned, so Leslie explained everything. After a little orange sherbet, Billy seemed to feel better and went to get ready for bed. 9:00 on the dot.

Leslie suddenly realized how tired she was and how much she had done in one day. Once Billy brushed his teeth and put on his pajamas, she tucked him in and went to get ready for bed, too. When she went downstairs to turn off the lights and TV, she noticed that Steve and Melanie's lights were all on and hoped everything was okay. Leslie thought about Melanie's morning sickness and decided to call tomorrow to check on her, then settled in bed with her journal. She had initially decided to allocate a certain number of pages per day but realized that some days there would be nothing to write and others would be like today. How did she ever have time to work?

As she wrote, she tried to keep things factual and not reveal her feelings too much, worried that someone might read it later. It would have been nice if her mother had kept a journal, recording what had happened in her life. After what Leslie had discovered about her mother in just one day, it really would not be surprising to find diaries or journals. Leslie had always felt that she and her mother were close and shared their feelings and thoughts openly, but maybe she had misjudged her mother. Leslie had felt sorry for Mom, who was never able to get over her husband going missing and assumed dead. Leslie often thought about how much easier life could have been for her mother if she had just moved past it and found another husband.

Leslie really didn't understand how strong her mother was until she became a single mother herself, but she was discovering that there was so much more to this incredible woman who never lost faith in her husband being found alive. It was the most beautiful love story, and Leslie wanted to tell it to the world. She was hoping that Jennifer Tillotson, the energetic young journalist, would see this in the same way so her article would tell a story about love and loyalty, not about how many people her dad killed.

Leslie fell asleep thinking about their story and woke up just before 3 AM because her phone was buzzing. She wondered who in the world would be texting her at that time of the morning and saw Jim Carlson's name on her screen. She read the text: "Call me when you get up in the morning. One of your dad's memories made its way out. The police just left." The police? Oh, no. Leslie texted back as quickly as her tired brain could: "What happened? Do you want me to call now?" Jim replied immediately: "No. He's okay. Let's talk tomorrow while he's at one of his appointments. The good news is that he definitely remembers Tillotson and Mackey, so maybe he can help us find them."

Leslie sat up in bed, her heart and mind racing. How could she go back to sleep now? She didn't want to wake Billy up by doing anything loud, so she decided to just finish writing in her journal. She wrote for over an hour, then checked the alarm to make sure it was set and closed her eyes. She needed to update her list of things to do, but she could do that tomorrow. As Leslie drifted off to sleep, she thought of Tillotson and Mackey and decided to ask Jennifer for more information about her grandfather. Maybe some pictures, too. Whatever might help Bill Lucas get his memory back.

...

Chapter Thirty-Eight

Leslie woke up to Billy shaking her. She sat up and looked at the time and asked how she slept through the alarm. "Maybe it doesn't work anymore," she mused. "Oh, it works," Billy replied. "It's super loud. I turned it off when I went to take a shower. When I got out of the shower and you were still sleeping, I got a mirror and held it under your nose to see if you were breathing. There was steam on it, so I knew you were," he added. "I saw that trick on TV."

Leslie laughed at his ingenuity. She threw on some clothes and brushed her teeth, skipping her shower until later. She helped Billy pack his lunch, checked his backpack to make sure he had what he needed, and they jumped in the car. As they pulled out of the driveway, Leslie noticed a sign in front of Steve and Melanie's house but couldn't see what it said. She made a mental note to look at it later, or at least ask Melanie about it when she called to check on her. She turned her attention back to Billy, who was eating a breakfast bar.

"Hey, buddy!" Leslie exclaimed. "You basically got ready by yourself this morning. Did you remember the deodorant?" Billy nodded his head and smiled. "I'm almost twelve, Mom. I'm practically a teenager." Leslie laughed and thanked Billy for waking her up in time to drive him. "Why were you so tired?" he asked. "Did you stay up too late?" Leslie remembered the text from Jim Carlson and decided that it wasn't something an almost-12-year-old needed to know. "I woke up around 3:00 this morning and just couldn't get back to sleep," she explained, wondering if everything was okay with her father. Billy accepted her answer and finished his breakfast just as they pulled up to the school. "Bye, Mom!" he yelled. "See you later!" Leslie smiled and waved after him. He was growing up so quickly.

As soon as Billy was out the door, Leslie dialed Jim Carlson's number. "What happened last night?" she asked. "Good morning to you, too," replied Jim. "So, remember when Dr. Edwards showed your dad those pictures yesterday and he didn't seem to recall Tillotson? Well, he does. After I had been asleep for a few hours, I woke up to someone yelling and screaming. I jumped out of bed and opened the door to the guest room, not sure what I'd see. Your dad was crouching behind the bed yelling at some imaginary person to 'run', then to 'come back', then to 'get down.' He tried to fight me when I was waking him up. You know, he's a lot stronger than he looks."

Leslie tried to process the scene in her mind. "So, he said all those things in English, without repeating anyone? That's good." Jim replied that it was great that Leslie saw the positive side of that, but this means that they would need to increase his PTSD counseling. "How did you finally stop him?" Leslie asked. Jim explained that he got Bill in a type of bear hug and tried to tell him it was a dream. When he used Bill's Buddhist name, "Erden," he seemed to calm down.

"How did you know it was about Tillotson?" asked Leslie. "Did he actually say his name?" Jim said that Bill kept repeating "Tilly," which is what they called Tillotson, and even mentioned Mackey a couple of times. "Do you think he knows what happened to them?" Leslie wondered aloud. Jim replied that he didn't know for sure, but this was a start. "The frustrating part is that when he finally snapped out of it, he didn't remember much and couldn't tell me about it. It's like the words are somehow locked up when he's awake." Leslie suggested that perhaps they could take her dad to someone who practices hypnosis and Jim laughed. "Maybe we could just take him to a fortune teller."

Leslie changed the subject and asked how the police got involved. "I live in an apartment building…a nice one, with our own security. Apparently, they heard the commotion and thought there was something going on. They thought your dad and I were a couple and they were concerned that this was a 'domestic violence' situation. What the hell is wrong with people?" Leslie laughed and said it was a sign of the times, then thanked Jim for taking care of her dad. Jim suggested that he should call Dr. Edwards to let him know what happened, so Leslie urged him to do that now and call her back later.

After she hung up, Leslie couldn't help but wonder how she was going to handle that type of situation when her dad came home. That scenario would be scary, not just for her but for Billy. She would talk to Michael about it after he and Jim discussed what happened. She pulled in the driveway, still thinking about that, and saw Gary out taking more measurements. She waved to him and thought about how much he had done to help her and Mom over the years. Leslie was really going to miss him.

She walked into the kitchen and saw that her "To Do" lists were still on the kitchen counter. She crossed off what she had done yesterday and made a new list for today, transferring whatever she didn't get done yesterday onto today's list. Satisfied with her organization and ready to begin another day, she jumped in the shower, thinking about what kind of treasure she might find at the bank when she took Mom's key over there.

After showering, Leslie walked past her mother's room and turned on the light. She wasn't sure if she should remove everything now or wait until the renovations began. She pulled a couple of large paintings off the wall and looked around. "I really thought Mom had more paintings in here," she thought aloud. She set the paintings in the corner of the room and covered them with the old bedspread. "Well, at least I have the 'Donate' pile started," she stated proudly, knowing that there were going to be enough items donated to keep the local charities in business. Mom kept everything!

Leslie decided to worry about it later, as she wanted to have time to grab a donut on her way to the bank. She brought a copy of Mom's death certificate and the power of attorney, not sure what kind of paperwork she would need at the bank, and of course the mysterious little key. Leslie didn't remember the bakery having a drive-thru before, but she found it convenient and quick. She savored the chocolate-covered donut, feeling a bit guilty for not buying one for Billy, and pulled into the bank parking lot. Leslie watched a silver car drive past, 99% sure that it was the same one that she had seen near her house and mentally added "Ask Steve about silver car" to today's list.

As she entered the bank, she felt the same way she had when she arrived at the Fisher House. They seemed to know who she was, although she didn't bank there, and asked if she would like something to drink. She was thirsty, so she asked if they had sweet tea and a young lady with beautiful platinum blond hair ran off to get it. Leslie looked around and felt like everyone was staring at her.

The bank president, Clarence Petry, came out of his office to greet her and Leslie asked if this was how they treated everyone. "Well, we are proud of our customer service," he said with a slight lisp that amused Leslie. "For certain guests, though, we go above and beyond. Your mother was one of our most loyal customers, and I've never met a more humble woman. I'm only a few years younger than her, and I can recall her working in the local soup kitchen when we were in high school. She also worked for her stepfather, so she had been saving money for most of her life." Leslie explained that she was an accountant and was embarrassed for not knowing how much money her own mother had, but it really wasn't her business. "Well, it's your business now," explained Mr. Petry. "As she wished and in accordance with her will, that money is now yours. I have a copy of your mother's will and she made her wishes clear. You know, she was quite proud of you." Leslie thanked him for the kind words, swallowing the lump in her throat. "Would you like to see the contents of her safe deposit box?" he asked. With his lisp, it sounded like he said 'boxes,' but Leslie only had one key. She pulled out the key and explained that she had found it yesterday, and Mr. Petry smiled and nodded. He explained that each box has two locks. His key opens the outside lock, and the key held by the bank's guests opens the inside lock. Leslie was amused that customers were referred to as "guests," but it made her feel special.

As they started down the white marble hallway, the young lady with platinum blond hair caught up with Leslie and handed her a bottle of sweet tea and a napkin. "Thank you, Allison," Leslie replied graciously, reading her name off the young lady's name tag. Mr. Petry thanked Allison as well. Such polite people, Leslie thought, as Mr. Petry unlocked a room that contained about 300 safe deposit boxes. There was a table in the center, a big granite slab with a box of tissues, a notepad, and a pen. Mr. Petry told Leslie that she could use the table to hold items as she was taking them out. He explained that the tissues were for emotions or cleaning, whatever was needed, and the notepad and pen were there if she needed to write anything down. "I was thinking that I would just take everything home," Leslie explained. Mr. Petry replied that she could certainly do that, if that's what she ultimately decided to do, but suggested looking through the contents first before deciding to remove anything from its secure location. If there is something valuable or precious, he explained, it would be safer in the fireproof vault than at someone's home. Leslie asked what kind of things people generally kept there and he replied that the most common items were old jewelry and original paperwork, but sometimes the items that people choose to lock up may seem odd to others who don't understand their value. "Like what?" asked Leslie. "What's the oddest thing you have seen in a safe deposit box?" Mr. Petry smiled. "I would never divulge secrets to which I have been entrusted," he stated emphatically. Leslie admired that but wondered if it was like the show she occasionally watched about abandoned storage units. There was some weird stuff stored in those units!

Mr. Petry unlocked the outside door to Box 64 and showed Leslie how her key opened the second door. He showed her a button on the wall to push for assistance, whether that meant asking for more tea or getting copies of documents or whatever. Leslie did her part and opened the box with the key she had found. As she pulled the box out of the space, she realized that it was much larger than she had expected. She saw Mr. Petry opening another outside door farther down the row and assumed that someone else was coming in to access their safe deposit box. He explained that he would give her some privacy and closed the door behind him. Leslie noticed that there were cameras everywhere, so she made sure not to do anything that she didn't want the world to see and opened the box. It appeared to be stereotypical paperwork and jewelry, and Leslie admired some of the beautiful broaches and necklaces. There was a list in a plastic sleeve attached to the jewelry box, explaining the history of each piece. Leslie smiled when she thought of her mother taking the time to do this, and decided that once she had her fence and security system she would take the jewelry home so she could read about it and admire it at her leisure.

There was a lot of paperwork in a file folder, mostly originals of birth and marriage and death certificates from several generations. At the bottom of the folder was a manila envelope that was sealed, and on the front it read "Please do not read until my passing. – Bill, Sr." It did not appear to have ever been opened, so Leslie broke the seal and removed the contents, wondering if her mother had ever opened it. There were black and white photographs of a baby girl and on the back were Aunt Judith's name and some dates that seemed to be from the first few months of her life. Leslie had never seen these photos before, but they were adorable. There was no denying that Aunt Judith was a beautiful baby, but the woman holding her in the pictures was not Grandma Lucas. There was some paperwork in the envelope, and Leslie started reading, curious about the pictures.

The first piece of paper was from a hospital in Ann Arbor, something about Grandma Lucas being diagnosed with ovarian cancer and having a complete hysterectomy. Leslie couldn't read the exact date because the day had been typed over, but the month was March and the year was 1947. Leslie was surprised because she had been told that her grandmother had died of ovarian cancer in 1970. How could that have been possible if her ovaries had been removed 23 years earlier? The date also didn't make sense because Aunt Judith was born in 1949, which was two years after the supposed hysterectomy, until Leslie read the next item in the envelope: Certificate of Adoption. It was dated August 1, 1949.

•••

Chapter Thirty-Nine

Leslie looked around the room, feeling like she was doing something she shouldn't. There were cushioned benches along one wall, and she took the Certificate of Adoption paperwork and sat down. This would explain why Aunt Judith didn't resemble either of her parents! Leslie read through the paperwork carefully, which was notarized and signed. "Judith Ann Lucas" was born "Judith Louise Perkins," and she was from Jackson, Mississippi! The birth mother's name was listed, but there was no father. Leslie laughed at first but then she could hear Mom's favorite saying, always there in the back of her conscience: "If you can be anything, be kind." Leslie wanted to be anything *but* kind, but she also didn't want to be the one who caused Aunt Judith to jump off a bridge. She went back to the table and set the adoption paperwork aside so she could get a copy. Mr. Petry was right about the value of having a safe deposit box and Leslie immediately understood why Mom didn't keep this paperwork at the house. Wow.

As she sifted through the remaining contents of the box, Leslie wondered if Aunt Judith knew that she was adopted. Leslie also wondered if Mom had ever known about the adoption, since the manila envelope didn't appear to have been opened. There were other items in the box that brought up more questions, such as life insurance policies and several stocks that Leslie would need to investigate. There was a small plastic box at the bottom that appeared to be ancient, yellowed and cracking. Leslie opened it carefully and there was a lock of her hair from her first haircut as well as all her baby teeth, along with stories and explanations. Although it was a bit creepy, she was flattered that her mother had kept these personal items for so many years and never said a word.

There was a tiny envelope at the bottom with "Bill" written on it, and Leslie was intrigued to find a small key inside that resembled her mother's safe deposit box key. She looked at the back of the key from the envelope and saw that the number was 12, which did not match the 64 on Mom's key. Leslie looked around and realized that Mr. Petry had opened the outside lock to Box 12, knowing that she was going to find the key. She opened the inside door for Box 12 with the new key, her heart pounding as if she were robbing the bank. This box was much smaller than the one from Box 64, and Leslie took it to the table to find out what was inside.

She opened it up, expecting more paperwork and hoping not to find more teeth and hair. There were two wooden cars (one smashed and one intact), an issue of *Boys' Life* magazine from June 1955, and a large unsealed envelope, each in a sealed plastic bag. Leslie opened the bag with the envelope and pulled out the contents carefully. There were several certificates and letters from the Boy Scouts of America, two $100 savings bonds, and a torn piece of notebook paper which simply read "Bill's Scout awards and letters, 1954-1958." It looked like a woman's handwriting, so Leslie assumed that it was written by Grandma Lucas a long time ago. The bonds were from 1954 and 1955, and initially Leslie, being the accountant that she was, wondered if they were still valuable. The thought dissipated quickly as she realized that she could never cash them in. Their true value was that they could help bring back some memories for her dad.

Leslie wasn't sure what to make of the homemade cars that felt so much heavier than they appeared to be and turned her attention to the magazine. Why would they save this one issue? On the front cover, there was a picture of a boy who looked a lot like Billy, holding his Pinewood Derby car and smiling. The caption read "Lucas Wins Again!" Leslie stared at it, then looked back at the cars. One of them was clearly the small red car held in the photo and Leslie was quite intrigued. She turned to the article inside the magazine, moving the brittle pages ever so carefully. By the time she finished reading the 3-page article, she was in tears. Her dad had won the National Pinewood Derby TWICE!

Bill Lucas was a curious and competitive kid who loved cars from an early age. After hearing about a new competition where Cub Scouts made their own cars and raced them, Bill started asking questions about how he could be part of it. After convincing his parents to sign him up for Cub Scouts, Bill immediately started creating his derby car. His father explained that it was supposed to be an activity that they shared, but Bill wanted to do this on his own. His father helped put on the wheels and made some suggestions, but Bill did everything else.

After winning the local and regional races, Bill easily won the state race and moved on to Nationals. His father proudly accompanied him, but his mother stayed home with his little sister. "I would wish you luck, honey, but I already know you're going to win," his mother assured Bill as they headed out for the long drive to California. Judith cried for the entire week that they were gone and gave Bill the silent treatment when he returned because he was getting so much attention. Three days after Bill returned home as National champion, Judith smashed his derby car with a hammer.

Although his parents were upset, Bill decided to view it as an opportunity to make a better car. He worked for almost a full year, making subtle adjustments and changing the color to red because all the fastest cars seemed to be red. It worked. He breezed through the local, regional, and state competitions, but the National race had heated up due to so many competitors. A couple of the cars were disqualified for being too heavy, and this time Bill won by a very small margin. But he won. The photographers snapped his picture and asked about next year, but Bill said he was moving up to Boy Scouts and wouldn't be participating.

When they returned to Michigan after the second National championship, Bill asked his father to put the car where Judith couldn't ruin it. Bill Sr. promised his son that he would keep it safe forever and secured a safe deposit box after he found Judith looking for the car "just to play with it." He added the magazine article and other awards as they were earned, planning to give these items back to Bill when he got older and perhaps had a son of his own.

Leslie thought this would be a great way for her dad to bond with Billy, who also loved cars. Leslie imagined them making a Pinewood Derby car together and her heart sored. These tangible items could also help her dad recover some of his memories, and having the actual cars was much better than just having pictures.

Leslie decided that she would get rid of Box 12 and take those items with her. She pressed the button marked "Assistance" and told the sweet young lady who answered that she would like to get copies of a document and take the items from the smaller box home. Leslie put everything back in Box 64, except for the adoption papers and pictures. Allison, who had brought the tea for Leslie, rushed into the room with a large bag and explained that Leslie could put the items she was taking home in the bag. As Leslie filled the bag, Allison took the Adoption Certificate to copy it.

Mr. Petry appeared and asked Leslie if she had any questions. She had a lot of questions, but simply replied that there were some items for her to explore another day. He noticed that the other box was on the table and explained to Leslie that Bill Sr., Leslie's Grandpa Lucas, had put those items there for safekeeping and seemed to have forgotten that they were there. Susan kept paying the fee to keep both boxes after Mr. Lucas passed away, but there was no record of her ever opening Box 12. Although it had been occupied for over 50 years, the rate never changed so the monthly charge was still only 50 cents. Leslie thought about how nice it was that the bank treated their "guests" so fairly and decided to consider switching her other accounts there.

Allison returned and handed Leslie the copy in a file folder. Leslie handed her the key for Box 12 and explained that she would no longer need that box, as it was empty, but would probably be keeping Box 64. Allison said she would be happy to remove the charge from Leslie's account immediately and left the room. Mr. Petry asked if Leslie would be keeping her accounts there or moving them and was relieved to hear that she had no intention of changing anything yet.

Leslie put the original Adoption Certificate back in the safe deposit box and put the copy and pictures in her plastic bag with the contents of Box 12. She was excited to show the cars to Billy and hoped it would spark his interest. She thanked Mr. Petry for his assistance and was impressed that he walked her all the way to the front door and opened it for her. Everyone who worked there was smiling and waving, and Leslie found it quite comforting. She understood now why her mother never wanted to switch banks, even when several opened closer to her house. These people treated Leslie like royalty, and she was sure that they had done the same for Mom.

Leslie put her plastic bag on the passenger seat and headed home, wondering what to do with this new information about Aunt Judith. If Mom were around, Leslie would have gone to her for advice. Sadly, that was no longer an option so Leslie asked herself what Mom would do. Before telling anyone else, Leslie decided that the appropriate thing to do was to tell Aunt Judith herself and then go from there. She pressed Aunt Judith's number on her control panel and it took a few rings before there was an answer.

The person who answered was Uncle Jack, not Aunt Judith, so Leslie wondered if she had dialed the home phone instead of Aunt Judith's cell phone. "Hi, Uncle Jack," Leslie began. "How are you?" Uncle Jack was usually much nicer than Aunt Judith, so Leslie decided that this wasn't so bad. "Hello, Leslie," he answered coldly. "I'm sorry to hear about your mother, but I imagine she left you with enough money that you'll forget about her soon enough." Leslie was shocked at his comments but realized that Uncle Jack was slurring his words. "Are you drunk?" she inquired. He laughed heartily and explained that he's always drunk. "Where's Aunt Judith?" asked Leslie. "Is she there?" Uncle Jack said he had no idea and hung up the phone.

Leslie wasn't sure what to do but decided that she would just call back later. Who in the world is drunk at 10:30 in the morning? She was still wondering about it when she pulled into her garage, pleased to see the familiar face of Gary working on the security system. "Hey, Gary," she greeted him. He smiled as he approached and said he should have the system in today. "Did you bring me a receipt?" asked Leslie. Gary handed her the receipt, showing what the system had cost. Leslie thanked him and asked if he knew anyone who was drunk by 10:30 in the morning. "Not off the top of my head," he replied. "Is that what you're planning to do with your retirement?" Leslie laughed and told him what happened when she called her Aunt Judith's phone a few minutes ago. "It's probably better that she wasn't there," Gary responded. "I've never understood how she came from that family; the rest of them were such wonderful people." Leslie was having a difficult time not telling her secret but chose not to tell Gary. She was trying to be fair and kind like Mom would ask her to be and needed to tell Aunt Judith first.

Leslie went inside to get her checkbook to pay Gary back for the security system and added $200 for installation fees. She didn't want to forget to pay him, so she walked right back out to the garage and handed it to him. She thanked him and walked away, ignoring his

"Hey, this is too much money!" and "I'm not even finished with it yet." Leslie knew that he would say those things and just said, "Okay, okay," as she went back inside to tidy up.

Since she hadn't really cleaned her house in weeks, Leslie expected it to be dirty but it really wasn't. Someone had definitely dusted the bookshelves and tables, and the logical choice was Melanie, who had probably done it while Leslie was in Maryland. Leslie remembered that she needed to call her to see how the pregnancy was going and ask about the sign in their yard, so she called while she was clearing things off the counters. Melanie sounded awful, which most women do in their first trimester, as she answered with a sleepy "Hello?" Leslie apologized for waking her, and Melanie explained that she didn't think she had slept all night so she was just trying to nap. Leslie started listing all the morning sickness cures she had read about, but Melanie stopped her, saying that her morning sickness was actually the least of her worries right now.

Leslie found that getting information from a tired pregnant woman was quite a chore, but she finally got to the root of the problem. Yesterday, Steve had received a letter in the mail that he'd been anticipating for about a year: he had been selected to attend the State Police Academy. "Oh, Melanie, that is great news!" said Leslie, excited for her young neighbor to start his career. "When does he leave?" Melanie explained that he had just over two months before his report date, and with a 5-month training period, he was due to graduate only three days before her due date. "Is that why you didn't sleep?" asked Leslie. "Are you worried about the timing?"

"Well, I was worried about the timing," Melanie explained, "but then things got worse. Someone from a real estate office showed up with a 'For Sale' sign and just put it in the yard. They didn't come up to the house or anything, so I called our landlord for an explanation. It turns out that he is in Hospice care and his daughter has a Power of Attorney to sell his properties. If she doesn't get a buyer, or at least some leads, in 90 days, the house will go to auction. Either way, we are going to have to move and I doubt that we can afford anything else in this area; our landlord gave us a cheap rate because Steve had recently been discharged from the Marines. We have lived here for three years!"

Leslie had a lot of questions, but honestly did not realize that they were renting. She thought they had bought the house. Melanie explained that she was worried about having to move, being alone for most of the pregnancy, the extra money Steve needed for a long list of items to take to the Academy, and the fact that she wasn't even sure how she felt about him becoming a police officer. "Wow, that's a lot to think about," agreed Leslie. "I have a few things to get done here, but maybe you and Steve could stop over later tonight to talk about this. We will put together a plan to make sure everything is covered, okay? Since I'm retired now, my new job will be Neighborhood Busybody. Go eat some soda crackers and take a nap." Melanie thanked Leslie and hung up.

Leslie continued cleaning up the kitchen, thinking about Melanie and Steve and how she could help, but then her mind drifted to Aunt Judith. She wrote on her list of things to do "Call Aunt Judith," then grabbed the cleaning supplies for her bathroom to make sure it was fresh when Linda stopped by.

•••

Chapter Forty

After Leslie cleaned the bathroom and straightened things up a bit, she realized that she was starving. She opted for a ham and cheese sandwich and some chips and was just finishing them when the doorbell rang. Leslie opened the door and there was Linda, even more beautiful than she appeared in pictures. "Hello, Linda! It's nice to meet you in person!" greeted Leslie. Linda thanked her and walked right in. "You really look like Susan," she commented. Before Leslie could reply, Linda spoke again. "This place is certainly trapped in time," she announced as she looked around. "I can't believe your mother still has that macramé owl plant hanger. That thing is older than you are!" Leslie had honestly forgotten that it was even there and just nodded.

"Have you ever seen my show?" Linda asked. Leslie was confused. "What show do you mean?" she asked. Linda laughed heartily and explained that she had her own show. Leslie shook her head. "No, I'm sorry, but I haven't," she answered. "I really don't watch much television." Linda suggested that it might be a good idea to pull up a few episodes to see what kind of work she does, and Leslie promised to do that. Without hesitation, Linda looked around and headed upstairs. "It's up here, right?" she asked as she barged right in. Leslie managed a quick "Yes" as she tried to keep up. Linda turned on the light and gasped.

"Oh, Leslie, sweetheart," Linda started, "I am not trying to make you feel bad about the choices that your mother made with her décor, so please don't take my comments personally. Susan was a gem, but she was quite thrifty. This room doesn't look much different than it did fifty years ago, but I have no doubt that I can transform this little time capsule into a retreat for your father. Do you know what you want to do in here?" Leslie looked around. "Honestly, I have no idea," she replied. "I just met my dad a few days ago. You probably know more about him than I do." Linda's smile looked forced, and she mumbled something about them figuring it out. She suggested that they take measurements first and reached into her bag for a notepad and measuring tape. "What's that pile under the blanket?"

asked Linda. "More old furniture?" Leslie explained that it was just a few items that she was going to donate, and that she would move it out in the next day or two.

Leslie asked if they could talk about other things after they discussed the plans for decorating, and Linda did not beat around the bush. "You mean about Jim and how he broke my heart?" she asked. "Not just that, but whatever you want" Leslie replied softly. "By the way, he's still so much in love with you, and he doesn't drink anymore." Linda changed the subject and launched right into her suggestions for the room. "Whatever you want to do is fine with me," replied Leslie. "Would you like something to drink?" Linda asked for bottled water, preferably Dasani at room temperature, and Leslie replied that was exactly what she drinks. Linda smiled in approval and Leslie went downstairs to get the water.

As she headed into the kitchen, Gary was walking in. Leslie asked if he would also like a bottle of water. He said that would be great, and that he needed Leslie's phone so he could program the security codes into it. He asked Leslie who was visiting and pointed to the bottles of wine and champagne on the counter. "Wow! You weren't kidding about day drinking, huh?" he asked. Leslie explained that the bottles just kept arriving, mostly from people she had never even met, and she wasn't sure what to do with them. Gary suggested that she save them for the party that she would throw for her dad when he got home. "Whose blue Lexus is that out there?" he asked. "Did you get another car without telling me?" Leslie laughed. "No, the car belongs to Linda Edwards," she explained. "She's going to help me redecorate Mom's room." Gary cocked his head and squinted his eyes a little. "*The* Linda Edwards? The designer?" he asked. Leslie wondered if she was the only person who had never seen Linda's show before. "Yes, that one," she replied. "How do you know her?" Gary said he watched her show every Monday night on TV.

As if on cue, Linda strolled into the kitchen. "Oh, you watch my show?" she asked Gary. He just stared at Linda with his mouth open, obviously mesmerized. Leslie handed a bottle of water to Linda and hit Gary in the arm with his water to break the spell. "Yes, Ma'am," he replied. He thanked Leslie and said he was going to check on the security system. "Is that your handyman?" Linda inquired. Leslie explained that he was their neighbor, but also their handyman and mechanic. Linda said she needed a new one and asked if Gary would be willing to drive the 20 miles to her house. "Probably, but he's moving in the next couple of weeks," Leslie explained. "He's heading out to Colorado to be closer to his daughter." Linda suggested that perhaps someone just as handy will move in, and Leslie didn't think about what she was saying until the words were out of her mouth: "Jim bought Gary's house."

Linda blinked her eyes dramatically. "Jim is moving back to Michigan?" she asked incredulously. "He swore he'd never do that." Leslie saw the opportunity to put in a good word and suggested that Jim said and did a lot of stupid things when he was younger. "We all did," agreed Linda quietly, as she gazed out the window. "Thanks for the water, Leslie," she mumbled as she headed back toward the stairs. "I will need to do some measuring and drawing, then I'll show you what I come up with, okay?" Leslie suggested that she leave Linda to her creativity so she could think. "I'll be here in the kitchen if you need me," Leslie added as Linda disappeared upstairs. Leslie still had a couple of hours before she needed to go pick up Billy, so she decided to work on the boxes of mail that she had picked up the day before.

After about an hour, Leslie had a trash bag full of junk mail and a small pile of bills to be paid. Linda walked in quietly and cleared her throat. "So, are you ready to hear my plans for the bedroom?" she asked excitedly. "Yes!" Leslie replied. "I can't wait to get started." Linda handed her a drawing and explained what she visualized for the bedroom. She assured Leslie that she had some great local contractors who would do everything except the decorating, which Linda would be doing herself.

Leslie loved Linda's ideas and couldn't believe how quickly she came up with them but requested to add one more thing. She wanted to replace the window overlooking the garden with a sliding glass door, adding a small deck with steps down to the yard. Since her father was so fond of gardening, this would allow him quick access to the garden area. Linda loved the idea and quickly sketched that in. Leslie asked how Linda wanted to start the process for this project and what it was going to cost her. Linda explained that she would need to have one of her contractors give an estimate for the work and that she was donating her time and would not be charging

Leslie. Leslie tried to argue but Linda shut her down. "We'll talk more about this later," she said. "Let's get our contractors out here. What's your availability look like this week?" Leslie offered that she had nothing concrete planned because she just retired, and Linda said that was the perfect availability.

Linda walked out of the kitchen to make some calls to her contractors, and Leslie grabbed a small pad of paper. She wrote a reminder note for herself, "Look up Linda's show," and wondered if Gary had used any ideas from Linda's show when he was renovating the basement. As soon as Linda was off the phone, Leslie mentioned that Gary had done some extensive redecorating in the basement and asked Linda if she wanted to see what he had done. Linda followed Leslie downstairs as she explained that her mother had created a room for her pictures and pointed out the lights on the walls and ceiling. Once they reached the bottom, Linda seemed to stop listening as she pulled out an old photo album. "Wow. This is from my first marriage," she explained as she plopped down at the desk. Leslie had no idea what to say.

Before Leslie knew what was happening, Linda had her head in her hands, sobbing uncontrollably. Leslie grabbed a box of tissues from the downstairs bedroom and put them on the desk, then put her hand on Linda's shoulder. "Let's go upstairs and look at this album," Leslie suggested. Linda nodded silently and carried the album upstairs like it was a baby. They sat on the couch and opened the album, and Leslie couldn't believe how absolutely beautiful Linda was in the pictures. Jim was quite handsome, too, and they looked like a fairytale couple. Linda told Leslie how they met, how he proposed, and all about the wedding.

"I thought I was living in a dream," Linda explained. "I had married this handsome, educated Marine pilot who treated me like a queen. I thought we would have children and grow old together…" Her voice trailed off a little and then she spoke up again. "He was home on leave when he got word of your dad going missing, so he cut his leave short to go back and start looking. I was lucky that he wasn't shot down over there, that he returned alive, but he never really returned. Not all of him. He blamed himself for your dad's disappearance and I tried to convince him that it wasn't his fault. He kept drinking more and more, and he seemed to stop caring about me. He got mad at the silliest things, and I just couldn't take it. Women didn't often file for divorce back then, but I had to get out. I couldn't help him, and I was honestly afraid he was going to die. For a few years, I felt like I had made the right decision, but I really missed the Jim that I married. Still do, I guess."

Leslie looked at the pictures as she listened to Linda's story. They looked so happy. "Alcohol sure tears a lot of families apart," Leslie lamented. "You know, my Uncle Jack was drunk this morning when I called to talk to Aunt Judith." Linda was surprised to hear that Leslie had called to talk to her aunt and complimented her for being the better person. "Well, I actually had some information that I thought she'd want," Leslie explained, "but she wasn't available." Linda seemed to snap out of her sadness and smiled at Leslie. "If you don't mind my asking, what kind of information did you have for her?" she inquired. Leslie said she would show her and ran to retrieve the Certificate of Adoption from the plastic bag they had given her at the bank. She explained how she found the key and told Linda about everything else she had found.

Linda stared at the document for a few seconds and then threw her head back and howled with laughter. "Oh, my God!" Linda finally managed. "Judith isn't your dad's biological sister! This explains so much." Leslie agreed and commented that she didn't know if Aunt Judith was even aware, then looked at her watch. "Oh, I have to go get Billy," she announced. "You are welcome to come along or stay here, or whatever you choose to do." Linda appreciated Leslie's hospitality, but said she needed to go run some errands. She left the photo album on the coffee table and told Leslie that the contractors would be there in two days, and she would return then. Leslie thanked her for her help and watched her drive off, followed by that silver car that she had seen so often lately. She grabbed her purse and headed to the school to pick up Billy, eager to hear how his first full day of wearing deodorant had gone.

•••

Chapter Forty-One

As Leslie drove to Billy's school, she dialed Katrina's number but it went right to voicemail. With everything going on, she wanted to keep Katrina in the loop and available to answer questions. Plus, now she had more time to spend with her old friend and it would be nice to hang out like they did when they were younger. Leslie left a short message and asked her to call back when she had a chance. The pickup line at school seemed more orderly today, and Leslie realized that more people waved at her than usual. One friendly lady even rolled down her window and waved a small American flag. Leslie smiled and waved back, reminding herself to follow up with Jennifer Tillotson about that press conference.

Billy was happy to see Leslie, and she noticed that he smelled better than he had in a long time. "Hey, how did that deodorant work?" Leslie asked when he got in the car. "It's awesome, Mom," replied Billy. "Girls are nicer when you don't smell like dirty socks." Leslie laughed at his firm grasp of the obvious and was surprised when he asked her how her day went. Leslie told him about going to the bank and finding some interesting things, and about Linda coming over to make some plans for renovating the bedroom. "It's sad that Grandma is gone," Billy commented, "but it is exciting that I am getting a Grandpa for a replacement." Leslie smiled at the wisdom and acceptance in his statement, and just nodded her head in agreement.

As they pulled in the driveway, Gary had the garage door open and was testing the cameras. He waved at Leslie and Billy, but he was obviously deep in thought so they didn't bother him. Billy took his backpack inside and set it down next to the plastic bag from the bank. "What's in there?" he asked. Leslie showed him the Pinewood Derby cars and the old *Boys' Life* magazine, which Billy thought was awesome. "Can I take this to my Scout meeting and show them?" he asked excitedly. Leslie said she would consider it but didn't want to push too much about the Derby cars. She said they would talk about it after he finished his homework. After the groaning subsided, Billy pulled out his math book and said he had a lot of homework. "It's a good thing I'm smart," he added. "I feel sorry for people who don't understand math. They must really hate homework." Leslie had never really thought about what Billy might want to do for a career, but if he liked math then maybe he would become an accountant like her. "Hey, I didn't realize you like math so much," she remarked. "Maybe you'll become an accountant." Billy looked like he'd just eaten something rotten. "I didn't say I like it," he explained. "I said I understand it. I think I might want to be a pilot."

Leslie's phone rang before she could reply. It was Katrina, calling her back. Leslie was happy to hear her voice and eager to fill her in on everything going on, especially the latest discovery about Aunt Judith, so she went into the living room to talk. Billy sat down at the kitchen table to do his homework, oblivious to the conversation that Leslie was having with her friend/attorney. Katrina said what was on her mind and could not stop laughing about the Adoption Certificate. "Oh, please let me be the one to tell her," Katrina begged. "I'll be tactful." After her laughter subsided, she asked Leslie when she could come by and really catch up. Their conversation was interrupted by another incoming call, so Leslie suggested that Katrina come by any time that works and clicked over to the other call. It was Michael.

"Oh, hello, Michael," she answered. "Hello, yourself," he replied. "You are not on speaker phone today. Your father was already here, and I'm quite concerned about that dream he had." Leslie agreed that it was scary and asked how she should handle that type of situation when her dad comes home. "Well, I understand that Jim bought out your neighbor and he will be right next door. Jim said he is fine with your dad staying with him if it would be easier, but I was wondering how you feel about that." Leslie explained that she wanted her dad to truly come home to the house that still has his name on the deed, but agreed that the decision would be his.

"I did have an interior designer here making plans for the renovations today," Leslie explained. "Apparently, your mother is a well-known celebrity." Michael laughed. "I thought you knew," he replied. "I'm so used to people who meet me asking about my mother that I assume everyone knows her. She can be a bit much, so I hope she was kind." Leslie said it went well and that she found Linda to be beautiful and funny and quite emotional.

"Seriously?" asked Michael. "Are we talking about the same lady?" Leslie explained what had happened with the photo album and how they had talked. She suggested that perhaps Linda had just never been able to fill that hole in her heart. "She's aware that her loneliness made her unhappy, perhaps even depressed," Leslie continued. "She even suggested that she's the reason that you studied Psychology." Michael said he couldn't argue with that. "Look at you, amateur psychologist, figuring out my mother on day one," he teased. "It took me years." Leslie suggested that if he had known about Jim, it would have been a lot easier. "Yeah, I guess," he replied. "I wonder if my dad knew." Leslie replied that it didn't really matter at this point, and asked Michael how he felt about Linda and Jim being reunited. "Hey, I am all for my mother being happy," he responded. "Plus, I like Jim; he's hilarious. A little intimidating, but still hilarious." Leslie was relieved to hear that, and asked, "So, did Mr. Hilarious tell you that the police thought he and my dad were a gay couple?" She didn't hear a response, so she asked, "Michael, are you there?" All Leslie could hear was laughter and what sounded like Michael pounding on his desk. "Hang on, hang on," was all he could manage. Finally, he got himself under control and explained that Jim did not tell him that, but he looked forward to asking him about it tomorrow.

Leslie informed Michael that Linda would be returning the day after tomorrow, as her contractors would be there to start renovations. "Did she tell you how much she charges?" he asked. "I can't believe people pay that much for a designer." Leslie explained that Linda was not charging her and Michael asked what kind of magic wand she had waved. He'd never heard of his mother working pro bono, not even for family members. Leslie said she was just lucky and promised not to take it for granted. Michael thanked her for being so gracious with his mother and for giving him the biggest laugh he'd had in a long time. "I can't wait to talk to Jim tomorrow," he said. "I'll bet he was so mad." Leslie promised that she would call him in a couple of days, but she wasn't sure if he heard her over his own laughter.

She walked into the kitchen to check on Billy. "Who was that laughing on the phone?" asked Billy. "I could hear it in here." Leslie explained that it was one of her dad's doctors, and Billy said he didn't know that being a doctor was so much fun. "Maybe I should be a doctor instead of a pilot," he mused. "You do whatever makes you happy," Leslie advised. "Just do something." Billy went back to his homework as Gary walked into the kitchen.

"Okay, we're all set," he announced. He showed Leslie how the system worked, how to log in on her phone, and how to check the cameras on the monitor. He had the monitor facing away from Billy's spot at the table and said he did that on purpose because he knows how short Billy's attention span is. "There's nothing wrong with my hearing," Billy chimed in. "I can hear you talking about me." Gary laughed and said it was nothing bad, and admitted that his attention span is short, too. He had a few little projects to do at his house, so he told Leslie to check out the system for the next few days and let him know if she had any questions. "Oh, one more thing," he added. "I've noticed a silver car around the past few days and I wrote the plate number down for you." Leslie thanked him and explained that Steve was having one of his police buddies run the plate. "You're always a step ahead," Gary said. "I like that."

When Gary left, Billy said to Leslie, "I think you're getting more popular, Mom. You're on the phone a lot and people are here all the time." Leslie said that being "popular" isn't important as an adult, and there are just more people around because there is a lot going on. Before she could finish voicing her opinion, the doorbell rang. "See what I mean?" asked Billy. "Popular." Leslie opened the door to find Steve and Melanie standing on the porch. "You know, you two can walk in any time," Leslie explained. Steve explained that he wasn't sure about the new security system and didn't want to set it off. Leslie thanked him for his consideration and acknowledged the fact that she needed some time to get used to having it. She invited them into the living room so Billy could finish his homework, and Steve messed up Billy's hair as he walked by. Billy yelled, "Hey!" but continued with his Math problems.

As they sat down in the living room, Steve told Leslie that his friend had run the plate for the silver "stalker" car, and it came back as a Federal Government plate. Unfortunately, that is the only information they could get because federal plates aren't traceable for the city police. Leslie asked if he'd write down the plate number so she could ask a friend who works for the federal government. He checked his phone and wrote it down on the pad of paper Leslie had given him. She flipped the page in case she needed to write anything else down.

"Will you be able to run federal plates when you work for the State Police?" she asked. Steve said he wasn't sure, then added that he hadn't accepted the offer of employment yet because the timing was awful. "Well, isn't this what you've wanted to do for a long time?" Leslie asked, confused about his response. Steve explained that he would graduate just a few days before the baby is due, and that meant that he would miss most of the pregnancy, leaving Melanie alone to handle everything. If the house was sold before he left, they'd have to move somewhere. He also had a lot of extra items to purchase and didn't have a lot of extra money.

Leslie had been taking a few notes as Steve talked. She could sense the conflicting emotions and agreed that he and Melanie had a lot on their plates, but she wanted to put the young couple at ease. "I know I sound like an old lady, but opportunities don't always come along at a convenient time," she began. "When my mother died, I already had so much on my mind when I got the call that they found my dad. The timing was horrible, but it's something I'd been wanting for my whole life, so I'll have to take everything one step at a time because it's worth it. You can do the same because I'm here to help you."

Steve and Melanie smiled at each other, and he thanked Leslie for being so generous. "Okay, so let's take your issues one at a time: First, the issue with your house. Do you want to stay there?" Steve said they did, but they couldn't afford a down payment, and they were renting for only $600/month, probably cheaper than a house payment. He explained that their landlord had served in the Korean War, and he had a soft spot for other veterans. He had reduced the rent to thank Steve for his service. Leslie asked if he had looked into a VA loan to buy the house, remembering from a presentation she attended with her mother that they usually don't require a down payment. He wasn't sure how it worked, but he promised to check into it right away.

"Next issue on the list," said Leslie. "The items you need to buy for the Academy. I just inherited more money than I could ever spend. You're putting up my fence and I'm paying you for your time, so I'll just factor in some extra money to pay for whatever you need to buy. I know you'll finish the fence as soon as you can. Just don't tell Tyler what I'm paying you because he won't be making the same. Sound good?" Steve said that would be great and he started looking a lot more relaxed. Melanie went to get more tissues to blow her nose because she was crying again.

As Melanie came back with more tissues, Leslie continued. "So, Steve, I know you're worried about Melanie being alone while you're gone. Regardless of what happens with your house, Melanie has me and Billy here and she can stay at our house if she chooses. We have that extra bedroom downstairs that Gary redid, and on weekends she can go home with you or you can come here with her. My father will be here by then, but I think we'll have plenty of room, with the basement being used as living space now. The only problem I see is that we only have one bathroom. We can talk more about it, but we'll figure it out as we go." Melanie blew her nose and nodded her head.

"Steve, I know you're worried about missing most of the pregnancy," Leslie continued. "In a couple of months, you may not see that as such a bad thing, depending how things go," she teased, "but we can take pictures and videos, and I can go with Melanie to doctor's appointments. You'll be around for the next kid. I will be the surrogate grandmother, I guess." Leslie suddenly felt old and remembered how emotionally vulnerable she was when she was pregnant, especially when she was packing up to move.

Leslie put the last cup from the kitchen cupboard into the box, taped it up, and wrote "Cups" on it. "You don't think that's too heavy?" asked Susan, concerned for Leslie's pregnancy. "It's fine, Mom," Leslie answered. "Besides, Mark can move all the heavy ones." Susan bit her tongue and nodded, wondering where Mark was while his pregnant wife was packing up the house. "At least you're going to Virginia, and not some other country," Susan finally managed. "With so many veterans' events in DC, I can kill two birds with one stone when I go to DC and then to visit you." The idea of killing birds with stones made Leslie sad and she started tearing up. Susan was adept at reading Leslie's mood, even if she wasn't always sure where it was coming from and changed the subject immediately.

"What are you going to do with the rest of your season tickets for Michigan football?" Susan inquired. "Do you want me to find someone to take them?" Leslie explained that her friend Katrina was going to use them. "After the first two games, especially that loss to Appalachian State, I didn't know if I'd be going to any more games this year," Leslie continued. "It's halfway through the season now and they've won the rest of the games so far, but I think it might be Carr's last year." The thought of her alma mater losing their coach could turn into more tears, so Susan steered the conversation away again.

"Did I tell you that Grandpa Joe came in to see me at the library the other day?" asked Susan as she grabbed another box to load for moving. "I told him that you're moving, and he was a bit surprised, but he knows you'll be fine. Just make sure you go visit him before you leave town." Leslie said she would do that and reminded her mother to make sure she takes him every Wednesday for his hot fudge sundae. "I'm going to miss taking him," Leslie admitted, "but I think I'll find a place to go for ice cream out there and try to go on Wednesdays; it will make me feel closer to him." This time Susan couldn't deflect the tears and Leslie started sobbing. "How am I going to be away from you and Grandpa Joe?" she wailed. "It's just not normal to be away from the people you love." Susan hugged her and explained that nobody knew that more than she does. "I'm sorry, Mom," Leslie sniffed, realizing what she had said. "I am going to work really hard to one day be as strong as you are."

Leslie remembered her tear-filled pregnancy with amusement as Melanie broke into tears again, as one might expect. Leslie wasn't prepared for Steve to do the same, though. She had never seen this side of him, and she knew that he didn't like feeling vulnerable or indebted to anyone and didn't want to dwell on it. She suggested that she should grab some water for everyone and promised she would be right back, giving them a couple of minutes to discuss what she had just proposed. Leslie took her time getting the bottles of water in the kitchen and handed one to Billy. She opened a package of Oreos and held it out to him. "How many can I have?"

he inquired. "As many as you can grab in one handful," Leslie answered. "Really?" Billy asked. "Mom, are you sure you haven't been drinking?" Leslie said she was sure and gave him a napkin for his handful of cookies.

She returned to the living room and handed Steve and Melanie each a bottle of water. "Would you like some Oreos?" she offered. Melanie put her hand over her mouth and Steve laughed. "I'll take a few, thank you," he replied. "The scent of them makes Melanie sick to her stomach, like everything else." Leslie said she would eat a few extra for Melanie but also offered to get her some crackers. "I'm fine, really," Melanie replied. "I'm still processing what you said. Are you serious about me staying here? I don't think I've ever even been in your basement." Steve asked Leslie if he could show Melanie the space that Gary had redecorated, and Leslie suggested that he give her the grand tour. She asked Steve if he could create an estimate for how much she should pay Gary for the labor while he was down there.

"What are they doing?" asked Billy, as he watched Steve and Melanie head to the basement. "Oh, Steve is showing Melanie how cool the basement looks now," Leslie explained. "If you want to take a break from homework and go down there, maybe you can help him." With a quick "Heck yes!" Billy jumped off the bar stool and ran down the stairs to help Steve. Leslie followed, thinking about how busy it was going to be to have her dad and Melanie both here, but it would only be a temporary situation. She was actually looking forward to it.

•••

Chapter Forty-Two

As Billy showed Melanie the Craft Room and the redesigned bedroom, she couldn't believe how beautiful it was. "The only thing missing is a bathroom," she commented. "Hey, Steve, could you put in a bathroom?" asked Leslie, as she handed him the paper and pen. "Gary will be leaving for Colorado soon and probably won't have time." Steve said he needed to get the fence done first, but then he could do it. He was going from room to room, asking Leslie what had been done in each and writing down the approximate time it might take for each task.

Melanie was really impressed by the scrapbooks and photo albums, and even more impressed when Leslie showed her the card catalog with all the thumb drives and explained that she wanted to put together a PowerPoint presentation for her father. Melanie said she would love to help, since she was creative and technologically savvy, which was a relief for Leslie. "Can you start on it tomorrow?" she asked. "I don't expect you to work for free, and I'll gladly pay you for the time it takes."

Melanie suggested that buying the items that Steve needed for the Academy and allowing her to stay there would be payment enough, and Leslie reluctantly agreed. "So, do you think you could stay in this basement?" Leslie asked. Melanie said she would be fine, but wondered about how cold it would be in the winter. "The fireplace is almost finished," Leslie explained, "so when Steve is home on the weekends maybe he can chop some firewood. I don't really know how cold it gets down here, but I'll make sure you don't freeze. Of course, I don't expect you to just stay in the basement. You're welcome to be upstairs with us."

Steve came in with his pad of paper and asked Leslie a few questions, then did some more calculations. "I would say that doing this work took between 120 and 140 hours, depending on what went wrong," he announced. Leslie thanked Steve and took the pad of paper to write it down, but Steve already had it written out. Leslie planned to write the check for Gary in the morning, and could only imagine the resistance she was going to get from that. "Mom, I hear your cell phone ringing upstairs," Billy yelled from the next room.

Leslie ran upstairs to answer her phone and saw that it was Jennifer Tillotson. "Hello, Jennifer!" she answered. "Hello!" Jennifer replied. "You sound out of breath. Did I catch you at a bad time? Were you working out?" Leslie laughed and assured Jennifer that she was definitely not working out. "So, how do you feel about having a press conference at the high school?" asked Jennifer. "I talked to the basketball coaches and they said you can have the gym tomorrow evening. Journalists thrive on these last-minute press conferences, but I need to make sure that you're available." Leslie said that would be fine and asked about the time so she could plan for dinner. They agreed on 7:30 and discussed details about what to wear, where to go, and who should participate. Leslie did not want Billy involved and said it would just be her. Jennifer said she would see her there, preferably a few minutes early, and Leslie thanked her and hung up the phone. She pulled a piece of paper out of the pad she was holding and wrote down the place and time and set it on the kitchen counter.

Steve and Melanie came up from the basement with Billy, and Leslie asked if Melanie could come over for a couple of hours tomorrow night to stay with Billy during the news conference. Steve said he would come with her so he could start looking at where to put in that bathroom. "I can show you my new G.I. Joes, too!" Billy announced. "My mom's doctor friend picked them out for me. He laughs a lot on the phone!" Melanie said she would love to know more about that friend and winked at Leslie, who immediately changed the subject.

"So, Melanie, whenever you're up and around tomorrow, I can show you what I want to do for that PowerPoint presentation," she said. "I'm sure you'll be way more creative about it than I would be. Also, I need to figure out what to wear for the press conference and I'm hoping you can help." Melanie said she would be glad to help with both and hugged Leslie. "Thank you for being so good to us," Melanie said, fighting back tears. "I think I'll sleep a lot better tonight." Leslie expressed that she was happy to help and walked them to the door. She reminded Steve to check into the VA loan tomorrow and he promised that he would as they left.

"What the heck is a 'VA loan'? asked Billy. "Doesn't 'VA' stand for 'Virginia'? Are they moving to Virginia?" Leslie said they were not moving to Virginia, especially since Steve just got a letter inviting him to become a State Trooper for Michigan. "Woah, that is so cool!" Billy exclaimed. "Why didn't he tell me?" Leslie explained that Steve had not yet decided if he was going to do it, and jokingly suggested that Steve might be afraid. "No way!" Billy replied. "Steve is the bravest guy I know!" Leslie agreed and explained that it takes several months of training so they would have to keep an eye on Melanie for him. Billy laughed. "That's funny. We're going to babysit my babysitter!"

Leslie agreed. "That is kind of ironic, isn't it?" she laughed. After explaining the meaning of 'ironic,' Leslie asked Billy if he wanted to go out for dinner. "But it's Taco Tuesday," he whined. "I love tacos!" Leslie said she had an exhausting day and suggested that they go to a Mexican restaurant to have tacos. "I'll try it," he agreed, "but I doubt that they make better tacos than you do. Are we going to eat out a lot now that you're popular and rich?" Leslie laughed and said she was hoping to do that, and maybe travel a little more.

After backing out of the garage, Leslie took out her cell phone and used the app to turn on the security system. She waved to the strangers in the silver car and found it amusing that they looked the other way instead of waving back. "Do you know those guys?" asked Billy. "They park out here a lot, and I think I saw them out the window at school the other day." Leslie explained that she didn't know them, but she knew someone who might. "I have a feeling that they're just keeping an eye on us because of your Grandpa Bill," she explained. "When someone important disappears, there will always be people who don't believe what really happened. I think they're watching the house and waiting for him. I don't think they're interested in you or me." Billy thought about it for a minute and his eyes widened. "Was Grandpa a spy?" he asked. "Basically," replied Leslie, "but he also helped the children in Vietnam by running a school for them. Grandma said he always wanted to be a teacher."

Billy still had his mouth open, like he couldn't close it himself. "Woah! Wait 'til I tell the kids at school!" Leslie suggested that he probably shouldn't tell them about the spying, but he could tell them about the school that his Grandpa started. "So, it's like a family secret?" he asked, eyes still wide. "Yes, exactly," explained Leslie. "I think it's a secret we should keep out of respect for your Grandpa." Billy's grin was priceless as he stared out the window. "Nobody ever tells me their secrets," he commented. "Did Grandma know about that?" Leslie explained that Grandma Susan had always talked about Grandpa Bill being a truck driver, so Grandma probably did not know. Billy thought about that for a minute and pondered, "Well, he couldn't just go around telling everyone what he did, right? I think he had to make up something to tell everyone." Leslie smiled and agreed. "Wow," she said, "you're pretty smart for an 11-year-old." Billy reminded her that he was turning twelve in a couple of weeks and changed the subject to his birthday party.

By the time they got to the restaurant, they had some tentative plans for Billy's party...who was coming, what to eat, what to do and not do, etc. Leslie hadn't been to this restaurant in years, so she was shocked when the waitress asked if she was the lady whose father was recently found. Leslie replied that she was, and thanked her for asking. They ordered Cokes to drink and Leslie was surprised when the person who brought out the drinks was the owner. He congratulated Leslie on the news about her father and asked if he was returning to the area. Leslie explained that he would be there in a couple of weeks and the owner asked her to bring her father there to eat. "Of course, he will not be charged," the owner explained. "We would just be honored to have him as our guest." Leslie thanked him and promised to bring her dad to the restaurant.

The waitress returned to take their order and then Leslie talked to Billy about all the changes going on. Billy seemed to accept everything so far and Leslie just wanted to make sure that he wasn't feeling overwhelmed. "I think it's okay to have *good* changes," Billy explained. "It's the bad ones that are hard, like Grandma dying. But getting a Grandpa and having Melanie stay with us and eating at restaurants is all good stuff." Leslie had been worried about him but hearing him talk about the positive aspects made her feel a lot better.

Their food arrived and Billy was excited that his tacos were served with rice and beans. He had already eaten a lot of tortilla chips, but he polished off everything on his plate as if he hadn't eaten in days. Leslie was pleased that he liked the food and suggested that they come back every Tuesday for tacos. "Yes!" Billy agreed. "I love these tacos! The cheese is so creamy! Not to be rude, Mom, but I think these are better than yours." Leslie laughed at his honesty and admitted that she thought so, too. She expected the bill every time the waitress passed by, and finally stopped her as she passed. "Oh, no charge," explained the waitress. "You and your family have paid enough. Your meal is on the house." Leslie thanked her and left $20 for a tip, explaining to Billy on the way out that 'on the house' means that it's free. Billy turned around as they reached the door. "We'll be back next week!" he announced with a wave. Nearly everyone in the restaurant waved back, customers as well as workers.

"Being a celebrity is going to take some getting used to," Leslie commented. "Mom, this is awesome!" Billy replied. "Everyone thinks it's so cool that Grandpa is coming back, and they want to be part of it!" Leslie explained that it would probably get even crazier after the press conference tomorrow night, as she would be on the local news. Billy suggested that she take some things with her, like the Pinewood Derby cars, to show that Grandpa Bill liked to do fun stuff before he disappeared. "Good idea!" agreed Leslie. "He was just a normal guy, doing what he was told for his country. Thanks, buddy!" Billy's suggestion gave Leslie a great idea, but she'd have to check with Gary to see if he was busy tomorrow evening or not.

• • •

Chapter Forty-Three

As they pulled into the driveway, Leslie hit the button on her garage door opener and an alarm went off on her phone. Leslie stopped and looked at it, then pressed the "Okay" button. "We need to get used to this system," she announced to Billy. "We have to tell it when we're coming in and out." They pulled into the garage and shut the door and her phone buzzed again so she pressed "Okay" and explained to Billy that the system was on, and he should not open any doors or windows after they got inside.

After a quick "I won't!" Billy climbed back onto the bar stool to finish his homework as Leslie went into the living room and called Jim Carlson. "Hi, Jim!" she greeted him. "Hi, Leslie!" she heard Jim say, followed by her dad saying "Hi, Leslie!" That was music to Leslie's ears. "Hey, that's awesome!" said Leslie. "Not always," explained Jim. "It's like having a parrot. I never realized how much I talk to myself, but your dad repeats a lot. His hearing is excellent, by the way. When I grumble under my breath, he understands what I'm saying and often repeats it." Leslie replied that she could see where that might be annoying, but also funny. "Funny, but sometimes embarrassing if I'm making an observation," Jim agreed. "I think he understands not to do that in front of any doctor besides Dr. Edwards. The other doctors don't realize that he can speak."

"Oh, speaking of Dr. Edwards," Leslie chimed in, "his mother was here today." There was a brief pause. "Linda was there?" Jim asked softly. "How did it go?" Leslie told him everything about the decorating and the pictures, and admitted that Linda was one of the most beautiful women she'd ever seen. "I know," Jim agreed, "and I blew it." Leslie explained that Linda seemed to be excited when she discovered that Jim was going to be Leslie's new neighbor. "I have a good feeling that there will be a reunion," she teased. "We'll see," Jim replied.

Leslie decided to change the subject and asked Jim if he could trace a federal plate. "How do you know it's a federal plate?" Jim asked. Leslie explained that her neighbor had a friend at the police station who looked it up and said it came back as belonging to the federal government. Since she had returned from Maryland, the silver sedan had been hanging around and following her. She had the plate number memorized and gave it to Jim. He told her to hang on a second, and in less than a minute he was back on the line. "For some reason, it's blocking me," he grumbled, obviously frustrated. "Maybe they already yanked my access, since I'm retiring. Let me check with one of my sources, but if the local police say that it's a fed, it probably is. Chances are fair that they're from the Agency, probably watching for your dad. The best thing to do is just walk up to their car and ask them why they're there." Leslie looked out the window. "They're out there now," she said. "Should I go ask them?" Jim suggested that she wait and do it in the morning, so it would throw off their whole day. "Text me after you do it," he requested, "and by then I should have their information so I can call them and ask how it's going."

Leslie was excited to be part of Jim's plans, and asked how he was going to handle leaving that area and his contacts. Jim laughed and explained that his contacts are spread out all over the world, and he will still have access to some of them. "I'm trying to use my last days on the job to get information I might need later, but won't have access to," he continued. "Between that and getting your dad to all his appointments and trying to pack up my belongings, I've been pretty busy. Your dad has really been a big help with packing. He seems to have a knack for wrapping things up and fitting them in boxes, which is an interesting skill for him to have. We may have run into an issue with his medical care, though."

Leslie wasn't familiar with the military healthcare system and asked how there could be issues, since her dad's identity was verified and Walter Reed was considered the top facility for military members. "That is the issue," Jim explained. "I put a rush on the paperwork to get your dad's status updated from MIA to veteran. Treatment at Walter Reed is for those who are still active military, so as soon as that paperwork is done they will transfer his treatment elsewhere." Leslie suggested that Jim discuss this with Michael to ensure continuity of treatment, and Jim mentioned that he would see Dr. Edwards tomorrow at an appointment. Leslie wished Jim a good evening and hung up, smiling as she thought about the fact that Michael was probably going to ask Jim how he felt about the assumption that he and Bill were a couple.

Leslie wished she could be a fly on the wall.

She headed upstairs to decide what to wear to the press conference and nothing seemed quite right. She decided that she needed to add "Go shopping" to her list of things to do tomorrow and went back downstairs. Billy was just finishing his homework. "Can you hire someone to do my homework?" he asked. "This stuff is boring!" Leslie laughed and told Billy that nobody was doing his homework for him, explaining that the reason for homework is to make sure that he understands what he's learning *outside* of the classroom. "Oh, I thought it was just to keep us busy," said Billy. "Can I write in that journal that you bought? I want to write about how much I don't like homework."

Leslie went to get Billy's journal and grabbed her own, too. Maybe they could start a routine of writing in their journals together after dinner. She handed Billy his journal and explained to him that he could write whatever he wanted or even draw pictures. "But I'm not a good artist," Billy argued. Leslie explained it didn't really matter because he was the only one who would see it. She remembered the beautiful pictures that her dad drew of the gardens and told Billy about them. "We should put them in frames and hang them up!" Billy said excitedly. "Maybe he can show me how to draw, too." Leslie loved that idea and looked forward to her son having a dependable role model around.

Before they could write anything, Leslie noticed the time and told Billy that he needed to get ready for bed. "When I turn 12, can we change my bedtime?" he asked. Leslie suggested that they increase it by 20 minutes every year, starting with him turning 12. "Awesome!" Billy shouted. "I can't wait!" He left his journal on the counter and ran upstairs to get ready for bed. Leslie looked over her lists for the next day, adding some things and deleting others, before grabbing her journal and heading upstairs to get ready for bed. After turning out Billy's light and writing a few pages in her journal, she brushed her teeth and collapsed into bed. She thought about everything she had going on in her life and wished that Mom were there to be part of it. She hoped that she could explain to her father what a great woman he had married and drifted off to sleep thinking about her parents.

•••

Chapter Forty-Four

Leslie woke up feeling refreshed and ready to take on the world. She could hear Billy in the shower as she headed down to make some tea. While her tea steeped, she looked out to see if the silver car was in front and was disappointed that it wasn't there. She saw Steve coming back from his morning run and waved, but he didn't seem to see her as he passed by the house. He was looking over his shoulder as he went into his house, and Leslie followed his gaze. He was watching the silver car, which stopped in front of her house, directly across the street. Leslie was still in her pajamas, but she decided to go out and greet them like Jim had suggested. She opened the door to go out and was met by an obnoxiously loud chirping sound, letting her know that she had forgotten about the alarm system. She pulled the door closed and ran up to get her phone to turn off the system.

Billy came out of the bathroom wrapped in a towel. "What was that noise?" he asked. "Is someone breaking in?" Leslie explained that she had opened the door and apologized if it scared him. She turned off the system from her phone and went back downstairs. The silver car was still there, so Leslie walked out and knocked on the window. The tint was so dark that she wondered it if was legal, but the window rolled down. The driver was an older man with short gray hair who looked like he hadn't shaved in days. She assumed that he'd be wearing a suit, as her stereotype of federal workers dictated, but he wore a turquoise polo shirt. "Hi, I'm Leslie," she began. "I've noticed you around a lot, even following me. My friend Jim Carlson says that you're probably harmless, but I thought I would come out to see what is going on." The driver stared at Leslie as if she had two heads but said nothing. The passenger, a beautiful young Asian woman, smiled and offered a reply. "Hello, Mrs. Mitchell. My name is Connie Wang. We're just keeping an eye on you and your family in case there is anyone who wishes you ill will. Nothing to worry about. Please tell Jim that I said 'Hello.'" Leslie thanked her and went back to the house, proud of herself for being proactive.

On her way up the sidewalk, Leslie could see Steve looking out his kitchen window and they exchanged waves. "What did you do?" Billy asked as Leslie stepped inside. "Did you just go talk to those strangers in the silver car?" When she confirmed that she had, Billy reminded her that she had always told him not to talk to strangers or approach a strange car. Leslie explained that the people outside said they were watching to make sure that nothing bad happens to her or Billy. "That's what criminals always say on TV," countered Billy. "They don't tell you that they're stalking you and then, boom, you end up in an alley dead." Leslie thought he was being ridiculous at first, but then wondered about the fact that someone who knew Jim Carlson professionally referred to him as "Jim," not "General" like Justine does. That seemed odd.

Leslie made sure that Billy had everything for school and helped him pack his lunch, then looked at the clock and realized that they were running behind. Her phone was still upstairs, but she didn't bother getting it since she would be right back after dropping off Billy. "Let's go, buddy," she said to Billy. "We're going to be late." As they pulled out of the driveway, Leslie noticed that the silver car had pulled forward, so it wasn't directly in front of her house. Maybe they saw the new cameras and were avoiding them, or they were rattled because she went out to speak to them. The thought of it made her smile.

Leslie also noticed that Steve's car was still in his driveway. She hoped that he wasn't sick, and was just enjoying a rare day off. It seemed like he worked so much lately. During the drive, she and Billy talked about the press conference that Leslie was doing later, and Billy was excited to spend more time with Melanie and Steve. The drop-off zone at school seemed unusually slow but Leslie didn't have to go to work so she tried to relax and not worry about it. She turned on some music and sang along, waiting for the traffic to clear. After a few minutes, things cleared up and Leslie headed home.

As she was turning into her driveway, she noticed that the silver car was gone. They often disappeared during the day, so that was no big deal. As she pulled up to the house, she saw that the front door was wide open, and her heart started racing. That was a big deal. Had she not closed it when she came back inside this morning? She entered the house cautiously and called out "Hello?" Steve's voice came from the living room: "Hey! In here!" Leslie went to see what he was doing and was shocked to see him sitting on top of someone. "What's going on?" asked Leslie. "I just caught this lady breaking into your house," Steve explained. "She's pretty strong, so I can't let go to use my phone. Call the police!"

Leslie called 9-1-1 on her landline and ran outside to flag them down while Steve held onto the woman. When they arrived, Leslie quickly explained the situation. Officer Hahn, who knew Steve, ran inside to help him while the other officer looked around outside. "Did your security system go off?" he asked. Leslie explained that she had turned it off this morning and rushed out to get her son to school on time. As they walked into the kitchen, Officer Hahn had handcuffed the intruder and was walking her out. "Oh, that's Connie Wang!" Leslie exclaimed. "I met her this morning." The woman didn't look at Leslie or say anything, so Officer Hahn asked his partner to take her out to the car.

Officer Hahn asked Leslie and Steve if they could provide him with more details and suggested that they sit down to relax. As they were heading to the living room, Leslie could hear her cell phone ringing repeatedly upstairs and excused herself to go turn it off. It was Jim Carlson. "Hello, Jim," she answered. "Can I call you right back?" Jim told Leslie not to hang up because he had something urgent to tell her. "The plate that you gave me *was* a federal plate, but it had been sent to recycling after a new plate was issued. They're having some problems with those plates making it to their destination because they're being sold to people who want everyone to think they are feds. Bad people. Do not approach the vehicle!" Leslie's breath caught in her throat. She explained to Jim what she had done that morning and said she had to go because the police were there. Jim asked Leslie to call him as soon as the police left. She promised that she would and turned off her phone as she walked downstairs.

"Are you okay?" asked Steve. "You look like you just saw a ghost!" Leslie told Steve and Officer Hahn about giving Jim the plate number and what had transpired since. She couldn't believe that she had boldly approached the vehicle and felt incredibly lucky that something horrible hadn't happened. Officer Hahn was the friend of Steve's who ran the plate and admitted that there was something odd about it in the system. He explained further that he was limited to his search because there hadn't been a crime committed, but with the most recent developments, he was hoping to find out more. He asked Leslie and Steve a lot of questions and took notes, then handed Leslie a business card with his contact information. He suggested that they keep their eyes peeled for the silver car and its other occupant and promised that he would be in touch. Leslie thanked him as she walked him to the door, and saw that Connie was in the back of the police car when the two officers drove away.

She turned to Steve and breathed a sigh of relief. "I'm so glad you were here!" she said. "This could have been so much worse!" Steve was obviously worried about what had happened and about the fact that the silver car and its driver had taken off. "Was the car here when you came over?" asked Leslie. Steve explained that he saw the woman get out of the silver car and approach the house. He suggested that these people were not feds or they wouldn't have broken in or fled the scene. "Maybe it's time for you to consider going to the range with me and carrying some protection," he added. "Until then, I strongly suggest that you take advantage of your new security system. I took the day off so I could work on your fence, and Tyler will be here shortly to help. You should probably grab something to drink and relax."

Leslie nodded in agreement. "So, I turned off the alarm to the security system this morning, but the cameras will still work, right?" she asked Steve. He suggested that she talk to Gary, since he installed it, and went to get his tools. Right on cue, Gary walked into the kitchen. "What happened?" he asked. "I was packing up some things and saw the police car in the driveway. Are you okay?" Leslie told Gary what had happened and he asked a lot of questions. He explained that the cameras should have caught everything, and that he would get his glasses and be right back to help with that.

Leslie dialed Jim Carlson's number and didn't even hear it ring. "Leslie?" he answered immediately. "Is everything okay?" Leslie explained everything that had occurred this morning, from her going out to the silver car to Gary saying it should all be on camera. "I feel awful," Jim admitted. "I gave you some bad advice and put you in a dangerous situation. I am so sorry." Leslie argued that she was a big girl and she should have known better. "My 11-year-old son gave me a lecture about approaching strangers, which I've told him to never do," Leslie continued. "Now I know why I told him that. Any idea who those people are?" Jim said that he had no idea, but assured Leslie that he would have federal agents looking into it, especially since it involved one of their old license plates.

Gary came back into the kitchen and Leslie told Jim she would call him back with any updates, and he said he would do the same. "I'll call you later this evening, whether or not I have anything new," he promised. "By the way, your dad's 'father' instincts seem to have kicked in. When I told him what you said before, he was so worried that he couldn't meditate. He is drawing furiously. Must be a good stress relief."

...

Chapter Forty-Five

After Leslie finished speaking with Jim Carlson, Gary showed her how to pull up the security cameras on the monitor in the kitchen. They went back to the beginning of the footage, which just started the day before, and saw that there were several shots of the silver car out in front of the house. Leslie was fascinated as they fast-forwarded through yesterday's activity, seeing the mailman when he delivered the mail and everyone else who passed by. Now that she knew how to do this, she thought it would be fun to review it periodically, maybe once a week.

When they got to the part where Leslie went out to the silver car, she grimaced a little. "That was probably not one of your best decisions," suggested Gary. "I know that now," admitted Leslie, "but still probably a better decision than marrying Mark." They had a good laugh, but Leslie was sick to her stomach, seeing her smug face as she returned to the house, remembering how proud she had felt about going out and talking to them. "Who do you think they are?" she asked Gary. His eyes never left the monitor as he watched the woman come up to the house and walk right in. "I don't know," he admitted, "but I find it oddly amusing that when Steve comes running in, that silver car drives off in a hurry, leaving the woman behind."

Leslie agreed and asked if she should call Officer Hahn to let him know that they saw the woman entering the house on the security footage. "Absolutely!" Gary said. "I'm sure he'll appreciate anything you can do to help. I need to go finish some packing but let me know if you need anything." Leslie thanked him and went to get Officer Hahn's business card. She dialed the number and told him about the security cameras. "Would you like to come over and check out the footage yourself?" she asked. "I would love to do that," he replied, "but it might not be until tomorrow. We're still questioning our mystery intruder, who isn't giving us any information, other than telling us that you two are friends and she was there to visit. She has no identification on her, and she has an empty holster but no weapon. You didn't happen to see any weapons around, did you?" Leslie suggested that she probably would have noticed a gun lying around but promised to look and then let him know. Officer Hahn affirmed that he would call tomorrow before they stopped by, and Leslie thanked him and hung up.

Steve and his friend Tyler knocked on the front door and Leslie opened it. She explained what Officer Hahn had just told her about the empty holster, and Steve said he'd do a sweep of the house to search for a weapon. Leslie introduced herself to Tyler and thanked him for helping with the fence. "We have had some odd things happen," she explained, "so hopefully you guys can get that fence up quickly." Tyler said they would do their best and suggested that they bring in a couple of other friends to help if Leslie wanted it done even faster. Leslie liked the idea and went to talk to Steve about it. She found him lying on his stomach by the couch, reaching underneath, and couldn't imagine the dust bunnies he was finding.

"Well, what do we have here?" he asked. "Leslie, can you grab a couple of sandwich bags?" She wasn't sure why he needed them, but she went into the kitchen and grabbed a few. She returned to the living room and handed them to Steve, who stuck his hand in a sandwich bag and reached under the couch. He carefully pulled out an old pistol, covered in dust bunnies, which he placed inside the other bag. "Whew! Got it!" he exclaimed proudly. "I need to call Hahn." Leslie couldn't believe what she had just seen. "Why would Connie Wang bring a gun into my house?" she asked, but there was no answer. She felt worse now than she had earlier.

Steve placed the bag on the top of the refrigerator, out of reach, and removed the other sandwich bag from his hand. He called Officer Hahn and explained what had happened. Leslie heard a lot of "Okay" and "Uh-huh" before Steve said, "No problem" and hung up. He announced that Hahn was sending an officer over to retrieve the evidence, and the officers planned to return tomorrow to see the security camera footage. "Do you have to work tomorrow?" Leslie asked. Steve explained that he was taking another day off, since they needed to get that fence in, and Tyler called some friends to help while Leslie and Steve waited for the other officer to arrive.

Leslie suddenly remembered that she needed to ask Gary something and asked Steve if he and Tyler would wait for the police officer. Leslie scurried next door and knocked, wondering when she had last been inside Gary's house. When he answered the door, he seemed excited to have her come in. "The house looks great, even with everything off the walls and all the boxes lying around," Leslie commented. Gary showed her a couple of recent projects and she informed him that she had Steve look at everything he had done at her house and give her an estimate for the labor costs. When she told him that she was going to pay him for all the work he did, he argued that she didn't owe him anything and said he would refuse it. Leslie said they could discuss it later and asked him if the '58 Impala was in running condition.

"Of course," Gary beamed. "That car is in perfect shape. Are you planning to drive it?" Leslie explained that she wanted to drive it to the press conference tonight, to make a statement. Gary said he'd be happy to check it to be certain, but everything should be fine. He reminded her that there is no power steering and that she would have to hand-crank the windows to roll them down, which Leslie already knew. She thanked him and said she would argue with him about the labor costs later.

As she walked back to her house, Officer Hahn had just pulled up. "I decided to come instead of sending someone else," he explained. Leslie took him into the kitchen and showed him where Steve put the pistol. Hahn placed it carefully inside an evidence bag, got statements from Leslie, Steve, and Tyler, then zipped out the door again. "See you tomorrow!" he called out. Steve and Tyler were right behind him, returning to work on the fence.

•••

Chapter Forty-Six

Melanie appeared at the door and knocked. "You don't need to knock!" Leslie called out. "Just come in." Melanie said she had just spoken to a friend of hers who worked as a lender for mortgages. "In order to get a VA loan, Steve needs an eligibility certificate," she explained. "I just filled it out online for him, and as soon as it comes, we can check into a loan for the house." Since their bank was the same as her mother's, Leslie suggested that they talk to Mr. Petry about getting everything in place beforehand. Melanie liked the idea and said she'd discuss it with Steve later.

"Okay, where should we start with the PowerPoint?" asked Melanie. Leslie had somehow forgotten all about it and was happy for the distraction from her crazy morning. Melanie had her laptop and a thumb drive that she would use for the project, and she honestly looked better than she had in a long time. Leslie showed her what was in the Craft Room and admitted that she hadn't yet looked through everything. "Your mother was so organized," Melanie claimed in awe. "I really think it will be easy to do. Maybe you can find actual items to go with the pictures while I work on them." Leslie liked the idea, but she told Melanie that she needed to make a quick phone call before she started looking for any time capsule items. Melanie got to work, looking through the thumb drives of pictures as Leslie went back to the kitchen.

Leslie looked up the phone number for her mother's bank and asked to speak to Mr. Petry. He seemed happy to speak to her, and Leslie explained the situation with Steve's house and asked if there was anything she could do to speed up the process for the loan. Mr. Petry said that he would be happy to help and that he had some inside information because his wife was the realtor that the owner's family had chosen to sell the house. Since Leslie's neighborhood is one of the more desirable areas in town and houses there rarely go up for sale, word got out quickly and apparently there were several buyers interested. "But there hasn't been anyone coming for a viewing and there haven't been any inspections" Leslie countered. "How could they buy the house?" Mr. Petry said those things would happen quickly and expressed his doubts that Steve would have his paperwork before someone made an offer. Leslie asked for his wife's number so she could ask some questions, and he was happy to share the information.

Leslie dialed Mrs. Petry's number, not really sure what she was going to ask. "Hello, Mrs. Petry, my name is Leslie Mitchell," she began. Mrs. Petry knew a lot about Leslie, it seemed, and extended her congratulations about her father and condolences for her mother. Leslie asked if she knew any more about the house next door and gave Mrs. Petry the address. "Oh, yes," she replied. "I have had three people call to schedule viewings, but I wanted to wait until this afternoon to call the renters." Leslie asked about the process and Mrs. Petry explained that after a viewing, there is usually an inspection, which is required for a mortgage. "What if someone pays cash?" asked Leslie. Mrs. Petry explained that she had not yet received any cash offers, but if someone had the money, they weren't required to get the inspection before the purchase. "I'll take it!" Leslie declared. "Where do I bring the check?" Mrs. Petry informed Leslie that she would need a cashier's check and offered to come by Leslie's house tomorrow with the paperwork. Leslie agreed that she could sign the paperwork the next day, and promised to have the check for her then.

As she hung up, Melanie came up the stairs to ask a question. "I just bought your house!" Leslie blurted out. "Now you don't have to move!" Melanie burst into tears and hugged Leslie, then opened the back door and yelled for Steve to come inside. He came running, already sweaty from digging post holes. "What happened?" he asked. "What's wrong, honey?" Melanie couldn't say anything, so Leslie explained, "Nothing is wrong. I'm buying your house to keep anyone else from buying it. When everything is in place, you can just buy it back from me." Steve wrapped his arms around Melanie first and then hugged Leslie. She passed on what Mrs. Petry had told her and apologized that she hadn't thought about doing it before, but it would be done tomorrow. Steve mumbled something about being the luckiest man alive and ran back out to work on the fence. Leslie knew she had done the right thing as she watched him throw his fist in the air and yell, "Woohoo!"

• • •

Chapter Forty-Seven

Leslie felt relieved, like a weight had been lifted, and knew that Mom would have been proud of what she just did. She asked Melanie if she needed something to drink and offered her a bottle of water. As Melanie sipped her water and calmed down, Leslie remembered that Melanie had come up to ask her a question. "I honestly don't remember what it was," said Melanie, "but it will probably come to me when I go back downstairs." Leslie laughed and remembered how forgetful she was when she was pregnant.

"Hey, before you go back downstairs, can you help me pick out something to wear tonight?" Leslie asked. "If nothing seems right, I'll go get a new outfit." Melanie said she'd be happy to help, and they headed upstairs. After looking through Leslie's closet, Melanie had a couple of ideas but then asked if she could look in Susan's closet to see if there was something there that might work. Leslie agreed, but she doubted there was anything of her mother's she would want to wear. They opened the door to Susan's room, and Melanie asked when the contractors would begin renovations. When Leslie replied that they were coming tomorrow, Melanie recommended that Leslie remove as many of the personal items as possible today. "I have a friend who tried to surprise her parents by having some remodeling done on their house while they were on vacation," Melanie explained. "When the contractors did their destruction, they didn't mess around. They destroyed a lot of her parents' belongings." Leslie didn't believe Linda would allow that to happen, but decided that she would remove everything after she and Melanie went through the clothing.

Susan had been an organized woman and her closet reflected that. The clothes were arranged neatly and some of the nicer items were covered in plastic. "One Hour Martinizing," Leslie read on one of the plastic coverings. "That must have been dry-cleaned when I was still in high school." It was fun, looking through fifty years' worth of clothing, and Melanie found several potential outfits for Leslie. Most of them were too small, since Leslie wasn't as slender as her mother had been, but there were a few dresses that fit. Leslie chose a simple pink short-sleeved dress and thanked Melanie for the suggestion. "Wearing Mom's dress and driving Dad's car," Leslie commented as she looked in the mirror. "You're taking the Impala?" asked Melanie. "Steve will be so jealous! He loves that car!"

Leslie felt good about the wardrobe choice they made and took the pink dress to her closet. She decided that she would go through all of Mom's clothes and decide what to keep for herself and what to donate to charity. Melanie went to work on the PowerPoint while Leslie went back to her mother's closet. She should have known that this would bring back memories that might tear at her heart, but she had to do it. There was the yellow pantsuit that Mom wore when Leslie graduated from college. Leslie smiled at the memory of Mom insisting that it wasn't yellow; it was *maize*. She wore a blue scarf and blue pumps with it, and she looked great. Next to the pantsuit was the peach-colored dress that Mom had worn when Leslie married Mark.

The dress was wrapped in a dry cleaner's plastic bag, which had yellowed a little, and Leslie noticed some writing on the back when she took it out of the closet. She laid the dress across the bed where the lighting was better and saw that "Worst day ever" was written on the plastic with a black marker. Leslie laughed until she cried. "Oh, Mom," she said aloud, "I miss you so much." She couldn't do much to stop the tears at that point. Her life had been so safe and predictable as long as Mom was around. So much had happened in the last month that Leslie didn't understand how she was handling it without her mother's strength and support. It seemed unfair that Mom didn't get to see her husband come home, or that she wasn't there for her grandson's first scuffle or girlfriend or deodorant.

Although she missed her mother terribly, Leslie decided that wearing some of these clothes would be an appropriate way to honor her mother. She found several articles of clothing that still had tags and others that she had never seen her mother wear. She made piles on the bed for herself and for charity, and tossed the items that would be thrown out on the old chair in the corner of the room. The chair would be going, too, but it was too heavy for her to move. There were more shoes and purses than Leslie would have expected, given that her mother never seemed to be interested in fashion. She considered having a garage sale, but then she remembered the work that goes into such a project and decided that she'd rather just donate the items. Like a true accountant, the words "tax deductible" came to mind.

Her thoughts were interrupted by the doorbell ringing, and she was surprised to see Gary at the door when she went down to answer it. "Why didn't you just come in?" asked Leslie. Gary explained that he didn't want to trigger the security system, and that he was going into the garage to check on the Impala. They walked through the breezeway, one of the few updates that her mother had allowed to the house, and Gary pulled the cover off the Impala. "She's as beautiful as ever," he declared. "I'll check everything out to make sure she's in working order." Leslie thanked him and opened the garage door so Gary could pull the Impala out into the light. As she headed back inside, she could see Steve heading over to check out the car. She thought about staying outside to talk to them, but her phone was ringing so she went to answer it.

"Hello, Officer Hahn," greeted Leslie. "How can I help you?" Officer Hahn informed Leslie that they still didn't have much information, but he was worried about the fact that the silver car and its driver had disappeared. "We did trace the fingerprints of the woman who says she is 'Connie Wang' and she has so many aliases that we're still not sure of her real name," he explained. "It appears that she's from Virginia. Do you know anyone who lives there?" Leslie replied that her ex-husband and her aunt both live in Virginia and pulled out her address book when Officer Hahn asked for their contact information. He suggested that she take extra safety precautions until they get some answers, and asked Leslie what she had planned for the next few days. For the press conference, he advised that she not go alone and promised that he would have someone from the evening shift patrol the area during the event. Leslie thanked him and went back to the garage to talk to Gary and Steve.

Steve was talking about the color of the car and asked if it was the original paint job. "Yes, sir," replied Gary. "Cashmere blue. I love this color." Leslie told Steve that she had just spoken to his friend at the police station, and shared what Officer Hahn had told her. "So, you'll be needing a chauffeur tonight, huh?" asked Steve. "I'm busy, but I could probably change my plans." Gary cleared his throat and put his hands on his hips. "Well, I'm moving soon, and this may be my last chance to drive this beauty, so I would also like to throw my hat in the ring," he announced. Leslie laughed and suggested that perhaps she needed a chauffeur and a bodyguard. "I'll let you guys figure it out," she called out as she headed back inside. "Just be ready to go around 6:45!"

Leslie walked into the kitchen and grabbed a Coke from the refrigerator. She yelled down the basement stairs, "Everything okay down there?" and Melanie yelled back, "Awesome! I love all these pictures!" Leslie wanted to see the photos, but she had a lot of other things to do first. She thought about how interesting it was going to be to see the pictures as she called Mr. Petry to ask about a cashier's check. He asked a few questions and informed Leslie that it would be done within the hour. She thanked him and went back to her sorting in Mom's room.

Leslie had cleared out a lot of clothes and could see the gun case now, which wasn't very big. She took the blanket from Mom's bed and laid it out on the floor, carefully tipping the gun case onto it. She dragged it to her room, next to her closet, and tipped it back up. She draped the blanket across the top and went back to check the nightstand drawer. Leslie took the entire drawer out and carried it to her room, not sure what she should do with the revolver. She remembered emptying a few shoe boxes in Mom's room and retrieved one, dumping everything from the drawer into the box. She pulled out the small key that was taped inside the bottom of the drawer and set it on her nightstand, shoving the shoebox under her bed near the top. She felt better about having those items out of her mother's room, since there would be strangers working in there tomorrow.

• • •

Chapter Forty-Eight

Leslie suddenly realized that she was hungry and headed back to the kitchen to make a sandwich. Her phone, which she had started carrying in her pocket, was ringing again. "Oh, hello, Jim," she answered. "How is everything?" Before she could get the words out, Jim was talking. "Did you tell Dr. Edwards about what the police thought when they came to my apartment?" he asked. Leslie admitted that she had because she thought it was funny, but Jim did not see the humor. He asked if there was any update about the silver car, and Leslie recounted the conversation with Officer Hahn.

"So, someone is going with you to the press conference?" asked Jim. Leslie confirmed that either Steve or Gary was driving, but she wasn't sure which one. She told Jim that she tried to pay Gary for the work he had done for her mother, but he wouldn't take her money. "Can you put money into his account again?" asked Leslie. "I can give you my account number and you can take it from there." Jim said he should be able to do it and wrote down Leslie's account information.

"When do you think you're going to get here to be my new neighbor?" she asked. Jim replied that he had received the confirmation that Bill's status was changed from "MIA" to "Veteran," and he had discussed the ongoing Treatment Plan with Dr. Edwards, so it would be very soon. "Honestly, you shouldn't need to come back here," Jim advised. "I can leave as soon as they'll release him, so I'll just take him home." Leslie asked him to keep her updated on the progress and told him about the contractors coming tomorrow to start some renovations. Jim was concerned that there would be strangers in the house, due to the recent break-in, but Leslie assured him that Steve and some friends would be there. "He's a Marine Corps veteran," Leslie added. "He'll make sure I'm safe." Jim admitted that made him feel better, and said he had to go find her dad. "What do you mean?" asked Leslie. "You lost him?" Jim explained that as Bill got more comfortable, he explored more and occasionally he wandered off. "He's a grown man," Jim reminded her. "He can come and go as he pleases."

Leslie told Jim about the situation with Steve and Melanie's house, and how she was buying it so nobody else could. "I love it!" Jim replied. "That shows outstanding character. Your mother would approve." Leslie thanked him and said she needed to finish her sandwich and go pick up the cashier's check. "Are you going alone to pick up that check?" he asked. Leslie said that she was, so Jim suggested that she take someone else along. Leslie agreed and said goodbye, rolling her eyes at the idea of having to take someone with her everywhere.

She finished her sandwich and was going to go pick up the check but realized that it wouldn't be long before she had to go pick up Billy at school. She decided to roll it into one trip and save time. She still had about a half hour, so she went back to her mother's closet to go through more of her items, finding more purses and some fashionable jewelry.

When she was ready to go, she grabbed her purse and went out to the garage. Gary was still out there and suggested that they put more gas in the Impala before going to the press conference. "Hey, I have an idea," Leslie answered. "Why don't you drive me to the bank and to pick up Billy from school, then we can stop for gas?" Gary loved the idea, and after checking to make sure he had his wallet he wiped off his hands and grabbed the keys for the Impala. "Let's go!" he announced. As they pulled out the driveway, Leslie noticed Steve watching them drive away, waving sadly. She suggested to Gary that he drive now and allow Steve to drive later. "You think he can drive an old three on the tree?" he asked. Leslie assumed that Steve knew how to drive it, but suggested that they might have to draw a diagram and tape it on the dashboard like Gary did when he taught Leslie how to drive it. "It worked, didn't it?" he laughed. Leslie smiled at the memory and asked Gary if he'd be willing to drive if she needed him to do it. "Honey, I'd rather drive this car than sleep or eat," he replied with a wink.

When they pulled into the bank parking lot, everyone was staring at the Impala. Gary said he would stay with the car while Leslie went inside to sign the cashier's check. She had to sign a withdrawal form, but the check was ready and the whole process only took five minutes. Mr. Petry claimed that he didn't like the idea of that check sitting in Leslie's house overnight and suggested that they leave it locked up at the bank and his wife would come by the next day to retrieve it. Leslie hadn't even thought about that but agreed that it would be a better option. She left the bank feeling positive and grateful for people who were looking out for her.

Since Billy's school didn't dismiss for another twenty minutes, Leslie suggested to Gary that they get gas first and then go pick up Billy. Gary drove the Impala as if it were made of porcelain and Leslie found it adorable. They pulled into the gas station and Leslie went inside to pay while Gary pumped gas. Everyone stopped and stared at the immaculate blue Impala.

As Leslie was walking back to the car, she thought she saw the driver of the silver car going past. He was driving a small white car and Leslie couldn't get the plate number, but it definitely was not a Michigan plate. She dialed Officer Hahn's number to let him know. "I can send someone right over," he offered. Leslie said she couldn't stay there to wait because she had to pick Billy up at school, but she informed Officer Hahn that Steve was going with her to the press conference and her neighbor Gary was with her now.

Leslie and Gary headed to Billy's school and waited in the pickup line. Their windows were rolled down and everyone had something to say about the car. When Billy came out, he didn't notice them right away because he was used to seeing Leslie's Equinox. She waved out the window and yelled his name. Billy's eyes lit up and he ran to the car. "Hey! I didn't know you were bringing the Impala to school! Can I show it to my friends?" Leslie explained that they had to keep moving in the pickup line but assured him that his friends could see it. She saw Jenna coming out and waved. "Hi, Jenna!" Leslie yelled as Jenna returned the wave and stared at the car. "Hey, Jenna!" yelled Billy. "Do you like our old car? It's a '58 Impala!" Jenna smiled. "I love it, Billy!" she yelled back.

"I think she said she loves you," Gary teased Billy, who blushed at the thought. "Nah, she loves the car," Billy replied. "We're just friends." They drove away from the school and Billy looked back over his shoulder. "Hey, remember the guy who used to sit in front of our house in a silver car?" he asked. "I just saw him drive past in a white car." Leslie said she had seen him, too, and tried to reassure Billy that there was nothing to worry about. She changed the subject by asking how his day went at school and was happy to hear that it had been a routine day. She reminded him that she had the press conference tonight, but there had been a little bit of a change in plans. Steve was going to drive her there and Billy would be spending that time with Melanie. Gary said he could stop by if needed, but Leslie said it shouldn't be necessary and thanked Gary for the offer.

As they pulled in the driveway, Steve walked over to greet them. "How does it drive?" he asked Gary. "Well," Gary replied with a grin, "you put the key in and start it up." They all laughed except Billy, who was already running inside with his backpack. "Actually, it runs pretty well," beamed Gary. "Do you know how to drive a 'three on the tree'?" Steve said he had only done it once, so he and Gary discussed it and Leslie went inside.

While Billy started on homework, Leslie went to finish getting the personal items out of Mom's closet. When Melanie came upstairs to use the bathroom, Billy was startled because he wasn't aware that she had been downstairs working on the PowerPoint. "Hey, a little warning," urged Billy. "Are you trying to give me a heart attack?" Melanie apologized and asked Billy about school. He told her that the most exciting thing about it was getting picked up in the Impala. Melanie said there were some great pictures of the Impala on the drives that she was organizing, and that she would show some of them to Billy later.

Leslie continued sorting through her mother's closet and then her dresser drawers. She would ask Linda about the furniture in the morning, but that mattress definitely had to go. Leslie grabbed a couple of trash bags and dumped all the bedding and pillows into them, blinking back tears when she realized that this was the last place that Mom was in the house. Leslie had heard that frugal people stuffed money under their mattresses, so she lifted it up to check. She found some fabric softener sheets and a little blue notebook, but no money. She thumbed through the notebook and shook her head in disbelief. All her mother's accounts and policies were listed, alphabetically of course, including account numbers and passwords. This was better than finding cash; it would help Leslie sort out what she had.

As Leslie was taking the notebook to her room, Billy called upstairs. "What are we having for dinner?" he asked. "Can we order pizza?" Leslie was happy to hear that Billy was growing out of his meal ritual and walked downstairs. "Sure, we can order pizza," she replied. "When you get a minute, go ask Melanie and Steve if they want pizza, too. If they do, find out what they want on it and I'll order it soon so I can eat before I go to the press conference." Billy looked at Leslie like she had two heads. "Wait, you don't know that Steve will eat everything and Melanie only wants cheese?" asked Billy. Leslie pondered it for a few seconds and admitted that she didn't know and asked Billy to check with them when he had a chance. She was heading back upstairs when she noticed the white car that she had seen earlier, so she grabbed her phone. "I better take this upstairs with me, so you don't get disturbed if it rings," she fibbed.

Billy went back to his homework and Leslie returned to her mother's room. She dialed Gary's number and told him that she thought she had seen the white car again. "Do you think I'm just paranoid?" she asked. "No, my dear, I think you're just being cautious," Gary replied. "Would you feel better if I come over to stay with Billy and Melanie tonight while you're gone? I talked to Steve and he seems to be confident about driving the car." Leslie admitted that she would feel better if Gary were there and asked if he'd like to join them for pizza. He declined, since he had a lot to do at his house but promised to be over shortly after Leslie and Steve left.

•••

Chapter Forty-Nine

Leslie thought about how much her life had changed in the past month and smiled. "Mom, I think you'd be proud of me for some of the decisions I'm making," she said aloud as she peeled the bedspread back from the pile of paintings underneath. She folded up the bedspread and carefully laid the two paintings on top of it. "It is too bad that we can't discuss your decisions when it comes to art, though," she laughed. Leslie recalled one of the few times that Mark defended her mother, praising the artwork that Susan inherited from her stepfather. "He took one art class, and called himself an expert," Leslie said aloud.

Steve appeared at the doorway. "Who are you talking to?" he inquired as he looked around. Leslie admitted that she talks to her mother occasionally and was just commenting aloud about the awful paintings that her mother seemed to love. Steve recommended that Leslie take the paintings to an art gallery or somewhere else where they could be appraised. "I heard about a lady who bought a painting at a garage sale for $3.00, and it was appraised at over a million," he added. "Don't be too quick to throw it out, even if it's ugly." Leslie laughed and asked if Billy had asked about pizza toppings. "No, he is really into his homework," Steve replied. "I walked right past him. He's pretty focused. The reason I came in is to tell you that Tyler had to leave. Also, I think I saw the guy from the silver car, but he's in a white car now." Leslie shared that she had seen him, too, and had asked Gary to come over while she and Steve were gone tonight. He liked the idea.

As they walked downstairs, Leslie asked Steve about having pizza, and he said he'd ask Melanie. "What do you like on your pizza?" asked Leslie. "Personally, I'll eat anything," he replied, "but Melanie usually just wants cheese. Being pregnant has changed her eating habits, though, so I'll have to ask her." Billy didn't even look up from his homework. "Told ya," he said proudly. Leslie laughed and patted him on the back. "Yes, you did," she replied. "Now use that brain to do your homework."

Leslie went downstairs with Steve to ask Melanie about pizza.

"Of course, I want pizza!" she replied. "But not just plain old cheese. I'd like pepperoni and green peppers, please." Steve shook his head. "I have never known you to eat any toppings on your pizza," he remarked. "Just keeping our life unpredictable," Melanie teased. Leslie loved how cute these two were together, obviously in love, and said she would leave them alone. "Wait! I want to show you something cool," Melanie said. "Look at this picture." She showed Leslie a photograph of two couples sitting on a bridge, probably four of the happiest-looking people she'd ever seen. "That's my mom and dad on the left," Leslie observed. After looking closely, she couldn't believe her eyes. "That's Jim and Linda on the right," she whispered. "They are gorgeous!" Melanie commented. "Can I print out a photo of them?" Leslie thought that was a great idea, and while Melanie connected to the printer, she talked about how much she loved black and white photos.

"Is there a good picture of my dad with the Impala?" asked Leslie. "Dozens of them," Melanie replied. "Should I print out one of those, too?" Leslie asked if she would do that and walked upstairs to order the pizza. She ordered two pizzas and told Billy to keep his ears and eyes open for the pizza delivery man. "You're not picking it up?" he asked. "I don't remember ever having someone deliver it." Leslie said that was because Grandma didn't believe in it; she believed that if someone else was going to make your food then you should at least go get it. "I like having someone bring it to the house," Billy replied. "It makes me feel like we have a chef. Hey, now that we're rich, can we get a chef?" Leslie laughed and said there was no reason to have a chef because she knows how to cook. "Now that I'm not working, I'll have more time to cook and clean," she explained. Billy argued that on TV, they always say that you should travel after you retire, not cook and clean. Leslie reminded him that they just spent two weeks in Florida, then she went to Maryland for a few days. "Let's plan on some trips for this summer," he suggested. Leslie told him that after he finished his homework, he could research summer vacation trips. "Woohoo!" exclaimed Billy. "I'm the trip planner!"

He went back to his homework and Leslie went downstairs to get the photos that Melanie had printed. "I'm going to take these with me to the press conference," Leslie said. "I think these pictures help to tell the story of my parents." She thanked Melanie and asked where Steve went. "He's looking at the spot for a bathroom again," Melanie replied. "Even if I don't end up staying down here, it's still a good idea." Leslie went to find Steve, who was measuring and mumbling to himself. They discussed measurements and layout until the doorbell rang and Leslie's phone buzzed in her pocket. "My phone is letting me know that someone is at the front door," she laughed.

Steve went upstairs with Leslie, who paid the delivery man and gave him a nice tip. "Really, a $10 tip?" Steve asked. "If you keep spending like that, you're going to run out of money." Leslie laughed and said she appreciated his concern, but this was her first time having pizza delivered to her house. Steve looked at her like she had just revealed a deep secret. "Seriously?" he asked. "What can I say?" she replied. "I've lived a sheltered life." She locked the door and called for Melanie to come up and eat some pizza.

Billy had just finished his math problems and grabbed some paper plates. All four of them filled their plates and headed into the living room with pizza and drinks. Leslie went over driving the Impala with Steve, who insisted that he knew how to drive a "three on the tree." Billy asked for an explanation, but Leslie's phone rang and she asked Steve to explain it to Billy while she walked out in the kitchen to talk on the phone.

"Hello, Michael," she answered. "Hello to you!" he replied. "Are you excited about the press conference?" "I am, honestly," admitted Leslie. "I have a couple of pictures to show everyone and I'm going to take the Impala." They discussed her father's appointment and Michael said Jim was not happy when he was asked about the police officer's assumption. "Yes, he told me," Leslie replied. "But it's still funny." Michael confirmed that they had officially updated Sergeant Lucas from "MIA" to "Veteran," so he could be discharged any minute. Leslie asked him to keep her updated and thanked him for calling. "I'll say Hello to your mother for you tomorrow," Leslie offered. "She and her contractors will be here in the morning."

Michael thanked Leslie and wished her luck at the press conference. "I'll be watching, as long as I can get the channel," he said before hanging up. Leslie smiled and headed back to the living room. "So?" asked Melanie. "So, what?" asked Leslie. "I told you she'd say that," said Billy. "You owe me a dollar, Steve." Steve handed Billy the dollar and smiled at Leslie. "It's nice to see you smiling again," Steve said. "Every time she talks to that doctor, she seems to smile like that," observed Melanie. Leslie said she had to go get ready for the press conference and walked upstairs to change clothes.

Just as she reached the top of the stairs, Leslie's phone buzzed to let her know that she had a text. "See you at 6:45!" read the message from Jennifer Tillotson. Her phone buzzed again and at first Leslie thought it was the same message because it read "I'll see you @ 6:45." She looked at the sender and it was Linda. 6:45 in the morning? That was way too early for Leslie, so she replied, "Could we make it a little later?" She had to laugh when the reply came back: "Okay, 7:00." Leslie texted back that 7:00 would be fine and went to get ready.

Leslie cleaned her face and put on some makeup, straightened the crazy parts of her hair, and put on the pink dress. With the moderate tan she still had from her Florida trip, the pink dress looked great. She went downstairs and asked Melanie to help her pick out some shoes. "Where are Steve and Billy?" she asked. Melanie explained that Steve went to change clothes and Billy went with him. "I hope he's not wearing a pink dress, too," Leslie joked as they headed back upstairs for shoes. Melanie chose simple black flats and a black purse but could not convince Leslie to add a black belt. "I'm not in my twenties or thirties," Leslie explained. "Women my age who try to dress like they're young make me sad." Melanie laughed and said she understood.

As they got back to the kitchen, Billy was walking in from the garage and pretended to blow a trumpet. "Doot-doo-doo!" he trumpeted. "Announcing tonight's security guard and driver!" Steve was cleaned up and wearing a charcoal gray suit. "I wanted to look official as your security detail," he explained. Melanie hugged him and said he looked incredible. Leslie agreed and looked at her watch. "We should probably get going," she suggested as she popped a mint in her mouth. She told Melanie to lock the doors when they left and reminded her that Gary would be over shortly. "No problem," said Melanie. "We'll be fine."

Leslie grabbed the file folder with the pictures inside and they headed out. Steve wanted her to sit in back, but she refused. "I'm not going to let people see me sitting in back and think I'm uppity," she explained. Steve laughed and said he thought it would be funny, but she could sit wherever she chose. They backed out of the driveway in the Impala and Steve was beaming. "This car is so awesome!" he announced. Leslie agreed and gave him some advice about steering and braking. The drive to the school was uneventful, but Leslie was shocked at the number of cars already in the parking lot. There was a spot up front reserved for her, and Steve escorted her up to the building so nobody could bother her.

Jennifer Tillotson was waiting just inside the door and Leslie said she couldn't believe that all these people were here. "It's a great story," Jennifer replied, "and they're here to hear it from you." They discussed what would happen and who was supposed to be there, and then went down the hall, behind the gymnasium, and out onto the stage in the gym. Leslie paused, listening to the crowd buzzing, then made her entrance.

As she walked out onto the stage, the crowd erupted into applause. Leslie sat down behind the podium and was glad that she had done the other press conferences and knew a little more about what to expect. Jennifer introduced Leslie and told a little bit about how her grandfather was with the same unit as Leslie's father, and expressed her hope that one day they would find him, too. Leslie went to the microphone and told the tale of this couple who was so much in love and showed everyone the picture of her parents with Jim and Linda. She told the crowd about the other couple, too, and said there was a chance that they could be reunited. She expressed her hopes that when her father was able to talk about everything, he could help them locate Jennifer's grandfather. She felt poised and confident and a little overwhelmed at the support, but made sure to thank everyone who believed in her mother.

While Leslie spoke, Steve kept guard silently at the end of the row. She noticed him texting at one point but did not draw any attention to him as he had requested. After taking a few questions and directing any media requests to Jennifer, Leslie left the stage with Steve. "That went better than I expected," she commented. "What did you think?" Steve seemed to be in a hurry. "I think we better get home," he said sternly. "I'll explain on the way."

• • •

Chapter Fifty

Leslie and Steve walked briskly to the car, brushing off reporters and anyone else in the way. As they pulled out of the parking lot, Steve told Leslie why they were in a hurry. Melanie had texted him about the security system going off about ten minutes after Steve and Leslie left. She and Billy were in the basement and heard a lot of commotion and then Gary called out their names, so they came upstairs. The man from the silver car was standing in the kitchen with his hands up and Gary was holding a shot gun. He told Melanie to call 911, and the police had just arrived at the house as the press conference was ending.

"Is everyone okay?" asked Leslie. "What do those people want from me? It doesn't make sense." Steve said everyone was fine, probably just a little shaken, and admitted that he had a lot of questions, too. While he drove, Leslie called Melanie and put her on speaker phone. "Hey, we're on the way home," Leslie informed her. "Are you okay?" Melanie assured Leslie that she was fine, and so was Billy. "You would have been so proud of him," she added. "When the alarm went off, he convinced me that we were safer in the basement, and urged me to go to the new bedroom because it had a sturdy lock on the door." Melanie said she would explain it all when they got there, but she had to go because Officer Hahn wanted to speak to her.

Leslie hung up and realized that Steve hadn't said a word. "Are you okay?" she asked. Steve assured her that he was fine, just mad and worried. "Once I heard Melanie's voice and she said she was okay, I felt better," he admitted. "I'm just processing everything." Leslie suggested that the man and woman had heard about her mother's death and perhaps they were looking for jewelry or money that she might have. "But if that were the case, why didn't they come right after she passed away, while you and Billy were gone?" asked Steve. "It's like they're trying to scare you on purpose." Leslie hadn't really thought about it, and said they'd have to see what information Officer Hahn had for them.

The trip home was not the luxury joy ride that the trip to the press conference was, but the Impala got them there quickly and safely. As they pulled in the driveway, two police cars were blocking the way so Steve parked in his driveway. He jumped out and ran across the lawn, with Leslie trying her best to keep up in that pink dress that was definitely not made for moving quickly. An officer was at the door into the kitchen and wanted to see some type of ID, but Melanie and Billy came running to greet Steve and Leslie, so the officer let them pass.

"Mom!" yelled Billy. "You would have been so proud of me! I didn't even freak out!" Leslie hugged him and said she was always proud of him, as Steve hugged Melanie and asked what happened. She told him that when he and Leslie left, she knew they had a few minutes before the press conference would be on TV so she went downstairs to show Billy a couple of pictures. An alarm went off and Melanie wanted to go upstairs to check it out, but Billy convinced her to go to the new bedroom because of the deadbolt-type lock. There was some banging around and yelling, then Gary called out their names and instructed them to come upstairs and call 911.

Leslie looked around and said it didn't look like much was out of place, but Melanie said she was pretty sure that the sounds she heard were mostly the intruder hitting the floor. "When you're in the basement, everything seems louder because they're walking over your head," explained Billy. Leslie thanked him for his analysis and asked where the man was now. "He's in the police car, handcuffed," said Billy. Leslie marveled at Billy's resilience and hugged him again. "I'm glad you're okay," she said. "Where's Gary?"

Billy pointed to the living room. "The police are talking to him in there," he replied. "He's pretty brave, knocking that man down and then pointing that shotgun at him until the police got here." Leslie went to the living room and Steve followed. Gary was sitting on the couch, and he appeared to have a swollen eye. "Are you okay?" Leslie asked. Gary explained that he was just getting ready to come over and he received an alert on his phone that the security system was triggered, so he grabbed the shotgun from behind his door and ran. He came through the garage into the kitchen and saw a man heading toward the stairs, so he ran in and grabbed a leg. "The other leg kicked me in the head," Gary explained, "but that big man fell like a pile of bricks. He almost kicked the shotgun out of my hand."

Gary continued that the man ran away from him, into the kitchen. "When I didn't see Billy or Melanie, I decided it was safe to raise my shotgun," Gary explained. "I told that asshole not to move or I'd shoot him, and I was surprised when he stopped and put his hands up." Leslie asked if she should get some ice for the swelling and Gary touched his brow. "Ouch! He got me good, didn't he?" he exclaimed. Leslie went to get some ice and Steve continued the discussion with Gary. "So, then you yelled for Melanie and Billy to come out?" he asked. Gary said he was worried because he didn't see or hear them, but he was relieved when they opened the door from the basement and came out.

"I think they were a little bit shocked to see me holding that shotgun," Gary explained. "I hope that didn't scare them too much." Steve commented that everyone did a great job and asked Officer Hahn if the intruder had been armed. "We didn't find anything on him except a cell phone," Officer Hahn replied. "Of course, we took that and we'll see if there are any clues. One of the other officers just found the white car, which also has stolen plates from Virginia, parked around the corner."

Leslie returned with the ice and put it on Gary's eye. "I'm sorry this happened," she said. "Do you wish you would have gone with me to the press conference instead?" Gary shook his head. "Heck no!" he replied. "This will make a much better story!" They all laughed, and Gary asked how the press conference went, since he missed it. Leslie said she had Melanie record it and they could watch it whenever he wanted, and Gary asked if they could watch it now. Officer Hahn stood up and said he had enough information, and that he would get back with Leslie tomorrow. He reminded her that he still needed security camera footage from the other break-in, which he would get when he returned.

Steve walked Officer Hahn outside and ran home to change after asking Leslie to wait until he got back before watching the press conference. Melanie and Billy joined Leslie and Gary in the living room and the other officers cleared out after making sure that Gary did not want to go to the hospital. Leslie breathed a sigh of relief. "Hopefully, all of this is over now," she announced. "I just don't understand what they want from me." Billy was staring at Gary and asked, "Didn't you say the man was heading upstairs?" Gary verified that he was, and Billy declared matter-of-factly, "Well, it's obviously something upstairs. What is up there that a stranger might want?"

Leslie thought about it. Nothing that she had was worth a lot, but her mother had some nice jewelry, and she wasn't sure what was in the gun case. How would these people know what was there, though? Were they people that her mother knew? Had she confided in them that she had jewelry or guns? Leslie had more questions than answers.

...

Chapter Fifty-One

Leslie ran upstairs to change into comfortable clothes while Steve was gone, as Melanie gathered some snacks and Billy described what had happened with Gary. When Leslie returned to the living room, she took a picture of Gary's eye with her phone. "Hey, send that picture to me," Gary requested. "It will prove that my story is true when I tell it." Leslie texted it to him and then to Jim with "More drama" as the subject. She didn't explain any more than that and assumed that he would call immediately to ask what happened. She knew that Jim would be concerned, but she would explain when he called.

When Steve returned, everyone assembled in the living room and Melanie played back the press conference. There was Leslie in her pretty pink dress, and the cameras obviously noticed the young driver/security guard who walked Leslie in and took his position at the end of the stage to keep watch. One reporter even commented about Leslie's fine taste in clothing and in choosing her security detail, with some cheeky comments about her relationship with this young bodyguard. "Why must they turn everything into something it's not?" she asked aloud. "To be fair," Steve chimed in, "you are buying me a house." They all laughed and watched as Leslie spoke about her father and answered a few questions, then Jennifer handled questions from the other reporters.

"Do you think my Grandpa knows what happened to that reporter's Grandpa?" asked Billy. "Maybe he could help her find him. Maybe he's still alive, too." Leslie replied that she certainly hoped so, but it was extremely unlikely, and they weren't sure how much her dad remembered. They discussed amnesia and how Grandpa Bill thought his name was Erden, but Dr. Edwards was going to help with that. "We just have to get past the language barrier first," Leslie said, "and then we can start asking more questions." Billy said he had a lot of questions, and Leslie cautioned him about pushing too hard, too soon. "He is going to remember some horrible things if his memories start coming back," Leslie suggested. "We need to make sure that we help him through that." Billy agreed but had a great question. "Won't he also remember some of the good things from his life?" he asked. "I sure hope so," Leslie replied. "He had a great childhood and married someone who truly loved him, so let's keep our fingers crossed that he remembers some of that, too."

Melanie yawned and apologized, but said she'd had enough excitement for today. She and Steve got up to head home and Steve said he would walk Melanie home and bring the Impala back over, since the driveway was clear. Gary got up to go, too, and Leslie asked if he was sure that he didn't want to go to the hospital for his eye. "You've been awfully quiet," said Leslie. "That's not really normal for you." Gary explained that he was just thinking about how much he was going to miss them when he moved. "All these years, being more of a family member than a neighbor," he recalled. "It was never as exciting as it has been in the past week, honestly, but you and your mom always made me feel like family."

Leslie teared up as she hugged Gary. "I appreciate you more than you know," she sniffled, "but you're always welcome to come back. There's always room for you here." Gary thanked Leslie and headed home through the garage. "Don't forget to turn the security system back on after we're gone," he advised. Leslie thanked him for worrying about her and said she would do that after Steve came back with the Impala.

She went to check on Billy and found him watching the press conference again. "What did you notice that you needed to see again?" she inquired. She knew Billy's habits well. "Look at this guy back here," said Billy, "pointing to a man in the crowd. "Doesn't he look like my Dad?" Leslie thought it did, but simply remarked, "Nah. Doppelganger." As she walked out of the room, Leslie recalled the conversation with Jim when he spotted Linda's picture and Leslie assumed it was a "doppelganger" situation. She thought it was odd that Jim had not called her about the press conference or about the picture she texted, so she dialed his number to make sure everything was alright.

"Hello, Leslie," Jim answered. "I found your dad. What's going on?" Leslie heard her dad say, "Hello, Leslie," and she laughed. "Hello, Dad," she replied, relieved that he had been found. She told Jim about the press conference and the second intruder, leaving out a few details so Jim wouldn't be too worried. "I apologize for missing the press conference, but I got caught up in finding your dad," Jim explained. "I can probably find it somewhere on social media, but don't delete it. Maybe we can watch it when we get there." Leslie agreed that it would be fun to watch it together. "We can talk more about it later, maybe tomorrow," Leslie suggested. Jim seemed awfully preoccupied, so Leslie apologized for calling so late and wished them a nice evening. She then went back to the living room to remind Billy that it was time for bed.

"Hey, buddy, you have school tomorrow and it's past your bedtime," she announced. Billy looked at the clock. "Holy crap, it's almost 9:30!" Billy observed as he ran up the steps, already removing clothing so he could change into his pajamas. "Don't forget to wash your face after you brush your teeth!" Leslie called up after him. She picked up the remote and went back to the man in the crowd, Mark's doppelganger. The guy really did look like him, but his hair was a bit wilder and he was wearing glasses. If it were him, though, Leslie assumed that he would have made himself known, since he was quite fond of the spotlight. She turned off the TV and went to make a list for the next morning.

Steve tapped on the door from the garage and walked in. "I brought back the keys to the Impala," he announced. Leslie thanked him for driving her and asked how he liked driving the Impala. "It was everything I expected," he replied. "I love old cars, but I'm so thankful for modern technology, like power steering." Leslie agreed and asked if he and his friends would like to cook out tomorrow after working on the fence. "That sounds like a good plan," said Steve. "The nights are still a little chilly, so having a cookout will be like kicking off summer early." He and Leslie discussed how many people would be there and what to have, and Leslie started her lists with "Cookout." After they figured out a time and menu, Steve left and Leslie made sure to lock the doors and set the security system. She texted Gary: "All secure." He replied by sending back the picture of his bruised eye, which made Leslie burst out laughing. She was really going to miss him, but for now she had a lot to do. Tomorrow was going to be a busy day.

Leslie went upstairs to turn off Billy's light and kiss him goodnight. She was surprised to see that his light was turned off and he was in bed. It looked like he was already asleep. She smiled at the thought of him growing up and becoming more responsible and decided not to bother him. As she turned away from his doorway, he called out, "Hey! Aren't you going to kiss me goodnight?" Leslie laughed and said she thought he was already asleep and had not wanted to wake him. "Mom, I always want you to kiss me goodnight," Billy explained. "I think it helps me sleep better." Leslie kissed him on the forehead and reminded him that Linda would be there early, so she was going to bed shortly. "Big day tomorrow," Leslie added. "Lots going on."

Leslie put on her pajamas and went through her nightly routine. As she rubbed the lotion into her skin and noticed the wrinkles starting to appear around her eyes, she thought about Linda and how beautiful her skin was. She would try to remember to ask what she uses on her skin. She finished her lists, plugged in her phone, and set her alarm for 6:00. She wanted to be up and showered when Linda and her contractors arrived in the morning.

•••

Chapter Fifty-Two

Leslie jumped out of bed at 6:00, startled by the early alarm. She hadn't set out any clothes before she went to bed and thinking about what to wear this early never worked for her, so she headed to the shower with just a robe and some panties. She showered and dried her hair, and came out of the bathroom to find Billy waiting to go in. "You're up early," she observed. "I want to be out of the shower before strangers come to the house," he mumbled, obviously tired. Ah, there was the Billy she knew and loved. He went to shower as Leslie headed to her room to get dressed. She looked out the window as a news van pulled up, then another. For goodness sake, the sun was just coming up! She closed the blinds and went to pick out an outfit.

Leslie knew she might be doing some dirty work when the contractors arrived, so she opted for some comfortable jeans and a simple t-shirt. She picked a shirt that would make a statement if one of the news cameras caught her, one with a map of Vietnam and something written in Vietnamese. It was her mother's shirt, given to her by a former POW, one that Mom never wore but could not seem to part with. It fit Leslie perfectly and she went downstairs to get some coffee going. She didn't like coffee, but it was more for her guests than herself. She heated some water for her tea in the microwave and dropped a couple of Pop-Tarts in the toaster. She caught some movement outside out of her kitchen window, but it was just Steve going out for his morning run. She laughed as he went directly to the news van to confront them and could only imagine how that conversation was going.

Leslie looked around the kitchen and wondered how it got dirty so quickly. She cleared off the counters and wiped them down, then did a quick sweep with a broom that was probably as old as she was. Mom had worked hard to keep everything as it had been when her husband left home, and Leslie was pretty sure that straw broom was the same one her mother had been using in the 60s. Leslie was ready to get rid of some things, but she didn't want to rush too quickly to replace everything because she had read about people with amnesia who recognized something as simple as a coffee cup from their past. She noticed Linda's car pulling up in front and looked at the microwave clock. It was 6:44.

Leslie turned off the security system and went to the front door to greet Linda. The news vans were still there and a cameraman jumped out when Linda was walking to the front door. "Good morning!" Leslie announced with a smile. "Good morning to you!" Linda replied. "How long has the paparazzi been hanging around?" Leslie said she wasn't sure, but it was probably in response to the press conference last night. "I saw that," said Linda, "and I can't believe you found that picture of us." Leslie apologized for not asking Linda if it was okay to share the photo, but it was a last-minute find. Linda didn't respond and brushed past Leslie into the kitchen. "I smell coffee," Linda announced. "Caramel?" Leslie wasn't sure, so she opened the cupboard. "Dulce de Leche," she read from the package. "Sorry, but I don't drink coffee. I just made it for you and your contractors."

A large white pickup pulled into the driveway and Linda looked at her watch. "Hey, would you look at that!" she announced. "They're ten minutes early." She went out to greet the contractors as Billy walked into the kitchen. He looked sharp in his khakis and blue polo shirt, and Leslie asked if he had something going on at school. "Not that I know of," replied Billy. "I just feel like today is going to be a special day, so I want to look good." Leslie hugged him and laughed as she took a few bites of her Pop-Tart. "And I am dressed in jeans and a t-shirt. Would you like me to fix you something for breakfast?" Billy said he would just make some toast because his stomach felt excited, like he had butterflies in there. Leslie took out the bread and handed it to him. "Okay, buddy, I'm going out to meet Linda's contractors," she said. "I'll be back in a few minutes." Leslie went to talk to Linda and the four men from the pickup truck as another news crew showed up. Linda introduced Leslie to her contractors, and they were all excited to be part of the remodel after hearing about Leslie's dad being found. One of them suggested that they contact HGTV to do a "Before and After" episode, but Linda said she would talk to Leslie about that after they discussed exactly what they would be renovating.

Coming Home

A cheesy reporter in a tweed sports coat started up the sidewalk and asked, "Is that Linda Edwards?" Linda waved and said, "In the flesh, honey." The cameraman was right behind the reporter, but before they made it up the sidewalk a small black car zipped into the driveway and almost hit them. Jennifer Tillotson jumped out and Leslie thought she was going to tackle the two men. "I told you guys that Miss Leslie is not to be bothered!" she announced. "She has given me exclusive rights to this story, and you need to respect that." Linda smiled. "Oh, I like her," she confided to Leslie. "She's a spitfire." Jennifer herded the men back to their van, lecturing them about respect and boundaries until they drove away. The other two news crews left before she even made it to their vehicles, as Leslie and Linda watched in awe.

Jennifer walked up the driveway, smoothing her hair, and apologized to Leslie. "I'm sorry, Leslie, but they know the situation and I was just trying to remind them," Jennifer explained. Linda shook Jennifer's hand. "Hi, I'm Linda," she began. "I saw you on the press conference last night and I have to admit that I'm quite impressed." Jennifer stared at Linda for a few seconds before she responded. "Oh, my God! You're the other beautiful lady in that picture that Leslie had last night!" Linda admitted that was her and Jennifer said she had so many questions. "Not right now, sweetie," cooed Linda. "My guys and I have some work to do. Maybe we can talk later." Jennifer was obviously excited and asked what they were doing. Leslie explained that there would be renovations, but first they were going to get some plans together and make some decisions. "We'll be starting on the outside first," Linda explained. "Probably around 1:00. You can come back then if you wish." Jennifer thanked her and apologized to Leslie for the other reporters before dashing off in her little black car.

"Okay, what now?" Leslie asked. Linda explained that she would walk around with the contractors to decide what needed to be done, then they would draw up the plans and go over them with Leslie before any final decisions were made. Leslie let them know that the security system was off and they were free to roam the property as needed, then went inside to check on Billy. He had made a cinnamon/sugar mixture to put on his toast and between that and the coffee, the kitchen smelled great. Leslie let Billy know that the contractors would be wandering around the house and suggested that he clean up his room a little before he went to school. He was on his way upstairs when he noticed something on the living room floor and picked it up. "Hey, Mom!" he called out. "I found one of your earrings in the living room." Leslie went to take it from him, and Billy ran upstairs to clean his room. Leslie looked at the earring and then looked around for another one. It looked like a diamond earring, but she didn't have any. She was still examining the earring when Linda walked in. "Nice!" exclaimed Linda. "Half carat?" Leslie said she wasn't sure and set it down on the kitchen counter, making a mental note to ask Melanie later if it belonged to her.

The contractors filed into the kitchen, and Linda told them that Leslie had made some "Dulce de Leche" coffee for them if they wanted any. Leslie showed them where to find cups, spoons, and sugar. As they were helping themselves, Linda picked up the earring. "How is a woman not sure about the size of a diamond earring?" she joked. Leslie explained that she didn't wear diamond earrings and hadn't owned any for years. Mark had bought some for her to wear for their wedding, but they sat in her jewelry box until the divorce, when he pawned them. "Wow, he sounds like quite a catch," Linda commented sarcastically. "No wonder your mother didn't want you to marry him."

"I just don't understand where the earring came from," Leslie wondered aloud. "Maybe it was Mom's. Do you want to go check with me?" Linda told the contractors to enjoy their coffee for a minute and headed upstairs with Leslie. "Hey, Billy," Leslie called out as she passed his room, "we're leaving for school in a few minutes." Billy said he needed to pack his lunch and headed downstairs as Linda walked into Susan's bedroom. "Oh, I took all of her jewelry into my room," Leslie explained, but Linda had seen something in the "trash" pile that caught her eye. "Oh, my goodness! Are these original?" she asked, obviously excited. Leslie went into her mother's room and found Linda holding the paintings that had hung in there for years, just blocks of color that Leslie didn't understand or appreciate. "I think so," explained Leslie. "Mom inherited them from Grandpa Joe." There were three paintings, one large and two smaller, and Linda was looking at them like they were beautiful paintings of flowers or rainbows. "Do you want them?" Leslie asked. Linda stared at Leslie like she had lost her mind. "These are

Rothko paintings, worth millions," Linda finally managed. "You need an art appraiser."

Linda picked up all three paintings and told Leslie to hide them in her closet, and not to tell anyone else about them until she could find the right person for the situation. "I have an art guy," explained Linda. "I'll check with him." Leslie wrapped the paintings in a blanket and set them in her closet, then put her mother's jewelry box on the bed to sort through it. They did not find diamond earrings, although there were other nice earrings and necklaces. Leslie said she would ask Melanie later and put the jewelry away. She needed to get Billy to school, so she and Linda walked out of the bedroom and Linda shut the door behind them. "Our secret," Linda whispered. Leslie giggled and agreed that it was their secret.

...

Chapter Fifty-Three

Billy had packed his lunch and was making toast for the contractors when Leslie and Linda returned to the kitchen. Leslie explained to the contractors that Billy had to go to school, so they were on their own, and told Linda she'd be right back. As Leslie was backing out of the driveway, Steve was returning from his run. He and Billy exchanged "Good morning" greetings and Leslie thanked Steve for going out to talk to the news crew earlier. "No problem," Steve replied. "I think they don't believe you that your dad isn't here, and they're trying to get a shot of him." Leslie laughed. "Not only is he not here, but I don't even know when he's coming." Steve nodded in acknowledgment and said that he and his friends would be over to start working on the fence in a half hour or so. "Do you mind if I take the Impala out of the garage so I have some space to work in there?" he asked. "That's fine," Leslie responded. "I won't pull into the garage when I get back from taking Billy; I'll just park in the driveway."

Billy reminded Leslie that they needed to go, and they headed to Billy's school. As they drove, Billy shared some thoughts. "Mom, I've been thinking," Billy started. "Since Grandpa thinks his name is Erden, why don't we just call him that?" Leslie explained that it wasn't really his name, and Billy brought up the fact that she calls him "Billy," but his name is William. They discussed nicknames and how some people have a lot of them. "Grandma told me once that Grandpa's closest friends called him 'Luke,' which is short for Lucas," Billy explained. "I guess some people have lots of nicknames." Leslie agreed and admitted that her dad had been called "Erden" longer than he had been called anything else.

Bill had been summoned to the private quarters of head monk Thich Dinh Ky. Everyone in the monastery was aware that their leader was probably in his last days and would be sharing his final bits of wisdom and light with them. Bill knew this might be the last time he got the chance to visit with the man who was a fatherly figure and tried not to let his emotions get the best of him.

Bill entered the room and bowed out of courtesy and Ky requested that he come closer. Bill went to Ky's bedside and knelt there, concerned at the weakness of this man who had always portrayed such strength and resilience. Ky announced that he had a confession to make before taking a deep breath and quietly admitting that he hoped Bill could forgive him. Bill couldn't imagine there was anything about this man that would disturb him. He urged him to continue.

Ky confessed that he bestowed upon Bill the name of 'Erden' many years ago because it means 'treasure,' but that his given name is William and he is an American. He brought Bill there to save his life and when he didn't remember that life Ky made the decision to let him stay and treat him like the son he could never have. He continued that we are taught not to dwell in the past and Bill was able to do that so easily because he didn't remember his past, which made him the best student who brought him such joy. Ky shared that Bill's silence may have to come to an end because soon he would no longer be there to protect him and asked for Bill's forgiveness. Ky kept calling Bill by his American name, William, which seemed odd.

Bill listened intently, nodding in agreement with whatever Ky was saying and assuming that this was some type of hallucination or his mind playing tricks on him. As Ky closed his eyes, Bill stared at the abbot – his mentor - for a moment before he slipped away politely to allow Ky some time to rest. Bill had been taught that peace can only come from within, and he hoped that Ky was able to be at peace with himself. He didn't have much time left.

As Bill headed back to tend his garden, he felt sad about the idea of losing the closest person in his life, but he couldn't help but wonder if there was any truth to what Ky shared with him. Bill had been taught not to dwell on his past, but if he was really someone else, wouldn't he remember something? Anything? He did have vivid dreams sometimes about people and places he didn't know, but he had no memory of being William. He resolved to focus on the present and continue to be Erden, as he had been called for so long. He wasn't one to be concerned about things that he couldn't change and resolved to be at peace, whoever he was.

"I guess we'll just leave that up to him," Leslie continued. "As soon as he is able to tell us what he wants to be called, that is what we'll honor." Billy nodded and Leslie took the opportunity to change the subject. "Are you excited about your Boy Scout meeting this weekend?" she asked. "YES!" Billy shouted. "I can't wait to tell them about Grandpa and his Pinewood Derby cars! Maybe Grandpa can go with me to the next meeting so they can talk to him." Leslie appreciated his excitement but reminded him that they need to ease her dad into social situations so he doesn't get overwhelmed. "Are you going to have a party for him?" asked Billy. "You know, a 'Welcome Home' party? I can share my birthday party with him." Leslie said she definitely wanted to throw a large party but wanted to keep it separate so a bunch of strangers weren't showing up for Billy's birthday. "As long as they bring presents, I don't mind," Billy confessed.

They pulled up to the school and Billy jumped out. "Have a good day!" Leslie yelled after him. "I hope something important happens that warrants khakis and polos!" Billy waved and scrambled into the building as Leslie headed home, thinking of everything she had to do today. She turned on some music to keep her mind from overloading. About halfway home, she noticed that a police car was following her. "Was I speeding?" Leslie wondered aloud. The police officer didn't pull her over, but he did follow her right into the driveway. Leslie sat still and rolled down her window. She was quite relieved when Officer Hahn came to the window and asked if she was getting out or not. "I thought I was in trouble," Leslie explained. "I was getting ready to take out my license and registration." As Officer Hahn opened her car door, Steve and Tyler straggled across the lawn with four of their friends to work on the fence. "Hey, Hahn," greeted Steve, "can you park in the street? We need to pull the Impala out and someone else already parked their truck here." Officer Hahn moved his car out to the street by Linda's and Leslie went inside to ask the contractors to move their truck.

Leslie found Linda and the contractors in the basement, admiring Gary's renovation work. After Leslie asked one of them to move the truck, she suggested to Linda that it would be easier for them to put in a bathroom down there because Steve really didn't have time. Linda admitted that bathrooms were her favorite room to design and asked where Leslie wanted it. "Wherever it works," Leslie commented, and Linda went on a mission to find the right spot.

Leslie went back upstairs and grabbed the keys to the Impala. She went out and handed them to Steve so he could move the car, and Officer Hahn returned to the house with Leslie. "I have some interesting information for you," he told Leslie, "And I'd like to see the security footage if you have time." Leslie grabbed some sweet tea from the refrigerator and offered Officer Hahn something to drink, but he politely declined. She showed him the security cameras and monitor and gave him permission to scroll through and take what he needed. "Gary even brought me these thumb drives to record anything I needed," Leslie explained, "so you can use one of those." Officer Hahn thanked her and asked if they could talk privately about the pistol that was retrieved.

This sounded serious, so Leslie asked if he wanted to go to the living room and talk. They sat down and Officer Hahn did not beat around the bush. "We checked the serial numbers from the pistol," he began, "and it was registered to Mark Mitchell." Leslie's eyes widened. "My ex-husband?" she asked. "Well, I assume so," Officer Hahn replied, "but the address that you gave us for him is not the same as the one on the registration. Do you recognize this address?" Leslie looked at the notebook in Officer Hahn's hands. "Yes, that's the address of our cabin up north," she replied. "Well, Mark's cabin. I let him keep it in the divorce because I have no need for it." Leslie was trying to understand the connection as Officer Hahn continued. "We have been talking to the woman and man who broke into your house. Apparently, they are from Virginia. The man was not armed because they only had one weapon and the girlfriend dropped it when Steve dropped her." He laughed and said the whole situation was a comedy of errors. "When we arrested her," he explained, "she was wearing one earring, which we have with her other personal effects, and she keeps accusing us of stealing her other earring. She even claims that they're real diamonds."

Leslie told Officer Hahn she'd be right back. She retrieved the earring from the kitchen and brought it back to him. "Does it look like this?" she asked. Officer Hahn looked it over and agreed that it did. "My son found this in our living room earlier," Leslie explained. "It's not mine or my mother's, and Linda Edwards said it's a real diamond." Officer Hahn tilted his head. "Linda Edwards, the designer?" he asked. "Yes, her," replied Leslie, and Linda appeared as if on cue. "Hey, Leslie, I have some great ideas when you have time," she interrupted, before noticing Officer Hahn. "Oh, who's your friend?" she asked sweetly. Leslie introduced Linda to Officer Hahn and tried to explain Linda's connection to the family, as Linda started asking questions about the break-ins. "What are they after?" she asked Hahn. "Did they say?" Officer Hahn explained that he is not allowed to comment on an active investigation, and Linda suggested that Leslie let him in on their secret. "I don't need to know your secrets," Officer Hahn said nervously, "unless they are connected to these B-n-E's." Linda asked Officer Hahn to follow her upstairs, and Leslie was wondering if Linda was onto something significant.

They went into Leslie's bedroom and Linda took the paintings out. "I believe these are original Rothko paintings," she explained. "If so, they're worth millions." Officer Hahn looked them over and asked if they had been appraised, but Leslie said she had just been told today that they might be valuable. Linda said she would go call Reginald, her "art guy," and ask if he could stop by as Officer Hahn took pictures of the paintings with his phone. "It is a possibility," he explained to Leslie. "I personally don't see it, but do you think your ex-husband sent these morons to steal the paintings?" Leslie sat down on the bed and tried to process it. "After the week I've had, I'm not ruling out anything," she commented. "He definitely knew that they were here, though."

Officer Hahn took some notes and Leslie asked if he could keep the information about the paintings as private as possible. "Of course," he promised. "Your secrets are safe with me." They walked downstairs so he could check out the security footage, and Linda met them in the kitchen. "Reginald is on his way over," Linda announced. "He is super excited about your discovery." Leslie expressed her concern about this no longer being a secret and Linda assured her that Reginald is very discreet.

Leslie's phone buzzed and she looked to see a text from Katrina. "I'm stopping by in a bit," she wrote. "I hope you're not too busy." Leslie laughed and decided that these paintings might be another topic of discussion with Katrina. "See you soon," Leslie wrote back.

• • •

Chapter Fifty-Four

Leslie picked up her tea to take a swig as the side door to the garage opened and Gary walked into the kitchen. "Wow, your eye is healing well," Leslie commented. "Is there more trouble here?" asked Gary. "Did you have to call the police again?" Leslie explained that Officer Hahn was there to go over some of the footage on the security camera and suggested that Gary could probably help, since he knew the system so well. Gary showed Hahn how to manipulate the controls to get what he needed and went back to the beginning of the recording a couple of days ago. "Seems easy enough," Officer Hahn stated. He scrolled through the recorded footage as Gary turned to Leslie.

"So, this might be a good time to ask you about the $2500 that showed up in my account," said Gary, raising his eyebrows and rubbing his chin. Leslie laughed. "I'm glad Jim was able to push it through," she replied. "That money is for all the work you did on the house. Mom owed it to you, so now we're square." Gary crossed his arms and said he had rejected her offer. "Well, I reject your rejection," Leslie responded, as she crossed her arms and stared back.

"Okay, not to change the subject," Gary said, "but I think I saw your ex-husband downtown earlier this morning. I haven't seen him many times, so I can't be sure, but it looked like him," Gary stated. "This guy was chunkier, and his hair was a little longer, though. Did he move back to the area?" Leslie shook her head. "No, he still lives in Virginia," she replied. "Sometimes, he goes to his cabin up north for vacations, but usually he lets me know so he can stop and visit Billy. It's been months seen I've seen him."

Leslie thought about the possibility that Mark might be in the area if he had sent people to take paintings out of her house. She asked Gary if he knew anything about some artwork that her Mom had. "Oh, she has some expensive pieces," he replied. "She has a few Rothko paintings upstairs and I believe she has a few other expensive works in the closet of the basement bedroom." Leslie stared at Gary like he was speaking a foreign language. "You knew about the artwork?" she asked. "Sure," Gary replied. "I'm the one who told Susan that the paintings that her stepfather gave her were priceless. She wasn't really a fan, and she was going to throw them out." Linda was just coming up the basement stairs. "Who was going to throw paintings out?" she asked, as she walked into the kitchen. Before Leslie could answer, she noticed a metallic green Miata pulling up to the curb and almost touching the bumper of Linda's car.

"Hey, there's Reginald!" Linda announced. "Hold that thought about the artwork!" As Linda went out to greet Reginald, Leslie explained to Gary that Linda had asked her "art guy" to come over to look at the Rothko paintings. "Are you going to sell them?" asked Gary. Leslie said she didn't plan to sell them, but wanted to know their value so she could insure them. "Oh, they're insured," Gary explained. "Did you find the little blue notebook that has all the policies in it? It's in there." Leslie laughed and asked Gary if there was anything else that she should know about. "I'm sure there is," Gary replied, "and I'll let you know if I remember anything that might be helpful."

Reginald came waltzing in like he owned the place, decked out in a peach satin shirt, and Linda introduced him to Leslie. "Can I get you something to drink?" Leslie offered. "Oh, sweetie, that's so hospitable," replied Reginald, "but I brought my flask." He winked at Leslie and asked where to find the paintings. "Come upstairs and I'll show you the goods," Linda offered. "Oh, I can't tell you the last time I heard that from a lady," teased Reginald. He and Linda laughed and headed upstairs as Leslie just stared after them, blinking. Gary cleared his throat and explained that he needed to get home to pack more boxes, reminding Leslie that the other paintings are in the basement.

Leslie headed upstairs to join Linda and Reginald and had to laugh when she heard Reginald squeal with delight upon seeing the paintings. As she walked into her bedroom, Reginald was laying the paintings out on her bed. "These are incredible!" he fawned. "Look at the rich colors, Linda! I can feel the warmth!" He rubbed his hands together over the paintings as if they were actual fire, which amused Leslie. She watched him as he took pictures and jotted down notes. He advised her to never touch the actual canvas, as the oil from her fingers would ruin the paint. "But aren't they oil paintings?" asked Leslie. Reginald rolled his eyes and attempted to educate Leslie on Rothko's paintings and how he used blocks of colors to represent emotions. Leslie tried to understand his passion, but it just didn't appeal to her. "I don't mean to be rude," she explained, "but I don't get it. I have a lot going on so I will let you two spend as much time as you would like up here, but I need to head downstairs. I just found out that there are more paintings in the basement, too."

As Leslie headed downstairs, she could hear Reginald's questions: "How did the family acquire these paintings?" "How am I going to sleep tonight, knowing these are here?" and then "My Lord, what is going on with this wallpaper?" She would let Linda explain everything, and then they could go check out the paintings in the basement.

Leslie looked at the clock when she got to the kitchen and couldn't believe it was only a few minutes before ten. She had already had a full day in the four hours that she was awake and there was still so much to do. She saw that Officer Hahn was busy with the security cameras, so she went outside to check on Steve and his friends to let Hahn have some space. She found one of the contractors talking to Steve about doing some work for him. "Sorry to interrupt," said Leslie, "but did you guys bring anything for lunch? I am running to the store to get stuff for the cookout and wondered if you need anything."

Steve checked with everyone and assured Leslie that they were all set. "Melanie is bringing some sandwiches over in a bit," he explained. "I'm sure she would like to help you with the cookout, if you want to go ask her." Leslie thanked Steve and saw Officer Hahn walk out and drive away in his patrol car without saying a word. "That is weird," Leslie remarked. "I wonder if he got what he needed already." She shrugged her shoulders and headed across the yard to talk to Melanie.

Leslie was pleasantly surprised to see how much better Melanie looked when she answered the door. "Oh, Melanie," Leslie gushed "your perkiness has returned!" Melanie invited Leslie inside and explained that she slept soundly and felt so much better about what was going to happen with the house and Steve's future career. Leslie laughed when she walked into the kitchen and saw the mountain of sandwiches and chips, and Melanie explained that she was making sure that everyone was fed so they would keep working. "I am going to get stuff for the cookout," Leslie said. "Did Steve tell you about it?" Melanie laughed and shook her head. "He doesn't usually tell me things until they are happening," she complained. "It's frustrating."

Leslie explained what she was getting for the cookout and asked Melanie if she'd like to help. "Of course," said Melanie, "I can make some pasta salad if you pick up some rotini while you're at the store, and I'll make some brownies and oatmeal Scotchies for dessert. I have everything for those." Leslie admitted that she'd never eaten oatmeal Scotchies and that her mother never made them. "Supposedly, they were my dad's favorite treat," Leslie explained, "and it was too painful for Mom to make them." Melanie said she was excited to make them for Leslie's dad whenever he returned, and Leslie smiled. "If I can get through this next week or so," Leslie lamented, "we can start planning a party for his return. There is so much going on today that my head hurts." Melanie asked if there was anything she could do to help, and Leslie cocked her head and thought about it. "Maybe you could pick up Billy from school today. I'm not sure what I'll be doing by then," she suggested. "Done!" said Melanie. Leslie thanked her and went to leave. "Hey, one more thing," said Melanie. "You might want to get some beer."

Leslie wondered about the beer as she walked back across the lawn. "Hey, Steve," she said when she was closer to where he was working, "what kind of beer should I get for the cookout?" Before Steve could answer, Tyler chimed in, "The kind that makes you drunk!" The guys all laughed and Leslie rolled her eyes. She didn't remember being like that when she was younger. "Okay," she replied. "I'll make sure to ask for that kind at the store."

She went inside to get her keys and purse as Linda and Reginald were walking into the kitchen, discussing the Rothko paintings. "Hey, I'm going to the store to get some things for our cookout," Leslie informed them. "Will you two be staying for that?" Reginald looked out the window. "I have a couple of appointments this afternoon, but I will return later," he explained. "It isn't often that you get that scenery around here." Leslie looked out the window and wondered what he meant. There were a few lilac bushes, but not much else to see. "Scenery?" she inquired. "Oh, honey," Linda cooed. "He means those boys working on the fence." Leslie laughed, but she could feel her face getting red. "I'm going now. Any special requests?" Reginald looked around the kitchen. "Any chance that you have some merlot?" he asked. Leslie said she would add it to the list and reminded Linda and Reginald about the other paintings in the basement. Reginald squealed with delight again, which made Leslie giggle as she was heading out the door.

Leslie turned off the radio so she could enjoy some peace and quiet on her drive. She had only driven about 7 minutes when her phone rang. "Hello, Mrs. Petry," Leslie answered. "How are you today?" Mrs. Petry said she was fine and wondered when she could come by with the paperwork for the house. "I'm heading to the store right now," explained Leslie. "I should be home in about an hour, so how about 11:00?" Mrs. Petry explained that she had another closing at 10:30 and asked if Leslie was available around 12:30. "Sure, that sounds fine," said Leslie. "I'll be home all day, so whenever you get there." Leslie enjoyed about five minutes of quiet before she arrived at the grocery store.

Before she got out of the car, Leslie added a few things to her list: rotini, beer, and merlot. She could handle the rotini, but she was going to need advice for the other two. As Leslie walked around the store, collecting the items on her list, she felt like a celebrity. Strangers were greeting her by name and asking if her father was home yet, congratulating her and wishing her well. An older gentleman with a "Vietnam Veteran" hat approached her while she was looking at the rotini, and he had tears in his eyes. "Is it true?" he asked Leslie. "Is Luke really alive and coming home?" Leslie explained that her dad was alive and well, but she wasn't sure exactly when he would be returning. "So, you knew my dad?" she asked, aware that the man was working hard to control his emotions. "I grew up with him and I was lucky enough to be stationed with him in Chu Lai," he explained. "Best Marine I ever knew. We couldn't believe the VC blew him up. We found the three who died, at least what was left of them, but there was no sign of Mackey or Tilly or Luke. We thought they were all dead." His gaze wandered off a little and Leslie wasn't sure what to say. "What's your name?" she asked. "Bill Kowalski," he replied, "but everyone calls me 'Ski."

Bill Kowalski had only been in Chu Lai for a few weeks and had heard incredible stories about his friend Bill Lucas. They finally ran into each other on a dusty day in early March 1967, as Kowalski was trying to find the parts he needed in a supply tent. "Well, if it isn't my hometown hero," Bill Kowalski announced as he and Bill Lucas shook hands. "Ski! When did you get here?" asked Bill Lucas, surprised to see someone from home.

They caught up quickly, with Kowalski filling in the details about going to work in a factory after graduation and dating Ginny Sanderson up until the day he left for basic training. "I got drafted and then got my 'Dear John' before I even left," he explained. "What about you and Susan?" Bill Lucas explained that they were married just six months ago, and they had a baby on the way. "So, you'll be heading back to Michigan when the baby comes?" Kowalski inquired. "For sure," Bill Lucas exclaimed. "But until then, I'm kicking some VC ass while I'm here. What MOS did they give you?"

Bill Kowalski seemed hesitant to say. "6114, Huey mechanic," he said quietly. "I wanted to be a grunt, just a basic rifleman, but I know how to fix engines so that's what I'm doing." Bill Lucas laughed. "Look, we're all riflemen; those 0311s just get to do it all the time. There aren't any rules that you can't be both," he said with a wink. He abruptly changed the subject and warned Kowalski that it was just a couple of weeks before the seasons change, and the monsoon rains would begin. "You'll start to wonder if you'll ever be dry again, but you will. Just find a way to keep your stuff dry," he advised.

Bill Kowalski thanked him for the advice and went about his mission of finding the engine pieces he needed. As he watched Bill Lucas grab his M-14 and slip away into the jungle, he wondered why his friend from home never discussed his MOS. Susan had mentioned that he was a truck driver, so it seemed odd that he hadn't brought it up. Kowalski decided that it really didn't matter much and went about his business.

Leslie explained that she was going to have a "Welcome Home" party for her dad and asked if he would like to come. She started writing down the address for him and he stopped her. "I just live down the block from you," he said with a wink. "I walk past your house every day." Leslie said she would keep an eye out for him and would let him know when they decided to have the party. He thanked her and wiped his eyes. "It's a miracle," he mumbled as he walked away. "Just a damn miracle." Leslie put the rotini in her cart and smiled. She would ask Jim later if he could find anyone else still around who was stationed with her dad. Maybe they could have a reunion of sorts.

She had everything else on the list except the drinks, and when she headed down the beer aisle she was overwhelmed by the choices. She decided to get the merlot first, and since she didn't know what kind to get, she asked one of the workers for help. "Can you help me find some merlot?" she asked. "Sweetie, I can help you find it *and* drink it," the woman replied with a wink. "Is it just for you, or is there a special occasion?" Leslie explained that she was having a lot of people at her house, which she wasn't used to, and she didn't drink alcohol very often. She mentioned that she just met Reginald, an art appraiser, when he came to her house and the woman laughed. "Ah, Reginald," she said with a knowing smile, "a frequent flyer. Here's his brand, but it ain't cheap." She pulled a bottle off the shelf and handed it to Leslie. "Oh, thank you! That was easy," beamed Leslie. "Can you help me with my last item?" She explained that she needed beer for the men who were putting in the fence, younger men who just wanted to get drunk. "Oh, okay," replied the woman as she led Leslie back to the beer aisle. "Millennials will go on and on about craft beers and IPAs, but our biggest sellers are still the old classics. You can't go wrong with Coors and Michelob Lite." She showed Leslie where to find them and then went to assist another customer. "Thank you!" Leslie yelled after her as she filled the bottom level of the cart with a few different beers, wondering if she should buy another large cooler. Her cart was too full to add one, but she was reasonably sure that Steve had one that she could use.

...

Chapter Fifty-Five

As Leslie was loading her groceries in the back of the Equinox, her phone rang and she let it go to voicemail. She looked at the message when she got in the car and saw that it was Officer Hahn who had called, so she listened to the message. "Hi, Leslie," said the message. "I had to run back to the office for something and I'm on my way back to your house now. Should just be a few minutes."

Leslie was able to enjoy about 15 minutes of peace as she drove home, wondering if Linda and Reginald had finished looking at the other paintings. As she pulled in the driveway, Leslie was pleased at the obvious progress on the fence. She started carrying the bags inside and Steve asked if she needed help. "No, I can get this stuff," she replied. "You guys keep doing that. The fence will be up in no time!" Leslie took all the food inside and decided to unload the beer right into a cooler. She got the large cooler from the garage and rinsed it out, then took the entire bin of ice from her freezer and dumped it in. She put the cooler in the garage and was adding the first 12-pack of beer when Officer Hahn pulled up. Leslie waved and continued what she was doing.

"Looks like you're having a party!" Hahn commented as he got out of the patrol car. "Or maybe you just drink a lot." Leslie laughed. "I haven't had a beer in years," she replied. "I don't really like it." She explained that she was having a cookout for Steve and his friends. "Hey, what time are you off work?" she asked. "Do you want to come by for a burger and one of these beers?" Officer Hahn replied that he was supposed to be off at 4:00, and he would love to come by when he was off duty.

Leslie and Officer Hahn filled up the cooler and obviously needed another one, so Leslie yelled for Steve to get the large cooler from his house. She and Officer Hahn went inside to talk, and a couple of Linda's contractors were in the kitchen drinking coffee. "Hello!" said Leslie. "What's going on?" One of them explained that they had done their measurements and had plans but needed her approval to move forward. Leslie told them that if Linda approved of the plans, then that was good enough for her. "But nobody touches the garden area," Leslie reminded them. "My dad and I will do that."

As the contractors set off to start the renovations, Officer Hahn sat down at the kitchen table and opened his laptop. Leslie grabbed a couple of teas from the refrigerator and sat down across from him. She took a drink and closed her eyes for a second. "Ahhhh..." she breathed as she relaxed into the chair. "So, let's talk about Mark," Hahn said grimly. "From what I am assuming, he enlisted the assistance of the incompetent couple to break in and steal something, possibly paintings. He gave them his gun and a key to the house, and we have those in our possession. We must find him and question him." Leslie explained that Billy thought he saw Mark in the recording of the press conference and Gary thought he saw Mark downtown earlier. "He must have thought he was getting what he wanted soon, and he's in the area," Officer Hahn surmised. "Stay vigilant, in case he's just waiting to get in here."

Leslie asked what the next step was, as they tried to find Mark. "Well, I am going back now to question the couple," he replied. "I have the other earring now, which I might be able to exchange for some information. I'll head back and see what I can do. I plan to be back after work for the cookout, and we'll talk more then."

Leslie thanked him as she walked him to the door. "See you this evening then!" she called out as she shut the door. She remembered that Melanie needed the rotini for pasta salad so she grabbed the bag off the counter and headed across the lawn. Leslie knocked and Melanie yelled for her to come in as she was busy zipping around the kitchen. Leslie gave her the rotini and asked where Steve put the large cooler so she could take it back to her house. Steve had pulled the cooler out of the garage rafters and set it on the floor, but it needed to be cleaned. Leslie carried it home to clean it and was hosing it off when Katrina pulled up.

"Hey!" shouted Katrina. "What are all these beefy young men doing in your yard? What's your secret?" Leslie laughed. "I have money now," she joked. Leslie went inside to get some PineSol and invited Katrina in. "Help yourself to a drink while I run this outside," said Leslie. Katrina saw bottles of wine and champagne on the counter and called out to Leslie, "Since when did you start drinking? I saw beer out there and there's a ton of wine and champagne here. What's going on?"

Leslie let the cooler soak for a few minutes and returned to the kitchen. "You know that I don't drink much alcohol," she announced. "The beer is for the guys putting up the fence and the bottles of wine and champagne are from well-wishers, most of whom I've never met. They also sent flowers and fruit baskets. Feel free to drink whatever you find, and please eat some of that fruit." Katrina pulled two glasses out of the cupboard and picked out a bottle of wine. She whistled as she poured some for herself and some for Leslie. "Just try it," she suggested as she handed a glass to Leslie, who sipped it and wrinkled her nose. "I'll stick to tea or Coke," she commented. "Suit yourself," replied Katrina as she took a drink of hers and smiled.

Katrina enjoyed her wine as Leslie made a peanut butter and jelly sandwich. "You do realize how much money you inherited, right?" asked Katrina. "Sure," Leslie replied. "Should I be eating more expensive peanut butter?" Katrina shook her head. "You're right," she said. "There is no replacing PB&J. Make me one, too." Leslie made the sandwiches as Katrina started asking questions about everything. Leslie set the two plates on the table and sat down. "Do you think I need a financial planner to help me with the money?" asked Leslie. Katrina gave Leslie a puzzled look and laughed. "Darling, until a few days ago, you were an experienced accountant," she reminded Leslie. "Just think about how you'd advise a client who became a millionaire and follow your own advice."

They were discussing the money and insurance policies when the door from the basement opened. "Did I hear a bottle of wine being opened?" asked Reginald. Leslie laughed. "I totally forgot that you two were down there," she replied, "and yes, that is wine. Here, you can have this one." She handed the glass to Reginald and asked Linda if she wanted anything. "Careful, honey, Linda is in shock," warned Reginald. "Tell her, Linda."

Linda looked at Katrina suspiciously, and Leslie explained, "Oh, sorry. Linda and Reginald, this is Katrina. She's my attorney." Linda seemed to relax, but Katrina freaked out a little. "Linda Edwards! I watch you on television, and I used your idea about the deodorant on my curtains. It really works." Reginald laughed and admitted that he does the same, then repeated what he had said with more urgency: "Tell her, Linda." Linda asked Leslie if she had ever been in the closet in the downstairs bedroom. "I just discovered all the renovations a couple of days ago," Leslie replied. "I saw a door that I assumed was a closet, but I didn't open it."

Linda went on to describe the gigantic climate-controlled closet that was filled with precious artwork. "Like a humidor, but for paintings instead of cigars?" asked Katrina. "Don't even think of bringing your stinky cigars over here," warned Leslie. Linda explained that it was similar, and that she and Reginald had been looking at the paintings and estimating their value. Reginald whistled and said "Around 17 million dollars, if you include the Rothko paintings. That is a very conservative estimate." Katrina gasped. "You have Rothko paintings?" she asked. Before Leslie could reply, the doorbell rang and Leslie went to answer it while Katrina talked to Linda and Reginald.

Leslie opened the door to find a plump older woman dressed in a mauve-colored skirt and blazer. "How may I help you?" asked Leslie. "Hello, Leslie," replied the woman, "I'm Gladys Petry." Leslie couldn't believe it was 12:30 already. "Come on in, Mrs. Petry," said Leslie with a smile. "I hope you don't mind that there are about 100 people milling around." Mrs. Petry said she had seen the young men working on the fence and Leslie said there were also four contractors, an art appraiser, an attorney, and an interior decorator.

"And a partridge in a pear tree," quipped Linda as she walked into the room. "Oh, my!" claimed Mrs. Petry. "You have Linda Edwards decorating your house?" Leslie laughed and explained that she was lucky that Linda was an old friend of the family and she was willing to help. "Will she be redecorating the other house that you're buying, too?" asked Mrs. Petry. Linda looked confused. "You're moving?" she asked. "No, I'm not moving," explained Leslie. "The young couple next door was going to get kicked out of their house because the owner died, so I bought it. When they're able, they'll buy it back from me." Linda commented that Leslie was more like her mother than she probably realized and went to go check on her contractors.

• • •

Chapter Fifty-Six

Leslie suggested that Mrs. Petry have a seat in the living room and went to get her phone and reading glasses in the kitchen. Reginald and Katrina were laughing like they had been friends for years, and Leslie suggested that they finish the bottle of wine while she signed papers for the house next door. "So, let me get this straight," Katrina began. "You inherited a few million, you have $17 million in paintings, you're buying the house next door, and your favorite lunch is still peanut butter and jelly?" Leslie grabbed her glasses and phone. "Yes, all correct," said Leslie. "I will be in the living room. You two, get to know each other, drink whatever you want, and solve the world's problems."

From the living room, Leslie couldn't hear everything being said between Katrina and Reginald, but she could hear his dramatic squeals, which made her laugh. Mrs. Petry had picked up the cashier's check and had all the paperwork completed, so Leslie just had to sign everything. "You should consider updating the paperwork for your own house," suggested Mrs. Petry. "Since it's still in the name of your parents, it might be more difficult to pass it on later." Leslie thought about it and smiled. "Well, I guess it's not really my house, since my father's name is on the deed and he is alive," Leslie mused. "What a great time to have my attorney here, huh?" Leslie turned toward the kitchen. "Hey, Katrina! I have a legal question," she yelled.

Katrina waltzed into the living room. "Did someone call for an attorney?" she sang out. Leslie could see that the wine was already taking its effect. "So, my mom left this house to me, but my dad's name is also on the deed," Leslie explained. "Is the house legally mine or my dad's?" Katrina laughed and rubbed her chin. "I believe it's your dad's," she replied, "but I will check into it." She laughed again and Leslie asked what was so funny. "So, you don't own the house you live in, and you own a house that you don't live in," she explained. "You're like a homeless millionaire."

Mrs. Petry didn't miss a beat. "I have several homes for you to view, if you're in the market," she offered. Leslie said she appreciated the offer, but she wasn't going anywhere. "I never thought I would say this," she continued, "but this is where I belong. My mother put her heart and soul into preserving this home and staying here, holding on to the chance that one day my father would return. Everyone thought she was a little crazy, including me if I'm being completely honest, and now everything she put into place has made it possible for my dad to return and enjoy the remainder of his life with no worries. I plan to be right here, enjoying whatever time I have with him."

Katrina came to sit on the couch next to Leslie. "I'm sorry, Leslie," she apologized. "I wasn't trying to be insensitive. We'll get the paperwork straight so your dad won't have to worry about anything, and then we can work on wills for both of you. You're going to have to think about who is getting those paintings when it's your time." Mrs. Petry looked around the room. "What paintings?" she asked. "Are you an art collector?"

Leslie shot Katrina a dirty look and laughed nervously. "No, I don't really have an eye for art," she explained. "My attorney is just using hypothetical situations." Katrina headed back to the kitchen so Leslie and Mrs. Petry could finish the paperwork. "I believe that your attorney is drunk," whispered Mrs. Petry. She suggested that Leslie get her house reappraised after all the renovations were completed, but Leslie politely declined. "I was an accountant for many years, Mrs. Petry, and I don't want to pay for an appraisal that will raise my taxes, just so I can brag about how much my house costs." Mrs. Petry said she certainly understood and explained that she would send Leslie a copy of all the paperwork that they had just finished.

As Leslie was letting Mrs. Petry out, a familiar black car pulled up in front. Leslie waved at Jennifer and quickly closed the door. She zipped into the kitchen and asked Reginald what time he needed to be at his next appointment. "Oh, I was supposed to be there ten minutes ago," he replied, "but I didn't want you to have to explain to that real estate agent who I am." Leslie thanked him and asked if he was okay to drive. He explained that he hadn't been drinking the wine, just pouring it for Katrina, and promised that he would be back later for the cookout. "We'll drink more then!" Katrina called out to him as he left the kitchen. As Jennifer walked up the driveway and into the open garage, Reginald walked quietly out the front door. Leslie smiled as she recalled Linda saying that he was discreet. Maybe he could teach Katrina some tricks.

"You should probably stay inside, Katrina," Leslie advised. "There is a reporter outside with a cameraman. Do not tell them about the paintings." Katrina laughed as she picked fruit out of one of the fruit baskets and tossed it into a pitcher. "I am going to make a delicious sangria for your cookout," she announced. Leslie shook her head and went out to the garage to greet Jennifer. They discussed everything that was happening, with Steve and his friends putting in the fence and Linda and her contractors working on other renovations. Leslie also explained that her neighbor had already done some renovations to her house, which she had just discovered. "This is great!" Jennifer replied. "Do you care if I walk around and ask some questions before we start filming anything?" Leslie thought that was a great idea, so she could get facts and explanations, and present it in an organized fashion.

"By the way, nice t-shirt," Jennifer commented. "Do you know what it says?" Leslie admitted that she didn't, and Jennifer translated: "Until they all come home." Leslie smiled. "Perfect," she replied proudly, secretly relieved that it wasn't something nonsensical. "So, you speak Vietnamese?" she inquired. Jennifer explained that she studied it for years and even spent a year of college in Vietnam. "Several times, I went inside the area of Marble Mountain where they found your father," she continued. "I was trying to find anything I could about my grandfather. I spoke with an old monk named Dinky or something like that, who suggested that Grandpa was probably in a 'better place' now. I think he had dementia."

Jennifer was almost finished with her year abroad and decided to visit Marble Mountain in one last attempt to find information about her grandfather. Her friends laughed at her when they chose their countries for studying abroad; everyone went to Austria, France, or Spain. Jennifer had been taking Vietnamese classes at a local community college for years and felt that going to Vietnam was the best choice for her. She knew a lot about Vietnamese culture and had even studied Buddhism to try to get a better understanding of those who followed it. She knew the awful politics and history of the American involvement in the Vietnam War and had lost her grandfather to that war. She never got the chance to meet him, and her dad grew up not knowing what really happened to his father.

As a small child, Jennifer had asked many questions about what happened to her grandfather and vowed to solve the mystery when she was old enough. As she trudged uphill on the back side of Marble Mountain, she thought about the great story she would write when she got the answers. As a perceptive budding journalist, she noticed things that others might not. The frail monk hunched over on a bench off the path was only visible because of his orange robe, but Jennifer pushed through the hanging branches to get to him.

She was breathless from the climb but greeted him and asked if he was okay. The old monk smiled politely and nodded his head. Jennifer told him her name and that she was a student from the United States. In a barely perceptible whisper, he offered that his name was Thich Dinh Ky, and that he was resting in the fresh air. She inquired about how long he had lived on the mountain. Thich Dinh Ky shared that he had lived there for many years but wasn't sure how many because he doesn't track time and only lives for today. Jennifer admired that, but she had some burning questions. When she asked if he lived there 50 years ago, during the war, he seemed reluctant to answer. He admitted that it was an ugly time in his world, but sadly he was here. He closed his eyes and appeared to be falling asleep.

Jennifer knew she might not have a better chance or audience for her questions. She shared that her grandfather disappeared in 1968 and may have been brought here. When there was no response from the monk, she continued that her grandfather was injured when his Jeep was ambushed and there were rumors about a hospital inside the mountain. When she asked if he knew about that, Ky looked down at his folded hands and closed his eyes again, but Jennifer noticed a slight gasp before he spoke. A spark of acknowledgment, perhaps. Thich Dinh Ky declared that he admired her quest for enlightenment but suggested that her suffering would continue as long as she was attached to the past. He urged Jennifer to make peace with the life she has, knowing that her grandfather is probably in a better place.

Jennifer scrambled to pull out her notepad in case anything relevant was shared. As she wrote down what Ky had told her, he rose to leave. She pleaded with him to wait, as she had more questions, but Ky merely bowed as he walked away silently. "Wow, what a crazy old man," she commented aloud. "Interesting, but nuts." She placed her pen and notebook in her backpack and started the trek back down the path, processing Ky's words.

Leslie was trying to recall the name of the monk who had died right before they found her father. "Jennifer, I think that's the monk who kept a daily journal and adopted my dad like a son," she explained. The extraction team brought the journals back when they went to get my dad." Jennifer's eyes widened. "Who has the journals now?" she asked. "Maybe there's something in there about my grandfather. Leslie wasn't sure who had the journals, but she told Jennifer that she would find out and made a mental note to ask Jim about it. She thought it was odd that she hadn't heard from him yet today, since he seemed so flustered last night.

"Okay, I will let you wander around and ask questions," said Leslie, "with just one request. Please do not disturb Billy's or my bedroom." Jennifer said she didn't need to go into their rooms, but she would be in the house shortly. Leslie went back inside to start getting things ready for the cookout. Katrina was organizing the bottles of wine and champagne on the kitchen counter. "Do you know who sent this over?" she asked, as she showed Leslie a bottle of champagne with the year 1989 on the label. "No, I don't," replied Leslie. "What a horrible coincidence, the year I married that jerk."

Katrina and Leslie stared at each other for a few seconds. "You don't think..." Leslie began, but Katrina cut her off. "I'll bet that asshole sent it!" Katrina shouted. "Oh, the nerve!" Linda walked into the kitchen and stopped. "What's going on?" she asked. Leslie showed her the bottle and Linda suggested that she pour it out, explaining that 30-year-old champagne would be awful. "It's not like a fine red wine that grows better with age," explained Katrina. "Or a fine woman," added Linda. They all laughed as Katrina uncorked the bottle and poured it down the sink.

"Leslie, honey, can you come upstairs for a second?" asked Linda. Leslie followed her upstairs and into her mother's bedroom. "I see that cute little reporter outside," Linda practically whispered. "I don't think she should see the paintings." Leslie explained that she had already told Jennifer that her room and Billy's room are off-limits. "Well, for some reporters, that is the first place they'll want to go, then," Linda replied matter-of-factly. Leslie wanted to trust Jennifer, but asked Linda to help her get everything else out of her mother's room so they could start the destruction phase of the renovation. They dragged everything into Leslie's room and Leslie grabbed a key out of her nightstand drawer. As she locked her bedroom door, Linda laughed. "You want to trust but can't?" she asked. "Looks like we have something in common."

Leslie phone rang and she pulled it out of her pocket. "Hey, something else we have in common," Leslie announced before answering. "Hello, Michael!" she said cheerfully. "Hey, sorry to bother you," Michael began, "but I can't get ahold of Jim or your dad. Do you think he's still mad at me for laughing at him?" Leslie said she didn't think Jim was mad, but she had not spoken to him today, either. "They're probably just out doing something fun," Leslie suggested. "But your mother is right here if you'd like to say hello." Without waiting for a reply, Leslie handed her phone to Linda. "Well, hello," Linda blurted, clearly surprised at the gesture. They had just reached the bottom of the stairs and Linda went into the living room to talk while Leslie headed to the kitchen.

Katrina was still straightening in the kitchen and asked what she could do to help. "Well, we're going to need hamburgers for the cookout," Leslie replied. "Can you add some spices and Worcestershire sauce to the ground sirloin and create as many patties as it will make?" Katrina said she would, but was hoping for something more fun. "Well, maybe you can distract yourself with the bottles that you just arranged, and decide which ones you want to take home with you," Leslie suggested. "Oh, that's more fun!" Katrina replied. "I have my eye on a couple of them." Leslie said she would keep a few for her dad's Welcome Home party and give some to Katrina, but the rest would be given away at the cookout to the fence-building crew. "Okay, I'll separate them into those categories," said Katrina with a little more enthusiasm.

Linda strolled into the kitchen and handed Leslie her phone. "Thank you," she said quietly. "We don't speak often." Linda walked outside as Leslie put her phone back in her pocket. "She seems so sad," Katrina observed. Leslie agreed, but she already had enough on her plate, so she continued her barbecue planning. She pulled out one of her pads of paper and Katrina laughed. "I have never seen anyone make as many lists as you," she teased. Leslie brushed off the comment and began a list of what they'd have for their cookout. "I haven't used the grill all winter," Leslie realized. "I need to go see if there is enough propane for it."

Leslie walked into the garage and pulled out the grill. The gauge for the remaining propane was low, so she went to ask Gary if he had any. She was surprised to find Linda standing outside by herself, just watching everyone. "Hey, is everything okay?" asked Leslie. "You're awfully quiet." Linda smiled and said she was just thinking. "Well, I'm a good listener if you want to talk," Leslie offered. Linda said she was just processing some things and Leslie asked if she'd like to go next door with her to ask Gary about some propane. "Yes, I'd love to," said Linda as she perked up a bit. "I might need to do some renovations at that house eventually, so I want to get an idea of what I'm up against." Leslie laughed and walked next door with Linda.

Gary came to the door before Leslie even knocked. "Well, hello, ladies," he greeted. "It's not every day that two beautiful women show up at my house." Linda giggled and Leslie rolled her eyes. She explained the propane situation and Gary admitted that he didn't have any, but he offered to run to the store and get some for the barbecue. Leslie thanked him and headed back across the lawn with Linda. "I didn't even get inside," Linda complained. "I must be losing my touch." Leslie promised that there would be plenty of opportunities to go inside some other time. "Are you kidding about losing your touch?" asked Leslie. "You look great!" Linda smiled and thanked Leslie, as Jennifer headed across the lawn toward them.

•••

Chapter Fifty-Seven

"Mrs. Edwards, might I steal you for a few minutes?" asked Jennifer as she approached. "Of course," Linda replied sweetly, "as long as you call me 'Linda' instead." Jennifer agreed to do so and walked away with Linda, so Leslie headed back inside to prepare for the cookout. Katrina was loading the dishwasher. "Everything okay?" asked Katrina. "You look like you have the weight of the world on your shoulders." Leslie explained that she was thinking about the absolute irony of the whole situation and how her life had changed so much in a month. "I just can't believe that Mom isn't here for this. My Dad coming back right after she died just seems so backwards." Katrina stepped closer to Leslie and her tone softened. "I think it's all part of a beautiful love story, and somehow your mother was able to succumb to her sickness because she knew that her goal had been achieved. Somehow, I think she knew that he was found." Leslie sat down on the bar stool and smiled. "She did know," Leslie said quietly. "She told me, and I dismissed it."

Leslie watched her mother's petite face as she slept, keeping an eye on the machines that were hooked up to monitor Susan's heart rate and blood pressure. She looked so helpless lying there with a morphine pump and an oxygen tube up her nose, and Leslie knew it wouldn't be much longer. She thought about how strong and stubborn her mother had always been, how she beat breast cancer with just a few rounds of chemotherapy. Leslie wished that was the case with pancreatic cancer, but that stubborn woman didn't tell anyone about the pains in her abdomen until the cancer was in Stage 4 and chemotherapy hadn't been very effective.

The nurse came in to check Susan's vitals and wrote some things in her chart. "She looks so peaceful," Leslie commented, "and I feel terrible that I can't do anything for her." The nurse smiled and assured Leslie that she had done plenty for her mother. "You're a single mother with a full-time job, and you found a way to be here every single day," the nurse replied. "What else could you do?" Leslie explained that she would do anything for her mother, but the one thing her mother wanted most was out of her reach. "Oh, you mean bringing your father back from the war?" the nurse asked. Leslie was surprised that she knew, but Susan had spent some time talking with the nurse about the details.

Susan's eyes suddenly opened about halfway and she reached her hand out to Leslie. "I waited," she began weakly. "Mom, save your strength," Leslie implored. "Just rest." Susan coughed weakly and grimaced, probably in pain. "Take care of Bill," she managed. Leslie squeezed Mom's hand and stood up. "I will, Mom," she replied. "I promise." The nurse smiled and assured Leslie that it's best to go along with whatever ideas or fantasies people leave this world with. "Your son's name is Bill, isn't it?" the nurse inquired. "It's Billy," Leslie replied, "but she didn't mean him." Susan's body relaxed completely as if she had fallen into a deep sleep and Leslie slumped into the chair, unaware of what the nurse was doing. Leslie knew her mother was gone, and she didn't know how she was going to tell Billy that Grandma wasn't coming home.

Leslie recounted the last conversation that she had with her mother and admitted that she had almost forgotten her last words because she didn't know that her father had been found yet. Katrina wiped a tear away and hugged Leslie. "That is sweet, but also heartbreaking," Katrina whispered. "How are you keeping it together?" Leslie thanked her and shrugged. "I don't see any other option," she explained. "I have to take care of Billy, tie up the loose ends of Mom's passing, and get ready for my Dad to come home. I don't have time to fall apart." Katrina admitted that she had always admired Leslie's ability to stay strong. "Well, except for that one time in Lit class," she teased. "Shut up!" Leslie replied. "That was so sad! It's not that I agreed with Poe, it's just the way that he described his sadness."

They laughed together and Katrina stopped abruptly. "Hey, I just had a great idea," she began. "You will have more free time now that you're retired. Why don't you do some writing? You were always good at it." Leslie said she would consider it as Linda and Jennifer walked in. "Uh-oh, what are you considering?" asked Linda. Leslie explained that she used to write stories and poetry, and Jennifer mentioned that she belonged to a writers' group if Leslie was interested. "I have a lot to do right now," Leslie explained. "But maybe after things calm down a little." Jennifer agreed that it was a good idea to wait a bit, then went over how she wanted to approach the story. She asked if she could see the rest of the house before she dragged her cameraman in. "Linda, can you show Jennifer around?" asked Leslie. "You know the house, and what you want to do, as far as updates." Linda said she would love to do that and headed upstairs with Jennifer.

"Okay, back to my list," Leslie said aloud. Just then, Melanie knocked lightly on the kitchen door as she entered. "Hey, I'm getting ready to go pick up Billy," she announced. "Do you need anything else while I'm out?" Leslie thanked her and said that she was all set, so Melanie headed to get Billy. Leslie continued to work on her list while Katrina went to relax on the couch, muttering something about grapes and headaches.

The contractors returned from lunch and joined Linda and Jennifer upstairs. They started marking the areas to demolish, with Jennifer asking them questions for a few minutes before coming downstairs. "Where's Linda?" asked Leslie. "Oh, she's supervising," replied Jennifer. "She never leaves the contractors during the 'demo' phase. Don't you watch her show?" Leslie admitted that she did not, so Jennifer went to the living room and grabbed the remote. "May I?" she asked. Leslie nodded her approval. "I think it's Channel 111," mumbled Katrina from the couch. They watched part of an older episode of Linda's show and Leslie was really impressed. Just as the show ended, Jennifer noticed the photo album on Leslie's coffee table. "Oh, I love looking at pictures," she declared. "I hope you don't mind."

Leslie realized that it was the wedding album of Linda's and Jim's and explained that to Jennifer as she opened it. Her comments were enough to rouse sleepy Katrina, who also wanted to see the beautiful couple. "I have to tell this story," Jennifer stated quietly. "Look how much in love they were." Leslie explained what had happened, or at least as much as she knew, and Jennifer was fascinated. Leslie expressed her hopes that there would be a reunion and a happy ending to their story and urged Jennifer to tread lightly with Linda about this subject. "She's been hurt enough," Leslie advised, "so I don't want her to have to live through it again."

Jennifer explained the power that journalism can have, and how people's opinions and emotions can be affected. "Oh, like how sad it is when a beautiful woman dies?" asked Katrina. "Oh, are you a Poe fan?" asked Jennifer excitedly. "No, she's just teasing me," Leslie explained. "One time, I cried in class when we read about Annabel Lee. I'm the Poe fan." Jennifer admitted that she was, too, and as they discussed their favorite stories and poems Linda returned and jumped right into the conversation. "Oh, Michael is a Poe fan, too," she explained. "Too sad for me." Katrina looked confused. "Who is Michael?" she asked. Leslie explained that Michael is one of her Dad's doctors and coincidentally, Linda's son.

"The doctor who sat next to you at the first press conference?" Katrina asked. Leslie shot her the "Shut up" look and said, "Yes, that's him." Jennifer laughed. "I saw a cover of a gossip magazine that showed a picture of you two, and it said that you were spotted at a local night club together." Leslie could feel Linda's stare and laughed nervously. "That's ridiculous," she said weakly. "I hardly know him." Linda patted Leslie's arm and smiled. "Honey, he calls you every day," she said sweetly. Leslie's face flushed and she changed the subject. "So, Jennifer, what is the plan for your story? Do you know how you're going to start it?" she asked. "I have some ideas," Jennifer replied, "but I am curious to hear more about Linda's son."

Billy came running into the room, a pleasant distraction for Leslie. "Mom! Guess what? Jenna wants to be my girlfriend!" he announced. "I knew it was going to be a good day!" Leslie laughed and suggested that he tell her all about it as she walked him into the kitchen, smiling slyly at Katrina. "You can't escape the questions forever!" Katrina yelled. "I'm the Queen of Cross-Examination!" Billy was already telling Leslie about what happened at school, and Melanie walked in briefly. "Hey, I'm going to finish making stuff for later," she told Leslie. "Billy is pretty excited about having a girlfriend." She winked at Billy and said, "See? That deodorant helped." Leslie thanked Melanie for picking him up and asked Billy about homework. "How can I do homework at a time like this?" he asked. "I need to go talk to Steve for a minute." Leslie said that was fine for just a few minutes, since Steve was busy working on the fence. "Steve will be here later for a cookout," she explained. "You can talk to him more then." Billy gave a quick "Okay!" and ran outside to talk to Steve.

• • •

Chapter Fifty-Eight

Leslie went to look at her list as Katrina waltzed into the kitchen, followed by Linda and Jennifer. "So, you didn't go to a night club with Linda's son?" asked Katrina. "No," Leslie replied, "but we did go to Target...all four of us. Two Targets, actually. It was so much fun!" As her audience of three listened, Leslie described what had happened on that adventure. "I'm still confused," admitted Jennifer. "The Jim who went to get your dad, who was his friend in college and then the Marines, is Linda's ex-husband?" Linda smiled and nodded. "Yes, correct," she replied. "And your dad's doctor happens to be Linda's son?" Jennifer continued. "Yes, also correct," answered Leslie. "But he's not just a doctor; he's a psycholinguist."

Jennifer took out her pad of paper and wrote down some notes. "Of all the people I know in the world, you are the last one I would have painted into this adventure," Katrina stated. "But I've never seen you more alive. I love it!" Leslie thanked her and suggested that she had spent enough years watching life pass her by. "Please take some advice from a wise old woman," Linda added. "Do what you love and pursue what makes you happy. I spent so many years being miserable, and I'm just figuring that out." Jennifer was writing down what Linda was saying, obviously taking it all in. "This is going to be the best story ever told!" she beamed. "I'm going to get my cameraman so we can get started."

Jennifer headed outside and Leslie thanked Linda for her advice. "You know, I think that's what my mother was doing all those years," Leslie continued. "She never gave up looking for my dad because that was the only thing that made her happy. She was the epitome of persistence." Katrina admitted that Susan's picture was probably in the dictionary next to the word "persistence," and Leslie noticed that Katrina had tears in her eyes. "Thinking about Poe again?" teased Leslie. Katrina shook her head. "No, I'm thinking about your mom and how much she must have loved your dad," she replied. "I just hope that one day I love someone that much."

Linda quietly walked out of the kitchen and Leslie smacked Katrina on the arm. "Nice job," Leslie whispered as she watched

Linda head back upstairs to supervise her contractors. Katrina said she was going to lie down on the couch again as Jennifer bounced back inside with her cameraman. She sure had a lot of energy. Leslie asked them to start out in front of the house, telling how a young couple purchased this home just before he left for Vietnam. "Great start!" Jennifer agreed, as they went back outside through the kitchen door.

Billy came back inside, still excited about having a girlfriend, and Leslie asked if he wanted to invite his girlfriend over for the cookout. "Probably not, since there won't be any other kids," he replied maturely. "Plus, I have homework and I need to practice for my 'Signs, Signals, and Codes' badge." Leslie explained that he might not be able to do much homework while there was so much going on around the house, but later it would be quiet. "Do you need some help with the cookout stuff?" asked Billy. "I can't cook, but I can carry food and drinks. What about games?" Leslie let Billy know that he was in charge of coming up with games, and Billy went off to figure out what they could do, thrilled about being in charge.

"You're a great mother," Linda stated as she walked into the kitchen to grab some water. "It seems like you two have a solid relationship." Leslie explained that Billy is autistic and was just beginning to interact with others, but for years he wouldn't talk to anyone but her. "He would open up to my mother when we would come back here to visit, and when we moved back here after I divorced Mark, Billy really started to flourish," Leslie explained. "This was always his safe haven." Linda explained that she and Michael were very close when he was younger, but when he decided on being part of the military she purposely distanced herself. "It's not that I didn't want to support his decision," Linda explained, "but there was still a lot of pain that I couldn't tell him about. We just grew apart."

Leslie felt sorry for Linda, but also hopeful. "I really see a happy ending to your story, Linda," she said confidently. "The odds of my dad being found alive and then returned by his best friend are incredible enough, but then to have one of his doctors to coincidentally be the son of that best friend's ex-wife is unbelievable. It's fate." Linda smiled. "I hear that doctor is actually a psycholinguist," she teased. Leslie laughed. "Yes, and he's going to help my dad get his voice back so we can find out exactly what he's been doing for the past 50 years." Linda thanked Leslie for being so supportive and hopeful, and admitted that she was looking forward to what life had in store for her immediate future. "I have to tell you that I have always thrown myself into my work to keep my mind from wandering into some dark places, but I'm feeling very positive. My therapist is probably not going to like it, though, since my issues have financed his lavish lifestyle for several years." They both laughed as Linda headed back upstairs.

Leslie went outside to check on the progress of the fence. "We're done for today," Steve stated. "There is just a small area next to the garden that isn't fenced, and Tyler and I can knock that out tomorrow." Leslie couldn't believe how much they had done and asked Steve to come up with a list of names and how much she owed them. "If they want to be paid in cash, they'll have to wait until I can go to the bank tomorrow," Leslie explained. "I can write checks now, though." Steve went to talk with everyone who had worked on the fence and Leslie was pleasantly surprised to see Billy talking to a few of them about games to play outside. He was really becoming a social butterfly.

Jennifer and her cameraman came over and asked about the Impala. Leslie told them what she knew and explained that she was hoping that it would help bring back some memories for her dad. "He won it before he was old enough to drive," she stated proudly. "I think something in his memory will awaken when he sees it. At least I hope it does." The cameraman walked around the Impala, capturing the full effect and beauty. "If you ever decide to get rid of this car, I will buy it in a minute," he said excitedly. "This is the most beautiful car I've ever seen." Leslie smiled. "It really is," she agreed. "That's why I'm never going to sell it."

...

Chapter Fifty-Nine

Gary pulled into his driveway next door, returning from buying more propane, and zipped across the lawn like he was on a mission. "Why are they filming the Impala?" he inquired. Jennifer asked Gary some questions about the car and the camera turned to him. He explained how he had been the caretaker of the car, had taught Leslie to drive it, and had ridden in parades with it. Before long, he was talking about some of the house renovations that he made and then shared that Jim Carlson had purchased his home. Jennifer just kept asking questions and Gary kept talking, so Leslie went over to his truck and pulled the propane out of the back.

Steve was returning to speak with Leslie and took the propane from her. "The guys are fine with checks," he explained. "I wrote down everyone's first and last name and the number of hours that they worked. You can pay them whatever you feel is fair." Leslie thanked Steve and went inside to write checks. Gary was done talking to Jennifer and headed over to hook up the propane, so Steve went to finish cleaning up fence pieces. As Gary finished with the propane, he saw Billy digging through the garage and asked what he was doing. "I need some things for my obstacle course," Billy answered. "I'm in charge of games. Want to help?" Gary said he would love to be Billy's assistant, as long as there were no magic tricks. "I don't know any magic tricks," Billy replied, "so you don't have to worry about that." Gary laughed and helped Billy find what he needed, discussing ideas for other obstacles.

Katrina talked to Leslie in the kitchen, helping her decide a fair amount to pay Steve and his friends, as Jennifer and her cameraman buzzed through on their way upstairs to film Linda and the renovations. "I feel like we're in a reality show," Katrina commented. Jennifer turned abruptly, mouth open, but before she could say anything Leslie shut down that idea. "Not going to happen," she said matter-of-factly. "My dad's been through enough." Jennifer furrowed her brow and continued up the stairs. "I love the new, confident Leslie," Katrina laughed. "What else do you need me to do?" Leslie finished writing the amounts in her check register and stood up. "There's an entire list here on the counter," she replied. "Find something that sounds fun." She headed outside with the checks as Katrina checked the list.

"None of this is fun," Katrina mumbled as she read the list. "I guess I'll make the damn burgers." She was taking the ingredients out of the refrigerator when one of the contractors walked in to ask about something to drink. As he grabbed a bottle of water, Katrina asked if he and the other contractors would be staying for the cookout. He thanked her and said he'd have to clear it with Linda, but he thought it sounded great. Leslie returned to the kitchen and Katrina let her know that the contractors would be staying, too. Leslie wondered if she had bought enough food but stopped worrying when she saw Melanie coming across the yard with a wagon full of goodies. "What are you doing?" Leslie asked when Melanie got to the door. "One thing I learned when Steve was in the Marine Corps is that you can never have too much food for a get-together," she explained. "Whatever you bought, plus this chuckwagon, should be enough."

Katrina laughed. "Well, how many of us will there be?" she asked. "Leslie, don't you have a list for that?" Leslie grabbed a piece of paper. "Now I do," she replied. She wrote down names and informed Katrina that there would be 20 of them, if they include Jennifer and her cameraman. "Did you count Reginald?" asked Katrina. "I think he's a hoot." Leslie said she had counted him and mentioned that Officer Hahn would be there so nobody was going to drive home drunk. "Is that directed at me?" asked Katrina. "If the shoe fits..." Leslie responded. "Hey, I was a lot younger then!" Katrina argued. "I'm a responsible adult now. It was nice of your mom to bail me out and never tell *my* mom, though."

"You know what I never understood?" Katrina inquired. "How did that charge just get wiped away? It was like there was a magical eraser. I couldn't find any evidence of it when I was doing all that research for law school." Leslie squinted her eyes and thought about it. "I honestly don't know," she finally answered, "but after some of the things I've learned and experienced this week, I think I know someone to ask." Katrina's eyes widened. "Scandalous!" she whispered. "What are you talking about?" Melanie asked. "Fill me in." Leslie told Katrina and Melanie what she had found out about her father, and how Jim Carlson put money into Gary's account twice. "But why would he help me?" Katrina asked. "Good question," Leslie mused. "Maybe there's some connection that we don't know about, but Jim was definitely there for our college graduation that weekend."

Linda came into the kitchen and interrupted their theories. "Leslie, did you invite my contractors to stay for the cookout?" she asked. "Actually, Katrina invited them," Leslie replied, "but Melanie brought over more food, so we definitely have enough." Leslie informed Linda that there would be twenty of them, including Jennifer and her cameraman. "Would you like me to go get anything?" Linda asked. Leslie explained that they had plenty, showing Linda the list of food and drinks that she had. "I've never seen anyone with so many lists," Linda observed. "I love how organized you are." She thanked Leslie and headed back upstairs.

"She loves how organized you are," mocked Katrina. "How is it that the only person I know that doesn't care about celebrities is friends with a celebrity?" Leslie laughed and shrugged. "How long have you and Leslie known each other?" asked Melanie. Leslie and Katrina looked at each other, trying to figure it out. "6th grade?" asked Leslie. "Yeah, that sounds about right," Katrina replied. "That was about the time my parents split up." Leslie told Melanie how Katrina had moved into the neighborhood and didn't have any friends, so Leslie tried to be her friend. "I was an angry kid," Katrina explained. "My mother got screwed in the divorce and I made up my mind then to become a divorce attorney so I could help others in the same situation." Melanie listened intently. "And you have, right?" she asked. "Yes, she has," Leslie chimed in. "And we didn't really become good friends until we went to the same college."

Katrina and Leslie spent some time reminiscing while Melanie went out to start the grill. Leslie heard her yelling, "Sooey! There's beer here!" and it made her laugh. "Did she just call them in like pigs?" she asked. "Yes, and it worked," Katrina replied. "Here they come! I'd say the barbecue has begun!"

...

Chapter Sixty

Steve was the first one to get to the garage and bragged about how fast he could still run. Melanie handed him a beer and proudly proclaimed, "First prize!" As each of the other five guys arrived, the last two just walking, Melanie yelled out something. "She's hilarious," Katrina remarked as she worked on making the burger patties. "I think she has a bright future in party planning." Leslie agreed as she continued to unpack the wagon full of food. "What are these?" she asked, holding up what appeared to be light-colored brownies. Melanie was just walking in. "Oatmeal Scotchies, silly," she replied. "Try one." Leslie folded back the plastic and took in the smell of the butterscotch chips. "They smell incredible!" she commented. "No wonder these were my dad's favorite." Leslie took a bite and closed her eyes. "I can't believe Mom kept these from me for my entire life."

Katrina was watching Leslie and asked what she was talking about. "I've never had these because Mom wouldn't make them; they were my Dad's favorite," explained Leslie. "Oh, that is so sad and so sweet," Katrina replied. "I haven't had them in years, but I remember that they're even better if you microwave them." Leslie said she would try that later and finished taking the food out of the wagon. "I'm not sure if we need this big bag of ice," Leslie commented. "Do you want me to put it in the freezer?" Melanie cut open a trash bag and laid it in the wagon, then cut open the bag of ice and poured it on top of the trash bag. "No, thanks," she replied. "The wagon becomes a portable area for items that need to stay cold, like the pasta salad, condiments, whatever." Leslie was impressed. "Have you ever thought about being a party planner?" she asked. "What a great idea!" Katrina replied. "I wish I'd thought of it."

Melanie tilted her head slightly and admitted that she had considered it, but before there was any more discussion, Billy ran into the kitchen. "I need some sidewalk chalk to draw the lines for my obstacle course!" he explained. "It's almost done!" Leslie directed him to his own bedroom closet, and he zipped up the steps.

"Third shelf on the right side!" she called after him. "You really are organized," Katrina laughed, "but maybe you should go help him. He seems to be in a hurry." Leslie headed upstairs as Katrina finished making the patties. "Who's cooking these?" she asked. "Oh, I can do that," Melanie replied. "At least I'll start them. As soon as Steve sees meat on the grill, he usually takes over."

Katrina handed over the plate of patties and said she would put the cheese on a plate to bring out. "Oh, you can put the cheese and condiments in the wagon," replied Melanie. "We can roll it out there by the grill. Where is everyone going to sit with their food?" Katrina suggested that Melanie ask "the List Lady" because she had no idea. Leslie was just returning to the kitchen from helping Billy. "Ask me what?" she inquired. "Where are 20 people supposed to sit?" asked Katrina. Leslie had a slight look of panic. "I have one picnic table and some bag chairs," she offered. Melanie laughed. "I'll send the guys over to get our card table and chairs, and I think Gary has a couple of tables," she explained. "We'll be fine." Leslie thanked her and apologized for not even thinking about it. "Hey, before you have your dad's Welcome Home party, you might want to get some tables and chairs," Katrina added. "No shit," Leslie replied, heading out to ask Gary about tables.

"I love the sassy, more-confident Leslie," Katrina laughed. "I haven't seen that side of her in a long time." Melanie agreed that it was great to see Leslie's confidence growing and expressed her gratitude for having Leslie as a neighbor. As she was talking, Jennifer and her cameraman came down from filming upstairs. "Do you mind if we take a few minutes of your time?" she asked Melanie. The three of them went into the living room as Billy came into the kitchen with some sidewalk chalk. "Hey, Katrina, my obstacle course is almost done," he announced. "Do you want to see it?" Katrina replied that she needed to get the burger patties out, but then she would definitely check out the obstacle course. "Oh, you just have to get those on the grill and then Steve will take over," Billy explained. "At least that's what always happens when Melanie cooks out."

Billy held the door open for Katrina to go out with the plate and Leslie had just started the grill. "Where's Melanie?" asked Leslie. "The reporter took her," replied Katrina, "so you're stuck with me."

Leslie took the patties from Katrina and set it on the grill's side table. "Sounds like a fair trade," Leslie commented. "From what I understand," Katrina continued, "if you put the burgers on the grill, Steve will magically appear and take over." Leslie laughed. "I've seen it happen, and I'm counting on it," she explained, "but right now he's getting a card table and some chairs from his garage." Gary walked across the lawn, carrying a folding banquet table. "I have two more of these and some chairs," he explained. "I'll be right back." Gary yelled for Billy to come with him, but Billy was distracted and didn't respond.

Leslie walked over to Billy, who was staring down the street. "What's wrong, honey?" she asked. "I swear, that was my dad who just drove past," Billy replied. "Did you see him, Mom?" Leslie said she had not, but suggested that if his dad were in the area, he would surely stop by to see him. She urged Billy to head over to help Gary with the tables. "Mom, I have to finish my obstacle course," Billy whined. "Gary helped you come up with the course, right?" asked Leslie. "He agreed to be your assistant for that, so you need to be his assistant for tables." Billy agreed that was fair and headed over to Gary's house. "Don't mess with my sidewalk chalk!" Billy yelled over his shoulder. "I'll be right back!"

Leslie rolled her eyes and returned to the garage just as Steve and his friends brought over a card table and several folding chairs. The guys started to set them up in the driveway, but Steve explained that Billy was setting up his course there, so they moved into the back yard. Steve then went to man the grill, as predicted, and his friends went to help Billy and Gary with more tables and chairs. Leslie and Katrina went inside to start bringing out food as Linda and her contractors were coming downstairs.

"Done for the day?" asked Leslie. Linda explained that they were done, and that two of her guys were leaving and two were staying for the cookout. "Perfect!" Leslie exclaimed. She asked Linda if they'd made much progress and Linda explained what they had done. Melanie and Jennifer came into the kitchen, apparently done with their interview, and Melanie grabbed a Kleenex from the kitchen counter. "Is everything okay?" asked Leslie. "I just told Jennifer what you did for me and Steve," replied Melanie, as she hugged Leslie. "You're such a great friend." Leslie explained that anyone in that position would have done the same thing, and Linda smiled. "It's sweet that you believe that," she commented, "but I have to disagree. Very few people would have done that."

At the risk of getting emotional in front of everyone, Leslie started assigning roles and tasks to get everyone involved. Melanie oversaw chips and buns and desserts and Katrina was in charge of drinks and ice, except for the ice in the wagon because Linda offered to handle the cold food. She loved the idea of ice in the wagon and assembled the cold items in it carefully. "Maybe you can use that idea on your show," Leslie suggested. "Melanie has a lot of good party ideas." Melanie laughed and said she would love to take her wagon on the show as she helped Linda take it out the door into the garage, discussing other party ideas.

Officer Hahn pulled up in his truck and Steve asked him to park it across the driveway at the bottom so he could block anyone else from pulling in. Leslie went out to offer Hahn something to drink, smiling as she watched Billy and Gary setting up the obstacle course. Jennifer and her cameraman had put aside their roles temporarily as they grabbed drinks and watched Billy with anticipation. Leslie looked around, counting heads. "Hey, where's Reginald?" she asked. Linda laughed. "Almost always late," she replied. "He claims that it's fashionable, but I think it's rude. At least he apologizes."

Almost as if on cue, Reginald pulled up in front and jumped out. Leslie caught a whiff of his enticing cologne as he approached, sporting a different outfit than earlier. "Hello, Reginald!" she greeted him. "I'm glad you came back. I love that purple shirt." Reginald batted his eyelashes and smiled. "Thank you for the invite. Sorry if I'm late." Leslie laughed and said there was no set time, so no harm done. Katrina handed him the bottle of merlot that Leslie had purchased for him and he squealed with delight. "You even bought my brand! How thoughtful!" he gushed.

"Only the best for my friends," Leslie replied with a wink. Her voice grew louder as she called everyone's attention. "I'm not very good at having a lot of people around," she explained, "but I want everyone to feel at home. Steve is making burgers on the grill, then we'll throw on some hot dogs and brats. You can see all the food that we have, thanks to Melanie, and there are desserts inside for later. Katrina is your bartender for the evening, but I would like to introduce you to Officer Hahn and suggest that you decide on designated drivers now or plan to sleep here." Everyone raised their glasses and bottles in agreement. "I'll have more announcements later!" Leslie added.

...

Chapter Sixty-One

Jennifer and her cameraman decided to record some of the obstacle course participants, with Steve timing everyone. Billy went through first, explaining to everyone how to navigate through each section. Gary had brought a clipboard with some paper on it to keep track of the times, and everyone seemed to love Billy's course. Leslie had to take over the grill because Steve's priority became timing everyone, but with Linda and Melanie helping it was easy. Katrina and Reginald sat in bag chairs and watched Steve and Tyler and their friends, giggling and making comments that Leslie hoped were not picked up in Jennifer's filming.

Everyone stopped to eat after the hamburgers and hot dogs and brats were cooked, and it smelled incredible. Leslie wondered out loud why she didn't have more parties. "This is awesome!" she commented. "I love seeing you all having fun and getting fed. Let's do this more often." Reginald suggested that they introduce themselves and tell their connection to Leslie. "I'll go first," he began, before Leslie had a chance to agree or not. "My name is Reginald and I'm a property appraiser. I haven't known Leslie very long, but I was introduced to her recently by Linda." Leslie breathed a sigh of relief that he didn't mention the artwork, and laughed when almost everyone said, "Hi, Reginald!" in unison.

Linda went next, telling everyone that she is an old friend of the family and an interior designer. "We're all aware, since we watch your show," Reginald quipped. "Hi, Linda!" everyone chanted. It was interesting to hear what each guest had to say, and Leslie didn't expect Billy to speak up because he wasn't fond of crowds. He seemed to feel comfortable with this group, though, and when everyone else had spoken, Billy took his turn. "I'm Billy Mitchell, and I live here. I need to go do my homework." He ran inside as the crowd yelled after him: "Hi, Billy!"

Leslie was last and looked around as she stood. "As you all know, I'm Leslie." They chanted together, "Hi, Leslie!" and she laughed. "I appreciate everyone's help with this. You all know the story about my Dad disappearing in Vietnam and my mother's insistence that he was still alive. In her last breath, she told me to take care of him, and I said that I would. Thank you, all of you, for your part in helping me keep that promise." Leslie's chin was quivering and she had to stop talking so she didn't break down. Surprisingly, Linda stood up next to her and took over. "Susan Lucas was the most loyal wife and mother and friend that anyone could imagine," she began. "She raised an incredible daughter, worked tirelessly to support veterans and military, all while having a job and taking care of a house. She put everything in place to prepare for her husband, whom she loved dearly, to be welcomed home."

Leslie thanked Linda and Steve spoke up next. "As a Marine, I can't tell you how excited I am to be able to meet Bill Lucas. He's a legendary Marine, and the more I find out about him, the more I am in awe that he will be my neighbor. I can't wait to hear his stories." From around the side of the house, a man pushed through the lilacs. "Well, today's your lucky day," he announced. "JIM!" yelled Leslie. "What are you doing here? Where's my Dad?" Jim Carlson walked over to hug Leslie, obviously relieved to be there. "He's here, too," Jim assured her. "He's asleep in the car. He thought you were in danger and kept trying to take the car to drive to you, so I finally relented. We've been driving since early this morning."

Leslie hugged Jim and introduced him to the crowd. "Everyone, this is Jim Carlson, the retired Marine General who brought my dad back from Vietnam." Everyone applauded and Steve yelled out sounds that only Marines understand. Jim put his hand up and everyone was quiet. "To be fair, it was kind of my fault that he went over there, so I felt obligated to bring him home. It became my life's mission." Linda stepped closer, as he hadn't even noticed that she was standing there. "At the cost of everything else," she added sadly. "Oh, my God! Linda!" Jim shouted. He threw his arms around her, and she couldn't fight it. Her arms wrapped around him, and she closed her eyes as she thoroughly enjoyed this reunion embrace.

Reginald burst into tears, but other than that, there was no sound for what seemed like forever. Finally, Steve spoke up. "Sir, are you General Carlson, the pilot who flew over 1000 combat missions in Vietnam?" Jim nodded his head, not letting go of Linda, and Steve explained to Tyler and anyone else who was listening that General

Carlson was also Marine Corps Royalty. "May I?" Leslie asked Linda. "I think it's a story that should be told." Linda nodded her approval and Leslie addressed the group: "So, this is a strange coincidence, but I think you'll enjoy this story," Leslie began. "Linda Edwards used to be Linda Carlson. Their marriage could not weather the psychological storm of survivor guilt..." Jim interrupted, "Or the alcoholism that came with it." Leslie agreed and finished explaining that Jim was part of the extraction team that brought her Dad back from Vietnam.

Jennifer and her cameraman had caught it all, including the heartwarming reunion hug and Reginald and Katrina handing out tissues. Jim explained that he had to come through the garden area because it was the only part that wasn't fenced off, and Leslie headed that way to get her Dad out of the car. Jim went inside with Linda, and when they passed through the kitchen Billy asked who he was. "You look familiar," Billy said, "but I don't know where I've seen you." Jim introduced himself and Billy liked him immediately. "I'm Billy, Leslie's son," he added. "I know all about you," Jim explained. "I'm friends with your Grandpa Bill." Billy nodded his approval and went back to his homework as Jim and Linda went to sit on the couch.

Leslie went around the side of the house to Jim's car and tapped on the window. Her Dad opened his eyes and flung open the door. "Leslie!" he yelled as he threw his arms around her. "Welcome home, Dad!" Leslie cried, bursting into tears as she hugged him. "You might not understand what I'm saying," she explained, "but I'm so happy you're here." Her dad smiled. "So happy!" he mimicked. It wasn't exactly what she had envisioned for his homecoming, but it was perfect.

•••

Milton Keynes UK
Ingram Content Group UK Ltd.
UKHW010940090124
435730UK00004B/285